SAMBUCA SCARLET

A PRIVATE INVESTIGATOR COMEDY MYSTERY

FRANKI AMATO MYSTERIES
BOOK 10

TRACI ANDRIGHETTI

Limoncello
Press

SAMBUCA SCARLET

by

TRACI ANDRIGHETTI

***

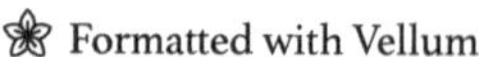 Formatted with Vellum

FREE MINI COMEDY MYSTERIES!

Want to know what Franki's up to between the books? Sign up for my newsletter to receive a free copy of the *Mini Comedy Mysteries*, a hilarious collection that contains "Prugnolino Purple" (Franki #1.5) and five other short Franki Amato mysteries. You'll also be the first to know about my new releases, deals, and giveaways.

Here's the blurb for "Prugnolino Purple:"

It's springtime in New Orleans, and Franki Amato's BFF and boss, Veronica Maggio, has dragged her to an art auction at one of the city's historic house museums. Up for sale, a provocative, not to mention peculiar, painting of their sixty-something ex-stripper landlady that is anything but priceless. Franki thinks the only crime at play is the image on the canvas until a cocktail waitress is found unconscious in front of an empty easel. After Franki finds a purple splotch on the presumed weapon, she and Veronica spring into action to ID the attacking art thief and locate the missing painting. But Franki's biggest surprise isn't the culprit—it's the "blooming idiot" who bought the portrait before the auction started.

And don't forget to follow me!

BookBub
https://www.bookbub.com/authors/traci-andrighetti

Goodreads
https://www.goodreads.com/author/show/7383577.
Traci_Andrighetti

Facebook
https://www.facebook.com/traciandrighettiauthor

Instagram
https://www.instagram.com/traciandrighetti/

To my reader krewe—especially those who came to the first parade and stayed all the way to Franki's wedding.
Here's to ten books of mysteries, madness, and meddling. May the good times keep rolling!

1

____

The slasher-flick scream that erupted from my lungs was proof I wasn't dreaming. And if I needed further evidence of my awake state, my Cairn terrier, Napoleon, provided it with a yowl-yelp before burrowing under the hot pink velvet duvet.

And rightly so.

Like me, he'd awoken to my mom and nonna standing silently beside my French bordello-style canopy bed. Their cheeks were flushed, and their eyes were glassy.

Because they were sick—with wedding fever.

But *I* was the bride.

"Honestly, Francesca." My mother huffed, smoothing her short, brown, Texas-sized hair. "You nearly scared your nonna and me to death with that outburst."

"*Sì, signorina!*" Nonna clutched a black bed post and the rosary at her bosom.

I flopped backwards onto my pillow and stared at the hot pink canopy. It was just like them to pin the blame on me when all I'd been doing was sleeping. "In my defense, it's more than a little startling to wake up to people hovering over you."

"In *our* defense, we thought you'd *never* wake up."

She acted as though I were a teen sleeping until noon, but I was thirty-two, and it was barely six a.m. I pointed at the old-school alarm clock on my nightstand. "Have you seen the time?"

Nonna nodded and raised a knobby index finger. "And-a it is-a wasting, Franki."

"Only five days until you walk down the aisle," my mother sing-songed, "and become Mrs. Bradley Hartmann."

Still on my elbows, I let my head fall back. I would've rather awoken to zombies from the creepy cemetery across the street than these two. With any luck, Thibodeaux's bar next door to said cemetery would help get me through my wedding week and their meddling antics.

Keeping my head hanging backwards between my shoulders, I said, "Since I've got more help than I need," I paused in the vain hope that message would sink in, "I'm caught up on wedding errands."

My mother dropped onto the bedside, sending my nose into the headboard.

"Ow!" I collapsed and grabbed my face.

"Be careful, Francesca! You don't want a bruise on your wedding day."

"No." My gaze was glacial. "I don't."

"Now, I know you think you're prepared, but problems have a way of popping up."

"I'm all too aware of that." I eyed her pointedly as I rubbed my aching nose. "But I'll deal with any problems if and when they happen—"

Nonna raised her chin. "Your mamma and-a I are glad-a to hear-a that, because-a something has-a come up-a."

"What?"

My mother folded her hands in her lap. "We almost forgot a Sicilian tradition."

Blowing out an exasperated breath, I propped myself on my elbows again. "We've already been over this—and over it, and over it again. The only traditions I'm observing are the normal ones, as in something old, something new, something borrowed, and something blue."

My mom and nonna opened their mouths to speak, but I wasn't having it. "Which rules out any and all Italian traditions like cutting up Bradley's tie and auctioning the pieces at the reception."

My nonna stood. "That's-a not—"

"And auctioning one of my shoes."

My mother rose beside her. "This isn't—"

"And kidnapping me and forcing Bradley to come to my rescue by solving riddles."

"Francesca Lucia Amato," my mother admonished. "Show us the courtesy of hearing us out."

We both knew the "courtesy" bit was a ploy to get me to listen to something I didn't want to hear. But because she'd phrased it that way, I had to acquiesce. "Fine. What's the tradition?"

Nonna patted the duvet. "*A cunzata du li lettu.*"

All I caught was the Sicilian word for "bed," which didn't bode well. "Do I want to know what that means?"

My mother pursed her lips. "It's called '*la cunzata del letto*' in Italian, which means 'the setting up of the marital bed.'"

I bolted forward like a bouquet thrown by a bride. "Stop right there."

Her eyes widened. "You said you'd hear us out."

"And given the subject, I'm setting a time limit on this discussion." I reached for the clock, and something stabbed my side. I pulled the culprit from between the sheets. The plastic baby from my late-night slice of king cake.

"Oh, Francesca!" My mother's shrill voice mimicked a drill running out of power.

"What? It's January sixth, and you of all people should know it's a New Orleans tradition to eat king cake on the Epiphany."

"But you have to fit into your wedding dress." No sooner had she uttered the words than the feverish look consumed her eyes. "Speaking of which," she grasped my forearm, "when are we going to see the one you picked out?"

My jaw set, and I wrested my arm from her grip. "On my wedding day, like everyone else."

"But I'm your *mother*."

"And you lost your dress privileges when you surprise-bought me that plantation-style gown—and parasol—at the Wedding Belles boutique last summer."

Nonna tsked. "It's-a bad-a luck not-a to show-a your wedding-a dress to your mamma and-a nonna."

"Everything is bad luck in Italian families," I snapped. "Now, you have one minute to tell me about this cunzata-del-letto thing, and then I'm going back to sleep."

"Well..." My mother paced in front of the adjoining bathroom.

Not a good start.

"The Thursday before the wedding, the mother of the bride and the mother-in-law supervise the preparation of the marital bed."

"Mom, that's weird."

Her head tilted, and her gaze went sideways. "It isn't, Francesca. According to the tradition, the mother and mother-in-law symbolize maturity and wisdom, so we know what we're doing."

If that were true, then they would know their involvement in the marital bed-making was a real romance killer. "What do you mean by 'preparation,' exactly?"

"The bed is made with sheets of fine white linen or silk."

Nonna nodded. "New and-a unused-a, like-a the bride."

My mom coughed, and I silenced her with a lethal look. Then I got back to business because I knew from hard-learned experience that there was more to the tradition than a set of nice sheets. Like a virgin. Or a fertility symbol. Otherwise, bad luck would inevitably result. "What else?"

"The bed has to be made by two virgins."

Right on target.

Nonna wagged a finger. "An odd-a number *porta male.*"

There's the bad luck.

"Once the sheets are on, a little girl jumps on the bed to ensure fertility."

And the fertility symbol.

"After that, all the relatives and friends are invited into the room. They put rice, grain, and coins between the sheets and decorate the bed with rose petals, Jordan almonds, chocolate, even bottles of liquor."

Money, chocolate, and booze? "Keep talking."

"For the final touch, they prepare a surprise for the couple."

My mom and nonna exchanged a look and giggled, suggesting a surprise I wouldn't like.

"And-a in-a the old-a days," Nonna's black eyes twinkled, "they attach-a bells and a cheese-a grater under the mattress."

Even though I was fully awake, this cunzata custom was worse than any nightmare I could remember, and I'd had some real brain busters. Not only was it embarrassing, but it also threatened to compromise my fondness for cheese. "Mark my words, I'll call off the wedding before I agree to that."

"It's important to adhere to tradition, dear. It portends a bright financial future with lots of children."

"What it *portends* is," I slid out of bed, "a weird and awkward start to our marriage."

My mom flailed an arm. "The weird, awkward start is you two spending your first night in this apartment before going on your honeymoon."

"I told you," I pulled a robe from the armoire at the foot of the bed, "the construction on Bradley's place is behind schedule. And because the reception will go late at the Piazza d'Italia, and we have an early flight to Rome, it doesn't make sense to go to a hotel."

She sniffed and surveyed the room. "I've always said Glenda's taste in furniture leaves something to be desired."

For the first time since I'd been so rudely awakened, I mustered something approaching a smile, i.e., a smirk. Desire was precisely the point of my ex-stripper landlady's brothel chic décor.

"You should take Anthony up on his generous offer to stay at Le Richelieu Hotel."

"Your mamma is-a right, Franki. Anthony give-a you a deal-a on the honeymoon-a suite."

Something about spending the night at a hotel my brother managed—which was not only around the corner from my office but also where my entire family was staying for my wedding—didn't say "honeymoon" to me. "Blue moon," yes.

No doubt about it, my apartment was the better option, even with a bed that was rigged and decorated by virgins.

I tightened the sash on my robe and slammed the armoire door. "I'm going to say this for the last time, Bradley and I are planning an Italian-tradition-free wedding, and we have everything under control."

My mother swooned, and my nonna gasped. Then she pointed her index and pinky fingers to the ground in a *scongiuri* gesture intended to ward off the bad luck I'd brashly cast over my wedding.

A loud thump and whoosh came from inside the armoire.

"What in the...?" I threw open the door. The wooden clothing rod had broken on one end, and my clothes had slid into a pile. At the bottom lay the satin bag that held my wedding dress—with the clothing rod rammed into it.

"All of this bad luck stuff is nonsense," I said, more for myself than for them. "Just silly superstition."

But my mom and nonna's faces were ashen.

Zombie colored.

I ushered them from the room.

The satin bag was torn, but the dress was intact. Logic told me that the incident was a fluke. Nevertheless, I had the awful sensation that it wouldn't be the last thing to go wrong with the wedding.

Or the worst.

⁓

"Oh, no." Veronica's fingers gripped the arms of the chair across from my desk at Private Chicks, and her face was as pale as her peach turtleneck. "No no no no no."

"Relax." I held up a hand. "The dress isn't damaged. Just my nerves."

She catapulted forward in relief, her blonde head dropping between her legs. "When I *think* of what we went through to pick out a dress without your mom and nonna finding out—"

"Don't forget the *nonne*."

Veronica shot up. "How could I forget your nonna's friends when at least one of them tailed us everywhere we went?"

The Café du Monde bag on my desk called to me, and I pulled out my second beignet of the afternoon, and I'd had a few that morning. "Fortunately, they weren't savvy enough spies to realize we'd recognize their FIATs."

"True, but if they hadn't been called to cook after that caterer canceled on Nedda Vitrano's granddaughter's reception, you wouldn't have a dress."

"You're leaving out my fitting during Richard Simmons' memorial mass and Sweatin' to the Oldies' workout." I licked powdered sugar off my fingers and, thanks to the mention of the famous fitness instructor, felt remorse—which I promptly brushed off.

Veronica fell silent. "I meant to ask you, did the nonne go to Richard Simmons' funeral because he converted to Catholicism? Or was it because it was held at St. Louis Cathedral?"

"Neither." I bit into the delightfully doughy beignet. "They're devout fans of his first book—actually, just its title, *Never Say Diet.*"

"Ah."

My phone rang. "Anthony," I said, checking the display. "Probably about our mother. She's not only telling me how to run my wedding, she's also telling him how to run the hotel."

Veronica smirked and shook her head.

"Hey," I answered. "What's up?"

"You gotta help me with Giada, Sis. I know she needs a job because of her divorce and all, but she ain't workin' out as a hotel cook."

The news was a surprise. Our cousin had a gourmet food blog that New Orleans society women loved. "Why not?"

"Giada De Laurentis she ain't. Since Le Richelieu used to be a macaroni factory, I asked her to create a special mac and cheese recipe to serve at our bar. And get this—she used cottage cheese."

Sacre bleu. "Tell Mom and Nonna to give her some pointers in the kitchen. They asked you to hire her, and God knows they need something to do."

"*A-ight*, but I don't think that's gonna help." He hung up.

Veronica glanced at her nails. "Giada's not working out?"

"Apparently not, which isn't good." I took another bite of beignet and brushed powdered sugar from my fingers. "Her soon-to-be ex is living up to his name, Wolf. She's still living in their Garden District mansion, but not for long. He's using his legal power to make sure she doesn't get a dime in the divorce. It doesn't help that they don't have kids."

"As an attorney myself, it really upsets me when I see a colleague capitalizing on the profession to cheat a spouse."

"The worst part is, they're splitting up right when I'm getting married."

Veronica leaned forward. "You can't feel guilty about that, Franki. You know Giada's happy for you. The last time I saw her, she mentioned how romantic it is that you're marrying Bradley on the anniversary of the day you met."

My heart fluttered at the memory of the day I walked into Pontchartrain Bank and met the love of my life. "It *is* romantic, but so improbable given our disastrous first date."

She grinned. "And you punching him in the face."

My mouth flat *refused* to grin back. "He deserved that for failing to mention that he was still married to Sheilah, even if the marriage *was* over."

"Speaking of the Sheilah-devil, is she coming to the wedding?"

"Nope." I polished off the beignet. "She and her second husband will be on a non-refundable trip down the Nile."

Veronica raised a brow. "Sounds fabulous."

"Not as fabulous as my Rome honeymoon."

"True. And as your best friend, I couldn't be happier for you. You kissed a few frogs before Bradley."

"Toadally," I joked. "Todd in college, Vince during my rookie-cop stint, and—"

Our eyes met. Neither of us dared to speak his name.

Some people were best left in the past.

My phone rang again. *St. Mary's Church* was on the display. I showed it to Veronica. "I hope there's not a problem with my ceremony." I answered the call on speaker. "Hello?"

"Franki," Nonna rasped, "you have-a to come-a to the church-a *subito*."

"Now? I'm at work. Can this wait?"

"No, it's-a *importantissimo*."

Suspicious that she hadn't offered an explanation, I decided to probe further. "Is this about a tradition? If so, the answer is 'no.'"

The call ended.

And I massaged my temples. "Will this wedding-tradition nonsense never end?"

"Not until the wedding does." She tilted her head. "But wow. The cunzata del letto is really something."

"Something I'm not even going to mention to Bradley."

Bradley entered the office, as handsome as ever in a black cashmere sweater and brown chinos. "What are you not going to mention to me?"

My eyes met his. "Yet another Sicilian tradition."

He walked around the desk and gave me a peck on the cheek.

"While we're on the subject of traditions," I said in a playful drawl, "what time is your bachelor party tonight?"

"Six p.m. Why?" A devilish smile danced at the corners of his mouth. "Are you worried?"

"Not at all." I leaned back in my chair and crossed my arms. "I trust you."

He bent over me, and his devilish smile descended on my lips and danced there for a time.

"*Ahem.*" Veronica cleared her throat. "Get a room, lovebirds."

My cheeks grew as hot as the kiss.

Bradley rose and squeezed my hand. "Veronica and I have a meeting right now about an insurance case she's going to handle while we're on our honeymoon."

He lingered on the last word, his blue eyes sparkling like the waters of Rome's Trevi Fountain.

And I dove in.

My phone rang, jolting me from my fountain frolic, and I frowned at the display. "The American Italian Cultural Center. Has to be Marcella."

Veronica looked at Bradley. "She's been fighting with Moira about the catering for your reception."

"I heard." He grimaced. "The stereotypical battle of the Italians and the Irish."

"It is." I reached for the phone. "And if I don't figure out a way to help them get along, Moira will cancel like the caterer for Nedda Vitrano's granddaughter's wedding, which means the nonne will man the cooking."

Veronica's eyes popped, and so did Bradley's. We all knew the chaos and calamity that would ensue if my nonna and her friends took over the reception food.

"We'll leave you to it." Veronica hurried from my office.

And Bradley followed.

Understandably. Marcella was a lot, even when she wasn't in Rocky Marciano mode. Sighing, I tapped *Answer*. "Hello?"

"It's Marcella." She paused, and based on her grim tone, I could see her flipping her black curtain of hair with her maroon-lined lips pursed. "Franki, I hate to do this because I know weddings are supposed to be happy occasions, but we have to talk about Moira."

"What hap—"

"After I gave her a list of the drinks and desserts the American Italian Cultural Center is contributing to your reception, she said our Italian flag cocktail won't work with her menu. I repeat, Won't. Work. With her menu."

Honestly, the drink wouldn't work with my wedding vision, but clearly this wasn't the time to say that.

"So I said, 'Tell me, Moira, what doesn't go with Crème de menthe, white chocolate liqueur, and red Sambuca?' And she said, 'Everything.' So I said, 'I beg your pardon, that drink is a knockout.' And she said, 'Yeah, the taste will knock out the guests' stomachs, and the colors will knock out their eyesight.'"

Entirely possible on both counts.

Marcella gave a hot huff. "Can you imagine anyone saying such a thing?"

"Y—"

"You know what I think, Franki?"

"N—"

"Moira insulted the Italian flag! And we both know it's because she's Irish. I mean, her last name is Mulligan! I'll bet she wants me to change the red Sambuca to something orange like Arancello so the drink will look like Ireland's flag, but the only way that's going to happen is over my dead American-Italian body. Because, let's be honest, the Irish flag looks like an Italian flag that's been in the sun too long. And who wants to sip a sad, faded cocktail at a wedding reception?"

"I—"

"*Mamma. Freakin'. Mia,*" she shrieked.

"Wh—?"

"Moira just sent me a text vetoing the Italian rainbow cookies. And you and I both know the reason."

"N—"

"They're the colors of the Italian flag too. What's that woman going to come for next? The *spumoni*? If she puts one finger on the carton, we'll settle this *my way*, to quote Sinatra. And by the time I'm done with her, Notre Dame is going to have to change the name of their mascot from the Fighting Irish to the Fleeing Irish."

I didn't know how the name change was going to go down, but I'd let Marcella tackle that issue with the football team. She could do it too, because she was the size of a linebacker.

Marcella growled. "The nerve of that wo—"

"I'll come down there right now and straighten this out."

"Oh." The growl had gone. "Why didn't you say so sooner?"

On that note, I hung up.

Then I turned off my phone—one way to keep my wedding under control.

Slinging my hobo bag onto my shoulder, I headed up the hallway to the lobby. Our two college-aged employees, David and Standish, aka The Vassal, were nowhere to be seen. Neither was Ruth, Bradley's assistant.

As I crossed the old brick-walled room, I looked with longing at the two opposing couches. I'd had many a nap there, not to mention the occasional night's sleep.

But I quashed the temptation. After all, I was on a peace-keeping mission. And based on Marcella's unauthorized drink and dessert choices, I was on a menu-keeping mission as well.

Grabbing my coat from the rack beside the door, I left the office and bounded down the three flights of stairs to the street below.

I stepped outside in the French Quarter and, per usual, caught a whiff of something peculiar. Not beignets or gumbo or chicory coffee, or even the sour odor of revelry from the night before.

It's smoky and vaguely fami—

Darkness descended over me.

"Hey," I yelled, struggling against a tomb of fabric.

Strong hands shoved my head down, and another pair slung me forward.

Onto a car seat.

The hands bent my legs at the knees, then someone sat beside me. The door slammed and tires squealed as the car set in motion.

My shock gave way to a sick feeling.

I'd been kidnapped!

2

———

The car moved in fits and starts through the Quarter, but the adrenaline maintained a steady surge in my veins. Its effect was that of a match dropped into a gas tank, igniting my nerves in a fiery blaze.

Who had kidnapped me?

And why?

My sight was limited by the fabric over my head, but my other senses fired on all cylinders. Especially my sense of smell, which was overwhelmed by a powerful scent.

Cheap cologne.

And that smoky odor.

Incense?

Then I got a whiff of a smell I knew all too well.

Garlic.

My confusion cleared, and the adrenaline spiked, now fueled by anger rather than fear. Because I knew what had happened—I'd been covered by a mourning dress and shoved into a getaway FIAT.

My jaw clenched, and I ripped off the dress.

The kidnappers were none other than nonne. And not just

any nonne but a couple of real goons. The one beside me in the backseat was so huge she had to hunch beneath the car ceiling, and she had fingers as thick as small salami. The nonna in the front passenger seat had the flattened nose of one who'd gone a couple of rounds in the ring with the late boxing great Jake LaMotta. Or Marcella from the American Italian Cultural Center.

And I couldn't believe who was at the wheel—the good-for-nothing son of Santina Messina, my nonna's best friend. "*Bruno!*"

He spun and flashed a cheesy smile over his shoulder. "Don't get mad, baby. My mamma made me do it."

My eyes rotated like the wheels of the FIAT, not only because he was pushing fifty and still a total *mammone*, a.k.a. mamma's boy, but also because he was wearing a black silk shirt unbuttoned to his navel in the dead of winter. "You think maybe it's time to cut the umbilical cord?"

"Bite your tongue, baby." Bruno's command was so emphatic his gold cross and horn necklaces jangled. "Mamma is my world."

She was, too, as in free room and board.

Flattened-Nose Nonna hit me with a dark stare. "His mamma is a saint," she growled through clenched teeth, "like her name."

Santina might mean "little saint," but the woman was about as saintly as my nonna—so, far freaking from it. "Since when do saints aid and abet in a kidnapping?"

"Eyyy! Ohhh!" Bruno stared stunned into the rearview mirror.

Salami-Fingered Nonna gasped and tried to pinch my bicep —but her fingers were too fat.

"Take it easy with the accusations, baby." Bruno shifted in

his seat and adjusted his shirt for maximum chest exposure. "We're just giving you a ride, like your nonna ordered."

Another Mafia-esque maneuver. "Wait a second... Didn't my nonna tell me you'd lost your driver's license after you ran a red light and caused an accident that injured your mother?"

"What're you, a cop?"

There was no point in answering. Bruno was as dense as the hair in his nostrils.

He pulled up in front of St. Mary's Catholic Church, a white stuccoed brick building built in 1845 on the site of the old Ursuline Convent, one block down Chartres Street from Le Richelieu Hotel. I tried the door handle, but it wouldn't open.

Bruno turned and winked. "Child-proof lock." He draped his arm over the seat and attempted a smoldering stare, but the squint and pout combined with his Neanderthal brow only made him look dazed and dim. "Listen, if you need any help with your bachelorette party," he gave me the onceover, "you know who to call."

"Ghostbusters?"

His face fell. "*Me*, baby."

"I'd sooner resurrect the Ursuline nun order."

His low brow cocked, triggering a corner of his mouth. "I wouldn't mind seeing you in a habit."

"Let's go, Jezebel." Salami-Fingered Nonna yanked me from the car, as though I were to blame for the Bruno encounter. Then she and Flattened-Nose Nonna led me into the church, where Nonna and a group of her nonna friends were packed in the pews near the altar.

St. Mary's Church had formerly been called St. Mary's *Italian* Church because it was the official Italian parish of the Archdiocese. But even though the name had changed and the Italian language services for the Sicilian immigrants who'd settled in the lower French Quarter had ceased decades ago, the nonne remained steadfast devotees. The problem was, the Church was now only used for weddings.

And the nonne planned to wear it out.

As I walked down the aisle to my waiting nonna, I gazed at the huge Baroque-inspired mural of the Assumption of the Virgin Mary. And I couldn't help but smirk. She was flanked by two angels, whereas I was flanked by the two goon nonne.

Nevertheless, a shiver ran down my spine. In five days' time I would make the trek down this aisle again to become Mrs. Bradley Hartmann. And I sincerely hoped the mood in the church would be different than it was at the moment, i.e., celebratory instead of somber Sicilian suffering.

The old Pilcher organ, built for the Ursulines, played in the church choir loft.

Incense burned.

Bible pages turned.

Rosaries churned.

The dark mood wasn't helped by the statues on either side of the altar, Saint Lucy, the patron saint of the sight-impaired, holding her eyeballs on a plate and a winged Saint George slaying the dragon with his spear.

"Franki." Nonna gave a curt nod and raised her chin. "I'm-a so glad you could-a make it."

My gaze sought Saint George's in silent plea. *I could really use your help with these nonne.*

Then I sank into a pew and glanced around at the nonne, most of whom I recognized but couldn't identify by name. They were all in black mourning dresses—except for Bruno's mother, Santina, who was suspect in a white chasuble worn by priests during solemn occasions. Apparently, her mourning dress was the one the goon nonne had used to kidnap me.

And I was well aware of the solemn occasion behind my kidnapping—a crash course on marriage traditions.

Led by Nonna and the nonne.

In a church.

At a former convent.

Not the way I'd planned to kick off a lifetime of marital bliss.

A sigh escaped my lips, and I raised my eyes to the mural of the Virgin Mary, ascending to heaven body and soul. *For the love of God, save me from these Sicilians.*

Nonna clasped her hands behind her back, lowered her head, and began to pace in front of the altar. "We commence-a."

A wide-hipped nonna rose in the middle of the pew with a sheet of paper in hand and made her way to the aisle, knocking over nonne one by one. She went to the pulpit, slipped on a pair of readers, and crossed herself. "Clothing and accessories." She glared at me over her glasses. "No pearls during wedding week. They symbolize tears."

A sob erupted from a nonna with a teardrop-shaped facial mole. "If only my Gina had taken that advice! She wouldn't be a widow now."

On that note, I reached for my phone and placed a call for help.

Wide-Hipped Nonna cleared her throat. "Franki, your nonna tells us you want to wear something blue." She paused to purse. "You also need something red to symbolize love and fertility. Otherwise, it's *arrivederci* to both, eh?"

A nonna with a face the exact shape and color of a San Marzano tomato nodded. "My niece, Rosa, didn't wear anything red, and now she's childless in Newark."

The word "childless" echoed in the church like a bell toll, but "Newark" dissipated into thin air despite its own ominous connotations.

A cannon-like crack echoed next. It was the nonne slamming down their kneelers to pray for Rosa's double misfortune.

Wide-Hipped Nonna waited for the prayers to finish, and

then she pushed up her glasses to highlight her piercing stare. "And whatever you do, don't forget to wear green the day before at the rehearsal dinner. We all know what *that* symbolizes."

Indeed. The almighty dollar.

Wide-Hipped Nonna returned to her pew, and the nonne she'd previously knocked over all scooted far from her.

A nonna wearing more rosaries than Madonna had throughout her entire *Like A Virgin* tour took her place at the pulpit. "On the way to the church," she wagged a finger at me, her beads clacking a foreboding warning, "woe unto you and Bradley if you see a priest, nun, or black cat."

Quite a crew.

"Also, you have to enter the church on the arm of your father with all of your relatives in procession behind you."

My jaw dropped. "My relatives aren't seated in the church?"

Nonna shot me a stern look. "We gotta let-a the groom-a know we mean-a business! Before these-a big-a fancy honey-moons of-a today, the guests would-a walk-a behind the bride and-a groom to their new-a house with-a *torches*."

The revelation proved what I'd suspected all my life—old-world Sicilian weddings were hostile occasions prone to mob violence.

Rosary-Bead Nonna resumed finger-wagging and subsequent bead-clacking. "Be sure to enter the church with your right foot. Otherwise..."

The nonne again dropped onto the kneeler and recited the Ave Maria.

"Finally," Rosary-Bead Nonna gripped her rosaries, "do *not* trip when you walk down the aisle, or you'll face obstacles in the marriage."

"I tripped," a nonna with a face as grim as a funeral procession announced in a lifeless tone. "And I've got obstacles." She laid a heavy gaze on me. "Try sharing a bed with a man with razor blades for toenails who kicks like Bruce Lee in his sleep. And try sharing a bathroom with that same man when he leaves his nose and ear-hair clippings in the sink. And he's got more than Danny DeVito and Jack Nicholson combined." She looked to the other nonne for support. "I've got fifty years of scars—physical and mental."

It was safe to say that I didn't want to try either of those things—except that it wasn't safe to say to Funeral-Faced Nonna.

A nonna with a personality as prickly as her profusion of chin hair stormed the pulpit, shoving Rosary-Bead Nonna aside. "Let's talk rings, Franki. Who are the *compari di anello*?"

"The, uh, 'godparents of the rings?'" I shrugged. "My best friend, Veronica, and her husband, Dirk."

"Well, you tell this Dirk that if Bradley drops your ring before he puts it on your finger," she blew out a breath, "*mamma mia*."

The nonne went down on the kneeler yet again and murmured prayers.

"And if the ring catches on your knuckle when he slides it on," Chin-Hair Nonna rubbed her stubble, "you'll wear the pants in the family."

Nonna grinned. "Which is-a good luck-a for our-a family." Then she ratcheted up the grin to a you-know-what-eating one. "But-a bad luck-a for his."

Chin-Hair Nonna wiped the smirk from her face. "When the priest introduces you as man and wife, you both have to turn to the guests at the *same time*." She pounded the pulpit. "God forbid one of you goes first, because that will be the first person to die in the marriage."

"Sweet Je—" I caught myself in the nick of time, narrowly avoiding a sacrilegious swear—and getting caught in the holy crossfire that would've ensued. "Are there any purely *good* luck scenarios?"

"Sure, sure." Nonna patted my shoulder. "If a bird does-a the poo on-a you on-a your wedding-a day."

"Um... That doesn't seem lucky."

Nonna threw up her hands. "You're getting-a *married*, Franki! What the hell-a did-a you expect? Wine and-a roses?"

This from a woman who'd been trying to sell me on marriage for over half my life. I glanced at my phone. My call for help had been answered. *But how to escape Nonna and the nonne's Catholic clutches?*

A dove flew into the church, eliciting gasps from the nonne. The bird flapped and circled and then landed on the head of Saint Lucy who, incidentally, was also the patron saint of virgins and Siracusa, Sicily.

"*È nu miraculu!*" Santina pressed her palms to her cheeks.

A nonna with a neck as thick as a ciabatta grabbed her throat. "It *is* a miracle!"

Ciabatta-Necked Nonna was only half right, because the dove was also a heaven-sent answer to my pleas. I slid from the pew, and with the stealth of a ninja nonna who'd crept up behind the dove for a closer look—or to catch it for a ragù—I fled the church.

The rear passenger door of a 1970s Pontiac Catalina opened, and I slipped inside, finally free of the FIAT and the stifling Sicilian wedding traditions.

But still uneasy.

Because more trouble was coming. And it was bigger than my Catholic class kidnapping.

I could feel it.

∿

"BACK TO THE OFFICE, EH?" My Uber driver beamed at me in the rearview mirror as he stroked his snow-white beard.

"Just to pick up my car." I decided not to tell him or the guy sitting next to him that I'd been kidnapped by goon nonne. I was in no mood to go into the whole Sicilian saga, and I was far too busy pouring myself an eggnog.

After adding a squirt of whipped cream, I leaned back against the cracked vinyl seat careful to avoid the dangers of the old-school decorations on the rear parcel deck—mercury-filled ornaments, the fiery-hot bulbs of methylene-chloride-filled bubble lights, and vintage tinsel, which not only contained toxic metal but could also conduct an electrical current from the lights.

Despite the hazards, I was happy. In the twinkling of an eye, I'd gone from the funerary church setting to Christmas in a car. In January.

When I was down and in need of a ride, I knew who to call—Santa Claus.

And his elf in the passenger seat.

Besides Santa and Hermey, who'd once given me a ride home from the airport after a disastrous Iowa glamping trip, the only other Uber driver I knew was Phil Redman, who was also the caretaker for Saint Cecilia Cemetery. And I'd rather take a joy ride in the Christmas Car any day of the year than endure a ride from hell in Phil's Uber Undertaker hearse—even though, when it came to jolly, Phil could give Santa a run for his money.

Smiling to myself, I grabbed a candy cane and breathed in the cinnamon-pine-gasoline scent. Then I settled in to listen to some holiday music. "Feliz Navidad" ended, and "Grandma Got Run Over by a Reindeer" came on the car stereo.

Hermey turned in his seat. Like his *Rudolph-the-Red-Nosed-Reindeer* namesake, he had black eyes that were too close together and wore a perpetually earnest expression. "We've got rum and brandy for the eggnog."

"I'd better not." The song was giving me ideas, and if I tied one on, I might be tempted to carry them out.

He raised a poinsettia-shaped plate. "Creole Christmas cake?"

"Why not? I mean, *eating* rum and brandy doesn't count." Using a napkin depicting gators pulling a sleigh, I took a piece. Then I bit into the iced, booze-infused fruitcake and had a vision of the St. Mary's mural of the Virgin ascending to heaven.

And a plan came to me.

"I'm getting married on the eleventh, and things are getting intense. So, I'll call you again when I need an escape. Maybe just to ride around, if that's alright."

Santa's face lit up like a Christmas tree. "Happy to oblige a bride-to-be."

Hermey nodded, but his face was hardly festive. "And these days, it's best you don't go walking around alone. Strange things have been happening in the Quarter."

I swallowed another boozy bite. "That's not exactly a news flash."

"Oh, this isn't about the usual crime or drunken antics." His eyes widened to the size of ball ornaments. "We're talking about a ghost."

"Also not news in New Orleans." I polished off the cake and surveyed the drink toppings, sugar cookies, and snacks in a tray attached to the back of the center console, opting for a handful of Reindeer Munch. "But for the record, I don't believe in ghosts."

"Santa and I don't either. That's the worrying part."

My eyes traveled from Hermey to Jolly Old Saint Nick, who'd turned uncharacteristically unjolly. "I'm not following you."

Santa coughed and rested his hand on his belly. "We're at a loss to explain it, but a spirit has indeed appeared in New

Orleans. Although, if you believe the local ghost tours, he never left."

"The pirate Jean LaFitte?" I guessed. "Or the ghost of Piere Antoine Lepardi Jourdan at Muriel's Restaurant?"

The car went over a bump, and a Grinch bobblehead on the dashboard went flying.

"No, Père Dagobert de Longuory, a Capuchin monk from Quebec." Santa turned onto Decatur Street. "The father was the rector of St. Louis Church, before it became the Cathedral. He died in 1776, but people claim you can still hear him singing hymns. His favorite is Kyrie eleison."

Lord, have mercy was both the translation of the hymn name and the thought that ran through my head.

Hermey gripped the back of his seat. "Not only did we *hear* him, we *saw* him when we took a passenger to the Bourbon Orleans Hotel early Thursday morning. He was wearing a brown monk's robe with a rope around the waist."

I popped some munch into my mouth. "It was probably some guy clowning around—or *Capuchining* around, as it were."

Neither Santa nor Hermey *ho-ho-ho*ed, maybe because they were in costumes themselves.

"I don't think it was a joke." Hermey flipped the blonde bangs that protruded from his elf hat. "It was three a.m., and bitterly cold. No one else was around."

Santa stopped at a red light. "Others have reported hearing Père Dagobert recently. It made *The Times-Picayune*."

I shrugged. "He's probably one of those religious zealots who hang around St. Louis Cathedral trying to save people."

"Could be." He stroked his beard. "Kyrie eleison is common in Christian liturgies."

Hermey laid a solemn look on Santa. "And the Mass for the Dead."

That comment gave me a jolt, as did neck contact with a

boiling bubble light. "Well," I rubbed a possible burn mark, "whoever or whatever this Père Dagobert is, I don't want to see him. It's not the ghost thing but a clergy issue. According to my Sicilian nonna, it's bad luck to see a priest on my wedding day."

Santa chuckled. "Then you'd best not get married in a Catholic Church, or you're doomed."

If you believed my nonna, I was doomed either way—and damned all kinds of ways. "She meant before I arrive at the church." I grabbed a couple of fluffy marshmallows for comfort. "And believe me, I can't take any chances. I haven't had an easy time of it when it comes to men and relationships."

"Hermey and I hear that all the time. The most common one is, 'Santa, I'd like an eligible man for Christmas, preferably one with health insurance.'"

"And a 401k," Hermey added.

Couldn't argue with those requests. "Sounds reasonable."

"Sure. But some women ask for a baby, and I can't help them there." He gave a hearty *ho-ho-ho*.

"Neither can I." Hermey offered no explanation, although I suspected it wasn't because he was an elf.

I glanced out the window. "A baby is the next thing my family will be on me about, but first I have to get down the aisle. My nonna has been calling me a *zitella* since I was in my teens, so if I don't get married this week, all *inferno* will break loose—as in legions of torch-carrying nonne conducting husband-hunts through the streets." That is, if they didn't try to marry me off to that hirsute brute, Bruno.

"*Zitella*..." Hermey pressed a finger to his pudgy chin. "Reminds me of 'zit.'"

My lips wrinkled. "It's worse than a pimple. It means 'old maid.' They got married young in Old World Sicily."

Hermey turned in his seat. "Families are tough, aren't they?"

Santa slowed the Christmas Car to a stop in front of the

Private Chicks building. "I'll say. Mrs. Claus has been after me for years to give up milk and cookies. Can you imagine?"

I shook my head. Not in this car, I couldn't.

"Thanks for the rescue." I deposited my eggnog cup and napkin in a red plastic bag on the back of Hermey's seat that read *Put your trash here or wind up on Santa's naughty list* and opened the car door. "I'll be in touch."

"We *ho-ho-hope* so," Santa cried. "Meeerrry Christmas!"

Hermey nodded. "Yes, enjoy the holidays."

"Uh, same to you." I closed the door, and the Christmas Car sped away, recorded sleigh bells jingling.

Back to a post-holiday reality, I walked to my Mustang.

And my head went sideways.

Lemons lined my windshield. A half dozen of them.

The memory of my co-worker David Savoie shooting lemons at me from a T-shirt cannon exploded into my head. He'd been put up to it by my mom and nonna who were bound and determined to get me to steal a lemon from a St. Joseph's Day altar, because Sicilian-Americans had somehow concluded that stealing such a lemon would land a single gal a marriage proposal.

But in this case the St. Joseph's Day tradition didn't make sense. For one thing, that was in March. And for another, I'd already gotten a proposal.

So, what do these lemons mean?

And who put them on my car?

The hair on the back of my neck stood up, and I couldn't blame the vintage tinsel.

Someone was behind me.

Close.

Before I could make a move, fabric covered my head.

"Let go of me!" I struggled, but the fabric trapped my arms.

A pillow case?

My assailant, who dragged me backwards with big man hands and the strength of ten men, didn't utter a word.

Writhing with all my might, I shouted, "If you're working for my nonna, I've already been to marriage-tradition class!"

In reply, I was hurled face first onto the floor of a car.

No, a van—with shag carpet.

The door slammed shut, and the van peeled out.

It was unthinkable, inconceivable, an absolute impossibility. And yet, here I was.

Kidnapped.

Again!

3

"Who are you?" My anxiety increased with the vehicle's speed. "And why'd you abduct me?"

The van careened around a corner, and I seized the opportunity to roll onto my back and wriggle into an upright position on the floor between the seats.

Someone pulled down the fabric encasing my head and torso. My head emerged through a hole in what I realized was a white sweatshirt, and I came face to face with my assailant's eye.

As in, one.

Made up with purple-black-and-gold eyeshadow?

"Surprise!" Marcella pulled back her black hair curtain, revealing her other smoky-eyeshadowed eye and a maroon-lined smile.

My friend from the American Italian Cultural Center wasn't the only shock. I was in Nadezhda Dmitriyeva's company van for her combined booze and bikini waxing business with the Russian-inspired spelling, Lucky's Liquor and Vaxing. And my ex-stripper landlady was her passenger.

"So, *you're* the ones who left the lemons on my windshield?"

Glenda eyed me from beneath inch-long leopard eyelashes. "I do believe Miss Franki's in shock."

Shock wasn't my only problem. My body was smarting from Marcella's manhandling, and so was my pride. Not only had I been kidnapped twice in two hours, but I'd also been abducted by Nadezhda and Glenda before, during an investigation of a nutty coffee shop owner and his witch of a nonna. Luckily, I wasn't working a homicide at present, because the demands of my upcoming wedding had clearly killed my survival instincts.

Angry at myself and them, I shoved my arms into the long sleeves of my sweatshirt. "Would one of you mind explaining why you nabbed me from the Private Chicks parking lot?"

Nadezhda's beady black eyes glared at me via the rearview mirror, her Boris-from-*Rocky-and-Bullwinkle* brow lowered. "Bachelor party. Vat else?"

"If you're talking about me," I slid into the seat behind her, "it's called a '*bachelorette* party.'"

She doubled over the steering wheel. "*Nyeh! Nyeh! Nyeh!*"

My eyes gravitated to Glenda. "Is that how Russians sneeze? Or is she choking?"

Nadezhda wiped away tears and looked at my landlady. "Who Frank kid vit voman bit?"

"Evidently, it was the latter, sugar. On laughter."

Red obscured my vision. Not the van's carpet—an homage to the rude Russian's Communist roots—but the proverbial color. Nadezhda persisted in insisting that I was a man, even after she'd given me a bikini wax for a strip club case I investigated. "If the two of you kidnap me again, I'll have you sent to jail."

Glenda ran fingers through her platinum Cher hair. "Child, I'm always up for a strip search."

Nadezhda sneered. "Frank iz big party poop."

"My name is *Franki*." I leaned into her headrest. "And watch out, Comrade Clueless. I'm riled *and* right behind you."

She bared huge veneers—and the eyetooth hole she hadn't filled. "I not vorried. I kidnap tvice."

It was my turn to bare my teeth.

Glenda practiced her sultry pout in the vanity mirror, probably for the future strip search. "Don't get mad at Miss Nadezhda, sugar. The kidnapping was my idea." She sighed and pushed the sun visor back into place. "Veronica said you didn't want a bachelorette party, but I had to do *something* for you after I organized Bradley's bachelor party."

"*You...*" My head spun as though I were watching a pole dancer, something my fiancé was undoubtedly doing thanks to Glenda, and I gripped the back of her seat. "...organized Bradley's bachelor party?"

"It should be starting soon. It's at Le Richelieu Hotel."

Nadezhda curled her lip. "He see tings he never see vit Frank."

That was either a dig at my femininity or a reference to whatever Glenda had planned. Scratch that—it was both. But I had bigger things to worry about than the bitter babushka's barbs. Namely, Bradley. "And what is he going to see, specifically?"

"No, ma'am." Marcella waved her arms. "We're not focusing on Bradley tonight—or that awful caterer, Moira, who you really should fire because she doesn't know a panettone from a pizzelle, which, incidentally, is going to ruin your reception. I repeat, Ruin. Your. Reception."

Apparently, we *were* focusing on Moira.

"That's what I was going to talk to you about today," she shot me a smoky-eyed side-eye, "*if* you'd come by the American Italian Cultural Center like you promised."

"Sorry about that. My Nonna made me stop by the Church," I said, which was putting my snatching by Bruno and the goon nonne mildly, "so I got sidetracked," I added, which was putting My Big Fat Sicilian Wedding Superstition Sermon mildly.

Marcella's shoulders relaxed. "No worries. We'll deal with Moira and her menu tomorrow. Right now, we're here to celebrate *you*. We all have matching bachelorette sweatshirts," she pointed to gold glitter letters on her chest, "but with different messages."

"I bring ze bail money?" I read.

Glenda turned and showed me hers—or what was left of it. She'd cut most of the fabric from the sweatshirt except for the seams that held it together and a thin strip across her braless breasts with the words *I bring ze bad decisions*.

Nadezhda stopped at a red light and rose from her seat. The spikes of her maroon hair stabbed the ceiling as she pulled out her sweatshirt. *I bring ze booze (and bikini vax for big discount)*.

Reluctantly, I lowered my eyes. *I bring ze bling*.

"Aren't they the *cutest*?" Marcella gushed. "Nadezhda made them."

No kidding. "I appreciate the effort, but what are we going to *do* at this party? Get drunk and rob a jewelry store?"

Marcella giggled and lobbed a punch on my arm that knocked me into the van wall. "Please. You're rocking a multi-stone masterpiece from Bradley." She eyed the ruby surrounded by diamonds on my ring finger and sighed. "Lucky girl."

"You'll have an engagement ring one day soon."

"Sure, and I'll also have abs, a villa in Positano, and a carb-free diet that doesn't make me homicidal. But go on, tell me more fairytales."

That was the last time I tried to comfort Marcella.

The light turned green, and Nadezhda stepped on the gas. "Ve go to beach on bourbon to ride vhale."

My eyes shifted to Glenda for a translation.

"It's a club called The Beach on Bourbon, Miss Franki. They've got a mechanical whale. After that, we're going to Bourbon Cowboy so you can ride their mechanical bull."

That clarified things—sort of. "Just out of curiosity, why are crime and riding mechanical animals the themes of my bachelorette?"

Glenda touched the tip of her tongue to her upper lip, amused. "It's practice for your wedding night."

Thankfully, we were near Bourbon Street because as soon as Nadezhda found a parking space, I planned to blow the bizarre bachelorette bus. "Does Veronica know about this party?"

"She does." Glenda produced a penis-shaped cigarette holder, introducing a third unfortunate theme for my bachelorette. "But we didn't tell her about your abduction. We merely told her to meet us at the club."

Marcella's eyes lit up. "Her shirt says, 'I bring ze alibi,' and Ruth's says—"

"You invited *Ruth*?" I interrupted, aghast.

"And that medium, Chandra Toccato."

The mention of Bradley's assistant and the psycho psychic sent me over the edge. I lunged past her and yanked the sliding door handle.

Locked. I was trapped like a non-mechanical animal.

Marcella shoved me back into my seat. "I know you're not exactly BFFs with Chandra and Ruth, but the shirts came as a set, and we needed someone to wear *I bring ze fun* and *I bring ze party*."

The fact that she'd picked none other than Ruth and Chandra to wear those messages made me take a hard look at Marcella. I'd always known she was passionate and excitable, but there was an aspect to her that I'd overlooked—her pizza was short a few pepperonis.

There was only one thing to do—get this bust of a bachelorette party started. "Nadezhda, where's the booze your shirt says you're bringing?"

"Marcella have Jell-O shots."

"*I do.*" Marcella gave my arm a slap. "See what I did there?"

Yeah. A red welt on my bicep.

She opened a mini cooler and pulled out IV solution-style bags labelled *Squeeze Shot* that were filled with a red-orange substance.

My lips revolted into a wrinkle. "Are these the blood bag energy drinks Chandra used to buy from Boutique du Vampyre?"

"No, this is a Jell-O cocktail I created called 'Rome-ing for a Ring.' Ruby red grapefruit juice and Prosecco to evoke your Rome honeymoon and that ruby-and-diamond rock on your finger."

The van hit a bump, then another, and we jiggled like the Jell-O.

"Ve park." Nadezhda shut off the engine.

Marcella handed me an IV bag and then squeezed a glob of shot into her mouth. "When we come back to the van, we're having a drink called Bling Rings, except for Nadezhda since she's driving."

"*Da.* I only have vodka."

That wasn't comforting, but it could've explained why she'd parked halfway on a sidewalk. "Can you unlock the door?"

Nadezhda grumbled but released the lock. "Ve leave Frank at bar."

My plan was the other way around, but her suggestion worked too. I passed Marcella and opened the door.

"Wait," Marcella shrieked and man-handled my arm.

Startled, I gaped at her. She sounded as though I were

heading into a war zone, which, I was—Bourbon Street. But still. "What's the matter?"

"You need your bachelorette party veil."

No, I didn't. The sweatshirt was enough—make that too much.

I climbed from the van. We weren't parked on Bourbon but rather one street over on Dauphine in front of a macabre business, the Museum of Death, which had a disturbing Broadway lights–style sign. *I hope that doesn't become the fourth unfortunate theme for my bachelorette.*

My body flinched, unsure why my brain had thought something so dark.

Glenda stepped out in a leopard-sequined thong—to go with her eyelashes—and fishnet stockings with platform stripper heels that said "ride" and "tribe."

The meaning was unclear, but odds were good she hadn't joined a cycling group.

She followed my gaze to her feet. "I scratched off the 'b' in 'bride,' sugar. No offense, but I can't have that word on my person. I wouldn't want to mislead my public when this body's still in business." She lit the cigarette in the penis-shaped holder to add emphasis to the last sentence.

"Da." Nadezhda ran her hands over her matryoshka middle. "Zis body in bizness too."

Fortunately, two thirtyish brunettes walked up in navy puffer vests, plaid shirts, and jeans, so I didn't have to comment.

"Hi, I'm Jody," the taller brunette said and pointed to her friend. "This is Logan."

The shorter brunette nodded.

Jody looked at Nadezhda. "We saw the slogan on your company van, 'Before you get your drink on get your hairs in order,' and the ad for the wax discount on your shirt. And we were wondering, can we get a couple of bikini waxes and some vodka tonics to go?"

Logan laid pleading eyes on Glenda. "We're from Alaska."

"*Lawd*, Miss Nadezhda." Glenda's hand was pressed to her breasts. "That's where the Bush People live. It's an emergency."

"*Da*. I handle." Nadezhda gave Glenda her bag and ushered the women inside the van. Then she pushed up her sleeves, flashed her eye-tooth hole, and climbed in.

"The Stripper" played on Glenda's phone.

"Excuse me, Miss Franki. I need to take this." She strutted up the sidewalk.

"Here we go!" Marcella rushed me, waving a headband with a veil covered in tiny lights and the gold glitter words, *Last fling before ze ring!*

Apparently, Nadezhda had made it as well. "Is everything about the ring?"

Marcella's jaw set as hard as a square-cut diamond. "Yes, Franki, it is. Particularly for those of us who don't have one."

"Let's put on my veil, shall we?" I asked as jolly as Santa from the Christmas Car. I'd forgotten she was unhappily single, and I wanted to avoid another manhandling. Thanks to my mother and that boiling bubble light, I already had a nose bruise and a neck burn.

Marcella situated the headband in my hair and handed me a compact mirror.

The veil lights glowed green, white, and red. It resembled the headpiece my nonna had made me wear to my first Communion—but decorated like a Christmas tree.

"Sweet spaghetti!" Marcella shouted. "A spicy Italian dish in the colors of the flag. How lucky is Bradley?"

He *was* lucky, but not because of the flag lights. And I didn't know how I felt about the odd food analogy.

Glenda strut-strode up. "That was Maybe Baby." She pout-pursed. "I don't have any specifics, but there's a situation at Bradley's bachelor party."

My pulse picked up—to the thumping beat of a strip-club soundtrack. "WHAT DO YOU MEAN, 'A SITUATION?'"

"Stay calm, Miss Franki. Whatever is going down, I'm sure it's not what you're thinking." She batted her spotted lashes. "And if it is, I'd like to remind you that sex is perfectly natural."

Marcella screamed.

Which didn't help the "situation."

"Get in the van." I snatched Nadezhda's bag from Glenda's hand and pulled out the keys. "I'm driving."

We piled inside, and I started the engine.

"Vhat you do?" Nadezhda shouted from the back. "I vax client."

"Yeah," Jody chimed in—with a considerable amount of concern in her voice, "I'm on the table here."

"Brace yourself." Keeping my eyes on the road because I didn't dare look in the rearview mirror, I floored the gas. "We're going to a bachelor party."

"Zis *iz* bachelor party," Nadezhda groused.

Later, I would get her for that. In the meantime, I turned to Glenda—or maybe "on" was the more appropriate preposition. "Tell me what Maybe Baby said—*verbatim*."

"She said, 'Come quick. It's emergent.'"

When it came to vocabulary, Maybe Baby was the slimmest dictionary on the shelf. Nevertheless, it was clear that some sort of emergency was taking place, more urgent than the one in Jody and Logan's jeans.

The question was, WHAT IN THE FOCCACCIA WAS HAPPENING AT MY FIANCÉ'S BACHELOR PARTY?

"I'M SORRY, ma'am, but the bachelor party is off limits." The late-twenty-something woman behind Le Richelieu Hotel's old-fashioned mahogany reception desk spoke in a tart tone despite her "Candy Kelly" nametag. She placed a room key into a cubby behind her. "Detective's orders."

"You don't understand." I removed my veil to show I meant business, not just bling. "I'm the bachelor's fiancé, and Anthony Amato, the manager of this hotel, is my brother. So, just tell me where the party is, okay?"

Candy pushed wavy auburn hair behind one ear, calling attention to features so sharp they could cut a person—a long nose, a hard jawline, and a pointed chin. One of her overplucked eyebrows formed an angry arch. "*You* don't understand. I'm the assistant manager, and the police gave me strict orders."

Turning, I shot a look at Glenda and Marcella, who stood behind me like two goon nonne. We were sans Nadezhda and the Alaskans, who were still in the Lucky's Liquor and Vaxing van. Based on the screams that had come from the table, the mobile bikini wax hadn't gone well.

"Listen," I said, turning back to Candy. "Something's going on at that party, and I'm not leaving until I know what it is. So, either you tell me where my fiancé is, or I storm this hotel with them." I moved to give her a better look at Marcella, because she was linebacker large, and Glenda, because she was nearly naked and holding a penis. If my instincts were right, they weren't a pair Candy would want roaming the hotel hallways.

Candy's full lips thinned. "In the Terrace Lounge." She pointed to a closed door. "Right there."

Given my current deficiency in the survival instincts department, it was a relief to learn that my people-reading office was sufficiently staffed—with an Italian-American bully and an aging flasher. But I was disappointed that I hadn't known the party was literally beside us.

The three of us entered the Terrace Lounge, but it was empty and decidedly three-star like the rest of Le Richelieu. The walls were white, an unusual choice for a colorful city like The Big Easy, and decorated with black-and-white photos of famous patrons, including Loretta Swit and Dan Aykroyd.

The bar itself was nothing special—wood with a mirrored backdrop and a yellow-brown granite counter surrounded by faux leather stools. Four two-tops lined the room, and in a corner next to the Monsieurs' bathroom was Glenda's portable pole—the one she'd once kept in our front yard for practice and spontaneous performances.

But my eyes locked onto something more egregious. On an adjoining patio overlooking a pool sat a white pop-out cake with the top tier open and the message, *One last slice before she takes your life!*

My head jerked to Glenda. "It's not like I'm going to *kill* Bradley after I marry him."

"For all intents and purposes, Miss Franki," she struck an unfortunate pose with her penis cigarette holder, "marriage *is* death."

My mind flashed back to the Museum of Death as my fingers flashed the scongiuri gesture to ward off the doom Glenda had cast on us with that comment. Good thing the nonne hadn't heard her, particularly Funeral-Faced Nonna. Otherwise, they'd turn our vow exchange into a memorial service.

Anthony blew into the lounge. He'd replaced his velvet tracksuit with cheap slacks, a white shirt, and a brown tie that—on him—resembled a noose. His dark hair was ruffled, and his brow was bathed in perspiration. "Yo, Sis," he said in the New Jersey accent he'd somehow acquired after a lifetime in Houston, "we've got a situation heuh."

"I'm aware. Now would you please tell me what this 'situation' is?"

He glanced at the cake and tugged his tie-noose. "A blonde wheeled that cake onto the patio with a woman inside, and she didn't pop out."

The blonde must've been Maybe Baby. "What do you mean, 'she didn't pop out?' Is she okay?"

Anthony sucked his teeth. "I'll put it dis way, she ain't gonna be the life of no more parties."

Glenda gasped. "That poor child."

Marcella screamed—again—and hid behind her hair.

The "life" seemed to leave my legs, and I braced myself on the bar. "What happened?"

He shrugged. "Dunno yet. A couple of cops took Bradley and the other guests to the kitchen." He pointed to the patio. "It's that building on the other side o' the pool."

"Oh, dear God." I wrung my hands. "Do we know the woman's name?"

Glenda nodded. "I do, sugar, because I hired her. Dana Del Ray."

"Why did you pick her?"

"She happened to be here having a drink when I came in to discuss the party with Anthony."

A fiftyish detective emerged from the kitchen outside followed by a prematurely bald male in a bartender apron. The detective dialed a number on his phone and entered the lounge, scowling at us. "You all need to leave, *stat*."

We stepped back into the lobby. Glenda and Marcella, both distraught, sat on a couch just outside the door. I stayed on my feet with Anthony so that I had a view into the lounge.

The bartender removed his apron and emptied the tip jar, probably closing shop, and the detective peered through a window at the cake on the patio as he spoke on the phone.

Anxiety gnawed at my gut, and I paced the lobby. "Glenda,

do you know if Dana had any health conditions? Or if she'd been ill recently?"

"Of course not, sugar. Only the best for Bradley."

"Oh, that's niiice," Marcella cooed.

I was glad *she* felt good about that, because I sure didn't.

Anthony pulled me aside into a large hallway with the elevators. "Between you and me, I think it was Giada's cookin'."

My brother's intelligence was questionable, as evidenced by his preference for Guido speak, but even I couldn't believe he'd be so insensitive. "A woman's dead, Anthony. This is no time to joke."

"Who's jokin'?" He looked over his shoulder, then stepped closer. "Giada fed Dana *spaghetti alla sambuca* before she got in the cake, and now her face is the color of the sauce."

"*Pff!* That's an obvious exaggeration."

His brow popped. "No, it ain't. That red sauce wasn't natural. It was neon-glow tomato, and Dana's face looks just like it."

I peered into the lobby from the hallway. The detective was still in the lounge on his phone. Then I returned to Anthony. "Did you see Dana before she got in the cake?"

"Yeah, I showed her to the kitchen."

"How'd she act? Was she agitated?"

"Nah," he wiped perspiration from his lip, "she was normal."

"Did she talk to anyone besides you and Giada?"

"Just Bradley."

"*Bradley?*" Now *I* was agitated.

"He was in the kitchen."

Probably to talk to Giada—he hoped.

The detective passed through the lobby and went outside to Chartres Street. A police car pulled up, and he leaned into the window.

Seizing the moment, I hurried out to the patio to the cake, which came to my chest, and peered inside.

A thin woman with long, shiny black hair, possibly a wig, was seated with her knees pulled into her chest in the small space. I couldn't see her eyes because her head was lowered, but that didn't matter.

Dana Del Ray was definitely dead.

A patch of her cheek was visible through a part in her hair, and Anthony hadn't been exaggerating about her skin color. It was neon glow, but scarlet, not tomato—and shockingly so.

Despite the strong vanilla scent of her perfume, one other odor was perceptible.

Sweet almond.

Cyanide!

Stunned by the discovery, I backed away from the cake. Then I went in the lounge and collapsed on a bar stool. I didn't know what any of it meant except that someone had murdered Dana.

But who?

And why do it at Bradley's bachelor party?

Nadezhda entered and tossed a red python handbag on the counter before sliding onto a stool at the opposite end of the bar. Her sweatshirt was askew, and a few of her maroon spikes had been flattened. "Marigny Mule. Make it double."

The bartender recoiled, which was understandable. The penny-pinching, booze-peddling, bikini-waxing Communist had that effect on people. "We're closed."

"Vhatever." She waved him off, pulled a bottle of vodka from her bag, and proceeded to guzzle.

Marcella entered the lounge and sat beside me. "I guess Nadezhda's as shaken as we are by the news."

Glenda sashayed over. "I haven't told her about Dana, Miss Marcella. She's all shook from those bikini waxes." She shuddered, and the holes in her sweatshirt presented a problem—two of them. "It was a gruesome scene on that waxing table."

Not as gruesome as the one in the cake.

Marcella's eyes widened. "Did one of the women get burned? The van ride was pretty hairy—I mean, scary." She glanced at me. "No pun intended at a time like this."

"Miss Nadezhda's too much of a pro to be thrown off her game by Miss Franki's driving." Glenda batted leopard lashes. "I was talking about those Alaskan lady parts. In cold climates, the women tend to have thick undercoats, similar to seals."

The upside to being in a state of shock was that Glenda's explanations had no effect—like water off an unwaxed Alaskan's back.

Veronica entered the lounge from the patio, her face as white as her *I bring ze alibi* sweatshirt.

"Veronica." I bolted from the stool. "What're you doing here?"

"Dirk called me from the party and told me what happened, so I rushed over from The Beach on Bourbon. I've been outside in the—"

She went silent, as a muscular forty-something officer I hadn't seen before entered the lounge from the patio.

Glenda ran a hand over her *I bring ze bad decisions* and raised her hand. "If you need someone to strip search, Officer honey, I volunteer."

The Officer remained expressionless as another officer emerged from the kitchen with Bradley in tow. When they entered the lounge, Bradley saw me and blanched. "Franki."

Veronica lunged forward and threw her arms around mine as the officers led him out toward the hotel entrance. "It's going to be fine."

But there was no need for her to restrain me. I was as still as Glenda's stripper pole, and I couldn't speak.

Because Bradley was in handcuffs.

"Stay calm, Franki." Veronica looked into my eyes. "The

detective says he found a bottle of liquid cyanide in Bradley's coat pocket."

Marcella screamed, her signature reaction.

The air left my lungs, but I didn't make a sound.

The room tilted and began to spin.

Am I on Glenda's pole? No, I'm on my feet... but not for long.

The Broadway lights of the Museum of Death sign danced in my head.

"Call the Christmas Car." I dropped to the floor.

Out like an old tree light.

4

———

The mattress felt good on my back—comforting, quasi cradling, which was odd for a French bordello bed that belonged to Glenda.

Wait. I'm in bed?

So, it was all just a dream? The superstition seminar, the bad bachelorette, Bradley's arrest?

My eyes opened—to my Mom and Nonna's wedding-fever faces.

Nope, the waking nightmare again.

Except that I wasn't at home. I was in a suite at Le Richelieu. And in addition to the mattress, the hotel's three-star furniture was a vast improvement over the French brothel décor of my apartment. A brown-and-maroon-striped armchair, a chest of drawers, and a chandelier. Even better, windows stretched the length of the room, opening onto a wrought-iron balcony. The only dubious feature was the mirrored wall in front of the bed.

"*Come stai,* Franki?" Nonna moved closer to the bed. "You passed out-a and-a hit-a your head."

My mother pressed her palm to my forehead. "I don't think she's concussed, Carmela. No fever."

The fever reference was ironic. I sat up and propped pillows behind me. "Nope, no concussion. Just painfully lucid."

"I'm glad, dear." My mother pinched the bridge of her nose. "Because as we discussed," she said in a feverish pitch, moving closer to the breaking point with each syllable, "a problem with the wedding has popped up."

The corners of my mouth nosedived. Technically it wasn't an 'I told you so,' but it was close. I couldn't blame her, though. I'd been delusional to think that Bradley and I could keep our wedding under control because: one, my family; two, New Orleans; and three, I'd sensed trouble was coming. Plus, given my track history, it should have been as plain as the bruised nose on my face that I wasn't going to get hitched without a hitch. "How did I get in this room?"

"Anthony and a couple of the bellhops carried you."

"You wouldn't wake up-a after the shock-a."

My brain hadn't wanted to, apparently. Now that I *was* awake, I should've been devastated, but I was too numb to feel anything. Bradley's arrest didn't seem real, and neither did Dana Del Ray's murder.

But both *were* real.

Chillingly so.

My mother paced along the windows. "I called Lillian to let her know her son has been arrested."

"Mom, I should've been the one to call her."

She spun to look at me. "Francesca, this is a matter between mothers. Remember what I said about the cunzata del letto—we represent wisdom and maturity."

The nature of a tradition that involved virgins making a bed and relatives rigging it was proof the wisdom-and-maturity theory was tenuous.

Nonna shuffled to the armchair. "I made a call-a too." She

took a seat and raised her chin. "It's-a time-a to bring out-a the big-a guns-a!"

Whatever or whomever the big guns were, I welcomed them. Hell, I'd even welcome the goon nonne with open arms. "How did Lillian take the news?"

"I believe she said," my mother cleared her throat, "'Bradley murdered a stripper?'"

The question was akin to a slap. I was numb, not dead.

Nonna's face assumed a long-suffering look—longer-suffering than her standard long-suffering look. "Tell-a Franki what-a his-a nonna Cordelia said-a."

"Something to the effect of," my mother gave her big hair a bump, "'Did he do it to cover up a tawdry affair?'"

My brow shot up. Not the questions I would've expected from his family, but everyone reacts in their own unique way—at least, that's what I was telling myself. "Did they say when they're coming?"

My mom pinched the bridge of her nose again. "A second problem has popped up. The Boston airports are shut down due to a blizzard, so it could be days."

They could miss the wedding. My stomach flipped. *What was I thinking? There probably isn't going to be a wedding.*

"But don't worry." My mother approached the bed and patted my hand. "The Hartmanns are going to call their family attorney, and with their money, I'm sure they have the finest in the country."

"Bradley's innocent," I said, because someone had to. "Whoever murdered Dana Del Ray obviously framed him."

Nonna raised her rosary. "Who would-a *do* such a thing-a to Brad-a-ley?"

The truth was, I had an idea.

But I couldn't let my mind go there.

I wouldn't.

Not until I was forced.

A knock sounded at the door.

My mother opened it, and Veronica entered, her face marked with worry. She sat on the side of the bed and took my hand.

I stared into her eyes searching for reassurance. "Is there anything you can do for him?"

She exhaled. "Not tonight. He'll have to go before a judge in the morning for a bail hearing, although...it's not likely to be granted." She squeezed my fingers. "But I'll be there first thing in the morning to see what I can do."

"I'm going with you."

My mother stopped pacing. "Now, Francesca, the best thing you could do for Bradley is to find out who killed that woman."

"I agree with your mom." Veronica tightened her squeeze. "Let me handle the legal stuff. Bradley needs you—and *I* need you—to investigate who murdered Dana. After all, I love him too."

For the first time, tears pricked at my eyelids. But I blinked them away. If I opened those flood gates, I would cry me a Mississippi River. And then a Lake Pontchartrain.

"You gotta do it, Franki." Nonna raised a fist. "To save-a the wedding!"

They were right. Even though I was still in shock, I needed to snap out of it, for Bradley's sake. "I'll start with the bachelor party guests."

Veronica released my fingers. "That'll be easy, because I've already talked to Dirk—"

"Where *is* Dirk?" I interrupted, anxious to hear what her husband knew about the ill-fated party.

"He went home to let Hercules out."

The mention of her Chihuahua reminded me that I needed to get home to Napoleon.

"Unfortunately, he arrived after Dana was found dead, so he

doesn't know anything. And Giada and Maybe Baby are still at the police station. But David and The Vassal were there for a while, so you could start with them."

It didn't surprise me that our college co-workers had gone to Bradley's bachelor party. They were Comp Sci geeks who didn't have much luck in the way of dates. What *did* surprise me was that they'd left, especially when a crime had been committed. "Why didn't they stay the whole time?"

Veronica bit her lip. "David said The Vassal was getting 'overstimulated.'"

"Makes sense." The Vassal had a history of getting overexcited about breasts that included offering his college fund to pay for a woman's implants and stealing a giant cast of Glenda's boobs from the front of the fourplex to hang in his and David's fraternity house. I could just see him, coke-bottle glasses fogged up, unfastening the top button of his plaid shirt as his jaw hung slack.

Nonna tugged the hem of her mourning dress. "Bruno Messina was-a there."

"What?" I frowned. "I didn't see him."

My mother turned from a window. "He must've left after Dana was discovered."

Figures he'd leave. "Why was he at the party in the first place? He's not friends with Bradley."

My mother pursed. "Anthony told us about the bachelor party, and your Nonna thought it would be a good idea to have a chaperone."

"What's-a the problem?" Nonna shrugged, palms raised, to stave off any protest from me. "I told-a Santina, and-a she told-a Bruno. He offer to do it-a, and I said-a fine."

"Very generous of him, dear."

Degenerate was more like it, which explains why he split before the cops got there. No live stripper, no Bruno. "What about Craig

Burns, Bradley's former client at Pontchartrain Bank? And his friends from college?"

Veronica rubbed her thighs. "Dirk said Craig had a family emergency, so he canceled at the last minute. And Bradley's friends didn't make it because their flight out of Boston was canceled due to the blizzard."

And I'd thought my *bachelorette* was a bust. The van party was a blast by comparison. Speaking of which, I was filled with regret at not saving my Rome-ing for a Ring Jell-O IV bag. I could use a booze injection about now.

Maybe there's a bar in the suite?

The door opened, and Anthony poked his head in. "Youse guys need to clear out. We just sent a car to pick up the people stayin' in heuh."

"This room is *rented*?" I asked, incredulous.

"What? I ain't gonna pay a maid to clean a vacant room when I already gotta pay her to clean this one." He pointed a hairy finger at me. "And you should be glad you got to stay in the Paul McCartney suite for free. It's the most expensive room in the hotel."

My eyes narrowed, and I slid off the bed. "I would say you're a real character, Anthony, but you have none."

"Fran-ces-caaa," my mother drawled, "be nice to your brother. After all, he carried you up here."

Anthony rubbed his collarbone. "Yeah, and I think I dislocated my shoulder."

My Mom went to check his arm.

My face flamed, possibly as neon red as Dana Del Ray's. When it came to their mothers, Italian men got away with murder.

Murder.

Bradley! I swooned and fell backwards onto the bed.

My mother turned. "You need to stay at the hotel tonight. You're in no condition to drive."

"Ma," Anthony whined, "she can't stay in this suite."

"Yeah," I shot him a cold stare, "we got that, Anthony."

Nonna nodded. "She can-a stay in-a my room-a. We say-a the rosary and-a watch-a the Pope-a do the Epiphany mass on-a YouTube-a."

Anthony recoiled and backed from the room.

And I related. I'd rather resurrect my bachelorette party—mechanical animals included. "Thanks, Nonna, but I have to go home and take care of Napoleon."

Veronica looked at my mother. "I'll make sure Franki gets home."

"That would be great." I managed a grim grin. "I need some time alone to process this."

My mother put her hands on my shoulders. "As God is my witness," she raised a Scarlett O'Hara-style fist, "your wedding is going to happen."

To my dismay, I got an image of her in the plantation-style wedding dress—and then Carol Burnett in that olive-green curtain.

"It is-a going-a to happen, Franki." Nonna rose and patted my cheek. "Believe-a your Nonna."

I wanted to believe her. My mom too. The will of the two women was stronger than a steel crucifix, but there was only so much they could do. Ultimately, saving Bradley and our wedding was up to me.

And I was terrified that I wasn't up to it.

Veronica opened the door, and I followed her into the hallway.

"Now that we're out of earshot," she pulled her phone from her Chanel bag, "I managed to snap a picture of the cyanide bottle before the detective bagged it."

We stopped at the elevator. She pressed the down button and handed me the phone.

On the screen was a photo of a green bottle, clearly vintage, with raised letters in the glass that spelled *potassium cyanide*. "It looks like an antique."

"There can't be many in circulation. That'll make it easier to trace."

It would, but the problem, as always, was where to start looking.

The elevator arrived, and we got in.

Veronica grimaced. "Brace yourself, because the bottle's not the only evidence."

My hand, on autopilot, shot to the elevator wall, as she pressed the first-floor button.

"And remember," she gave me a hard stare, "there is most assuredly a logical explanation for what I'm about to tell you."

My eyes shot sideways. "Not a good intro, Veronica."

Her mouth took on a grim set. "Just hear me out, okay?"

The doors closed, and I tried not to take that as another bad sign. "Shoot."

"The police went through Bradley's wallet," she paused, "and they found Dana Del Ray's business card."

My stomach plummeted before the elevator began to lower.

THE ELEVATOR DOORS OPENED, and my stomach dropped further than when Veronica told me about Dana Del Ray's business card in Bradley's wallet. At the reception was none other than Ruth Walker, Bradley's annoying assistant, and she was hopping mad. Case in point—the toe of one of her Keds was tapping so hard on the black-and-white tiled floor that her jowls were jumping.

Ruth rang the bell—despite the fact that Candy was behind

the desk. "Hello?" She rang it again. "Is there anyone in this down-at-the-heels hotel who'll help me?"

Candy leaned hard on her palms, and not only were her eyes shooting daggers, but all of her sharp features were stabby. "You can try every one of our employees, but you're not setting foot in the Terrace Lounge."

Reluctantly, I followed Veronica to the reception.

As I passed a lone Corinthian column at the end of the desk, Ruth fixed me with a stare as withered as her sixty-something skin. "Bradley's in jail, and you went to relax in a suite?"

My eyes shifted to a gilded mirror on the wall, and the look on my face resembled Saint George's as he was slaying the dragon at St. Mary's Church. Of course, I couldn't *slay* Ruth, but I did consider clawing out her eyes and adding them to the Saint Lucy statue's eyeballs plate.

"Ruth," Veronica's tone was cold and clipped, "we're all shocked and upset about what has happened, but your behavior is uncalled for."

Her whiskered chin drew up, and her turkey neck trembled. "I'll tell you what's uncalled for. I come up here to find out who set up my employer for murder, and not only is our ace PI—and Bradley's fiancé—MIA, but this crackerjack clerk won't let me investigate."

Candy's face turned as red and hard as a candy apple.

Ruth put her hands on her hips and surveyed us with contempt. "Whatever happened to breaking the law for a good cause, people? Bradley's arrest calls for some good old-fashioned vigilante justice."

Part of me agreed with her, which was distressing. The other part of me wanted to go home and sleep off this nightmare. I desperately wanted to help my fiancé, but I needed to decompress before I could trust myself to think rationally, i.e., not like Ruth.

Anthony emerged from a hallway and yanked up the waist of his slacks. "What's all the bell ringing about?"

"Uh, Anthony," I gestured to Ruth. "This is Bradley's assistant, Ruth Walker."

Candy's plucked brow went up. "Ms. Walker wants access to the crime scene."

"Damn right I do," Ruth shouted. "The Louisiana flag you're flying out front has the word 'justice' on it, that's what I want for my employer."

"Can't help you, lady," my brother said in his best hotel-manager speak. "We've already got enough problems, so we're following Detective DiMaio's orders. You'll have to wait until he gives the all-clear."

Ruth turned to me and jerked a thumb at Anthony. "This your brother?"

I nodded.

She sniffed. "Figures." She puckered and looked down at the marble floor. "I'll just have to conduct my own investigation—starting now." Her head shot up. "What's this business about a 'Christmas Car?'"

The reference shocked me—like an electric current transmitted via vintage tinsel. No way I was giving away my jolly holiday escape, especially not after the devastating developments. "I don't know what you're talking about."

"Nadezhda told me you said it right before you fainted."

"That's what trauma does to you. By the way, where *is* Nadezhda and the rest of my bachelorette party?"

Ruth's eyes narrowed to slits as thin as her lips. "Just like you to think of partying at a time like this. But if you must know, Nadezhda took Glenda and Marcella to Central Lockup. The police are still questioning that stripper, Maybe Baby, who helped organize the bachelor party, and Glenda wants to find out if they're going to arrest her."

Veronica slid her bag onto her shoulder. "What about Giada?"

Ruth shrugged. "They didn't mention her."

Giada had plenty of family who would come to her rescue. I was concerned about a certain Crescent City Medium with a spirit-channeling charm bracelet. "Does Chandra know what happened to Dana?"

"Certainly. She was with me when Nadezhda called. But she refused to help—like the rest of you lot—because she says this hotel is haunted."

My eyes rolled, and not because of Ruth's rudeness. It was because Chandra had a bad case of phasmophobia, not to mention phasmo*phonia*.

Candy smirked at Anthony. "I'll bet this Chandra person is talking about Ellen."

His jaw tightened, and he rubbed the back of his neck. "Never mind her."

"Who's Ellen?" Ruth barked. "The ghost of the sad sack who decorated this reception back in the 1800s?"

Candy tucked auburn hair behind her ear. "Ellen is the ghost of a former employee who still reports to work. She likes to chat with guests and clean rooms. Her favorite things to do are make beds and tidy up personal belongings."

Sounded like Anthony *didn't* have to hire a maid to clean up after me. He had a free ghost who was happy to do it.

Ruth leaned on the desk. "Chandra didn't mention any Ellen. She kept rattling on about soldier ghosts."

Candy pulled a brochure from a display rack on a counter beneath the key cubbies. "This has a history of the hotel. It was the site of the Spanish barracks from 1763 to 1803, when France ceded Louisiana to pay a war debt. We have guests who claim they see soldiers in the hallways."

The soldiers were news to me, but that explained why the hotel cross street was named Barracks.

"Before the barracks," Candy opened the brochure and laid it on the counter, "it was Royal Hospital, run by Ursuline nuns. Most of their patients were soldiers, but they also treated civilians and slaves for malaria and yellow fever. Some guests say the specter of an old nun—"

"Enough o' this ghost bunk." Anthony, who'd turned as white as Casper the Friendly Ghost in a snowstorm, snatched the brochure and returned it to the display. "Don't you got work to do, Candy?"

Her eyes flamed with fury that she quickly tamped down.

But I couldn't blame my brother for his reaction. In Italy, it was bad luck for a single man to see a nun. And after my Sicilian superstition sermon at the church, I sure as hell didn't want to see a nun, either, regardless of whether it was my wedding day or not. Given the run of bad luck Bradley and I were already having, I just wasn't willing to risk any more.

Ruth puckered as though she'd eaten a lemon. "Hades must be hosting a snowball fight, because I agree with an Amato— Anthony, that is. We've got work to do to prove Bradley's innocence, so we've got no time nor energy to waste on old ghost stories."

The floor gave way beneath me.

No, it was my knees.

Veronica linked her arm in mine. "Let's get you home." She turned to Ruth. "We'll start investigating tomorrow, after we all get some rest. I'm parked beside Franki at the office, so I'll walk her to her car."

Probably a good idea given my two kidnappings. And I was glad to have her support. A gnawing fear had settled in the pit of my stomach about the reason Bradley had been set up, and the haunted hotel history had only intensified it. Because it raised a terrible, awful question.

Had a ghost from my past come back to haunt us?

MY FINGERS TIGHTENED around the steering wheel, even though the engine was off. Veronica had left Private Chicks hours ago, but I was still immobile in my car.

Numb.

In a daze.

But I had to react. For Bradley's sake—and mine.

And Napoleon's! I checked my phone. Almost three a.m. I had to get home.

Sighing, I started the car and pulled from my parking spot. A foggy mist had rolled in, so I turned on my windshield wipers.

As I turned onto Decatur, the French Quarter was eerily silent. I reminded myself that was normal for early January. In the weeks before Mardi Gras, the city was always dead.

Dead.

Dana inside the cake.

Bradley in a jail cell.

"Who did this to them?" I shifted in my seat as a disturbing thought surfaced. "Was it—"

A black cat darted in front of the Mustang.

Screaming bloody cat murder, I swerved into the opposite lane, narrowly avoiding the animal before swerving back. My heart pounded in sync with Rosary-Bead Nonna's frantic bead-clacking, her warning blaring in my head.

On the way to the church, woe unto you and Bradley if you see a priest, nun, or black cat.

The light at St. Ann turned red. I slammed on the brakes and skidded to a stop. I lowered my head on the steering wheel.

"Don't buy into the superstition nonsense," I told myself. "Also, you're not on your way to church, so you're fine either way."

Wait.

My forehead rolled right, and I stared at the black gothic spires of St. Louis Cathedral emerging from the thick fog behind Jackson Square. "So, you *were* on your way to a church, just not on your wedding day."

"Okay." I sat up. "This is out of hand. Get a hold of yourself."

But a black cat did *cross your path, and that in and of itself is bad luck—wedding or no.*

"Dang it, Franki! Why'd you have to think 'wedding *or no*'?"

Exasperated, I hit the steering wheel. What was I doing to my sanity? And why was I waiting for a light to turn green in the middle of the night? I looked around to make sure the coast was clear before running it. There wasn't a soul in sight.

But someone was in the vicinity.

A man.

Singing.

The sound came from the cathedral—where the ghost of the Capuchin monk, Père Dagobert, was said to appear.

"That's 'ghost bunk,' like Anthony said." Although, he *was* frightened by it.

The singing became fainter, so I rolled down the window and strained my ears to hear the words. The hair on my arms stood at attention like ghost soldiers reporting for un-dead duty.

Kyrie eleison.

The mass for the dead.

"Oh, God," I whispered. "Is he singing for Dana Del Ray?"

Since Père Dagobert was a priest, I had zero plans to stick around and find out. I floored the gas pedal. Whatever was going on at St. Louis Cathedral, I *couldn't* get involved. I *wouldn't.*

But as I sped away, a little voice told me I might not have a say.

5

———————

"**H**oly. Freaking. Hot tub." Unlike the day before when I'd woken to the ceiling of the Le Richelieu Hotel suite, this time I awoke to a poster-sized photo of Glenda dressed as a stripper ski bunny—white furry pasties and a matching thong paired with a rabbit-eared cap, elbow-length *Playboy* bunny gloves, and thigh-high boots with the words "ski" and "me," respectively. Of course, I was more than accustomed to seeing my landlady half naked, but what struck me about this photo was the effort she'd taken to stay warm without putting on any clothes.

"Morning, Miss Franki. Like my new artwork?"

Turning in the giant champagne glass in Glenda's all-white living room—her only piece of furniture—I peered over the rim, glad to see my landlady was wearing her pasty pajamas and thong under her sheer robe. "It's a winter wonderland...of sorts."

Glenda raised a flute of champagne in a toast, but rather than drink she dragged on her Mae West-style holder. "I got the idea to hang it on the ceiling from Miss Nadezhda. She put an eye-candy pic above her mobile waxing table."

Glad I missed that while I was in her van. Nadezhda's taste in eye candy was nothing short of cornea scarring, e.g., a pale, flabby, and shockingly chest-hairless Putin on horseback.

"Before I forget, Napoleon has already had breakfast—the quiche from Thibodeaux's. And he absolutely adored their steak frites for his dinner last night."

I was sure he did—more than he adored me, in fact. "Thanks for feeding him and for letting me crash in your glass. I thought I wanted to be alone, but... not so much."

"Perfectly understandable, sugar. Plus, curling up inside a cocktail glass is surprisingly comforting."

Especially with a soft cashmere blanket the color of bubbly. I felt around the bottom of the glass and found my phone.

"If you're checking for a text from Miss Ronnie, she's down at Central Lockup." She flipped her platinum hair. "While we wait for news on Bradley, I've got something to kickstart your day."

"Please tell me it's a jumbo jar of Nutella and a shovel spoon like the one I had made for my *bomboniere*."

"No, child." She waved her cigarette holder, and her breasts wagged at me. "This has nothing to do with your wedding favors. Shoveling chocolate hazelnut spread into your mouth when you're down and out just *screams* wallowing in self-pity."

"And?" I prompted, puzzled by why that would be a problem considering the arrest of my fiancé days before our wedding.

Glenda fixed me with a stare sharper than a broken acrylic nail. "*Aaand* you're getting my Glitter Grit Getter kit. It contains three things that'll get you back on your feet." She handed me the flute. "Starting with champagne."

"How does getting drunk help me get my grit back?"

"Getting drunk isn't the objective, Miss Franki. Champagne replaces that bitter aftertaste of defeat with a better bitter flavor —one that's expensive."

"Sounds like a plan." I took a swig. She was right. This bitter tasted better.

Glenda pulled a cosmetics jar from the pocket of her robe. "This is Red Hot Body Glitter to give you back your sparkle. It's edible—just in case." She passed it to me and raised her hand. "Before you point out the obvious, I know Bradley's in jail. But he'll get out in time to eat that body glitter on your wedding night, you watch."

Try as I might, I could not envision it. No way Bradley was a glitter eater.

"Be careful not to use too much. It's a tad spicy."

Funny. Marcella had called me a spicy Italian dish, and it appeared that was coming true.

"Finally, the *pièce de résistance.*" Glenda pulled a print copy of her memoirs, *Like a Polecat at a Garden Party*, from her other robe pocket. "Chapter thirteen. I've marked it for you."

I'd read her bestselling memoirs, but it had been a while—and there were quite a few stories I'd worked hard to forget. But since I was so down that I'd sought out the bottom of Glenda's cocktail glass, I took the book and flipped to the chapter. "'The Time I Broke a Heel and Still Made Two Thousand Dollars?'"

"That's two thousand dollars in the *seventies*, sugar. An inspiring story, if I've ever heard one. And with Bradley in jail, you need that kind of motivation to get you out of my glass and on the hunt for Dana Del Ray's real killer."

My eyes lowered to the book. I *did* need a proverbial kick in the rear, and a broken stripper shoe might be just the thing to do it.

"I'll leave you alone to read. But before I do, I have some information for you."

"What is it?"

Glenda took a deep drag and grimaced. "Maybe Baby is still at Central Lockup, and when I was there last night, I got the impression the police think she was in cahoots with Bradley to kill Dana." She blew out some smoke. "Can you imagine?"

"Definitely not." Conspiracy required sustained mental effort, and Maybe Baby only thought in short spurts. "How did she know Dana Del Ray, anyway? From dancing?"

"No," she exhaled a smoke ring, "Dana didn't work in any of the clubs. Only private parties. They met on the Krewe du View."

I sipped champagne. "You mean, the Krewe du *Vieux*? As in the *Vieux* Carré?"

"It's a play on the French pronunciation, sugar. 'Vieux' sounds similar to 'view.' And both the 'Old Quarter' and the 'View Quarter' are appropriate names for the French Quarter these days."

"True dat," I replied in local speak. Anyone walking past the strippers standing outside the clubs on Bourbon Street could see that—plainly.

"Evidently, Dana wanted to quit dancing, so she was funding a parading krewe for girls in the profession."

Mardi Gras krewes were big business in New Orleans, but they cost a fortune to get going. The floats alone could run from thousands to millions. "How was she managing that?"

Glenda put her hand on her hip. "Maybe Baby said Dana had come into money, which I found odd."

"How so?"

"Well, I barely knew Dana, but I'm sure she told me she didn't have any family."

"She could've inherited money from a client or some other acquaintance, like Maybe Baby. You told me a while back that hospital patient she met at her candy-striper job said he was going to leave her his estate."

Glenda pointed her cigarette holder at me. "Oh, I forgot to tell you, sugar. He passed. Left her his party supply business, bounce houses and banquet chairs."

The news took me a moment to digest—not the man's death

but Maybe Baby's career pivot. As a former stripper, she knew a thing or two about bouncing and chairs.

"Anyhoo," Glenda flipped her platinum hair—and a breast, "from time to time clients remember us girls in their wills. But when that happens, believe you me, we all know about it. Getting money from men is our entire business model."

I had no cause to doubt that. Some of Glenda's stripper colleagues had recently paid The Vassal to input the client intel they'd scribbled on bar napkins into a shared database, and the results were nothing short of CIA dossiers.

"If I've learned anything in my years of dancing, it's to follow the dollars, Miss Franki, onstage and off. Money always has a story to tell, and it's rarely as uplifting as my chapter thirteen." She raised her cigarette holder and strutted from the room in her platform stripper slippers.

Picking up the book, I slid to the bottom of the glass to read —for inspiration and I wasn't sure what else.

"MIGHT I SAY, that red glitter is quite Christmasy."

"Thank you, Santa." My eyes met his in the rearview mirror, and my face flushed. Not only was I embarrassed, I was also a little tipsy from my champagne breakfast—hence my decision to call the Christmas Car. Well, that and the promise of holiday music for some Yuletide cheer. So far, though, the playlist had been a literal buzzkill. Prime example, "Blue Christmas" was playing, and right before it was a soul-crushing rendition of "White Christmas."

My gaze strayed to my phone. Still no news from Veronica on Bradley. I rested the side of my head on the window.

"Hermey and I admire your grit after the shock of seeing your fiancé arrested."

Even though he wasn't really Santa Claus, it felt wrong to tell him I owed the grit to an ex-stripper. I raised my head—careful to avoid neck contact with one of the hazardous decorations behind me. "I'm going to do whatever it takes to prove his innocence."

"Atta girl! Where do you plan to start?"

"My cousin Giada. That's why I'm headed to Le Richelieu Hotel. She's the chef, and I need to search the kitchen and talk to her about the sambuca spaghetti she served Dana. Plus, I'm hoping Giada chatted with her and got the name of a friend or acquaintance I can contact."

Santa stopped at a red light. "If not, you could ask around at the clubs to see if any of the other dancers signed up for her Mardi Gras krewe."

Hermey pressed a finger to his tiny mouth. "Too bad City Hall doesn't keep a public database of the krewes. The permit application includes a space for officers."

"How do you know that?" I picked up a mug of hot cocoa on the rear console.

His eyelids dropped to midpoint. "I presume you've heard of the Krewe of the Rolling Elvi?"

"Yeah, the 'Las Vegas Elvis' impersonators on mini bikes. I've seen them in a couple of Mardi Gras parades."

Hermey huffed and adjusted his furry white collar. "The 'Thieving Elvi' is a better name for them. They stole 'Rolling Elvi' from me and my krewe of elves. We were going to be 'Santa and the Rolling Elvi' and follow his sleigh on scooters, like the one meant for Jimmy on the Island of Misfit Toys."

As I poured myself some cocoa, an image of the old-school wooden scooter with black felt eyes and a red felt mouth emerged from the recesses of my brain. I rarely missed the annual rerun of *Rudolph the Red-Nosed Reindeer*.

"Before Hermey and I met," Santa cast an apologetic glance at his partner, "he used to ride with an Elvis impersonator."

Hermey sniffed. "He took the name after I refused to merge our krewes."

"Why did you refuse? You could've called the krewe 'Elfis.'"

Hermey gasped and pressed his palms to his round cheeks. "Elves are *helpers*. We wouldn't *dare* share in the limelight." He turned and stared out the window. "Besides, elves only work for Santa. But even if that weren't the case, can you imagine an elf riding behind an Elvis in a rhinestone cape? Those things are dangerous."

Valid point. The faceted stones could not only do damage, but as slight as Hermey was, they could knock him off the bike. And Elvis just wouldn't be The King in a plain white cape.

Hermey snapped his fingers. "Social media! I'll bet Dana mentioned her krewe officers on a post or a website."

"I'll definitely do a search." I sipped some cocoa.

He eyed my cup. "Peppermint schnapps to top that off?"

It was tempting, but I shook my head. Better not after the champagne.

Santa leaned toward the windshield and stared at the sky. "A cold front's coming in. If this misty rain holds up, it could turn to snow."

Hermey glanced at Santa. "That would be a Christmas miracle."

Except that it wasn't Christmas—at least, not outside the car.

"Speaking of snow..." Hermey raised a bakery box with the words "Sneaux King Cake."

"Say no more." I took a precut slice. The faux Cajun French spelling of "snow" was a nod to the coconut flakes on the powdered sugar icing, and I was here for them. And the cake.

"All I Want for Christmas Is You" came on the stereo—to spite me.

And I shoved half the slice into my mouth.

The sad lyrics reminded me of Père Dagobert's eerie rendition of Kyrie eleison. Since Santa and Hermey claimed to have seen him, I figured it couldn't hurt to mention what I'd heard outside St. Louis Cathedral. "Um, when I was driving home early this morning, I might've had an encounter with Père Dagobert."

Santa set the car in motion and frowned in the rearview mirror. "Was he rotund and jolly? That's how he's described in historical documents."

Hermey shot me a round-eyed side-eye. "Who does that sound like?"

"*Ho, ho, ho!*" Santa slapped the steering wheel. "Père Dagobert was a renowned lover of wine and food who frequented the taverns. And as we've established, I'm a milk-and-cookies man who hangs out in chimneys."

And this Pontiac Catalina.

Hermey laid a serious stare on Santa. "I meant that, like you, Père Dagobert was quite famous in his day and beloved by the people for his charitable work. He also wore unconventional clothing." He turned to the backseat. "Was he by any chance wearing his tricorn?"

"Actually, I didn't see him. The fog was thick, and I was in my car, so I only heard him singing. But he sounded anything but jolly."

Santa pulled to a stop in front of the hotel. "That's concerning."

A *ghost* was concerning, singing or dead silent. "Why do you say that?"

He turned in his seat. "Sightings of Père Dagobert are most common on misty or stormy nights, particularly during times of distress in the city. Pardon the pun, but after Hurricane Katrina, Dagobert sang up a storm."

"Would Dana's murder qualify as distress to the city?"

"Maybe." Santa stroked his beard. "But if you believe in legends, and I do," his eyes twinkled, "then whatever is going on has wider implications."

That was his opinion, and I didn't like it one bit. Because it implied that Dana Del Ray wasn't the killer's sole target. And since Bradley had been framed for her murder, the other target could only be one person.

Me.

"Oh, ho ho *no*." I let go of the handle to the Le Richelieu Hotel entrance and flattened myself against the old brick wall between the door and a green-shuttered window. Ruth Walker was at the reception desk—a "Ruth awakening" after the cozy cocoon of the Christmas Car.

No amount of champagne, body glitter, or Glenda's memoirs could give me the grit I needed to deal with Bradley's assistant when she was in save-my-boss mode. I'd sooner go into battle with a ghost soldier. Or interact with Ellen. Hell, even Père Dagobert.

My gaze lowered to the high-heeled boots I'd worn thanks to chapter thirteen. I didn't think they'd help me find the killer or make two thousand dollars in seventies money, but they *would* remind me that despite a serious obstacle on the way to the altar, the wedding show *had* to go on.

Slowly, I peered into the window. Ruth was gone, so I headed for the door.

"Franki! Ovah heuh."

My boots froze in their tracks, and the familiar Boston accent sent tremor down my spine. Nevertheless, I turned and saw Chandra Toccato, the mad medium, peering from the shadowed alcove of a private residence across the street. Her frosted brown hair was teased so high it doubled as a hat—or an astronaut helmet. The rest of her short, chubby body was bundled in a maxi-length black puffer coat, its silver crescent moons coordinated perfectly with her moon boots.

She motioned for me to approach. "I need to talk to you. It's about what happened to Bradley."

I'd dealt with the fast-talking phasmophobe enough to know that this was a psychic setup. "Why? Ruth said you didn't want to get involved."

Chandra wrung her puffy hands. "I know, but he's my relative. It wouldn't be right to deny him my clairvoyant counsel."

Or profitable. My hand shot to the door handle. "Stay where you are, or I'll open this."

"Have you lost your mind? That hotel is haunted."

Chandra had a lot of nerve asking me that, especially when her last name meant "touched," as in "crazy." "That's right. A ghost could come out. Like a soldier. Or Ellen, the maid."

Her paddle nails pressed into her moon-pie face. "A gh- gh-*ghost* maid?"

Oddly enough, she seemed to be more afraid of Ellen than the Spanish soldiers. Emboldened by this discovery, I went in for the kill. It was either that or face the music of her charm bracelet. "Uh-huh. She chats with guests and rearranges their stuff."

Her face turned lunar white. "Dear Gawd, I knew I had to warn you."

"No, you don't. This conversation is closed." I pulled open the door.

"Don't go in that gawdforsaken hotel!"

"Chandra, these boots *aren't* made for walking, but that's what they're gonna do—right into the lobby."

Her arm shot up, and the charm bracelet began jangling.

"Nope." I ducked inside Le Richelieu. Before the door closed behind me, I heard an ear-splitting scream followed by a telltale thud.

Spinning, I looked through the glass door pane and saw Chandra flat on her back in the middle of Chartres Street, lying beside a green plastic Hand Grenade glass and a broken strand of Mardi Gras beads. But her arm was still upright, and the charm bracelet was jangling.

Damnit. I can't leave her there…

Can I?

Chandra began wailing and flailing on the filthy asphalt, and her cheeks turned hot pink.

A shade reminiscent of Dana Del Ray's scarlet skin.

A sigh hissed from my lips. Chandra was fully aware of her surroundings, but accidents did happen, so I couldn't leave her for dead—even though I was sorely tempted. The crystal ball con artist had been orbiting my life since my second homicide investigation. And given the recent shock-discovery that she was related to Bradley, my chances of breaking free of her were about as good as Saturn ditching its rings.

But I *could* expose the fortune-telling phony.

My patience as thin as the polish on her paddle nails, I yanked open the door and stormed into the street. "Enough of this charade, Chandra. You've got to get up."

She didn't budge, but her bracelet did. "It's not a charade, Franki! It's Dana Del Ray's spirit." Chandra wailed and flailed some more. "She says you're in terrible danger."

"Of course she does." I made sure no cars were coming and squatted beside her, knowing full well that she'd interrogated Ruth about Dana's murder and studied the news for details. "Let me guess," my tone dripped sarcasm like cyanide from a bottle, "Dana says she was poisoned."

"No!" Her head rolled out of sync with the rest of her body.

"She wants me to tell you that it's so much worse than you know."

I smirked. "What is? The situation with Bradley?"

Chandra stopped rolling, but her eyes didn't. "I mean, what else would she be talking about?"

Annoyed, I pursed. "You don't have to be a smart alec about it."

She pushed onto her elbows. "In my defense, I'm thrashing around on this dirty street in the grips of a spirit, trying to help you out. I'd like to get on with it so I can get up."

My lids lowered. For someone in the clutches of a ghost, she was awfully in control. Plus, we both knew that whenever Chandra was trying to help me out, it wasn't out of the goodness of her heart but rather the fatness of her billfold. "Fine. Tell Dana to cut to the chase."

"Okay." She fell back and flailed.

If there were an award for worst psychic, Chandra would win, but she wouldn't see it coming.

"Franki!" She latched onto my arm. "Dana says, 'Beware the pear!'"

And I'd been worried about the lemons on my windshield. "Uh, what does fruit have to do with her death?"

"Let me check." Chandra resumed writhing.

A group of thirty-something men drinking Pat O'Brien's Hurricanes and wearing sweatshirts that said "New Orleans is for livers" stopped on the hotel sidewalk to watch the sham psychic scene.

"Oooh," she breathed. "Thanks for the clarification."

My brow cocked, and I grimaced. "Well? People are staring."

She glanced at the men and stopped squirming long enough to smooth her tousled tease. "Dana wasn't talking about a pear, as in the fruit. She meant the French word for 'priest,' *père*."

Dagobert? I bolted up in my boots, blew past the boozers

hell-bent on damaging their livers, and burst into the hotel. The second I was inside, I pressed my back to the door to steady myself. Not because of my high heels, but because my legs were the consistency of Marcella's Rome-ing for a Ring Jell-O IV shot.

The truth was, I was rattled. I'd only talked to two people about Père Dagobert.

And Chandra wasn't one of them.

6

———————

"Uh, Sis?" Anthony eyed me from behind the Le Richelieu reception desk. "Are you sparklin'?"

My face flamed the color of the red hot body glitter. I wasn't only embarrassed—I was also a little light-headed. Not from my champagne breakfast or the Chandra business, but from the hot cocoa and Sneaux King Cake. "It's a long story."

"Then how 'bout you tell me what you were doin' in the street? You made Le Richelieu look low rent."

"*Me?* How about the *murder* that happened here? Or the helmet-haired woman in the moon outfit ranting about channeling a dead woman's spirit?"

He blanched and pointed at me. "Don't youse start wit' the ghost garbage. I get enough o' that from Candy and all the paranormal kooks who come in after the Haunted History tours."

Fortunately, I didn't have to worry about Chandra coming in, or the supposed spirit of Dana Del Ray. What I *did* have to worry about was his assistant manager stopping me from investigating. "Where *is* Candy, by the way?"

"She works the evenin' shift. I've gotta hire someone to work days. We just lost a guy to the morgue."

My head lurched forward. "He died *too*?"

"You got death on the brain, or somethin'? He took a job as a transport tech."

Shame. He could've moved bodies here—both Dana's and Anthony's after I killed him. "Is Giada around?"

He grimaced. "She's in the kitchen with that uptight lady who works for Bradley."

Ruth. After the Chandra shock, I'd forgotten about seeing her in the lobby. I drummed my fingers on the counter, trying to figure out a way to get rid of her. She was a bigger problem than Candy and Chandra combined.

An elderly woman with a masculine face and the hooked nose of Italy's Christmas witch, La Befana, entered the hotel decked out in full Italian Widow Winter—a brown mink coat, a black Dolce & Gabbana lace dress, and fine jewelry from their rosary line (not costume like Rosary-Bead Nonna's). She carried one of the brand's signature Miss Sicily bags, this one in black lizard with a flap that featured a gold crown with red and green jewels, star studs, and blue and white wings. On the body of the bag, a white banner read *SANTA* in big red block letters, with *Sicily* below in cursive.

Holy Sicily, indeed. The bag would've been perfect for Saint Lucy both because she was the patron saint of Siracusa and because she'd had her eyes plucked out so she wouldn't have to see the thing.

The woman took a seat in one of the two ornate wingback chairs in front of the reception counter and pulled her phone from her bag. She furrowed black bushy brows, a stark contrast with her white hair, and typed a text message. Then she raised her chin and snapped thick fingers at Anthony. "Bellhop, I need a chair."

He pointed at the chair opposite hers. "We got one right there."

She squared her already square jaw. "It's for my handbag."

My brother's right brow arched so hard it formed a quasi-question mark. Then he shot me the silent plea that he reserved for situations involving female issues—the same look my dad gave my mother the entire time I was going through puberty.

At a loss, I raised my palms. The handbag chair was new to me too. But when Maybe Baby got out of jail, I planned to tell her about it for her party supply business.

"Uh, apologies, lady," Anthony offered in his finest manager speak. "We don't got any chairs for purses—just people."

Her head bobbled backwards, fingers flexing for her rosary. "You don't got a handbag chair? What kinda dump is this?"

This time I had a ready answer. "A *three-star* dump."

Nonna shuffled into the lobby, followed by my mother. She looked at the white-haired woman. "*Nonnone.*"

Big Nonna? I mentally translated. *Is she the 'big-a guns-a' Nonna said she'd call in to help Bradley?*

"Carmela." Nonnone embraced my nonna and then pointed to her Santa Sicily bag. "I brought cannoli."

Nonna bowed her head, like a low-level gangster preparing to kiss a Mafia Don's ring. "*La ringrazio.*"

My mother curtseyed. "Yes, thank you for coming all this way and on such short notice. Your presence is a great comfort, especially since the groom's family can't make it because of the blizzard."

Anthony glanced at me, and I shrugged. I didn't know who Nonnone was either, but based on the body language of my family, she was either a nonna gangster or the Dowager Contessa of Cannoli.

My brother scratched his side, as a good hotel manager would when greeting a guest. "You from Jersey?"

Nonnone frowned, highlighting the fact that the tip of her hooked nose hung over her mouth. "No, Kenner."

"The suburb twenty minutes from here?" I asked.

"You should visit." Nonnone's thin lips spread. "We've got the Treasure Chest Casino, the Planetarium, and the Brick Oven Cafe."

With attractions like that, it was a wonder tourists came to New Orleans.

"Don't worry, Carmela. I didn't come armed only with cannoli." She lowered her brows in a knowing look. "I've got *a guy*."

My nonna nodded at me, and Nonnone turned.

"You must be the bride." She pinched my cheek, hard. Every time a nonna did it, there was a violence to it—like punishment for still having estrogen. "Instead of that red glitter, you should be wearing mourning dress, what with your *fidanzato* in the slammer."

"Reaaally, Francescaaa," my mother drawled. "What were you *thinking*?"

To be on the safe side, I shrugged. It was far safer than admitting I was thinking of Glenda's stripper memoirs and the two grand in seventies money she'd made when she broke her heel.

Nonnone gave my cheek a pat that verged on a slap. "Don't worry about that groom, eh? We'll get him out. And if we don't," she nodded, screwing up her mouth, "I've got a guy."

My eyes widened. Her guy wasn't a fixer, he was a *fiancé*. "Thank you," I grumbled, "but I have my heart set on marrying Bradley."

"You do *now* but talk to me in twenty years. Or even in ten." Nonnone glanced at my mom and nonna, and they all roared with laughter.

The comment took me back to Funeral-Faced Nonna and her husband's razor-blade toenails and nose-hair trimmings.

"Besides," Nonnone patted my shoulder, "you've got time. Don't forget that the average age of a Sicilian bride is between thirty-three and forty."

My heels wobbled, and I leaned against the column for support. For over half my life, my nonna had made me feel like a zitella. And now, all these years later, I find out I'm *below* the average marrying age in Sicily?

Anthony appeared with a kiddie chair, and I dropped onto it, too stunned to do anything else.

"Slow your seat, Sis! That's for the bag." He yanked the chair out from under me.

Landing flat on my bottom on the floor, which, frankly, was a better fit, I resolved once more to free Bradley in time for the wedding. I needed a new family, and quickly.

As I pushed myself up from the black-and-white tiled floor, I shot my nonna and my mother a look as scorching as a Sicilian summer.

Nonna raised her chin. "Don't-a glare at-a me! It took-a you thirteen-a years to find a husband."

"She's right, Francesa." My mother smoothed her hair. "Imagine if we'd waited until now to start prodding you to get married."

"Good point, Mom. Without your early intervention, I might've ended up one of those poor, carefree women with a fulfilling life."

Nonnone sat her Santa Sicily bag on the little chair. "You want fulfillment? Then you shoulda joined a convent because marriage is a lifetime of sacrifice." Her black eyes grew serious. "But it's too late for that. Money has changed hands, and guests will arrive in a few days. The wedding must go on."

"Oh, you're speaking our language, Nonnone," my mother intoned, her voice hushed and solemn, as if a priest had proclaimed the gospel from a pulpit.

Nonna nodded. "That's-a why we set up-a a Command-a Center in a suite."

"*Bene.*" Nonnone's square jaw set. "It's time to call in reinforcements and get to work."

"Yes," I stressed. "Finding Dana Del Ray's real killer."

"No, doll," Nonnone's nose sunk beneath her mouth, "finalizing the wedding details. We got traditions to uphold. Your nonna tells me the cunzata del letto has been arranged, but what about the *serenata*? Who's going to serenade you outside your bedroom window if the groom's in jail?"

"*Madonna mia!*" Nonna pressed all ten of her fingers to her forehead. "We forgot about-a the serenata, Brenda."

My mother turned to me and threw up her hands. "Like I told you, Francesca," she said in an I-told-you-so tone, "no matter how much you think you have the wedding planning under control, problems have a way of popping up."

"The *serenade*?" I spat, incredulous. "You all think *that's* the problem here?"

Nonnone's fists went to her mink-furred hips. "It ain't just that. We need a new wedding dress."

Panic gripped my chest. "What for?"

"There's been a disgrace. You can't wear the old one." She turned to my mother. "Where is it?"

A river of shame washed over my mom's face, and she lowered her head. "We haven't seen it yet."

Nonnone's head bobbled, and her fingers flexed for her rosary. She looked as shocked by this revelation as she was by the absence of a handbag chair. When she recovered, she spun on her low heels, her Christmas-witch face as hard as a broom handle. "You didn't show your mamma and nonna your wedding dress?"

"It's, uh, complicated." I'd wanted to say that *they* were complicated, but I didn't want to risk another cheek pinching, or a whack from a jeweled and studded cannoli-filled handbag.

Nonnone pushed her handbag from the kiddie chair and sank her five-foot frame into the seat. "That's why your fiancé was framed for murder. You cursed your own wedding gown!"

Blamed again—this time for Bradley's arrest. Women had been shouldering the blame in Italian families since time immemorial. Italy had taken the whole Eve-biting-the-apple incident a lot harder than other cultures. And as much as they revered the Virgin Mary, she was still suspect for getting knocked up without Joseph.

"*Mamma mia, che disgrazia!*" She fanned herself with the Santa Sicily bag's crowned flap. "The only way to rectify this is with a new dress—one your mamma picks out."

My mother's eyes lit up like the boiling bubble lights from the rear dash of the Christmas Car. "I know just the one."

So did I—the dreaded plantation-style wedding gown. The double whammy of the age revelation and the dress curse was too much. I swooned and collapsed into one of the wingbacks, like a Southern belle in a too-tight corset.

"Well?" Nonnone prodded. "Where's this dress?"

My mother flailed an arm at the elevator, frantic to get backup for the hoop skirt horror show. "In the Command Center upstairs. I'd been hoping Francesca would wear two dresses in accordance with tradition in the Veneto."

My head hit the wingback. I'd been so besieged by Sicilian traditions, I'd forgotten all about my mother's Northern-Italian roots.

"Plus," my mother's shifty eyes shifted to me, "wearing two dresses is all the rage right now."

The word "rage" finally triggered my reaction—of rage. I rose up on my mother like a Spanish soldier ghost. "I am *not* wearing a plantation dress. That tradition is best left dead and buried."

"But it's just a big frilly ball gown. That kind of dress never went out of style here."

"It did, Mom. When the South lost the Civil War."

Nonnone rose and pushed up her sleeves. "I'll be the judge of that. Take me to this wedding dress."

They headed for the elevator without me, naturally. Which was fine. I had to get the investigation underway. The clock was ticking, literally. I checked my phone for a text from Veronica. Still nothing.

As I pocketed the device, I caught sight of a scrap of paper at the base of the reception counter. *I should leave it there after Anthony knocked me from the kiddie chair.*

Then I sighed. He'd already accused me of making the hotel look low rent after my encounter with Chandra, so I stooped to pick it up. The paper was stuck between the wood and the floor. I knelt and eased it out.

And promptly fell backwards onto my bottom.

One word in pen was visible on the half-inch scrap.

Eleison.

My eyes darted from side to side, as if searching for a ghost, but I knew darn good and well that Père Dagobert hadn't returned from the dead to write the word.

The question was, who had?

And what the hell were they doing at this hotel?

"Really, Franki?" My cousin Giada's dark eyes bore into mine as she dried her hands at the sink in the hotel kitchen. "Glitter so soon after a murder?"

I'd expected her to sympathize about Bradley's arrest or complain about her police questioning but not scold me about my sparkle. Although now that she'd mentioned it, the red hot body glitter *was* in poor taste given Dana Del Ray's scarlet skin color. "It was a gift from my landlady."

"Ah. Glenda." She pulled back her recently dyed brown hair with a headband, which emphasized her high cheekbones, not to mention her resemblance to the actress Claudia Cardinale. "I thought it was from that Christmas car."

I flinched. "How do you know about my Uber ride?"

"Ruth stopped by earlier, and she asked me if I knew about it. She's suspicious."

"Of a car decorated with Christmas ornaments?" I pressed my fingers to my forehead. "That sourpuss makes Scrooge seem like the embodiment of holiday cheer. Where'd she go, anyway?"

"She didn't say. But watch out." Giada pointed a sauce pan at me. "She's bound and determined to find Dana's killer, and she's sparing nothing and no one."

No surprise there. Ruth would go to any lengths to protect her job as Bradley's assistant, including murdering *me*.

Giada's phone vibrated on a stainless-steel island. "One second." She put the pan on the gas stove and picked up the phone. "Hey," she answered, turning on a burner, "I'm with Franki. Can I call you back?" Her eyelashes fluttered. "Moira, I know she's difficult—"

Me? I mouthed.

Giada shook her head and covered the phone. "She's talking about Marcella. She's treating your wedding like it's her own."

The way my wedding was going, Marcella could have it.

My phone rang, and I checked the display. *Speak of the devil.* I pressed the phone to my ear. "Hi, Mar—"

"What time are you coming by today?" Marcella's tone was as heated as the stove. "The situation with Moira is untenable."

My gaze shifted to my cousin, who was holding her phone at arm's length to protect her eardrum from Moira's shouting. "After I finish talking to Giada."

Marcella gasped. "Moira's on the phone with Giada now. What's she saying?"

There was no way I was going to repeat what was blaring from Giada's phone. If I did, Marcella might come and hurt *me.* "She's as frustrated as you."

"Because I won't let her have her way with your reception menu. I'm warning you, Franki. If you don't get down here soon, your Italian wedding will turn into an Irish wake." Marcella hung up.

I wasn't sure whether Marcella had just threatened to murder Moira or merely described her menu. To be honest, I kind of hoped it was the former. If my reception meal consisted of bangers and mash, the nonne would wage a holy war that would make The Troubles look like a minor disagreement over Sunday mass times. Then again, they would also halt the wedding until they'd cooked a proper Italian feast, which would buy me a few more days to get Bradley out of jail.

"Well, the Catholic-Protestant conflict is escalating fast." Giada deposited her phone on the island and reached for an onion. "What should we do?"

"Focus on solving the murder, starting with the old bottle of cyanide the police found in Bradley's coat pocket." I glanced around the kitchen. "Any chance the cyanide came from the hotel?"

"Doubtful. That bottle was an antique." Giada picked up a

knife and sliced the onion. "Plus, the officer who questioned me is convinced Bradley brought it to the party."

"That's impossible."

"Which is exactly what I told him." She reached for a head of garlic and began separating the cloves. "I also said that I'm more inclined to think the killer is Dana's boyfriend."

My heart skipped a beat. "What boyfriend? Was he here?"

"He called her, and whatever he said completely changed her demeanor. She went stiff and pushed her plate away." Giada shot me a look. "I got the abusive vibe."

"Please tell me you heard his name."

She shook her head. "I wish I had."

Me too. Because so far, the only suspect in Dana Del Ray's murder was Bradley.

Giada's phone vibrated. She answered on speaker. "Moira—"

"That Italian ogre stole my potatoes and Guinness and hid them somewhere."

Words that would strike fear in all of Ireland.

My phone began to ring. The so-called Italian ogre again. I tapped *Answer*. "Mar—"

"That pushy Paddy plans to serve *mini boxty* with sundried tomatoes and basil. Can you imagine? A *potato pancake* instead of *crostini*? Not only that, I just found a recipe on her desk for Guinness-braised ossobuco."

Even though I'd resolved to stay impartial, my jaw couldn't help but drop. A Milanese dish with Irish stout would be a bigger offense to my family than me wearing one of Glenda's stripper costumes to the altar.

The second the thought crossed my mind, my hand flew to my heart. Given my wedding dress crisis, I promptly struck the analogy from my mental record.

Marcella harrumphed. "This is the American *Italian* Cultural Center, for crying out loud. If Moira had said Roman-style gnocchi and Peroni, we could talk. But that culinary catastrophe? Over *her* dead body." She hung up.

Evidently, Marcella's earlier comment had been both a threat *and* a menu description.

Giada chewed her lip. "Should we go over to the Center?"

"Don't worry." I pocketed my phone. "I'm heading there after this."

Despite my reassurance, I *was* worried. Marcella and Moira were like oil and ale—apparently, a highly combustible combination.

"All right, then." Giada pulled Campbell's tomato soup from a cabinet. "Time to get the sauce on the stove for our lunch special." She tossed the sliced onion and garlic cloves into the pan and poured in the soup. Next, she mixed in a half cup of vinegar and several tablespoons of sugar. "*Voilà!*"

Voilà wasn't the V word I would have chosen. Anthony had been right to think her cooking was the murder weapon. That soup sauce was potentially lethal. "Um, what was in the spaghetti alla sambuca you served to Dana?"

"Shrimp, garlic, thyme, and tomato." She raised a finger. "Oh, and red sambuca."

My lips revolted. "You used *red* sambuca?"

"What's wrong with that? It's red like tomatoes, isn't it?"

Yeah, and the same shocking color as Dana's skin. If I didn't know cyanide had produced the discoloration, I might've blamed the liqueur. Red sambuca was made from the essential oils of star anise like the clear version, but with cinnamon notes. "Out of curiosity, why did you choose that dish?"

Giada stirred her sauce. "Anthony wants me to make pasta since the hotel was a macaroni factory, and I wanted to make something unusual."

She'd certainly succeeded at that—*every* time she cooked. "Did you leave the sauce unattended at any point?"

"Mmm..." She tapped her chin. "I left the kitchen twice while it was simmering."

"Did you or Anthony tell anyone you were making that dish?"

"He didn't know, but I posted the recipe on my food blog."

That meant *anyone* could have seen her post and slipped into the kitchen to poison the sambuca or the sauce. "Who was in here with you when Dana arrived?"

"No one."

"What about Bradley? Was he in the kitchen at any point?"

Her face fell. "Yes. I went inside to the Terrace Lounge to get a few martini olives for garnish, and when I came back, he was talking to Dana."

My stomach knotted—not only about Bradley, but about the pairing of martini olives with red sambuca. "What were they talking about?"

"Oh, chitchat about the weather. He came to say hello and talk to me about Moira and the catering."

Made sense. Veronica and I had mentioned the Marcella-Moira battle to him at the office. "Did Dana pass out her business card?"

"Not that I saw."

My stomach was now twisted like *nodino* bread. That meant Bradley had the card *before* his bachelor party. *But why?*

Giada's phone vibrated, and mine began to ring.

Moira and Marcella.

We answered anyway.

Arguing ensued—but not with Giada or me. Marcella and Moira were too busy fighting with each other to talk to us.

Giada and I exchanged a look, then hung up.

I silenced my phone. "How did you end up serving Dana a meal, anyway?"

"She said she was planning to eat here, so I served her a

plate." Giada added a splash of orange blossom water to the sauce. "She didn't want anything to drink before she got inside the cake."

My lips curled—not from the bathroom implication, but from the delayed punch of the floral spice. "What happened to the leftovers?"

"After Dana stopped eating, I put the rest down the garbage disposal. The police took the pan with the sauce."

That was disappointing, but I already knew it was the murder weapon.

Giada's text tone sounded, and she scowled at the display. Moira says to check the refrigerator.

"What for?"

"She must think Marcella hid her potatoes and Guinness here at Le Richelieu."

"Marcella did crash the bachelor party with me last night," I said, following my cousin to a large walk-in, "but we never went near the kitchen. We had a hard enough time getting that assistant manager, Candy, to let us into the lounge."

"She's controlling, that one."

I'd noticed. And I resolved to find out why when I talked to her about the scrap of paper I'd found—and Père Dagobert.

Giada scanned the shelves and put her hands on her hips. "I don't see Moira's potatoes and beer."

"That reminds me, where's the sambuca? In the bar?"

"No, the police took that too. But we keep the chilled liqueurs over there." She pointed to a milk crate in a corner.

A crate of lemons?

Giada picked one up. "I didn't order these. And where are the liqueurs?"

All I could think of were the lemons that had lined my windshield before Marcella had helped kidnap me for my bad bachelorette party. Then it hit me—Glenda had never answered me when I'd asked whether they'd put the lemons on my car. But by now it was clear that they hadn't.

So was something else.

The lemons weren't a bachelorette party prank, nor were they part of an Italian wedding tradition.

Someone was sending me a message.

A message that chilled me to the bone.

7

"Someone's a spicy pepperoncino in that red body glitter!" Marcella smirked from her seat behind the gift shop counter at the American Italian Cultural Center.

"Uh... thanks?" I didn't dare tell her it was edible or her Italian food analogies would never stop. To be fair, though, I *had* mentally compared her brain to a pizza missing a few pepperonis.

Her smoky-shadowed eyes were alight as she opened a drawer beneath the counter. "I have just the thing to go with that glitter."

My objective wasn't to accessorize the sparkle, but I was glad to see she was upbeat. She and Moira had evidently worked things out. Not that I was about to ask and risk setting her off.

"Here we go." She slapped a green satin bag on the counter. "A *borsa* for your wedding weekend."

In Italy, the borsa was a discreet little bag brides used to hold gifts of money from wedding guests. This one, however, was bedazzled with "I Love Italians and Cash" in red and gold rhinestones.

"Wear that with a green dress at your rehearsal dinner, and bada bing bada boom, you're rich!"

If Marcella ever had kids, she had a bright future as a nonna.

"Now that you're finally here, let's talk reception menu." She slid a marked-up copy across the table. Scrawled across the top in bold red letters—"NO IRISH FOOD. THIS IS A CULTURAL CENTER, NOT A FREAKING PUB."

Not wanting to ignite the Second Italian-Irish Wedding War, I pivoted. "Actually, I wanted to ask you about the lemons that were on my windshield when you kidnapped me for my bachelorette party. Did you or Nadezhda or Glenda put them there?"

"No, I thought *you* had."

"Um..." I blinked. "Why would I do that?"

"To keep them there until you could get in the car."

I stared at her, waiting for that to make sense. It never did.

My mind returned to the more unsettling possibility—the killer had left the lemons, just like the ones in the walk-in at Le Richelieu Hotel.

"Now that you mention it, though," Marcella reached for a green Sharpie, "we need to add a lemon recipe to your reception menu."

My eyes went wary. "Because of the St. Joseph's Day lemon tradition?"

"No," she scribbled a note in the margin. "Because lots of macaroni factories and spaghetti houses had their roots in lemons, like the D'Agostino Pasta Co."

"I'm not following you."

Her maroon-lined lips pursed, and she put down the Sharpie with a *thwack*. "This calls for the Giacomo Cusimano exhibit."

My gut clenched. I didn't have time for one of Marcella's American-Italian history lessons. "Listen, I'm in a huge hurry—"

"This will only take a minute." She grabbed my arm and

steered me toward an exhibit. "You need to know about Giacomo Cusimano. Thanks to Sicilian lemon traders like him, the Sicilian population in New Orleans grew to 45,000 by 1910. Since they ate pasta, enterprising men like Cusimano started making it. His factory," she pointed at a black-and-white photo of pasta drying on a rack, "produced 10,000 pounds a day. And it's now the site of Le Richelieu Hotel, where Anthony works."

Was I to infer that Giacomo Cusimano's ghost was the one leaving me lemons?

Marcella picked up a dusty old soup can. "I'll bet you're wondering why this Progresso Italian-Style Bean & Pasta is in the exhibit."

Honestly, I wasn't. But I was sure she'd tell me.

"Cusimano loaned money to a fellow paesano down on his luck—Giuseppe Uddo, who used it to start Progresso Foods. Not only that, Cusimano's plant manager was none other than Leon Tujague, who founded the Southern Macaroni Factory. Their luxury brand pasta is still sold in stores today."

"Huh." That *was* kind of surprising. "Is Leon the one who started Tujague's restaurant on Decatur?"

"Yes, it was one of the original spaghetti houses. Toney's on Bourbon was another. New Orleans' spaghetti houses propelled pasta to national popularity, and our macaroni factories were supplying it."

Despite being frantic to free my fiancé and save my wedding, I paused to silently thank my Sicilian forebears for this culinary triumph, which my belly and I enjoyed immensely. "This is all super interesting, but what does it have to do with my wedding?"

Marcella gave a shocked laugh. "You'll want to celebrate that heritage at your reception, *obviously*. We'll replace that godawful Guinness ossobuco with a nice veal scaloppini in lemon caper sauce. And, *of course*, you'll want a tricolor pasta to go with the Italian flag cocktail."

Truthfully, none of that was what I'd envisioned. But if Marcella had her way, my entire wedding would showcase the achievements of New Orleans Sicilians. And everyone at my wedding would not only eat and drink the Italian flag, we would also wave it and wear it too.

"Marcella, I really appreciate the, uh, *deep* personal interest you've taken in the reception menu. But this is *my* wedding, and given the situation with Bradley, it might not even happen."

Her face went stiff, borderline hostile. Then she threw back her hair curtain. "This calls for the Tony Canzoneri exhibit."

"Who was he?"

Marcella's jaw dropped. "*Only* a five-time world champion Sicilian-American boxer from Slidell."

Odd that she'd pick a boxer. Or was it? "And why do I need to see his exhibit?"

"To inspire your fighting spirit!" She balled her fists and raised them in a fighting stance. "You need to fight for your man, Franki, if not for yourself then for single gals everywhere. If you don't, I *will*."

And she'd keep him too.

Pounding erupted somewhere in the building, as if on cue.

"What's that?" I asked.

Marcella pulled a book the size of a cinderblock from a nearby exhibit—the *Dictionary of Italian Hand Gestures*. "I'm sorry. What?"

"The banging sound. Don't you hear it?"

"Oh, just some workers." She flipped a page in the dictionary. "Nothing to worry about."

My text tone went off, and I pulled my phone from my bag.

Marcella cocked a brow. "News about Bradley?"

I nodded, my insides coiled like a spring. "Veronica's leaving Central Lockup. I need to meet her at the office."

"You'd better be on your way." She put down the dictionary,

grabbed my arm, and hustled me to the exit. "Your man needs you."

The banging had become more persistent, and I heard a muffled cry. "Should you check on those workers? It sounds like someone's injured."

"No, they're good."

Unease prickled my spine. Something was off about her behavior. Then a dark scenario took shape in my mind. "Marcella... Where's Moira?"

Her eyes flicked left. Then she ducked her head behind her hair curtain. "I locked her in the janitor's closet."

"You *what*?" The last word came out a shout.

Her head shot up, and she latched onto my bicep. "It was just for a few minutes so I could show you *my* menu."

A food comparison was in order after all. I'd thought her pizza was missing a few pepperonis, but the problem was far more serious—as in, her pasta just wasn't *al dente*. "That's *false imprisonment*. You could go to *real* prison."

"Gahhh! Dramatic much? *Moira's* the one who should go to prison—for culinary crimes."

"The police will be the judge of that. Now let. Her. Out."

"Oof! Some people are *so* serious." Marcella pulled a key from her bra and stalked toward the noise.

And I followed—at a distance. I didn't want to end up like Moira.

Marcella stopped at the janitor's closet, its door rattling from the pounding. Then she sighed and unlocked it.

Moira burst out like an Irish rainstorm, wild and unrelenting. An Italian flag dangled from her wrist, knotted like a makeshift bind, and another was still in her mouth. She gazed at us wild-eyed and fled down the hall.

I ran to catch her—and to get the hell away from Marcella.

Moira skidded to a stop at a rear exit and wrangled the flag from her mouth. "You might want to investigate *that one* for the murder of that dancer, Dana Del Ray. The cake she stuffed her into couldn't be much smaller than the janitor's closet."

"Now, Moira, you know Marcella didn't put Dana in the cake. And she's definitely not a murderer. She's just...crazily committed to her culture."

"You got the 'committed' right. She should *be* committed—to a psych ward."

I glanced over my shoulder to make sure Marcella wasn't behind me. "Yeaaah, but given the stress I'm under with Bradley's arrest, I would appreciate it if you would stay on as caterer—from your house, I mean. Otherwise, my nonna and her friends will take over."

Moira yanked her coat and bag from a rack. "Let me put this in a language you'll understand. *Fuggedaboutit.*"

My head snapped back. I knew she was angry, but the Italian stereotype was uncalled for.

"Mocking our culture again, eh?" Marcella's voice made Moira and I both jump. "Did I warn you about her, or what, Franki?"

Moira opened the door. "Someone should have warned me about *you*." She looked at me. "Before Princess Fiona here locked me in the closet, she tried to lock me in the walk-in. So, I'm out." She stormed across the Piazza d'Italia.

The walk-in reference reminded me of the text she'd sent to my cousin. "Moira! Wait." I ran after her. "Why did you tell Giada to check the hotel walk-in?"

Moira turned. "What are you talking about?"

"The text you sent her this morning."

She pulled her phone from her purse and scrolled through her texts. "I didn't send this." She glared at Marcella, who'd followed us. "You broke into my phone?"

"What? No! I wouldn't do a thing like that. That's violating."

"Oh, and locking me in a closet wasn't?"

They started arguing, but I tuned them out. The only thing I heard clearly was the question ringing in my head.

Had the killer used Moira's phone to text Giada?

As I CLIMBED the stairs to Private Chicks, I was still rattled by the events at the American Italian Cultural Center—Marcella locking Moira in the closet, and the killer entering the building *and* Moira's phone.

One thing was clear—no one was playing by the rules.

And that included Moira adding Guinness-braised ossobuco to my reception menu. The only thing more shocking would have been lasagna with Lucky Charms.

When I reached the third-floor landing, my breath caught in my throat.

A hulking figure lurked behind the frosted glass of the Private Chicks office door!

"The killer?" I whispered.

Veronica's car wasn't in the parking lot, and I hadn't seen David's either. I was on my own.

The figure shifted—big, broad, and wearing a dark hoodie.

Armed with my bag, my boots, and the glittery grit Glenda had instilled in me, I pressed flat beside the door, ready to clock the killer the second they exited.

A tense minute ticked by.

Then another.

With my breath locked in my lungs, I peered through the glass. The figure had turned to the side, probably rummaging through the reception desk just inside the door. And I made out something familiar.

A swinging chain.

The breath I'd been holding broke out in a huff.

It wasn't the killer—just the Grim Reaper, a.k.a., Ruth, in her cat-eye glasses and hooded puffer coat.

I shoved open the door.

Ruth scowled and tugged on a mitten. "Good of you to show up to work at eleven a.m., what with your fiancé in jail and all." She pulled on the other mitten. "Do tell, did you come to investigate his case? Or to nap on the couch?"

"Save your breath, Ruth." I slipped out of my coat. "It reeks of garlic, and I'm already investigating Dana's murder."

The Vassal nudged David, who glanced over his shoulder at me.

"What?" I tossed my coat on the rack.

David turned his chair and flipped his bangs to the side. "You're, uh, sparkling. Like one of those vampires from *Twilight*."

The Vassal pushed up his glasses. "Except that you're red."

Ruth hissed, and her hawk eyes swept my body. Then her turkey neck drew in, as tight as her bun. "Did you take a roll in the sleigh with that Santa you've been carousing with?"

My spine straightened in my high-heel boots, reminding her I had a solid six inches on her. "I'm not going to dignify that with an answer."

She raised her nose. "The truth hurts, doesn't it?"

"No, the *Ruth* hurts."

David snickered, but The Vassal's slack jaw dropped in shock at the confrontation. He was as chill as a New Orleans sno-ball —unless there were breasts involved.

The chains on Ruth's readers swung like pendulums. "What would Bradley think if he heard you joking while his freedom hangs in the balance?"

"He would know I'm *not* joking. It's the bitter Ruth."

A wheeze escaped The Vassal's slack jaw.

Ruth's cheeks flushed redder than my body glitter. "I don't

know what you're up to, missy, but you leave my name out of it. What I do know is, I'm going to expose you to Bradley once and for all."

I took a step toward her. "And what I know—but you can't seem to grasp—is that your time would be better spent trying to help Bradley."

She matched my step. "That's exactly what I'm doing."

"If that were true," my voice was low and lethal, "you'd focus on the killer, not me." I shouldered past her and went to David and The Vassal's corner work station. "Now, I need you guys to find a contact for Dana Del Ray."

Ruth harrumphed. "I asked them to do that not five minutes ago. If you'd bothered to come in earlier, you'd know."

"Dana will have social media accounts," I said, refusing to further acknowledge Ruth. "She was starting a Mardi Gras krewe for dancers, and I'm hoping she listed her officers. It's called Krewe de View."

The Vassal's eyes grew wide behind his lenses, probably thrilled by the promise of pastie pics. He closed his mouth and sat tall in his chair. "Anything else?"

"Yes. Research the history of a Capuchin monk named Père Dagobert de Longuory and any hymns or songs he liked to sing, starting with Kyrie eleison."

"Well, Our Father who art in heaven," Ruth drawled. "Please tell me this isn't about the ghost."

There was no way I was going to fill her in on Chandra's spirit charade on Chartres Street. She'd think I'd lost my mind, which was entirely possible given the stress I was under. "There have been Père Dagobert sightings, and I have reason to believe they could be connected to Dana's murder."

David and The Vassal's eyes popped, then they turned, exchanging wide smiles, and high-fived. They were about to get paid to live out their geeky *Ghostbusters* fantasies.

"I've heard of wild goose chases," Ruth grabbed her bag from the reception desk, "but a wild *ghost* chase? That takes the stripper cake." She pushed open the door. "With theories like that, I'm Bradley's only hope." She left, slamming the door.

And I glared after her. "That woman's so toxic, she's a walking EPA violation."

The Vassal tapped his R2-D2 stylus on his thigh. "On the subject of toxic, any thoughts about the cyanide bottle?"

I turned to look at him and David. "That's a question for the two of you since you were at the bachelor party. Where was Bradley's coat?"

"On the back of his chair."

"Did he leave it unattended at any point?" I began to pace. "Like when he went into the kitchen to talk to Giada?"

David's eyes darted to his friend. "Yeah, but that's when we left."

"Why did you leave then?"

"Uh, well, Dana went into the kitchen after Bradley did, and..."

That news was like a boot-kick to the gut. *Had she followed him because they knew one another?*

"And..." The Vassal cleared his throat. "...I tried to storm the kitchen."

"No more questions." The last thing I wanted was more details of his boob quest. "I'm going to go wash off this glitter."

The office door opened, and Veronica entered.

I reversed course and rushed to her. "How's Bradley?"

"He's totally fine." She removed her camel-colored coat. "He's more worried about you than himself."

A pang pierced my chest. It was so like him to put me first. "Can I go see him?"

"Let's have a seat." She gestured to the waiting area in the middle of the old brick room.

My head retracted. "I don't like where this is going, Veronica."

"It's nothing serious." She led me to the couches. "There's a backlog at Central Lockup. He's gone through intake and processing, but he still has to be formally booked and assigned a housing unit. So, maybe in twenty-four hours?"

My heart sank, and my legs followed. I flopped onto a couch.

Veronica sat across from me. "I know it's upsetting, but you can spend that time investigating. Bring him some good news."

"*How* when he's the only suspect?"

"Don't forget Maybe Baby. She's still in custody."

"Please." I gave her a get-real look. "She couldn't kill *time* without help."

Veronica suppressed a smile.

I leaned forward. "What did Bradley say about all of this? Does he have any idea who poisoned Dana?"

"Not a clue. He doesn't know how the cyanide got into his coat pocket either."

My stomach was flip-flopping, so I grabbed a decorative pillow and pressed it to my abdomen. "What about her business card in his wallet?"

"Same."

"Glenda recommended Dana. Maybe she gave it to him, and he forgot."

Veronica shook her head. "She didn't. I already asked her."

"The killer must've put it there." I chewed my thumbnail. "The card isn't the only thing the killer has left."

Her brow rose. "What are you talking about?"

"Lemons on my windshield and in the Le Richelieu Hotel refrigerator." I stared into her confused eyes. "The last time I saw lemons in a walk-in was on the Steamboat Galliano. You know what this means?"

"Gigi Scalino's in prison, Franki."

"I'm not talking about the mob boss."

Her eyes studied my face. "Let's not go there, Franki. Lemons don't prove anything."

"Not even if the killer used Moira's phone at the American Italian Cultural Center to text Giada to check the hotel kitchen walk-in?"

Veronica stiffened. "How would the killer know her password?"

"Any number of ways."

She shook her head. "I'll admit that the lemons on your windshield are a little weird, but lemons in a walk-in? That's the norm in this city."

When she put it that way, I had to agree. We were in seafood country. Still, I had a bad history with the fruit, and I was starting to think it was the root of all evil—make that the *Ruth* of all evil.

But I did appreciate Limoncello. And a good lemon square.

With a sigh, I tossed the pillow aside. "By the way, Moira quit the catering gig after Marcella locked her in a closet."

Veronica slapped a hand over her mouth, but her eyes went wide with horror. "She *what*?"

"You heard me." I tapped the coffee table between us to underscore the vital importance of what I was about to say to her. "And we're not going to breathe a word of this to my mom and Nonna."

She blinked. "Where are you going to find another caterer at this late date?"

"Veronica, I don't need reception food. I just need the groom."

She gave a long slow exhale. "You're right. Let's start by identifying a suspect list. Someone at the hotel could have set him up."

"I'm starting to wonder about Candy. But if I'm right about

the lemons being connected to the murder, how would she know about my history with them?"

"She works with Anthony. He could've told her the story of your and Bradley's engagement."

Great point. Candy could also have been stalking Giada's food blog and seen her post about the spaghetti alla sambuca. "She works the evening shift, so I'll swing by the hotel tonight to question her."

"Don't forget the bachelor party guests. You have a suspect there too."

I stared at her like she'd just suggested Nonna take up stripping. Surely, she didn't suspect her husband, Dirk. Or David and The Vassal. That only left...

"*Bruno?*"

~

As I sat in my Mustang in the Private Chicks parking lot trying to figure out where to start my investigation, stress coursed through my veins like the gas to the engine. I'd considered calling the Christmas Car to drive me, but Ruth was most likely lurking in the vicinity, hoping to catch me in some lurid act with Santa and Hermey.

Well, just Santa.

The "lurid" reminded me of Bruno. I'd always thought of him as harmless, but the guy had the morals of a pimp-turned-preacher I'd once met. And then there was the matter of the car accident that had left his mother, Santina, in a wheelchair. It had cost Bruno his license, and yet he was still driving, as evidenced by my recent goon nonne abduction.

But did he set up Bradley for Dana Del Ray's murder?

My body gave an involuntary shudder. First Bradley's arrest, then the Nonnone's insistence that my mom pick me a new wedding dress, followed by Moira quitting the catering. And now I had to investigate my nonna's best friend's son?

The totality of it was more terrifying than ghosts and—

No, don't say the name.

The hair on the back of my neck stood. I spun and checked the back seat.

He's not here. He's dead.

"Calm down, Franki." I squeezed the steering wheel. "You can't help Bradley when you're this worked up."

If Glenda were with me, she'd tell me to summon my grit. I didn't have champagne from her Glitter Grit Getter kit, but I did have the Red Hot Body Glitter and the high-heeled boots inspired by her chapter thirteen.

She'd advised me to "follow the dollars," but that didn't seem to apply in this case. At least, not as far as I was aware. The obvious place to begin was with the cyanide, and I knew exactly where to go.

I put the car in drive and headed down Decatur—just in time to see Candy exiting a shop.

Sassy Spells?

Normally, I went the opposite direction, so I hadn't noticed the place before. There were already so many witch shops on Decatur, you couldn't swing a black cat without hitting one.

"Veronica should change the business name to 'Private Chicks and Wicks' and offer both investigations and incantations."

Parking on the street, I hurried from the car and jogged to catch up with Candy. "Hey, can I talk to you for a sec?"

Irritation sharpened her already pointed features. "Sure. What about?"

"Well, I found this scrap of paper in front of the reception desk at the hotel." Using my fingernails, I pulled it from my wallet. "It says 'eleison.'"

Her grip on her shoulder bag tightened. "Doesn't ring a bell. Maybe it's the last name of a hotel guest."

"That would be easy to check." I paused and watched regret flash across her face. "But I think it's a hymn, Kyrie eleison."

She shrugged. "Okay."

Even though she was doing her darnedest to appear indifferent, the hand gripping her bag had started to tremble. "It's sung by the ghost of Père Dagobert."

She blanched as though she'd just spotted the long-dead priest on the street. "Sorry. I've gotta run to an eye appointment."

Candy hurried off, and I watched her go, wondering what had prompted her fear. It wasn't that Père Dagobert was a ghost because she'd enjoyed seeing Anthony squirm when she'd mentioned Le Richelieu's ghost legends.

So, what did she know about that scrap of paper?

And why didn't she tell me what that was?

My gaze drifted to the Sassy Spells sign, and I entered the shop. The place was jam-packed with tall display shelves, but the most striking feature was that one side was old brick, like Private Chicks, and the other was painted bright pink. Awfully girlie for a witch shop.

"You here for body glitter?" a dark-haired male asked from behind the counter.

I really needed to wash mine off. "No, I was hoping you could give me some information. I'm a PI."

His jaw hardened, and his fleshy lips stayed shut even after I'd approached.

My gaze went from the large pink lump between his weirdly pale eyes to his priest collar and black button-down shirt—with the word "Mortician" and a white stitched coffin with a cross. If his gig at the shop didn't work out, he could go to work with the guy who'd quit the day shift at Le Richelieu to drive bodies to the morgue.

"So," I cleared my throat, "I was wondering about the woman with the auburn hair who left a few minutes ago. What was she doing here?"

He looked down his nose. "We don't discuss our clients' proclivities."

When he put it that way, I was almost glad because it sounded as tawdry as Ruth's claim that I'd taken a roll in the sleigh with Santa. What I wasn't glad about was his refusal to talk to me about Candy. "I'll just have a look around."

"As you wish." He left the counter and disappeared into the tall shelves.

And I wandered around Sassy Spells, trying to spot something suspicious. But they sold the usual witch stuff—your basic potions, wands, spell kits.

Candy hadn't been carrying a bag from the store. Either she'd left without making a purchase, or she hadn't come to shop.

She'd come for something else.

But what?

I scanned the space, looking for another room. Sure enough, behind a display, there was a double door on the rear wall.

Casually sauntering over, I spotted a "Private Clients Only" sign in a creepy, cursive font. *What went on in that room? Tarot card readings? Or something sinister like coven cabal meetings?*

Time to find out. Turning my back to the doors, I checked to see whether anyone was watching.

A hand clamped down on my mouth.

And dragged me into the dark.

8

"Why did you come here?" a blasted Boston accent whisper-huffed in my ear. "To blow my cover?"

My shock turned to rage. Nevertheless, I calmly peeled Chandra's pudgy, paddle-nailed fingers from my lips. Thanks to the pink light of an oversized crystal ball and a John Wick candle, I confirmed that she wasn't wearing her charm bracelet—then I let her have it.

"I don't know what cover you're talking about," I whisper-shouted, "but you'd better *take* cover after dragging me into this room like a freaking lunatic."

Chandra's tiny mouth screwed into a scowl, which really emphasized the height of her hair, and she crossed her arms against her silver sequin smock. "As a Cancer and someone whose name is Hindi for 'shining moon,' I don't appreciate you using a term that smears the lunar cycle."

"Well, let me tell you what *I* don't appreciate—getting kidnapped left and right and accosted in a weird witch shop. So, you'd best start explaining what you're doing in here, and *pronto.*"

Her scowl shifted into a peeved purse. "I'm doing readings undercover to investigate Dana Del Ray's murder."

My head fell back, and I gazed at the glow-in-the dark stars on the ceiling. The last thing I needed was both Ruth *and* Chandra on the case, causing more chaos. "I'm the PI, remember? Please leave the investigating to me."

"No offense," she gave her big bob a bump, "but I'm Bradley's relative. And until that wedding happens, which is looking none too likely, you're not."

Chandra would do well to remember that we were alone in a dark room, and no one knew I was here but her. "Why are you investigating Sassy Spells?" I gestured at a lit incense stick. "And what is that smell? Burnt blue jeans?"

"It's their Attract Money scent."

I sniffed, disgusted—but also to get the stench out of my nostrils. Despite her Crescent City Medium moniker, Chandra wasn't interested in getting the spirits to open up during a reading. Her sole focus was to get her clients to open up, and specifically, their wallets.

"And I'm not investigating the shop. I'm investigating Candy."

"Okay, but why? What do you know about her?"

"Uh, *hello*?" She waved her hands in front of my face. "I don't know anything! Why do you think I'm undercover?"

Bradley's chances of getting out of jail were looking as "none too likely" as our wedding happening on Saturday. "What I mean is, how would you know to get a job at Sassy Spells to investigate her?"

"Actually, I was already working here, and she came in."

My annoyance took a back seat to panic. Chandra had a joint business with her plumber husband called Crescent City Plumbing and Palmistry, and I had a vested interest in making sure it—and they—hadn't gone belly up. "You didn't leave Lou again, did you?"

Her fists balled on her wide hips. "Now why would you bring that up?"

What I wanted to say was, *Because the last time you left him, you moved into Veronica's old apartment next door and did psychic readings from a U-Haul in our driveway, and I would rather Glenda rent the place to my mom, nonna, and Anthony than go through that again.*

But I settled for, "Because you own a business together, and yet you're working here."

"Oh, this is just a side gig to help get my name out. Plus, Sassy Spells offers readings online and over the phone, which is super convenient, and I get a discount on products." She cocked an arm and approached me with her pit. "Their supernatural Crescent deodorant from Sea Witch Botanicals is out of this world!"

I didn't know what made it supernatural, but after spending the past few minutes in the small space with her, I could attest that "out of this room" was a more apropos description. "Can we get back to Candy?"

"Okay, okay. Jeez." She flailed her paddle nails. "Someone's pushy."

My teeth clenched. I almost pointed out that I hadn't been the one to drag me in here, but why bother? "Now, what made you suspect her?"

"For a PI, you ask a lot of dumb questions."

Frustration coursed through my body, and I reached for the crystal ball—not to gaze into her future, but to threaten it.

"Watch out! That costs ten thousand dollars."

My fingers flew off the ball like they'd been burned. "Ten K for a piece of pink glass?"

"Did you not hear me say 'crystal?'" She huffed. Then she

picked up a cloth and rubbed it over the ball. "It's large and perfectly spherical rose quartz, which is a rare find. Plus, rose quartz is one of the best for scrying."

I was scrying at the price. "Okay, whatever. Did you do a reading for Candy?"

"No, she had a private session with The Father. You probably saw him, the dark-haired man working the counter?"

The panic made a rousing comeback. I wasn't supposed to see a priest before my wedding. "Is he an actual clergyman?"

She shrugged. "He's a Bishop from the Universal Ecclesia and a member of the Aurum Solis."

That was a relief—I thought. "Which means what?"

Chandra sighed and rolled her eyes. "He's with the Universal Church, and the Aurum Solis is a Western esoteric tradition from the UK that focuses on Hermeticism, Neoplatonism, and ceremonial magic."

She lost me between "church" and "magic." "So, what does he do, exactly?"

"He teaches occult and energy courses. And he performs reiki, which is Japanese touch therapy. He also creates relics—"

"Wait." I glanced over my shoulder to make sure the door was still closed. "As in, the ones made from saints' body parts and personal belongings?"

"Those are the ones."

I puckered. That sounded like real Catholic priest stuff.

"He's also the world's only publicly verified traditional sin-eater."

That didn't sound remotely Catholic priestish. Although, gluttony was a sin. But given the occult nature of the shop, I didn't think sin-eating had anything to do with me eating Nutella from the jar with a shovel spoon. Also, I did that in private—and there would be no public verification. "Can you elaborate on that?"

"Dear Gawd, you ask a lot of questions." Chandra flopped into a chair in front of the crystal ball. "It's a ceremony to eat the sins of the dead."

I blinked. Not only was it unclear what that was, it was unclear why anyone would do it. "Sounds freaky, Chandra."

"Because you're a brick."

My head pulled back like a slingshot ready to strike. "Is that a comment about my weight?"

"Well," her eyes scanned my figure, "you could stand to lose a few pounds before the wedding, but it's a term we psychics use for people who are spiritually closed off."

Again, she would do well to remember that we were "closed off" in a dark room.

"Back to sin-eating, though, because I need to speed this along," she angled her head at me, as though *I* were the reason for the length of this conversation, "it's both an extraction magic and a form of sympathetic magic to help the deceased."

Still freaky. "What does that involve?"

"That's what I'm trying to find out. All I got from their website was that you use bread, ale, salt, a wooden bowl, and a wooden plate. Oh, and that sin-eating is most likely from an Egyptian mystery tradition to prepare the dead for the afterlife."

"The Father is nothing if not multi-cultural."

"Yeah, he's Canadian."

My head tilted. I'd never thought of Canadians as being multicultural, but then again, they *had* given the world poutine. Nevertheless, the Father's cultural training wasn't my concern.

What *was* my concern—whether Candy's visit to the shop had anything to do with the mysterious Egyptian ceremony. Because if it did, I had a feeling I knew whose sins she was eating.

Dana Del Ray's.

But why?

"Sweet Saint Expedite!" Francine the pharmacist's dark eyes were so wide I thought the barrette holding back her long black hair would rocket off her head.

The so-called saint was actually a statue of a Roman centurion who'd arrived in New Orleans in a box labeled "Expedite," but he'd become the go-to favorite for quick legal resolutions. *Had she somehow heard about Bradley's predicament?*

Francine rushed from behind the counter. "You look like you got kicked in the face by one of the Ruby Slippers!"

That explained it. Expedite was also invoked for speedy recoveries from illness. At any rate, I really had to wash off Glenda's glitter. "This isn't—"

"Don't say a word." She raised a thin hand. "You've got to conserve your energy."

Unease gripped my chest. *Or was it a heart contraction?* "I do?"

"Ssshhh!" Her fortyish face took on the solemnity of a surgeon preparing for a triple bypass, which I might need if she kept looking at me like that.

Francine shoved her hands into the pockets of her white lab coat and scrutinized the bruise on my nose. "This is either a blocked third eye chakra trying to break through the physical plane, or it's unresolved conflict with a dominant maternal figure."

She wasn't wrong. The bruise *was* courtesy of my mother's careless bed flop, and I was still upset about it.

"As for that red glitter," she sucked in a breath and pulled back the corners of her mouth, "that's a cry for root chakra stabilization. You're clearly feeling ungrounded. Or you're trying to attract a fire sign."

She wasn't wrong about that either. I *had* been feeling

uprooted since Bradley's arrest, and he *was* a fire sign that I wanted to get out of jail.

"The diagnosis—a classic case of spiritual whiplash."

My mouth dropped, semi-stunned. I hadn't been the same since Chandra channeled the spirit of Dana Del Ray and mentioned Père Dagobert.

"Hold this." She pulled a bottle of magnesium spray from a shelf and shoved it into my palm. Then she closed her eyes and linked her index fingers and thumbs.

Francine was muscle testing me—with her mind. She'd done it the last time I'd come to the pharmacy, when I was investigating an attempted mermaid murder—or *mermurder*. Back then, I dismissed her method as baloney. But so far, she'd been spot on without even touching me.

"Nope. You didn't test for that." She took the spray, replaced it with a dropper bottle, and repeated the gesture. Her eyes opened and drilled into mine. "I recommend two drops of this Rescue Remedy, reiki, and a rose quartz soak. Do it soon because if I ran a ZYTO scan on you, it would be lit up like a Christmas tree."

All I could do was gape. I had no idea what a ZYTO scan was —and whether she could do it with her mind or needed a device. But in less than a minute, Francine had zeroed in on my trauma from my Mom, Bradley, and Chandra, and she seemed to know about Glenda, the Father at Sassy Spells, and possibly Santa and Hermey.

And to think that I'd only come to the pharmacy to ask about the cyanide and get some decent deodorant for Chandra.

"Thanks for diagnosing me." I put the Rescue Remedy on the counter. "But this isn't a health visit. I'm investigating another homicide."

She grinned and pulled her signature lean, which would give the Tower of Pisa vertigo. "Do tell."

"I need your professional opinion about the murder weapon. It's—"

"Let me guess." She slapped my arm. "Poisoned VapoRub? Combustible hemorrhoid wipes? Or," her eyes went sly, and she smiled crocodile style, "the old suppository switcharoo."

My cheeks clenched—and not the ones on my face. Those weren't the guesses I would've expected, and I had so many questions that I absolutely *did* not want to ask. But since Francine knew a lot about alternative healing, I decided to run my conversation with Chandra by her. "Have you heard of sin-eating?"

"Utter malarkey." Her mouth went as flat as a po-boy roll. "I mean, if bread absolves sins, then why do I feel so much guilt about eating it?"

Good thing my nonna and the nonne hadn't heard her say that. They consumed communion wafers like deli crackers to absolve their guilt, and they—and the entire Catholic Church— would not appreciate any insinuation that it didn't work.

"Now that you mention it, though," Francine tapped her narrow chin, "I wonder if a sin-eater's bicep would be weak if I muscle-tested them after a ceremony? That's a heavy load of energetic baggage to carry."

Couldn't argue with her there.

She jerked her head in the direction of a chubby middle-aged male perusing weight-loss supplements. "Speaking of heavy loads..."

I glanced at the guy, hoping he hadn't overheard her. For a pharmacist, Francine was brutally frank.

He pulled a bottle from the shelf and squinted at the label.

Francine went into muscle-testing mode. "Those aren't going to help you, sir."

The guy looked at her and then over his shoulder.

"Yes, I'm talking to you," she sing-songed. "That's no spare tire around your waist. It's a tumor."

The man blanched and dropped the bottle.

"Don't worry. I'm pretty sure it's benign." Francine flashed a smile as she retrieved the supplements from the floor. "But instead of wasting your time and money on pills, I'd recommend a doctor of internal medicine."

Sage advice, and better than the invasive medicine she dispensed here.

The man spun on his heels and bolted from the pharmacy.

Frankly, I wanted to join him before Francine diagnosed me with something else. "Sooo... about that murder weapon."

She leaned hard and flashed another reptile smile. "Another possibility—body glitter made of toxic metal."

Given her earlier glitter diagnosis, she could have spared me that one. I pulled out my phone and showed her the photo Veronica had taken of the green cyanide bottle. "It was this."

"Hm." Her mouth drooped, unimpressed. "Potassium cyanide."

"And antique based on the vintage bottle. Would cyanide this old be able to poison a person?"

"Sure! It can be toxic for decades, especially if it's kept in an airtight container away from light and heat." She gave a chuckle. "I don't know if you've visited the old Pharmacy Museum, but if you go, check out their rectal dilators. Those never get old!"

My cheeks clenched again. Yes, they did, as in too old and barbaric to use. "Why would you mention the museum?"

"Because that's where the bottle is from."

I blinked. "How do you know?"

"Their tour specialist came in earlier." She frowned and shook her head. "Bad case of beignet bloat, if you know what I'm saying."

My hand went to my gut. I didn't, but as a beignet binger, I made a mental note to google that. "Can we go back to the cyanide?"

Francine straightened. "That's what I'm talking about. She wouldn't go into specifics, but she said that under the circumstances it's a terrible time for her to be out sick."

"Wait. What circumstances?"

"Yesterday, a visitor stole a toxic substance from the Pharmacy Museum's vintage medicine display." Francine nodded at my phone. "That cyanide has to be it."

THE HISTORICAL PHARMACY MUSEUM was empty, which came as no surprise. Despite its name, the place wasn't a pharmacy—it was a torture chamber.

Literally.

La Pharmacie Française, as it was called on its misleadingly quaint mortar-and-pestle sign, was opened in 1804 by Louis J. Dufilho, the first licensed pharmacist in the U.S. Apparently, he not only made up medicine as he went along—kind of like Francine, the mental muscle tester—but legend had it that he also performed sadistic experiments on patients. And that his ghost, and those of the innocent people he'd killed, allegedly haunted the place.

At the moment, the museum was also torturing me because there wasn't a staff member in sight, and I desperately needed to identify the person who'd stolen the cyanide bottle. The employees could've been in a meeting about the theft, so I decided to wait another minute before going in search of the tour specialist.

Steering clear of the huge white jar labeled LEECHES on the counter, I walked around looking for the vintage medicine display.

The pharmacy was more like Dr. Frankenstein's lab than a healing space. The air was stale, and the light was dim. Floor-to-ceiling cabinets made of stained, carved wood held shelves of glass bottles filled with herbs and powders—everything from poultices to voodoo potions. And all of it was coated in a thick layer of dust, which I was pretty sure was part rat feces and part centuries-old medicine.

Pausing to peer into a glass case, I spotted a device that made the rectal dilators—and even the uterine dilators—seem harmless. It was a terrifying multi-knifed bloodletter called a scarifier. "Fitting name."

Moving along, I came upon a bottle of opium-soaked tampons. "Talk about 'the old suppository switcheroo.'"

A young woman entered and walked behind the counter. She had a choppy pinkish-blonde lob and a diamond stud in her left nostril. Instead of a lab coat, she wore a tight yellow sweater with orange and pink stripes circling the sleeves.

Not what I'd expected, but that was the norm in The Big Easy. "Hi. Do you know where I can find the tour specialist?"

"She's out sick today."

Apparently, Francine hadn't been able to treat the woman's beignet bloat. "Would it be possible to speak to the pharmacist who normally works here? The older gentleman?"

She stared at me for a moment, her blue eyes pensive. "Can I get your name?"

"Franki Amato." I almost leaned against the counter, but I caught myself—before I caught hantavirus. "I'm a PI, investigating a homicide."

She drew in a breath. "Okay. The thing is," her brows knit, "I don't know who you're talking about."

This was getting weird. "He helped me with a case last Mardi Gras. He has wild gray hair, a sunken face, and super-pale skin, like a ghost."

"Yeah, well," she rubbed her arm, "I've worked here for two years, and I've never seen anyone who looks like that."

There was no way I'd hallucinated the old pharmacist. He was real.

Unless...

No, Franki. This isn't the time to rethink your ghosts-don't-exist position. You've got a fiancé to free. Plus, you'd have to leave New Orleans because it's more haunted than a Halloween party at Dracula's mansion. "Maybe you can help me. It's about the vintage medicine bottle that was stolen yesterday."

She swallowed. "I'm not sure I can talk about that."

"Why not? Were you here when it happened?"

"Yes, but..." She bit her lip. "There's an investigation, and I talked to a cop."

"No worries." I smiled to put her at ease. "Can you at least confirm that this was the poison stolen?" I pulled out my phone and held up the picture of the cyanide bottle.

Her lips parted. "Where'd you get that?"

"From the crime scene." I didn't want to say more. "Listen, since you talked to the police, you know that the cyanide was used in a murder. And I know for a fact that the main suspect is innocent. So, can you please tell me who stole the bottle?"

"He didn't tell me his name."

The thief was a male. *Could it be?*

No, Veronica said not to go there, and she's right. I have no evidence. "Can you describe this man?"

"Mm, I guess." She rubbed her arm again. "He was tall with brown hair. And hot. Awesome smile."

That description fit any number of men, including Bradley. But, of course, he hadn't stolen the cyanide. I sighed—but not too deeply. I didn't want to stir up that dust and risk arsenic poisoning.

"He, uh," the young woman glanced at the battered double

doors that led into the pharmacy, "put the bottle in his coat pocket."

"What kind of coat?"

"Black, maybe wool. I don't know the brand, but it was thigh length."

It was winter, and a lot of men wore coats like that. Still, I raised my phone to do a search.

The girl jumped backwards, knocking a bottle from the shelf that hit the floor with a crash. "Are you kidding me right now?"

"What is it?" I shouted, fearing the worst, both in terms of Bradley and whatever was in that bottle.

She pointed at my phone. "You know the guy who stole the cyanide!"

"Huh?" I glanced at the display. And I felt as though the ghost of Louis J. Dufilho had given me a Victorian-style blood-letting with the scarifier.

Instead of the cyanide bottle, the picture was the last one I'd taken, a New Year's Eve selfie of me—and Bradley.

A door slammed.

My head shot up. The young woman was running through the courtyard. I stared after her, desperately wanting to run too.

Run away.

To anywhere.

But there was nowhere I could go to escape what I'd learned.

Bradley, the man I loved and hoped to marry within a matter of days, had stolen the potassium cyanide that had killed Dana Del Ray.

9

———

"**B**radley couldn't have stolen that cyanide. He just *couldn't* have." Tears clouded my eyes as I grabbed a jar of marshmallow fluff from the Christmas Car's rear console and shoved another spoonful into my mouth—then chased it with Peppermint Schnapps.

Santa and Hermey traded a glance, their faces tight with worry.

"And I do not want to cry, damn it." For one thing, it was embarrassing to sob in front of a man known for being jolly. And for another, the tears were blurring my vision so much that I could barely see the marshmallow fluff, let alone scoop it up.

Santa leaned toward Hermey. "This calls for Milk Punch, the Cajun version."

Hermey nibbled his lower lip. "Are you sure, Santa?"

"As sure as Rudolph's nose is red." He adjusted his white fur collar. "That kick of Tabasco will do her good."

Would it? After all, I'd just been kicked in the gut by that woman at the Pharmacy Museum. I shoveled more fluff.

Hermey cast an alarmed glance at the jar. "Well, the beignet rim is certainly in order, but I'm concerned the Tabasco will interact with her spicy body glitter."

Dana Del Ray's scarlet skin flashed before my eyes. Then I squeezed them shut and pointed at my face with a spoonful of fluff. "Don't worry about this glitter. It's coming off as soon as you get me home. This look has done nothing but cause me problems all day long."

Hermey produced a cocktail shaker and began mixing ingredients.

And I resumed stuffing my face with fluff. It was nice of Santa and Hermey to look out for me. Glenda's Glitter Grit Getter kit had lost its sparkle, and my high-heeled boots had not only failed to get me two thousand dollars in seventies money, they were also killing my feet. I was in no condition to walk or drive, which is why I'd needed Santa and Hermey's sleigh alternative.

Something else I needed came to mind—Ms. Linda Green's famous hangover cure. "Santa, would you mind taking a detour to the Bywater Bakery? I could go for some Ya-Ka-Mein."

"Old Sober?" he asked, using the local nickname for Ms. Linda's Chinese-African fusion noodle soup. "You don't seem blitzened to me."

"I'm not—yet." In keeping with the reindeer game I added, "But I'll be donnered in an hour."

Santa hunched over the steering wheel and hooked a couple of right turns onto Bourbon. "You know, it's possible that Bradley wasn't the cyanide thief. Looks can be deceiving."

If the big brass band we'd just passed was any indication, I had to agree. All the musicians had alligator heads.

Hermey handed me a tall glass that read "Ole St. Nick's North Pole Distillery, Handcrafted by Elves."

"Thanks." I used the red-and-white striped straw to stir the Cajun Milk Punch. "Problem is, Santa, the girl at the museum was so sure Bradley had stolen the bottle, she ran from me like *I'd* killed Dana."

"You're a PI. You know people pick the wrong person out of a lineup, even when they're sure they're right."

That did happen, and all too often.

Hermey nodded knowingly, as though he'd been ID'd in a lineup.

Santa twisted his mustache. "And think of the Père Dagobert sightings. He can't be a real ghost, but people are convinced he is."

My mind drifted to Chandra, who couldn't be a real psychic. "I almost forgot... the Crescent City Medium, Chandra Toccato, claims she channeled Dana Del Ray's spirit, and she said Dana mentioned a père. Of course, I'm not buying her spirit baloney, but the reference is odd."

Santa's eyes twinkled in the rearview mirror. "As a Christmas man, I'm inclined to believe in magic."

Even Hermey smirked at that.

Santa glanced over his shoulder. "Hey, we're close to Le Richelieu Hotel. Want me to stop so you can get some home cooking from your cousin, instead of Ya-Ka-Mein?"

I huffed so hard my lips flapped like Mr. Ed's. After watching Giada concoct her Campbell's soup sauce, I'd be better off with the ancient can of Progresso from the American Italian Cultural Center. "I'll stick with the Old Sober. I could use some Creole soul food, and Giada's cooking could put me in a coma."

Santa gave a wry smile. "That bad?"

"Potentially. But please, keep that to yourself until I solve Dana's murder."

"What about after?" he asked.

Giada was family, but I could hardly let her poison people with bad food and/or botulism. I breathed in the car's cinnamon-pine-gasoline scent. "Shout it from the rooftops, Santa."

Hermey stared into the back seat, his elf-hatted head the only visible part of his body. "What's your next step in the investigation?"

"After I eat and feed my dog, I've got to track down someone who knows Dana."

"Might I offer a suggestion?" he asked.

"Certainly." I sipped my drink.

"Go to St. Louis Cathedral tonight and look for Père Dagobert."

That suggestion was as big a surprise as the Tabasco kick. "Surely you don't believe there's a connection between Dana's murder and this Capuchin ghost nonsense?"

He shrugged as Santa turned onto Esplanade. "Stranger things have happened in New Orleans."

I'd not only heard that before, I'd said it. But I was reluctant to buy what the money-grubbing medium was selling. "I don't know how Chandra knew to mention a père, but she didn't hear it from a spirit—unless that spirit was booze talking to her."

Santa shot me a look as cold and pointed as an icicle. "But you'd never forgive yourself if you didn't investigate, and it turned out she was right."

I slugged my milk punch. Santa was one smart cookie.

"If you *do* go," Hermey said, "watch out for the ghost nun."

I started, and a tin star stabbed me in the skull. I winced and rubbed my head. "Who the hell is *she*?"

"A nun from the Ursuline convent who met a tragic end. She floats around the chapel before disappearing into thin air."

Candy had mentioned guests at Le Richelieu seeing the specter of an old nun. Maybe it was the same one. "Next thing I know, you'll tell me there's a ghost black cat. And remember, I can't see a priest, nun, or black cat before my wedding. It's an old Sicilian tradition."

Santa hit me with another frosty stare. "Let's say that's true. What's more important to you? Getting married on Saturday?"

Hermey cocked a tiny brow. "Or getting your fiancé out of jail?"

Now I could see why these two rode together, and it had nothing to do with that thieving Elvis impersonator. They were a great team, like Simon and Garfunkel. Or maybe Donny and Marie.

Santa pulled up to a pickup truck parked outside the Bywater Bakery. Ms. Linda was serving food from the back.

My door flew open before I could reach for the handle.

Marcella pushed me across the cracked vinyl and flopped onto the seat, spilling what was left of my milk punch. "Fancy seeing you here! I'll bet you came for the tiramisù."

"No," I opened a package of Santa's Filthy Sack Wipes to sop up the spill, "Ms. Linda's Ya-Ka-Mein."

Her maroon-lined lips drew back in horror. "If you want noodles, why on earth wouldn't you go for Italian wedding soup?"

In Marcella's America, you were either with Italy or against it. So, it was a lucky break for Santa and Hermey that Christmas and the Italian flag shared the same colors.

"Speaking of weddings," Marcella gripped her linebacker-sized thighs, "I'm here about your cake." She raised her hands in surrender. "I know, I know. It's not Gambino's. And to be painfully clear—That's. All. Moira's. Fault."

Once again, I didn't know how, but she was going to tell me.

"That woman ordered your cake from a bakery in the Irish Channel. Not only is that culturally inappropriate, it's *such* a *stereotype*. I mean, does Moira's every action have to be connected to her Irish heritage?"

Talk about the moka pot calling the Kelly Kettle black.

"Unfortunately, Gambino's is so booked not even Connie

Massetti in Event Space Rentals could get you a cake. And if Connie can't get you a cake..." Her mouth flatlined like a Holter monitor registering a heart attack.

Santa shifted uncomfortably in his seat, probably thinking of Mrs. Claus's warnings about binging on milk and cookies.

Hermey just stared at Marcella, his black eyes unblinking.

"But don't worry, Franki." Marcella patted my shoulder. "The Bywater Bakery has you covered. A three-layer cake—vanilla, strawberry, chocolate—with Chantilly Italian icing."

"Oh," Hermey said. "A Neapolitan cake?"

Marcella exhaled and pressed green-white-and-red nails to her forehead. "I know what you're getting at. How could we do Neapolitan when all the Italians in New Orleans are Sicilian? But like I said, the Bywater Bakery has our girl's back." She gave me a pat on said back that shot me into Hermey's seat. "Instead of a plastic bride and groom cake topper, they're going to make one out of—" Her lips pursed with excitement and her smoky-eyeshadowed eyes popped. "—*two cannoli.*"

The Christmas Car was so silent not even a carol dared play on the stereo.

"How classy is that?" she shrieked, making us all jump.

The Nonnone would approve of the cannoli cake topper. As for me, my head hit the seat back and a hot piece of tinsel. I no longer cared. I just let my hair sizzle.

"Now, I'll tell you what's not classy," Marcella pulled a box from her "NOLA Sicilians: Spicy Like Our Red Gravy" tote bag, "this wedding gift someone sent you. It came to the AICC today with no return address. Otherwise, I'd call the sender and give them a piece of my mind."

Hermey gasped. "You opened it?"

Santa's eyes had lost their twinkle. "A gift for someone else?"

Marcella pulled back her hair curtain and proceeded to scowl-shame two members of the largest gift-giving operation in the world. "Of course. I had to make sure it wasn't a covert message from Moira."

My eyes slid sideways. "She *could* just call me, you know."

"Oh." Marcella went still. "I hadn't thought of that."

Sitting forward, I took the box from her hand and lifted the lid. And I went as still as she had. Then I shoved the box to the floorboard.

The so-called wedding gift was a brass skull with tentacles wrapped around it—those of a kraken.

The object was so hideous that I remembered exactly where I'd seen it before.

The gift shop on the Steamboat Galliano.

And I knew for certain that an uninvited guest had come to town for my wedding. The question was, which one?

"You're ho-ho-home, Franki!" Santa boomed into the backseat. "Are you going to get out?"

My gut response—*When Frosty takes a beach vacation.* The kraken skull had shaken me to my core, but the sight in my driveway was shaking me to the cellular level.

My parents' Ford Taurus station wagon.

"What the *heaven*, God?" I whispered. "Haven't I been through enough?"

Santa let out a yelp, and for a second I wondered whether he knew my family.

"Son of a nutcracker," he shouted and fled the Christmas Car.

Hermey gaped, coal eyed. "Gumdropsss!"

Then he split too.

Bewildered, I squinted out the fake-snow-sprayed windows, trying to figure out who or what had scared them away. It was dark out, so it took my eyes a moment to adjust. When they did, I gasped and jerked back, getting a jolt from some electrically charged tinsel.

And the raging Medusa staring into the windshield. Otherwise known as Ruth Walker, covered in dirt and leaves with moss filaments protruding from her hair like serpents.

"Apparently not," I said, answering the question I'd posed to God.

Ruth yanked open the car door and slid into the backseat beside me.

And I did the best thing I knew to do. I pushed down the lock beside me and reached over and locked her door too—in case Chandra Toccato popped out of a crypt or drove around the corner with a U-Haul and crystal ball. Then, semi-holding my breath, I leaned against my door to keep a healthy distance from whatever germs and bacteria were crawling on her. "Where'd you come from? Hades?"

Ruth flicked a beetle from one of her cat-eye lenses. "The cemetery."

I always knew Ruth was the Grim Reaper.

"Why'd the Christmas Casanovas run off?" she hummed. "Guilty consciences?"

"What do they have to be guilty for? You're the one who does underhanded things like spy on people."

"Trying to deflect, as usual. Admit it, missy." She tapped my chest. "You're looking to replace Bradley with one of those ho-ho-hos."

"Keep your grubby graveyard hands off me." I rubbed my breastbone. "And did you just call a Santa and his gay elf *whores*?"

"Mkay, scratch the wee merry one from my last sentence. But it's as clear as a Christmas condom that you're getting your jollies with Santa."

"Whoa!" My stomach gagged, as repulsed as I was. "You're way off base—like North-Pole off base. There is nothing remotely inappropriate going on between me and Santa."

"Alright. If you're not cruising Kris Kringle's candy cane, then what in the South Pole is going on in this Yuletide Ride?"

"*Gaaahhh!* What are you trying to do? Ruin Christmas *forever*?"

"For your information, I'm trying to find out why you're spending so much time in the Mistlehoe Mobile instead of investigating Bradley's case."

My hand went up, and I swallowed hard. "If you don't stop with the holiday-themed innuendos, I will yak up the Ya-Ka-Mein I just ate."

She slid backwards, spreading dirt and decay in her wake.

And I pulled my hair from my neck. The Christmas Car was as steamy as a hot toddy, but it had nothing to do with anything tawdry. I blamed the boiling bubble lights and Grim Reaper Ruth's death breath. "Listen, all I'm trying to do is prolong the magic of the season, because I'm under serious stress."

"*Me, me, me,*" she mocked with a look that could wither a freshly cut Christmas tree. "What about your fiancé? I'd say he's pretty darn stressed too, but he's not at liberty to take a jollyride since he's *behind bars.*"

When she put it that way, I *did* sound selfish, and maybe even whiny. Nevertheless, I much preferred Glenda's glittery grit approach to my attitude than Ruth's horny holiday one. "I've got some leads, okay? But right now, you and I have bigger turkeys to roast."

"Look who's using holiday-themed references now," she snapped.

"At least mine involve food, which is what normal people associate with the holidays."

She crossed her arms. "You and I both know there's nothing normal about Christmas in January."

No comeback for that.

Her brow arched, dislodging a clump of dirt. "Now what, pray tell, is a bigger 'turkey to roast' than solving Dana Del Ray's murder and freeing my employer from the hoosegow?"

Because Ruth—in a twist so ironic that Alanis Morissette could have written a song about it—had been hired to be the cruise director on the Steamboat Galliano, I picked up the skull kraken box and put it between us on the seat. "This wedding gift was sent to me and Bradley today. Anonymously."

She lifted the lid. Her head shot up, flinging moss filaments. "Did this come from Marian Guidry's gift shop on the Galliano? Or did that Mafia boss, Gigi Scalino, send it?"

"There's another possibility…"

Ruth threw open the door and bolted from the car.

My sentiments exactly.

I climbed out to look for Santa and Hermey, and I didn't have to look long. They were inside Thibodeaux's, doing brightly colored shots at the bar.

"Poor guys." The sight of Grim Reaper Ruth in her cemetery greenery had to be more terrifying than a real-life Grinch.

With a sigh, I slammed the car door and walked around to close Ruth's. But first I retrieved the box with the skull kraken. If the thing could drive Ruth away, I wanted to keep it.

Box in hand, I headed across my front yard, pulling my scarf around my face. Jack Frost was nipping at my bruised nose.

"Francesca?"

My feet stopped in their tracks. That was my mother's voice —but she wasn't on my front porch.

"Why don't you come upstairs, dear?" she called from above.

And I stared at the second-floor balcony. *Why is my mom outside Glenda's apartment with a wineglass?*

In a Zsa Zsa Gabor nightgown?

Then it occurred to me what this was about—a diversion from the cunzata del letto tradition. "Are virgins making my bed?"

"That's on Thursday, dear. Today is Tuesday."

True, but something was amiss. "So, what are you and Glenda doing?"

"She's not here. She went to get supplies for tonight."

Given everything I knew about my landlady, I didn't want to know anything about those supplies. "Then, why do you want me to come up there?"

My mother swigged some wine.

"Glenda loaned me her costume closet for the evening."

Despite the cold, I began to sweat. There was no reason for my mom and I to meet where Glenda kept her stripper outfits—and her aptly nicknamed "acsexories."

My mom took yet another gulp and swayed a little. "I thought we would have a mother-daughter chat..."

Okay, I didn't like the sway, but at least my nonna wasn't with her.

"...about your wedding night."

Clutching my gut, I staggered backwards like I'd been shot. And I had, by an ew-arrow. Because I would have rather attended a week-long Sicilian Superstition Seminar with Nonna, the nonne, and the Nonnone than talk to my mom about intimate things she'd probably done with my dad.

"It might surprise you, dear, but your mother knows a lot about lovemaking..."

My head flew back, and my wounded stomach heaved, its contents rallying for an uprising.

"...and pleasuring a man."

The motley mob of marshmallow fluff, Schnapps, Ya-Ka-Mein, and milk punch stormed my esophagus. I gripped the stair railing and swallowed hard. "Mom, I think I'm gonna be sick."

She giggled. "You said the same thing when I told you about the birds and bees."

"This is different. I ate too much Ya-Ka-Mein."

"Oooh, Francesca." She threw up her free hand. "Is that why you're staggering around? You've been drinking?"

I'd been staggering from the TMI-tipped darts she was shooting at me, but I couldn't tell her that. "I think I have good reason to drink right now, Mom."

"Alcohol is never the answer, dear." She swallowed some wine. "It'll make your skin sallow and emphasize your dark circles."

"Which will complement my nose bruise."

She sighed and descended the stairs, pink ostrich feathers swirling around her ankles. "You shouldn't joke at a time like this."

"Who's joking? My fiancé's in jail. There might not even *be* a wedding, much less a wedding night."

"There will, dear." She gave me a hug. "You'll solve the case before Saturday." Then she pulled back and stared into my eyes with that wedding-fever look. She really needed to believe that I could save my big day.

And so did I.

But after an entire day of investigating, I still knew nothing about Dana, and I wasn't even sure who my suspects were. Dana's as-yet-unidentified boyfriend? Candy? Bruno? A ghost priest? Or was it an escaped convict or missing person from my steamboat case?

A Honda Civic pulled into the driveway.

My mother looked up from the bottom of her wineglass. "Are you expecting someone?"

"No, it's probably Glenda with whatever those supplies are."

The driver door opened, and a young guy in a cap and T-shirt bearing the logo of Le Fleuriste NOLA got out holding a long flower box. "Either of you Franki Amato?"

"Me," I said.

"Solid." He swaggered to me with the box. "These have your name on them."

"Hang on." I put the skull kraken box on the ground and reached into my bag for my wallet.

"Appreciate ya, baby, but your Romeo handled the tip." The guy flashed a smile stamped with the initials J and D on his front teeth and shoved the box into my arms. "Big spender too."

"Ooohhh." My mom's eyes popped with exaggerated excitement. "Bradley must've had his family send them. By the way, Lillian called and said she and Cordelia still can't get a flight out of Boston. Thank goodness it's not snowing here."

Snow in New Orleans would be a bigger Christmas miracle than Bradley getting out of jail. I opened the flower box.

And promptly dropped it on the ground.

"Francesca! They're not the flowers *I* would've chosen, but that's no reason to throw them down. At least read the card."

"There isn't one." My voice was hollow.

Dead.

"You haven't even looked." She knelt and rummaged through the tissue paper. "How would you know?"

Because Bradley didn't give me yellow roses.

Former Detective Wesley Sullivan did.

10

"There's no card." My mother stood with the Le Fleuriste NOLA box. "Strange."

Strange? No, *sinister.* But I didn't correct her. If Sullivan was back, she was better off not knowing.

She swung the box toward me like a Tommy gun. "I'll put these roses in a vase, then meet you upstairs for our little chat."

My body tensed to DEFCON 1. *How am I going to escape* that *trauma talk?*

My mom took a few steps toward my apartment and cast a sultry stare over her marabou-feathered shoulder. "Glenda's got a few things in her costume closet I'd like to show you."

My stomach nose-dived, as would my libido after a mother-daughter acsexories demo.

Desperate for an escape, I glanced around. I had three options—take refuge in the Thibodeaux's bathroom, hide behind a tomb in the cemetery, or hop in my Mustang and leave town. Given everything that was going down in New Orleans, the latter seemed the best option.

But I couldn't leave Bradley.

Or my wedding guests, who'd be arriving in a few days and expecting to see me walk down the aisle to wedded bliss.

I shivered, and not from the cold. *Can this wedding really happen? Or am I delusional to think I can solve this case by Saturday?*

And what if I can't? What happens to Bradley?

To us?

The Lucky's Liquor and Vaxing van rounded the corner.

One of the supplies Glenda had gone to get was immediately apparent—her Mardi Gras decorations, as in the giant cast she'd had made of her boobs. It, or rather they, were perched on the van roof.

As the van pulled into the driveway, the breasts shifted. The one that naturally hung lower—on Glenda's real rack—now drooped over the door.

My gaze lowered to the windshield. Between Nadezhda and Glenda's seats sat a penis balloon the size of a six-year-old.

It wasn't clear whether this was a do-over for my bachelorette or just a normal night out for them, and I didn't care. The yellow roses had rattled me—but not as much as the threat of a mother-daughter chat.

My eyes darted to my apartment door to check for my mom. Then I dashed to the van and yanked the handle, but it wouldn't budge. "Unlock the door! I want to be kidnapped!"

Glenda leaned her head out the window. "It's not locked, Miss Franki. It's my Mardi Gras decorations. You'll have to move them."

When it came to her breasts, I'd dealt with worse. I gave the sagging mammary a shove, pulled open the door, and dove inside the van.

My survival instincts weren't off. They were right where they should be.

I slid the door shut and came face-to-face with the balloon. "Can we please move the penis to the back?"

Glenda turned in the passenger seat. Instead of her usual pasties, she wore a top made of two chain-linked champagne flutes. And her cups runneth over.

Way over.

"Have at it, sugar."

Wishing she'd picked another phrase, I grabbed the risqué balloon and wedged it between the back of my seat and the waxing table. "So. What're we drinking?"

Nadezhda eyed me via the rearview mirror. "Vodka."

"No mixers?"

"Nyet."

For someone who owned a liquor store, she made a lousy drink.

She poured me some vodka and shoved it at me. Unlike the bachelorette sweatshirts and blinged-out wedding veil, she hadn't designed the cup. It was decorated with penises and three appropriately misspelled phrases—*Wedding balls! Horny-moon! Much hapPENIS!*

Slowly, I reached out and took the thing, and she popped in a straw.

"Is that a—" I stopped myself.

It was.

Grimacing, I removed the salacious straw and tossed it behind me with the matching balloon. I sorely missed Marcella's Jell-O IV shots. She'd been all about the ring, but Glenda and Nadezhda were all about the sex organs.

And the night was young.

The van door opened, and I jumped, fearing a Mom ambush.

My cousin Giada climbed in—accompanied by a blast of cold air and the soundtrack of sleigh bells.

"Uh..." I looked out my window as the Christmas Car sped away. "You know Santa and Hermey?"

"Kind of." Giada unbuttoned her wool coat. "I call them when I'm stressed out."

I'd heard of genetic similarities, but the fact that we both destressed by immersing ourselves in a 1970s Pontiac Catalina Christmas was downright scary.

Nadezhda glared into the rearview mirror. "Vhy you stress?"

Giada returned the glare and yanked off her coat. "The associate manager of Le Richelieu just fired me."

"Candy?" I turned in my seat. "Anthony's the manager. Where was he?"

"Off work. I asked to speak with him, but Candy said the decision came from corporate. Supposedly, my cooking isn't up to snuff. But you know that's not right, Franki."

"Of course not," I huffed. Giada's cooking *was* up to snuff— as in it could snuff out a life.

She smoothed her brown hair. "They're obviously blaming me for Dana Del Ray's murder since I let a killer into the kitchen." Her head hit the seat back. "What am I going to dooo? I'm in the middle of a divorce. I need this job."

"Don't worry. We're family. I can help you out."

"Thanks, but I need to figure this out for myself." Giada raised her head and pointed to the windshield. "Is that your mother?"

My head snapped back. My mom jogged toward the van, her Zsa Zsa gown shedding feathers. "Get this vodka vessel rolling!"

Nadezhda sneered over her shoulder. "I not take orders."

"If you don't, you're going to have to listen to my mom's wedding-night sex talk, complete with an acsexories demo."

"Oh, hell nyet. Zere not enough vodka in Russia," Nadezhda muttered, starting the engine. She threw the van into reverse and peeled out.

Glenda leaned around her seat, her champagne flutes threatening to spill their contents. "If you have dance experience, Miss Giada, I can get you a gig at Madame Moiselle's."

My cousin gripped the armrests, unprepared for the strip-job offer. "That's kind of you, but my friend Moira is looking for work too, and we're thinking of going into business together."

"An Irish-Italian duo? *Chiiild*, the clientele will go wild!" Glenda shimmied for emphasis, and I leaned back in case those flutes shattered. "I'm thinking a food-themed striptease. Instead of Bangers and Mash, we'll call it Bangers and Gnocchi—"

"Under the circumstances," I cut in, "it's best if Giada lays low—and avoids anything food related." I turned to my cousin. "While we're on the subject, I hope Moira knows how sorry I am about Marcella locking her in the janitor's closet over the menu. I'll pay her for her time."

"She'll appreciate that, Franki. And you probably know this, but if not—Marcella has commandeered the kitchen at the hotel and put the nonne to work cooking for your reception. Nonnone has also gotten involved. She raised holy hell because there were no cannoli on your menu."

Apart from the bride and groom on the cake. "That's okay. I predicted as much."

Giada pressed fingertips to her forehead. "My family is due to arrive at Le Richelieu tomorrow, and they're already worked up about my divorce. Wait until they hear I'm jobless too."

"Now, Miss Giada," Glenda said, "that's a tomorrow problem. Let's focus on fun tonight. Let off some steam."

Giada sighed. "You're right."

Glenda *was* right, but I had no intention of backing her up. Her version of letting off steam was different from ours—and usually literal.

"Miss Chandra's on a psychic call until late, so she's going to meet us after she picks up Ruth."

My eyes rolled like the wheels of the Lucky's Liquor and

Vaxing van. Why did everyone persist in thinking that Chandra and Ruth were a) fun, and b) part of my bachelorette party posse?

Giada looked at me. "Where's Veronica?"

"Thank you for that reminder, Miss Giada." Glenda turned in her seat. "Miss Ronnie's on a Zoom call with Bradley's family attorney."

My chest tightened. "Why didn't she tell me about that?"

"She wants you to keep investigating, Miss Franki. And I'm glad you've got your glitter on because that's what we're about to do."

Thanks to my mother, I still hadn't managed to wash that stuff off.

"I got a tip that we need to go to The Big Teasy Strip Club because a dancer who knew Dana works there."

The tip was big news, but I was more interested in whether there'd been a development in Bradley's case. I pulled out my phone and called Veronica.

Straight to voicemail.

Sighing, I texted her to call me and shoved the phone in my coat pocket. "By the way, Glenda, why are your Mardi Gras decorations on the roof if this isn't my bachelorette party?"

"Bachelor," Nadezhda corrected.

"No one said it wasn't your bachelorette, sugar."

"*I* said." Nadezhda looked at Glenda. "It bachelor party."

Glenda cackled and slapped her thigh. "Miss Nadezhda's a real riot, isn't she?"

Sure, if your kind of comedian has the personality of Joseph Stalin.

"Anyhoo, Miss Franki," Glenda flipped her platinum hair, "I had The Vassal get my Mardi Gras decorations from his frat house because we're going to The Big Teasy strip club. I auditioned there a few times, and they never would hire me. I intend to show them what they've been missing all these years."

Given that her actual breasts were less covered than the ones on the roof, she was going to do precisely that.

Nadezhda turned onto I-10 East.

The penis balloon floated from behind my seat, and I batted it back. "Where is this place?"

"Kenner."

Nonnone's neighborhood. I wasn't surprised that a Sicilian nonna hadn't listed The Big Teasy as part of the suburb's attractions. Although, it was probably more interesting than the casino—and definitely the planetarium. "So, who gave you the tip?"

"Well, sugar, I put out an APB on Stripchat—"

"You mean, Snapchat."

"No, Stripchat. It's Snapchat for strippers."

Giada shot me an amused look. "Instead of Snapchat's disappearing messages, does Stripchat involve disappearing clothes?"

A much-needed laugh escaped my lips, and I high-fived my cousin.

Glenda blinked. "Why, yes. How else would it work?"

Our hands dropped.

And so did my smile. I was now concerned that APB stood for *All Penis Bulletin*. Still, whatever awaited us at The Big Teasy was still preferable to that mother-daughter chat.

Glenda glanced at her phone. "Ladies! Another tip has come in—one of Dana Del Ray's private clients is a Tuesday night regular."

I reached for Glenda's phone but retracted my hand. I was already juggling Glenda's Mardi Gras decorations, her champagne-flute top, and a penis balloon and cup, so I was in no mood to get flashed by Stripchat. "Does it say anything else about the client?"

"He's middle-aged and sleazy."

Giada sniffed. "That describes eighty percent of strip club clientele."

She was right about that. "Who's the dancer we're going to meet?"

"A member of Dana Del Ray's Mardi Gras krewe. Her name is Sunny Bare."

"Clearly a play on 'Honey Bear.'"

"No, Miss Franki. It's 'bare' like naked. It's her real name, and she lives up to it. She worked at Madame Moiselle's off and on, and she was always running around the dressing room in her birthday suit. I kept telling her to put a damn thong on, but she flat refused."

"Hold on." I gripped the armrests. "Her nudity was a problem for you?"

"The dressing room is our office, sugar. I didn't want to see her lower lady part while I was trying to work. It got so bad, I asked the manager not to give her any more shifts."

Stunned, I sat back. Glenda not liking nudists was more of a shock than finding out I wasn't a zitella.

For the next ten or so miles, I sipped my vodka and thought of all the things that could've been different if I'd known my landlady had boundaries sooner.

"Ve close to club," Nadezhda announced.

"Miss Franki, can you grab the box of supplies by the waxing table?"

"Sure." I stoop-walked to the mobile waxing table and, against all reason, glanced at the ceiling to see the picture Nadezhda put up for her clients. Rather than eye candy, it was an eyesore—NHL hockey great Alexander Ovechkin shirtless with a rose between his broken and missing teeth—and what looked like a hockey stick in his pants.

Grimacing, I dragged the box to Glenda's seat.

She rummaged through the contents. "Miss Nadezhda and I made you a bridal boa to go with your veil."

Nadezhda sneered—or smiled. Hard to tell.

Glenda raised the boa, which had not one feather. Just fake one-hundred dollar bills, empty liquor bottles, and condoms. "What do you think, sugar?"

Honestly, I thought it was all the things my friends and relatives would rig my bed with for the *cunzata del letto*. "Very… thoughtful."

Nadezhda flashed her eyetooth hole. "Everyting man need for vedding night."

The "man" was clearly me, but I didn't bother with a comeback. I was too busy trying to figure out why fake bills were a wedding-night essential in Russia.

Giada reached into the box and produced the "I bring ze bling" sweatshirt and blinged-out veil I'd worn during my ill-fated original bachelorette party. "Let me help you with this."

Without a word of protest, I slipped on the sweatshirt and let her put the veil on me. It was so cold out, I could use the head covering. Plus, a small part of me was worried that it might be the only veil I'd ever wear.

My landlady climbed out of the van, and suddenly her champagne-flute top made perfect sense. She'd paired it with a Dom Pérignon-label-turned-thong and six-inch cork stripper heels. After draping a sheer white tulle boa around her shoulders, she hit a switch—and white lights blinked on—complete with liquid that bubbled up her body.

Without so much as a glance back, Glenda hiked up her flutes and strutted past two muscle-bound bouncers checking IDs, tracing the tip of her penis cigarette holder across both their chests. Then she threw open the door and made her grand entrance like Dom Pérignon with a vengeance—sparkly, curvy, and ready to pop the cork on anyone who'd ever said she wasn't the right vintage.

"Zat big hairy bear," Nadezhda announced, then exited the van.

My cousin, mid-buttoning her coat, froze. "Did she say *bear*, like the animal?"

"Nah." I waved it off. "She probably saw Sunny Bare and thinks she needs a wax."

Giada slid open the van door, and I spotted the bear Nadezhda had referenced—Bruno Messina waiting in line at the entrance. Even in the freezing cold he wore a black satin shirt unbuttoned to his navel, and he had enough chest hair to hibernate through a Siberian winter. Although, given his red velour pants, he looked less like a creature of nature and more like a Soviet lounge singer.

Odd that Bruno would be at The Big Teasy, especially after Veronica ID'd him as a suspect.

Nadezhda handed him a business card. "I vax chest pelt vit vone strip. You keep, hang above fireplace like taxidermy."

"No way, baby." Bruno backed up, hands raised in horror. "I ain't depriving the ladies of my man fur."

Another thought occurred to me—after I'd shuddered at the man-fur comment—that I didn't like one bit. I climbed from the van. "You're here to see Sunny Bare, aren't you?"

Bruno started, surprised to see me. He reached for his gold saint medallion and broke into a sweat despite the freezing temperature.

"Answer me, Bruno."

He did—by shoving Nadezhda at me. Then he pushed a waiting frat boy into the bouncers and ran inside the club.

∼

"FREEZE, BRUNO!" I used my old rookie cop voice, but I doubted he'd heard me over the blaring music inside the club.

Bouncer One went in after him.

I tried to do the same, but Nadezhda's matryoshka body tripped me up like a bowling pin. I fell onto my back, and she kicked me in the shin. "Ow!" I pushed up onto my hands. "What's your problem?"

"I tell my problem. You step on Valentino vit big foot." She pointed to her snakeskin Rockstud pump. "You owe vone tousand dollar."

"*Vone tousand dollar?*" I echoed, aghast. "You were crazy to pay that, and you're even crazier to think *I'll* pay you that." I stood and stooped to get in her face. "Now move so I can go after Bruno."

Bouncer Two approached, patting the air with his palms in a take-it-down-a-notch gesture. "I'm gonna need you to cool it, ladies."

"She not lady. She Saskvatch." Nadezhda opened the door.

Bouncer Two grabbed her by the shoulder. "No one's going in until my partner comes back and gives the all-clear."

She whacked him in the gut with her snakeskin bag. "You touch again, I make kolbasa vit fingers."

Nadezhda would, too.

A group of forty-something men in golf shirts exited the club, and I darted behind Bouncer Two through the open door.

"Come back here," he yelled. "I at least need some ID."

Of course, I ignored him. But I *was* excited that he wanted to card me.

The club was packed, which was good cover from the bouncers. But it took a few seconds for my eyes to adjust to the dark, the neon lights, and the kaleidoscope of glittered and oiled skin.

Also glaring? Bruno's red velour pants. They—and he—were headed up a staircase next to a bar in the back of the club.

Hands raised to avoid skin-to-skin contact, I gave chase. As I wove my way through crowded tables, I bumped into a redhead doing a lap dance and knocked her to the floor.

She landed on her backside. "Could you be more careful, honey?" She pointed to her pastied chest. "You could've popped a boob."

"Uh... Sorry."

The guy scowled and got up. "No one is sorrier than I am, lady."

Debatable, but I had other things to worry about.

By the time I made it to the stairs, Bruno had disappeared. At the top of the landing, I stopped. On either side of me was a row of curtained rooms, and no one was in the hallway.

My mind went back to the time I investigated a murder at Madame Moiselle's where Glenda used to work. Strip clubs certainly weren't game shows, so there were no prizes behind those curtains. They concealed VIP rooms, and weird things went on inside them.

Steeling myself, I peered into the first room.

A stripper in a green wig sat on a fuzzy leopard couch—with a fully clothed male on her lap. He was easily fifty, and she was reading him a children's book. I squinted to see the title, *Are You My Mother?*

I let the curtain close.

There were several more rooms on either side of the hallway, but after the scene I'd just witnessed, I had no desire to know what was going on in any of them.

But if I knew one thing about Bruno, it was that he was predictable. And that coward would run as far as he could get.

Striding to the end of the aisle, I decided to try the room on the left. I peered through the curtain.

Neon purple light from a mini stripper pole stage blinded

me. When my eyes adjusted, I saw a blonde on a leopard couch behind it. A fake blonde.

Bruno in a wig.

And I ripped open the curtain. "You know," I shouted above the music, "there are a lot of reasons I wouldn't mistake you for a stripper—starting with your hairy chest and ending with those tacky pants."

He winced. "They're athleisure."

"They're ath*lame*." I walked around the mini stage to stand over him. "Now tell me how you know Sunny Bare and why you came to see her."

He lowered his gaze. "That's personal."

"You know what else is personal?" I grabbed him by one side of his collar. "My fiancé getting thrown in jail for a murder he didn't commit five days before our wedding. So, tell me what you had to do with Dana Del Ray, or you'll be wearing that wig in your throat."

"Like I said before, baby," he said, his voice tight, "you've got to slow down with the accusations. And the threats." Bruno spun, slid from his satin shirt, and stood.

Dropping the dated disco wear, I extended my arms into a T and backed up to block his exit.

To my surprise, Bruno didn't try to escape. He stepped onto the mini stage and grabbed the pole. Then he arched at the waist, and his knees buckled in slow motion—like a standing caterpillar having a crisis.

"Do you... have a cramp?"

"No, baby, I'm showing you my moves." He tossed the wig and launched into a body roll that ended with a dramatic pelvis pop. "How's that for bachelorette party entertainment?"

Almost as traumatizing as an acsexories demo from my mother. "I don't have time for this, Bruno. So, if you don't start talking, I'll make sure you never move again. *Capisci?*"

He deflated like a punctured silicone implant. "I'm a regular here. I was going to ask Sunny to keep quiet."

So, Bruno was the sleazy middle-aged regular mentioned in Glenda's Stripchat tip. "What does that have to do with Dana?"

"Dana and Sunny came to the house a couple of weeks ago." Bruno flopped onto the couch. "If my mamma finds out, she'll have me excommunicated."

Pretty sure the Church was already on it. "Uh, if you're trying to hide from your mother, why would you hang out at a club in Nonnone's backyard?"

He glanced up. "Who's that?"

"Big Nonna."

"Mm." He rubbed his thick lips. "I don't know no Nonnone."

Then I wasn't the only one. "Tell me about Bradley's bachelor party. Did you know Dana would be there?"

"No, she told me she wasn't going to do private parties anymore. When they found her in the cake, I panicked."

I sat on the stage. "Is that when you left?"

"Yeah, after I—" His low brow popped. "I meant just 'yeah.'"

Bruno was hiding something, and I knew it was bad. I scooped up the wig and leapt onto his lap. "Eeey, this is more like it. Can you put that bridal veil across your mouth like a belly dancer?"

"This is no lap dance, pal." With my free hand, I grabbed his bottom lip. "Tell me what you did, or this wig goes down your throat."

His eyes were pastie sized. "I didn't kill Dana! Wut I had her wusiness card, so I wut it in Wwadley's wallet."

In shock, I released his lip. "You set up my fiancé?"

"What'd you expect me to do? Throw the card in the trash where the police could find it?"

My pulse was pounding as hard as the bass on the strip club

sound system. "You thought it would be better if they found it in *Bradley's* wallet?"

"How could I know that would happen?"

Glenda yanked open the curtain, which was a good thing for Bruno—and for me. Because I was about to kill him. Death by wig-in-throat suffocation.

She strutted into the room followed by Nadezhda and ran her eyes over Bruno's torso and the blonde wig in my hand and then over Bruno's torso again. "Well, Miss Franki, I see things are getting wild at your bachelorette party."

I leapt to my feet. "Not wild. Hairy."

"He *is* a hairy hunk of man meat, sugar."

"No, hairy as in a problem."

"Da." Nadezhda sucked her eyetooth hole. "Meat old. Need vax and vipe vit bleach."

"Eyyy. Ohhh." Bruno reached for his shirt. "I'm feelin' objectified here. And a little disturbed."

Nadezhda handed him her business card. "You call. I give deal."

I looked at Glenda, who'd decided that the chain linking her two flutes was the best place to store her penis cigarette holder. "Where's Giada?"

"Outside, sugar. She got a call she had to take."

Bruno held up Nadezhda's card. "A combination liquor store and waxing salon?" He nodded in appreciation. "That's genius, baby. All you need is a wedding chapel."

Nadezhda's maroon spikes bobbed. "Iz good."

Honestly, it *was* a good idea. The place would do a bang-up business in New Orleans, but Nadezhda was going to have a hell of a time working a wedding business into her existing slogan, *Before you get your drink on, get your hairs in order.*

Bruno returned the card. "I even got the slogans for you," he said, as though he'd read my mind. "For the men, *Get waxed, get wasted, get wifed.*" He grinned and slipped on his shirt. "And for the ladies, *Get waxed, relaxed, and legally attached.*"

Glenda licked her lips and kicked out a leg. "Because nothing says commitment like a bottle of booze and a Brazilian."

Even I had to admit the slogans were spot on—just not aloud.

Nadezhda held out the card he'd returned. "You call. Ve talk."

Bruno fastened a total of two buttons on his shirt and took the card.

I sat beside him to up the pressure. "Let's get back to the investigation. First thing tomorrow, you're going to tell the police about Dana's business card. If you don't, I'll turn you in for her murder."

The sweat returned to Bruno's brow.

"Second, you're going to tell me why Dana wasn't doing private parties anymore. Did something happen? Or did she get another job?"

He shrugged. "She said she was coming into serious cash."

Glenda threw up her arm—and let it slap her behind on the descent. "What did I tell you, Miss Franki? Follow the money."

"And vat I tell you, Frank?" Nadezhda raised her Valentinoed foot. "You owe vone tousand dollar."

Ignoring the mansult and the cash grab, I kept my eyes locked on Bruno. "So, was Dana getting an inheritance?"

"Nah, the money was from her boyfriend. An older guy who'd just moved back to town."

The hair on the back of my neck stood. The profile fit someone I knew. "Did she tell you his name?"

"She just called him W."

My fingers dug into the couch cushion. Of all the W's in the world, Dana's boyfriend sure as hell wasn't George W. Bush. The W stood for Wesley.

Wesley Sullivan.

11

My fingers drummed on The Big Teasy's bar. "Well, this is a bust."

"Damn right it is." A stripper next to me thrust out her surgically enhanced breasts. "I paid ten grand for this Miami Special, but I haven't made a dime."

First of all, *hers* wasn't the kind of bust I was talking about. And second, someone at the club should've told her that the surgeon gave her the *Milwaukee* Special—not built for the stage, but for leaning over a Schlitz.

Right on the enhanced-bust theme, Glenda fondled one of her champagne flutes as she scanned the club. "Sunny has to get here soon, Miss Franki. The manager said she goes on at midnight."

"Let's just hope she shows. One dancer has already been murdered."

Glenda bit her lower lip. "I'll go check the dressing room again. But first," she slid the penis cigarette holder from her flutes, "I need a smoke before I confront her bare lady part."

I'd need more than a smoke for that scene—and to recover from where she'd stored that cigarette holder.

Glenda sashayed away, and I spun my barstool to face the stage in the center of the club. Two hours and one stripper had crawled by since I'd chased down Bruno. He'd since gone home to his mamma, and frankly, I envied him. Thanks to the neon lights and music, I had a Technicolor headache synced to the beat of a striptease.

My cousin collapsed onto the barstool beside me. "I just got off the phone with my father—and before that, my mother. Apparently, to protest my impending divorce, the Montalbano side of the family is wearing black to your wedding."

Despite the dark circumstance, I half laughed. "Don't sweat it, Giada. They'll fit right in with the nonne. Plus, if I don't solve this case, we'll be wearing black to the wedding."

"Don't say that, Franki. You'll prove Bradley's innocent. I know it."

My confidence wasn't exactly flowing, so I fell silent. Plus, I was distracted by a stripper who was sitting on a man's lap, knitting. I mean, it *was* unusually cold this winter. But still.

Giada signaled to the bartender. "Time to get this party started. By the way, where is everyone?"

"Glenda went to look for Sunny, and Nadezhda's passing out business cards."

She tugged at her ear and stole a glance over her shoulder. "Smart move. She could make a killing off this club, and I'm not talking about the strippers. What about Ruth and Chandra?"

"Good question. They're awfully late." I checked my phone. "Crap! I missed a call and a text from Veronica. Damn music."

Giada leaned in. "What did she say?"

"No new developments, but I should be able to visit Bradley tomorrow."

"That's great!" She patted my back. "He might know something that could help his case."

If he did, he hadn't told Veronica. And sure, Bruno had

explained how Dana Del Ray's business card ended up in Bradley's wallet, but that didn't change the fact that the woman at the Pharmacy Museum had positively ID'd him as the cyanide thief. And that was no small thing.

Ruth and Chandra entered the club.

"Ze fun and ze party are here," I said, quoting their badly chosen bachelorette-party sweatshirts.

Ruth made a beeline for the bar closest to the entrance.

Chandra waddled up. "Sorry we're late. I had a séance call that ran over. A man asked me to summon his late wife, but the wrong woman showed up—his former mistress."

It was tempting to ask whether the spirit of his wife had found out, but I had more pressing issues, like making sure Chandra wasn't going to pull one of her psychic stunts at the club. My eyes lowered to her wrist. "Where's your charm bracelet?"

"In the car." She pulled her bag to her chest and flashed a frown at a couple of men at a nearby table. "I couldn't run the risk of channeling a spirit in a strip club."

Naturally, I was relieved, but as usual, I couldn't follow her logic. "Why not? Dana was a stripper, so this is the perfect place to talk to her."

"You saw what happened when I channeled her spirit outside Le Richelieu Hotel," she huffed, aghast at my ignorance. "I was rolling around in the street. If a spirit possesses me here, I could end up riding a pole in front of an audience of men just waiting to leer at me."

There *was* an audience, but if they noticed Chandra, it was only because her huge hair was blocking their view of a stripper who was rolling in powdered sugar like she was auditioning for the dessert menu.

Ruth walked up with two drinks. "Here's your 'Grind and Tonic.'"

Chandra took the glass.

Giada frowned. "I'm going to the other bar. I can't seem to get served here. Want anything, Franki?"

"Nah, I'm good."

Ruth held up her drink. "If you want something non-alcoholic while we're working, Giada, I suggest this Long Island Iced Tea."

My cousin glanced at me, and I smirked. "Ruth, that so-called 'tea' has more booze than a Mardi Gras parade float."

"Well, I see someone's already liquored up because this is good old-fashioned Lipton's with a healthy dose of lemon."

"One, I've only had one drink—vodka in the van. Two, unless Lipton's started steeping their tea in tequila, vodka, gin, and rum, I'm calling BS."

She harrumphed. "Maybe if you spent as much time investigating Bradley's arrest as you did the contents of my drink, he'd be out of jail."

Ruth might've been sipping fiction, but her drink theory held water.

Chandra took a slug from her glass. "What have you found out about that tip Glenda got on Stripchat?"

"Bruno was the suspect, but he's not the killer. He knew Dana, and he happened to have her business card on him at the bachelor party. When she turned up dead, he put it in Bradley's wallet so the cops wouldn't find it on him and tell his mother."

Ruth's lips pursed, and so did her turkey neck. "Why that lily-livered coward."

"It gets worse. Dana's boyfriend was ex-Detective Wesley Sullivan, risen from the river."

Ruth chugged her Long Island Iced Tea, planted it on the bar, and sprinted from the club.

She was just as lily-livered as Bruno, and lush-livered too.

Chandra stirred her drink with a paddle nail, then turned to me like Ruth hadn't just fled the building. "Personally, I think Candy was the killer, and I said as much to Marcella when I ran into her at Le Richelieu Hotel earlier."

"You went to the hotel? Even though it's haunted?"

"With a ghost maid? Gawd, no!"

Her fear of Ellen still baffled me. But if the ghost maid would keep Chandra at bay, I was ready to hire her full time.

"After I picked up Ruth, I stopped at Le Richelieu and had her go inside to see whether Candy was at work. She was. When I was waiting for Ruth to come out, Marcella and a woman who called herself Nonnone pulled up with a carload of groceries. I filled them in on Candy's mysterious visit to Sassy Spells to see the Father. They're going to keep tabs on her."

"That's great," I said, shocked that Chandra had done something useful.

Glenda walked up, snatched Chandra's Grind and Tonic, and downed it.

"What's the big idea?" Chandra boomed, proving that The Big Teasy stereo system had nothing on her lungs.

"Apologies, Miss Chandra. The manager told me Sunny's in the dressing room. I need to prepare for a war zone, as in a full-frontal assault."

"I'm in," I said, rising, "but I'm not looking down. Bare lady parts are Nadezhda's department."

We tailed Glenda through the haze of vanilla and neon. Giada caught up with us as we reached an unmarked door near the stage. Inside, the dressing room was dimly lit with a row of bulb-lined mirrors, flimsy articles of clothing draped over chairs and on the floor, and the strong scent of body spray and dirty money in the air.

Only one woman was prepping to perform—and judging by her birthday suit, we'd found our tipster.

Sunny Bare lounged at a vanity in nothing but bronzer. Her

skin was leathery from too many years under stage lights and too few under SPF, and her bleached blonde hair was piled into a teased bouffant that defied both gravity and common sense. She looked like Glenda's tougher cousin—the kind who'd fight you in a parking lot and then ask you for a light.

"Well, well, well," Sunny Bare cracked open a compact, "if it isn't Texarkana Rose, the dressing-room snitch who cost me a gig."

Chandra's pudgy hands went to her hips. "I hate to correct your geography, but it's *Tokyo* Rose."

Sunny hack-laughed like she'd joined Glenda for one too many penis cigarette holder smokes. "Tokyo Rose brought nations to their knees. Texarkana here can't even bring a tip."

Glenda cocked a hip and batted her lashes. "I bring tips—and a thong to the workplace."

Sunny stood and hiked a stripper-shoed foot onto a chair, lobbing the full frontal assault Glenda had feared.

"Zat not vax job," Nadezhda erupted from the doorway, "zat var crime." She entered and handed Sunny her business card.

Glenda pulled up her Dom Perignon thong. "On that note, I'll wait outside, Miss Franki. I haven't had enough champagne to stomach this coochie coup."

"Yeah," Chandra said, "I need a drink, and Glenda drank mine."

They left, and Sunny Bare eyed Giada and then me. "The red face glitter's a nice touch, honey, but it's not hiding that ugly nose bruise. You might want to lower your bridal veil."

Sunny Bare was not only inconsiderate, she talked with a full-body shoulder shimmy—like Ann Margret warming up for a Vegas comeback. "You have a show to do, so I'll make this quick."

"Please do." She returned to her seat.

"What do you know about Dana Del Ray's boyfriend?"

"Never met the guy." She brushed bronzer across her bosom. "But she said he was older, lived near Baton Rouge."

"Any link to her learning about the bachelor party at Le Richelieu?"

"No, she heard about that while she was having a drink at the hotel bar."

That coincided with what Glenda, a.k.a. Texarkana, had told me.

Sunny snapped the compact shut. "Dana was hell bent on doing that party, too. Said it was going to be a game-changer."

How, I had no idea. The pay would have been a few hundred bucks at most. "Anything else?"

"She told me all this over coffee the morning of the party. Some woman from the hotel called to confirm details. Dana put it on speaker."

My pulse picked up. "Was it the assistant manager, Candy Kelly?"

"She didn't give a name that I remember."

Giada stepped forward. "Even if it was Candy, she was probably just doing her job. The hotel would've been concerned about the liability of having a woman pop out of a cake."

"That's exactly what the woman said," Sunny said with a shimmy that weaponized her breasts. "Dana had to eat a full meal before they'd let her jump out of the cake."

Giada and I locked eyes. We were both thinking of the spaghetti.

Sunny picked up an aerosol can. "The hotel was worried she'd faint and hurt herself. We thought it was weird, but we're no lawyers. But now that she's dead, it looks suspicious."

Before I could respond, she rose from the vanity and sprayed her nether region like she was Febrezing a crime scene.

Giada recoiled, and I flinched away from Sunny as though

she were a solar eclipse—too much exposure and a strong chance of blindness.

But the phone call looked more than suspicious. It looked like murder—premeditated and plated up with a side of liability. What I couldn't figure out was Sullivan's involvement.

If the caller *was* Candy, did she conspire with Sullivan to kill Dana?

∽

"SURPRISE, SUGAR!" Glenda shouted from the front passenger seat of the Lucky's Liquor and Vaxing van.

It was almost three a.m., so I was stretched out on the van's shag carpet. I lifted the blinged-out wedding veil from my eyes and raised my head from the penis balloon, which made a decent pillow except for the rubbery squeaks. "Why are we at Le Richelieu Hotel?"

"You can't stay at the fourplex tonight, Miss Franki."

Was she working with my mom on the cunzata del letto tradition? No chance. The ritual called for virgins to rig the wedding bed, and Glenda had seen more mattress mileage than a roadside motel. "Why can't I go home?"

"Ve plan bachelor party." Nadezhda sneer-smiled. "Vodka shots, sauna vit birch branch vhacking, and wrestle vit bear."

Giada leaned down to my level. "This time, I think she means the actual animal."

I thought the same thing. Louisiana was home to the black bear, and this being New Orleans, no one would be surprised to see one partying at my bachelorette.

"I'm sorry, ladies." Glenda turned in her seat, and her champagne flutes clinked. "But we missed our window for the hotel festivities when we went to The Big Teasy to investigate."

Nadezhda tapped a Soviet red fingernail on a matryoshkashaped bottle. "Ve still have vodka and birch branch. I drink and vhack Frank on vax table." She gave a curt nod. "Is tradition."

"For grooms-to-be in Russia, maybe," I said in a droll tone. "But when it comes to tradition, I'm female and strictly Sicilian." I almost added, *and we do normal things*, but then I remembered the Big Fat Sicilian Wedding Superstition Sermon I'd heard at St. Mary's Church. I settled for, "and I'm already beat."

"The room's paid for, Miss Franki. You go on in and get some beauty rest. We'll see Miss Giada home."

"It was nice of you to arrange this, but I don't have my things. And I need to get home to Napoleon."

"Your mother and I have taken care of everything, sugar. I packed you a bag, and she's going to stay at your apartment."

My eyes darted to the hotel. The only pro I could come up with for staying in the godforsaken place was that Candy was probably working, and after the bombshell about a woman from the hotel arranging Dana's last meal, I had questions.

The cons, on the other hand, were as plentiful as Glenda's pastie collection. Chief among them? A fresh murder, Candy being in cahoots with Sullivan, and a whole hotel crawling with nonne led by Marcella, the natural-born nonna and linebacker-sized boxer.

"Vell?" Nadezhda prodded. "Vhat you vait for? President Putin to ride up vit vhite horse?"

She was rude, but right—except for the Putin and the horse part. "Alright. We'll resume the investigation tomorrow." I stepped from the van, and the cold hit me like a birch branch. I lowered my head and hurried into the lobby.

Despite the warmth, I froze.

A vase of yellow roses sat on the reception desk. The memory of the identical arrangement delivered to my apartment flashed in my mind. *Did Sullivan really send them?* When Veronica and I went to Sicily for a conference, Gigi Scalino sent us a bottle of Cremoncello. But Sullivan seemed the likelier option since he'd sent Bradley to jail twice before.

My stomach plummeted, and I dropped onto the couch in front of the door to the Terrace Lounge. *Oh, God. Was the third time the charm? Is Bradley going away for good?*

A dark shadow of despair loomed over me.

Correction—the shadow was a mountain of a man, at least six-feet-seven and four hundred pounds in a navy tracksuit and shiny puffer vest, who'd exited the Terrace Lounge and was blocking the light. He was hairy and stunk of vodka and BO— and pickles.

My eyes met his, narrow and piercing with the unforgiving chill of a Siberian winter that made the air freeze in my lungs. They were James Gandolfini eyes, if Tony Soprano had grown up wrestling bears on the steppes.

He made a growling sound. "You are Frank?"

The thick Russian accent and that "Frank" told me Nadezhda had something to do with his presence. "And you are?"

"Yakov. Ve wrestle."

My lips curled. Yakov was "the bear." "Sorry," I smiled to be on the safe side, "the party was canceled."

His terrifying eyes turned sad and soulful, like those of a Borzoi puppy. "Ve not wrestle?"

"Nyet, Yakov." I used in his native language to make sure there was no miscommunication.

"Vhat about vodka?"

"In the bar." I made a shooing gesture. "Take the bottle. It's on me."

His eyes lit up, and he lumbered back into the lounge.

Anthony skidded into the lobby from the hallway, his tie askew. "Franki! Thank God!"

I rose from the couch. "What is it?"

"None—none's taking over the hotel, and your friend Marcella ain't no better." He wrung his hands." You've gotta help me wit' them, Sis. Our home office already fired Giada because 'o that murder. I could be next." His hands shot to my shoulders, and his panicked eyes stared into mine. "If that happens, I'll have to go home to live with Mom and Dad."

The fear on his face reflected my sentiment—a haunted hotel where murders happened was preferable to my parents' home in Houston. "Look, I get it, Anthony. But I've got my hands full with Bradley's arrest. Plus, you're the manager." I peeled his fingers from my shoulders. "You need to learn to deal with difficult clients."

"And difficult employees." He threw up his hands. "Candy's disappeared."

I blinked. "What do you mean?"

"Just what I said. I can't find her nowhere, and her shift ain't over."

Candy had probably stepped away from the desk for a few minutes, and I decided to take advantage of her absence. "Did you put Candy in charge of the bachelor party?"

"We didn't have nothing to do with that. It was all your landlady."

"But weren't you concerned about the liability of having Dana jump out of the cake?"

"No. Why?"

Knowing Anthony, he'd slept through that section of his hotel management course. "Did you ever see Dana in the hotel before the party?"

"Not that I remember. But lots of people come in heuh."

I pulled the scrap of paper with the word "eleison" from my wallet. "I found this on the floor in front of the reception desk."

Anthony leaned in, squinting. "I don't know no Allison."

Figures he thinks "eleison" is a woman's name. He probably thinks "subpoena" is some sort of Italian sandwich.

"Now that you mention it, Sis... that *is* Candy's handwriting." He pointed to the word, "See the way her 's' isn't part of the rest o' the word? She does that on notes she writes me—everything's in cursive till she gets to the 's.'"

All I could do was stare at Anthony. It was one thing to suspect Candy of murder but another to have proof that she was involved.

Yakov stepped from the bar, clutching four bottles of vodka to his chest as though protecting babies from the cold.

Anthony's head tilted up—and up—to take in the full height of Yakov. Then his hands shot up in surrender. "Cash register's on the desk, bro. Help yourself."

Another section of his hotel management course he'd apparently missed. "He's not a robber, Anthony." I sighed. "He's a wrestler." I turned to the bear. "I said *one* bottle, Yakov. Not four."

His gaze went full Russian wolfhound again.

"Yo." Anthony gave Yakov the onceover. "Nice tracksuit."

My eyes rolled like a vodka bottle. *Anthony* would *notice that.*

My brother patted his suit coat. "You the guy that was out front singin' earlier?"

"Nyet. I wrestle."

Anthony paled and stepped back. "Yo, you win, man. I'm out."

"He came to wrestle *me*, Anthony, not you."

"In that case, bro..." My brother puffed out his chest and removed his suit coat. "You might be big, but I cain't let you wrestle my sister."

"Nobody is wrestling anybody," I huffed, even though I was touched by Anthony's offer to wrestle the bear on my behalf. "What did you mean by 'singing?'"

"Oh. Some guy was out front in like a monk's robe, singing a hymn or somethin'."

My blood went cold. "Was this before Candy disappeared?"

"Yeah," Anthony ran a hand through his slicked back hair. "Like twenty minutes ago."

I stared past him, out the glass door into the frozen night. *Kyrie eleison* wasn't just a hymn. It was a summons. Sullivan had come for Candy dressed as Père Dagobert.

The question was, What did he want from her this time?

THE ANSWER to my question came to me, and it was so terrifying that my blood *didn't* run cold. It froze solid.

Wesley Sullivan was outside, using the ghostly monk getup to stalk me. That's why he'd summoned Candy.

I was his next victim.

Panic gripped my gut like Yakov did the four vodka bottles. I sank onto the brocade couch outside the Terrace Lounge. Every cell in my body screamed at me to run, hide, but I couldn't. I had to stop Sullivan. My brother and my nonna were in the hotel.

"You a-ight, Franki?" Anthony rushed to me.

I stood and took his hands. "Lock the doors when I leave. Don't let anyone in or out. Understand?"

"Where are you goin'?"

"After the monk. It's that ex-detective, Wesley Sullivan, posing as the ghost of Père Dagobert."

The color drained from Anthony's face faster than Yakov drained his first vodka bottle. "Whoa, whoa, hold on. You can't go out there alone. The guy's a homicidal maniac."

My jaw, which had been set, wobbled. "That's why I have to do this. You've got to stay here and protect nonna."

"Let's call the cops."

"There's no time, and they won't believe me," I snapped. "The entire New Orleans PD thinks he's dead, remember?"

"But it's the middle o' the night and colder than a freakin' Russian winter out there." He shot a nervous glance at our resident bear. "No offense, or nuthin."

"No vorries. I take none."

Anthony's eyes, and mine, landed on Yakov.

He beamed. "Ve wrestle now?"

"Nyet," I replied in my best Nadezhda. "You want those other three bottles of vodka?"

"Iz Pope American?"

He'll do just fine, I thought. I gave Anthony a final determined nod, turned, and exited the hotel with the human bear in tow.

As I headed the half mile to St. Louis Cathedral, Yakov caught up, clutching the vodka bottles like holy relics. We walked in silence down a deserted Chartres Street.

My gaze darted to the halo of a gas lamp, as though it were a ghost. Something cold and wet hit my face. Twice.

Snow.

A "Christmas miracle," to quote Hermey the elf. Within seconds, the miracle turned menace as the flakes became a full-on deluge. My coat was no match for real winter weather.

Yakov, however, lumbered along as if on a pleasant spring stroll, no doubt because of his Russian blood and vodka-fortified veins. Lucky for him, because it was snowing harder, as if the blizzard in Boston had moved down South.

As we neared our destination, the three Gothic spires of the cathedral pierced the snowy sky. I braced myself to hear Sullivan's deep baritone singing "Kyrie eleison."

But the night was eerily silent. And Yakov cast a long, terrifying shadow in the lamplight.

A scent snaked through the freezing air—the faint aroma of church incense.

A chill that had nothing to do with the temperature crawled up my arms.

The devil is here.

Just as the thought formed, I saw a flicker of movement—a flash of black fabric disappearing around the side of the cathedral.

Not a monk's robe—a nun's habit.

Could it be the specter of the floating nun that Candy and Hermey had mentioned?

Surely not.

Yakov's bottles began to clink, and his teeth chattered.

One look at his big Borzoi eyes told me it wasn't from the cold. Like me, he thought he'd seen a ghost too.

Now shivering, I swallowed hard. "We have to follow... it. St. Anthony's Garden is around back."

"Garden? Zey grow beets?" His eyes returned to Tony Soprano mode. "I make mean borscht."

"Focus, Yakov," I hissed, grabbing his arm. "Follow that nun. Now!"

Seeing a nun—ghost or otherwise—was bad luck for my wedding, according to the superstition sermon. But then again, so was having a resurrected killer stalking me.

We crept around the cathedral, down Pirate's Alley to the wrought-iron gate of the garden. What was a space for quiet contemplation by day became a spotlighted stage by night. A lamp at the base of the Sacred Heart of Jesus statue cast a massive shadow of the figure's outstretched arms against the cathedral's white rear wall.

When I moved to New Orleans, I'd assumed the statue was St. Anthony, given the garden's name. I'd since learned that the *potager*, to use the French term, was named for St. Anthony of Padua, the patron of the Capuchin monks who'd first cultivated the space in 1720. The Jesus statue was a more recent addition that locals viewed as a symbol of New Orleans' resilience after Hurricane Katrina.

Tonight, though, the statue was a symbol of something else entirely.

My eyes followed the beam of light from the ground up the stone figure. My brain struggled to process the profane sight.

It was too unthinkable.

But as the image sharpened, the horror crashed over me in a suffocating wave.

My knees gave out. I dropped into the virgin snow.

"Oy!" came from Yakov, and vodka bottles crashed on the pavement.

He'd seen it too.

Candy was bound to the statue, her lifeless arms tied to its outstretched ones, a gruesome parody of Christ on the cross.

12

—————

"For the last time, DiMaio," I growled from across the interrogation room table, "I don't know who killed Candy Kelly."

The fifty-something detective's laser glare could've set fire to the table. "You'll change your tune when you see what I've got for you." He stalked out.

Whatever he was talking about, it definitely wasn't evidence. I buried my face in my hands. The room's stale air was as suffocating as my situation. I wasn't sure what was more shocking—finding Candy splayed across the Sacred Heart of Jesus statue like a sacrificial pin-up or finding myself in here. At the rate Bradley and I were going, neither one of us would make it to our wedding.

And seriously—how was Yakov, the bear-sized vodka-swilling Russian who lived to wrestle, *not* a suspect?

Then again, it was obvious Yakov hadn't murdered Candy. The only suspect who made sense was Sullivan. He'd roped Dana and Candy into framing Bradley, then permanently removed the witnesses. The question was, what was he planning next?

The door slammed open, and I jolted upright.

My jaw dropped. My heart stopped.

Wesley Sullivan. His muscular frame filled the doorway, and his brown hair was slightly disheveled. The cold fury in his ice-blue eyes told me he'd come to settle our almost two-year-old score.

Is this what DiMaio meant? He's back on the force? Or was he working undercover?

No way. The guy was a known killer, and he'd committed other felonies before disappearing from the deck of the Steamboat Galliano.

"Look at these photographs, Amato." He slapped down close-ups of Dana dead in the cake and Candy strung up on the statue. "The neon red of Dana's cheeks. What does it remind you of?"

The sambuca sauce my cousin Giada had fed her, but I couldn't say that. "Cyanide poisoning?"

"No!" His fist pounded the table. "Red Hot Body Glitter."

Something was really off.

Sullivan leaned in, his eyes as frigid as the snowy weather. "You and Bradley murdered those women. Admit it!"

"You know you did it," I shot back. "And I'm going to prove it."

He let out a laugh as cold as the Mississippi River. "Good luck. I've been planning this since our rendezvous on the Steamboat Galliano." He leaned in, smelling of aftershave and vendetta. "I had a good thing going—a side hustle to supplement my police salary. I was going to buy a boat and retire early. You should've kept your mouth shut and gone along with it. Like a traditional woman."

In my experience, traditional women were the reason therapy was invented. Exhibit A—my Big Fat Sicilian Wedding Superstition Sermon, from the kidnapping to the razor-blade toenail warning. "Speaking of which," I said, my voice acidic, "is your mother proud of the man you've become?"

His face tightened, but a psychotic smirk surfaced. "No point in changing the subject. Bradley's going away for good. As for you... you're going in front of a firing squad."

A firing squad? In New Orleans? This city couldn't coordinate trash pickup after a parade, much less a military-style execution.

That clinched it. Something was very wrong with this interrogation, and I suspected I knew what it was. I leaned back in my chair and crossed my legs. "You know I didn't do anything wrong."

"You must have, because I had plenty of volunteers offer to shoot you dead." He opened a door I hadn't noticed, revealing a dark courtyard. "Move!" He pulled me from the chair and shoved me into the pre-dawn gloom. "Your firing squad is waiting."

As my eyes adjusted, I got a good look at the volunteers. A row of Ruths, cheeks Dana-Del-Ray red from too many Long Island Iced Teas, swayed in their Keds with rifles in their hands.

Suspicion confirmed. This is a bona fide nightmare.

The Father from Sassy Spells stepped from the shadows, his priest collar crisp against the black button-down shirt with the coffin and cross. "Now that Candy is dead," he intoned, "who's going to eat your sins?"

Nightmare or no, that dude is scary. I bolted upright in my bed at Le Richelieu Hotel, heart pounding like a brass band on Frenchman.

"Dammit! Why can't I dream about something normal? Like falling off a cliff? Or giving a presentation in my underwear?"

The clock read eleven a.m. I'd stayed at the crime scene until seven, but now I needed to get to Private Chicks. It was already Wednesday, which meant I had to assemble the troops. And at this point, I'd even take an army of drunk, rifle-toting Ruths if it meant clearing Bradley and nailing Sullivan.

As I swung my legs over the side of the bed, a flash of red on my pillowcase froze me mid-motion.

A stain.

Dinner-plate sized.

Blood?

I scrambled to the mirror. No cuts. No wounds. But the red was smeared across the *I bring ze bling* sweatshirt I'd slept in, and it was too bright for blood. More like…

Dana's cheeks.

I lifted the fabric to my nose.

Sambuca.

Fear speared my gut.

Sullivan. *Had he been in my room? Maybe even inspired my nightmare?* One thing was certain—it damn sure wasn't Ellen the Ghost Maid.

I had to find Anthony, but I couldn't go to the lobby looking like Carrie post-prom.

My gaze landed on the overnight bag Glenda and my mom had packed. I dug through it. Toothbrush and clean underwear —definitely my mother. Red Hot Body Glitter, boots, and champagne—Glenda. Oh, and a bonus pair of chili pepper pasties.

The stained sweatshirt would have to do.

The hallway was deserted. I took the elevator to the lobby, where my mom and nonna sat slumped on the brocade couch looking like flour-dusted fugitives.

My mother covered a yawn. "Hi, dear."

Nonna didn't speak. First sign of the apocalypse.

This wasn't the reaction I'd expected after stumbling upon Candy crucified in a garden. "Aren't you going to ask how I'm doing? You know, post-traumatic statue discovery?"

Nonna waved a limp hand. "Who's-a gotta the energy? That-a Marcella work-a us like-a pack animals."

"She's right," my mother mumbled, flicking dough from her apron. "Marcella's got us cooking around the clock. We only get four fifteen-minute breaks."

I planted my hands on my hips. "A hundred and fifty guests is a lot, but isn't that a little much?"

"Honestly, Francesca." My mom shook her head, releasing a cloud of flour. "How would it reflect on our family if we didn't have enough food?"

"Define 'enough,'" I said.

Nonna raised her chin. "In-a my day-a, we saved our whole-a lives for the wedding-a *pranzo*. Thirty courses—ten-a *primi*, ten-a *secondi*, and-a ten-a *dolci*."

I sank onto the arm of the couch, overwhelmed by the calorie count alone. "Why ten of everything?"

"Because of-a the Ten-a Command-a-ments, *naturalmente*. And-a we had-a few command-a-ments of our own-a, like-a 'Thou shalt-a have-a the seconds' and-a 'Thou shalt-a not ask-a for the gluten-a-free.'"

Nonna once again proved my theory—Old-World Sicilian weddings were violent, hostile occasions.

Marcella burst into the lobby from the Terrace Lounge, wearing a bold Baroque-print dress and an even bolder message on her apron—*Nonna is my sous chef*.

"Run, Carmela!" My mom pushed my nonna from the couch, and they hid behind the reception desk.

Marcella didn't notice. She marched to the entrance, giving them time to slip into the Terrace Lounge, presumably en route to the kitchen warzone.

Nonnone entered the hotel, decked out in her signature black-lace Dolce & Gabbana. On her arm, she carried a box bag with the words *Souvenir della Sicilia* in red, adorned with lemons and snapshots of tourist sites. The pièce de résistance—dangling from the bag's red patent leather strap was a cannolo keychain the size of the actual pastry.

She hoisted the bag higher. "You're doing a marvelous job, Marcella. The work of a saint."

Marcella's face lit up like the Vatican on Christmas Eve.

"But we need to double the cannoli."

The light dimmed. "Double? But... we also have the wedding cake and the spumoni. Isn't that enough?"

Nonnone looked down her hooked nose. "I'm surprised at you, Marcella. You know the significance of the cannoli to Sicily."

Marcella bowed her head. "It's a symbol of *Carnevale*—our Mardi Gras."

"Not only that!" Nonnone stomped the heel of a D&G mule. "The shell and the ricotta filling? They're a metaphor. Fertility. Abundance. A celebration of life! That's why at a wedding it's not just a pastry. It's a wish—a blessing for the bride and groom to have a fruitful and plentiful new life."

That was a lot to put on a pastry, but generally speaking, Italians had high expectations of their food.

Nonnone leaned into Marcella. "Now go. Make. Triple!"

Marcella saluted. "I *do*, Nonnone, I mean, I *will*!"

Then Nonnone spotted me and clutched her bosom as though I was the ghost of weddings ruined. "What the hell happened to you?" Her witchy nose twitched as she sniffed the air. "Now I see," she said, eyeing my sweatshirt. "You bring the bling *and* the booze." She shifted her bag. "I don't care what you do in your free time, but I got you a four o'clock fitting at Wedding Belles you're not gonna miss."

"Thanks, but I already have a dress."

Her eyebrow arched like a Roman aqueduct. "Are you trying to kill your mother?"

"No."

"Then you'll wear the plantation dress she picked out." Her black eyes swept my frame. "You've already done enough to disappoint her."

My head snapped back. "Excuse me?"

"All women are a disappointment, doll. Eve and the apple!"

Saint Marcella nodded, and I was surprised neither of them mentioned the funny business with the Virgin Mary's Immaculate Conception.

Nonnone's phone beeped. "*Uffà!* I've got to run an errand." She tapped my chest. "Your four o'clock fitting." Then she pointed at Marcella. "Triple."

And just like that, she was gone.

Marcella took my arm. "Come with me to the kitchen. I want you to see the reception meal prep in action."

Because my life isn't chaotic enough right now.

We passed the pool and walked through the kitchen doors, where a wall of heat and fragrance hit me. It was the holy trinity of Italian cooking—garlic sizzling in olive oil, tomato sauce simmering on the stove, and the yeasty scent of baking bread. The air was thick enough to chew, and the entire space was packed with nonne.

Judging by the women's grim expressions, they didn't appreciate the message on Marcella's apron. Nevertheless, they carried out their duties with the determination of soldiers supporting a war effort.

Mom and Nonna manned the cannoli station, as yet unaware their workload had tripled.

Marcella beamed. "Since the murder, the hotel guests have cleared out, so we've taken over the kitchen." She led me to the far side of the room. "Here's what I wanted you to see. Nonnone suggested we use a piece of history to make the pasta for your wedding."

Before me was a hulking table-like contraption, maybe fifteen feet in length. On one end, there was a hopper for flour and water that fed onto a wide, heavy-duty canvas conveyor belt. And on the other, a series of massive, powerful, steel rollers that grew progressively smaller before the dough reached the cutter. "So, this is the pasta machine."

"An original from Giacomo Cusimano's factory. The man, the myth, the macaroni-maker. Ten thousand pounds of pasta a day—thanks to the Dingley Tariff Act of 1897."

I sighed. No matter how rushed Marcella was—or I was, for that matter—she always made time for an American-Italian history lesson.

"The tariff doubled the price of imported pasta, so domestic demand soared. By 1901, New Orleans had eight macaroni factories, six owned by Italians, and all but one in the Quarter. And now, well over a century later, The Big Easy is making macaroni again thanks to your wedding." Marcella pressed clasped hands to her cheek. "You should be so proud!"

"Totally," I uttered. "But I have a groom to liberate, and you've got Nonnone's order to fulfill."

Marcella straightened like a drill sergeant. "Carmela! Brenda! Triple those cannoli!"

My nonna crossed herself, and my mom went to the veal scaloppini station and drank straight from a white wine bottle.

And I fled.

Yakov sat in the Terrace Lounge, looking like he'd wrestled several bachelors since I'd last seen him.

"You alright?" I gave his arm a pat, which was like trying to comfort a boulder. "Last night was really rough."

"Da. I lose pendant."

Apparently, he'd bounced back from Candy's murder. "Did you check the hotel's Lost and Found?"

His Tony Soprano eyes turned downcast. "Zey no have."

"I'll keep an eye out. What does it look like?"

"Gold ballet slipper." A faint smile touched his lips. "My dream vas audition for Bolshoi."

Try as I might, I couldn't envision him dancing in *The Nutcracker*, but I could clearly see him functioning *as* one. "Did you... get an invitation to audition?"

"Nyet."

We stood in silence, contemplating the marble floor and broken dreams. I didn't have it in me to tell a four-hundred-pound wrestling machine that the ballet might not be ready for him. And I sure as heck wasn't going to crush the dream of a man who could probably bend a Vespa.

"Oy." He scratched his beard stubble. "I need drink. But bar not have vodka."

No, because he'd cleared the shelves. Sensing he shouldn't be alone, I decided to say something I never thought would pass my lips. "You should go see Nadezhda at Lucky's Liquor." I left off the "and vaxing" in case he thought I was suggesting a bear-fur removal treatment. "She'll take care of you."

"Da. Iz good."

Yakov rose, and I walked him to the lobby. "I'll let you know if your pendant turns up."

He held out his hand for a shake but then enveloped my five-foot-ten frame in a bear hug that could've collapsed a lung. "Call if you vant wrestle."

"Will do," I wheezed into his puffer vest.

He released me and lumbered out.

The elevator dinged, and Anthony exited, looking more strung out than Candy on the statue. "Yo, any developments yet?"

"No news on Candy's killer, but it was most likely Sullivan. And tonight I'm doing a stakeout at St. Louis Cathedral to try to catch him."

He drew in a breath. "I don't think that's smart, Sis."

"I have no choice, Anthony. Sullivan put Bradley in jail and murdered two people, and now he's after me. I'm almost positive he entered my room while I was asleep, because it sure as hell wasn't a maid—flesh or spirit."

"Did you see him?"

"No, but when I woke up, my pillow had a big red stain."

Anthony turned marble white. "That ain't Sullivan." He grabbed my arm, his eyes wide with terror. "It's him—Bloody O'Reilly!"

I'd been through a lot in a short period of time, so the name "Bloody" hit too close to home. "Anthony, this is *not* the time to tell me some serial killer frequents the hotel."

"He's a ghost, Sis! A real Spanish general. Candy warned me about him when I took over as manager."

Why couldn't I just be haunted by Ellen? She could rifle through my overnight bag all she wanted.

Anthony glanced around to make sure no one was listening. "Candy said the ghost's signature move was leavin' bloodstains on pillows to scare people off."

It sounded certifiably insane, but there *was* a Sambuca stain on my pillow. "That's a little far-fetched, don't you think?"

"Is it? There's reviews about it on TripAdvisor. Plus, Candy was always sayin' Bloody O'Reilly didn't like male managers. She said he ran off the guy before me. Maybe he's trying to get rid of me by messin' wit' you."

More likely—Sullivan had read the TripAdvisor reviews and decided to make it real. But that didn't explain why Candy was pushing the Bloody O'Reilly ghost narrative on Anthony. Or why Sullivan went along with it.

The obvious answer?

They were trying to scare us away from Le Richelieu Hotel.

But what were they hiding?

"Did you ride to work in the Candy Cane Cruiser?" Ruth asked the second I entered Private Chicks.

As I hung my coat on the rack, I felt her hawk eyes boring into my back. "Given what happened to Candy, the nickname is in poor taste, even for you."

Ruth's graying-brown bun was as tight as her cheeks—and not the ones on her face. "Only a sourpuss like you would equate the two. But since that's who you are, I'll retract it in favor of 'Santa's Sleigh Ride.'"

I smirked. "Funny you'd use the word 'retract' after your hasty exit from The Big Teasy last night."

"I had a personal matter to attend to."

"Uh-huh—cowardice."

Her lips thinned and she stood, her posture stripper-pole straight. "I don't have to take this rudeness."

I shrugged. "Face the Ruth or consequences."

"Well!" Her reader chains swung as she snatched up a stack of papers. "I'm going to continue my investigation in Bradley's office." She spun on her Keds and stormed out.

And I didn't feel the least bit bad about it after her and the other Ruths' behavior in my nightmare. Because as sure as the woman recorded Judge Judy comments like they were Supreme Court opinions, if I ever did have to face a firing squad, she'd volunteer for it.

My dream reminded me that I needed to keep tabs on The Father, so I went to the window and looked down at Sassy Spells. I had no idea whether the man was connected to Sullivan and his shady dealings, but I'd certainly mentioned Candy's sin-eating session to police at the crime scene.

Nothing unusual outside, unless you counted the woman

walking six chihuahuas that were all wearing pink coats and tutus.

Crap. I'd forgotten to ask Anthony if he'd seen Yakov's gold ballet slipper. Even though Yakov was essentially a hairy Siberian sumo wrestler, there was something about the guy that made me want to help him—probably the fact that he had the soul of a sugarplum fairy.

A whirring came from across the room, followed by the odor of burnt plastic.

David and The Vassal had emerged from the hallway with bizarre apparatuses on their backs. David's looked like a geek soldier's Coachella survival kit—a military-surplus frame with an old beige PC tower bolted to it, alight with glow sticks. The Vassal wore a vintage 1970s canister vacuum covered in Christmas lights, perfect for sucking up cookie crumbs from Santa's Pontiac Catalina.

"What in the high-tech ho-ho-ho is going on here?" I asked. "It smells like you tried to roast a motherboard."

The Vassal pushed up his glasses. "No fire. Just a minor malfunction with my stakeout equipment."

"Which is?"

Slack-jawed, he sank into the chair at their corner desk. "The ghost vacuum invented by Egon Spengler? In *Ghostbusters*?"

David turned off a switch on a wand connected to his apparatus, silencing the whirring. "Mine is a proton pack to, uh, subdue ghosts for the stakeout."

Naturally.

The Vassal's eyes were grave. "We still have to fine-tune our PKE meters and seal the ghost containment unit."

"PKE?"

"Psychokinetic energy. A handheld device to detect paranormal activity."

"Ah. Well, for all our sakes, I hope one of your ghostbusting tools involves a pair of handcuffs."

The Vassal chuckled like that was funny.

David flipped his bangs. "By the way, you just missed Veronica. She's headed to Central Lockup. She said Bradley can have visitors in a couple of hours."

My breath caught. *Finally!* The past two days without him had felt like years. Tears pricked my eyelids—and turned hot. *Figures Ruth didn't mention that.*

"We also checked Dana's socials. Maybe Baby is the only krewe officer she mentioned. Veronica said she's still in jail, too."

I wiped my eyes. "Then after Bradley, I'll go see her. See what I can find out."

The Vassal looked up from his ghost-vac. "Want us to research anything else?"

"Actually, yes. A Spanish general named Bloody O'Reilly."

David glanced at The Vassal. "Oh, uh, we studied him in a History class. He crushed the Louisiana Rebellion of 1768."

I leaned against the brick wall by the desk. "What was that about?"

"Well, France ceded Louisiana to Spain after the Seven Years' War. Some French Creoles freaked out and rebelled, so the original Spanish governor fled. His replacement was Alejandro—a.k.a. 'Bloody'—O'Reilly."

I crossed my arms. "I'm guessing from the nickname that he wasn't sent here to hand out pardons."

"Hardly." David applied a Stay Puft Marshmallow Man sticker to his proton pack. "He captured the ringleaders, took them to the Spanish barracks—where the U.S. Mint and Le Richelieu Hotel are now—and had them executed. Firing squad."

A chill slid down my spine like the cold butt of a rifle. I was creeped out that I'd dreamed about a firing squad.

"To make it worse," The Vassal said, "he ordered the bodies left unburied on the levee across from the cathedral. As a warning. Two thousand soldiers guarded the corpses."

I gasped. "That's horrific."

"Père Dagobert must've thought that same thing."

"Wait." I gaped at The Vassal. "What does he have to do with this?"

"He gathered the rebels' families at the church and made sure the men had a proper Catholic burial. It's the reason he's still considered a hero in New Orleans."

"But how did he do it?" I asked, still stunned the monk and the general were connected. "What about the two thousand soldiers?"

David leaned forward, resting his elbows on his thighs. "Yeah, so, according to legend, the soldiers, like, never saw or heard a thing. He led a group of men to the bodies. And after the mass in the church, they buried them at St. Louis Cemetery No. 1. The whole time he sang 'Kyrie eleison.'"

Candy. That scrap of paper I'd found with the word "eleison." She must have figured out Anthony was afraid of ghosts and tipped off Sullivan. Then the two of them concocted a haunting. Maybe she researched local ghosts during her shift to pass to Sullivan.

"Oh! I know." The Vassal raised a hand like a student in class. "It was supposedly storming that night, so perhaps the rain cloaked their movements?"

David's brow wrinkled. "Still seems impossible. But everyone claimed Père Dagobert had performed a miracle."

A breath I didn't know I was holding whooshed from my lungs. The story was horrifying and beautiful at once. But it was also confusing. *Was there a link between these ghosts and whatever Sullivan and crew were doing? Or were they just convenient legends?*

David set down his proton pack. "Some people say they've

seen the funeral procession—like, Père Dagobert leading the coffins to the cemetery."

Although I couldn't quite buy any of the ghost stories, the hair stood on my arms.

"So," David rubbed his palms on his jeans, "for our stakeout, I figured we'd follow Père Dagobert's usual path. From the front of the cathedral, down Pirate's Alley, and into St. Anthony's Garden, where he disappears at the back door."

"Sounds good," I said, spooked that Yakov and I had walked in Dagobert's footsteps hours earlier and anxious to avoid the levee. It wasn't the kind of place you wanted to be after dark. "Two a.m. tonight in St. Anthony's Garden?"

They nodded.

My text tone chimed. I fished my phone from my purse, praying it was Veronica.

But it was an unknown number.

With a photo.

Of me, asleep in my room at Le Richelieu Hotel. My hair fanned out on the pillow, and next to my mouth was the plate-sized red stain.

My heart stopped as I read the message.

Buongiorno, Sleeping Beauty. Next time, it won't be Sambuca that spills on your pillow.

13

———

"The police don't believe Sullivan is back." Veronica did a quick check of the Central Lockup hallway. "And they don't think Candy's murder is connected to Dana's, either."

"How can they not see it?" I whisper-shouted. "It's all so *obvious!*"

"To *us*, Franki. But they found the potassium cyanide that killed Dana in his coat pocket. There's no way they can release him just because he was in jail when Candy was murdered."

"Like evidence has never been planted?"

"We'll have to prove it, and that photo of me sleeping that Sullivan texted won't work."

"Why not?" Veronica asked.

"David and The Vassal already checked it out. The photo was routed through an encrypted messaging app based overseas. No metadata, no location data, and the number was spoofed."

Veronica's eyes met mine, and her lips parted. "At this point, I think it's best if you left town for a while. Bradley would agree."

"I'm not going anywhere." I dropped the whisper and just

shouted. "Because I'm going to hunt Sullivan down, and when I do, he'll go to the bottom of the Mississippi once and for all."

She exhaled and checked the hallway again. "Let's not talk about felony murder in a police station, okay?" She forced a grin. "We can do that in private after you see Bradley. Speaking of which, it's time. Oh, and I pulled some strings—you have a call with Maybe Baby after Bradley. Want me to wait since David dropped you off?"

"No, you go." I already knew I was going to need a hardcore cookie-and-carol therapy session in the Christmas Car after I saw Bradley. *Maybe bourbon balls and Bing Crosby.*

She hugged me, which only aggravated my fragile state. Tears threatened to spill, and I was reminded that compared to her petite frame I was basically Yakov the man-bear. "Meet me at my hotel suite in two hours?"

"I'll be there." Veronica gave my arm an encouraging squeeze and headed down the hallway.

The visiting room hadn't changed since the last time I'd been —a sterile box of white cinderblock walls and a row of stainless-steel video screens that promised all the intimacy of a fast-food drive-thru. I took my seat on a stool and waited for Bradley to appear onscreen.

Actually, there was one new addition to the room—a flyer for Voodoo You-th Spa Services. I leaned in to read the specials. "Mention Central Lockup and get twenty percent off Bayou Botox or a Swamp Thing Seaweed Facial."

Hm. I tore off one of the phone number tabs. A facial might help with my nose bruise.

The video blinked, and there he was—the love of my life in an infamous orange jumpsuit. As a Texas Longhorn, I was normally a fan of the color. But I hated it in that moment.

I pasted on a smile and picked up the receiver. "How are you?"

"I'm doing fine, Franki. Really." His eyes told me he was lying, but his voice was steady. "Don't worry."

A lump formed in my throat. "Alright."

"How are *you*, babe?"

The question was suspended in the air. The truth would upset him, but I couldn't say "hanging in there" after what had happened to Candy. "I'm sure Veronica told you, but Sullivan is back."

Bradley's face was impassive. "I should've known he was the one who set me up. The cyanide, Dana's business card…"

"Actually, the business card was Bruno's doing."

He flinched. "What?"

"By sheer coincidence, he knew Dana and panicked when she was found dead in the cake."

"Did he put the potassium cyanide in my pocket too?"

"That was stolen from the old Pharmacy Museum."

"Okay, that's good news." He leaned closer to the screen. "I've never been there."

"Bradley, I went, and a woman I spoke to claims you stole it. She ID'd you from a photo on my phone."

"She's lying." His jaw clenched. "Sullivan must've paid her off." He leaned back. "But I don't want to talk about him. We need to get you out of town."

"That's not an option, Bradley."

"Only because you refuse to take it."

"Investigating scumbags like Sullivan is what I do for a living. I can handle him."

He exhaled sharply. "I know. I just wish I could help."

"You can. Stay safe. Remember, he used to work here."

Bradley caught the implication. "I'll be careful." He glanced offscreen. "Time's almost up."

Devastated, I looked down.

"Babe?"

I raised my head. "Yes?"

His eyes locked on mine, intense and unwavering. "I'll see you at the altar."

The word "altar" pierced my heart like an arrow. But I managed a smile. "Yes. You will."

The screen went dark, and my tough facade crumbled. I rested my head on the cold, stainless steel, and the sobs I'd been holding back surged like a broken levee. Leaving Bradley behind bars was torture, especially knowing Sullivan might still have people inside Central Lockup.

People who would do his evil bidding.

The cinderblock walls seemed to close in. My lungs struggled for air, and panic tightened my chest. I sat up and tried to breathe.

Then I shook my head. As illogical as it was, I half expected Sullivan to stroll into the room. The mere thought of his face made my fingers curl into fists.

The tears dried up.

And in their wake was rage.

Wedding or no, I was going to destroy Wesley Sullivan.

Fueled by fury, I rose. I had a few minutes to kill before my video call with Maybe Baby, so I exited the visiting room—and almost ran over my landlady. "Glenda?"

She stopped and struck a seductive pose. "In the flesh, Miss Franki."

Per usual. She wore pasties emblazoned with the words "Strip" and "Search" and a kind of loincloth held together by handcuff bracelets. On her feet, platform pumps with police siren heels. "Did you come to see Maybe Baby?"

"I was summoned, sugar. The police questioned me about my connection to Dana. They think it's suspicious that I hired her for the bachelor party, considering Bradley supposedly knew her."

"But he didn't know her!"

"That's what I told them, but they didn't believe a word I said."

"Predictable, but still disappointing."

"Disappointing?" Glenda huffed. "Sugar, I was expecting an aggressive interrogation under a hot lamp. Instead, I got Officer Good Cop and a damn 60-watt bulb."

"Dang," I commiserated. Navigating Glenda's ego was like swimming with gators—you had to stay calm and never show fear. "Tough break."

"Talk about tough!" She sniffed. "No strip search, no pat down—not even a casual frisk. I wore my tearaway skirt for *nothing*."

"Wow. That's tragic." I cleared my throat. "Did they say anything about Maybe Baby?"

"That's the kicker. The cop was going on and on about *her*—like this wasn't my moment in the spotlight."

"That's outrageous."

"I'll tell you what's outrageous, Miss Franki. They think *Maybe Baby* is the mastermind behind Dana Del Ray's murder."

Master and *mind* weren't words I'd associate with Maybe Baby separately, let alone combined. "What do they think was her motive?"

"Beats me, sugar. But like I said, follow the dollars, and you'll find the answer." She hiked up her handcuffs—and I wished she hadn't. "Gotta run. Miss Nadezhda's picking me up."

She knelt and turned on her police sirens. As officers rushed into the hall, she strutted past, head high, with lights—and lower lady parts—flashing.

For Yakov's sake, I hoped he wasn't in the van with Nadezhda. My landlady was a man-eater on a *good* day. But denied her strip search? She was liable to swallow that big ballet-loving bear whole.

I returned to the visiting room and took my seat. The video screen stayed stubbornly dark. While I waited, I perused Voodoo You-th's other spa services. When this investigation was over, I could really go for the Marie Laveau Mud Wrap and Hex Appeal Hot Stone Massage.

Maybe Baby appeared onscreen, her signature bleached blonde hair looked like it had been styled with a leaf blower.

I picked up the receiver. "How you doin', Maybe?"

"Well, I'm an *innate* now."

She meant *inmate*, but I let it slide. It wasn't the time to explain vocabulary—or irony.

"What brings you to the jail?"

As usual, we were off to a slow start. "I'm trying to find out who killed Dana, and I need your help. Did you ever meet her boyfriend, W.?"

"Nooo. She said he had *agora-fomo*. He was scared to go out because he'd miss something fun."

She meant *agoraphobia*, but what she'd described was the exact opposite.

Taking Glenda's suggestion, I decided to start by following the dollars. "Do you know if this W. gave her the money to start her Mardi Gras krewe?"

"Uh-huh." She inspected a cuticle.

And I waited. And waited. "Um, can you tell me?"

"All you have to do is ask."

I did, I thought, my molars grinding.

"Dana got some money from him, but she told him she needed a lot more. Krewes are crazy expensive. I know because she made me treasurer."

First a mastermind, and now a money manager? I had questions, but one thing was clear—the krewe treasurer position was the reason police thought she was the mastermind behind

Dana's murder. "Do you know if W. agreed to give Dana the money?"

"Uh-huh."

I closed my eyes, counted to three, and resisted the urge to test the durability of the receiver against the cinderblock. "Did he?"

"No. He had to make more money from his side hustle."

My skin tingled. *Side hustle.* Sullivan had said that in my nightmare and in real life. "What kind of business was he doing?"

"Dana never told me."

"Was he working alone?"

"No, Dana said it was with some of his family."

I was about to say, *Do you know which ones?*, but I went with the more pointed, "Which ones?"

"Mm..." She twisted a lock of hair around her finger. "His half-sister for sure, and... I think maybe his Mother Superior."

It was one thing to learn Sullivan had a sister, but a nun? Even though he *was* Irish Catholic, it was a stretch. "Do you maybe mean his 'stepmother?'"

She shrugged. "You'd have to ask Dana." Her blue eyes widened. "And you can't."

True, unfortunately.

"But his half-sister was her old roommate."

My pulse jumped. "Do you know where I can find her?"

"At Le Richelieu Hotel."

"Uh..." My mind raced. "I don't think that's right."

"Sure it is! She's the assistant manager."

Candy?

"How are you ho-ho-holding up, Franki?" Santa asked, catching my eye in the rearview mirror as he steered us toward Le Richelieu Hotel.

"Still a wreck about seeing Bradley on a Central Lockup screen, but the eggnog bread pudding with bourbon sauce helped somewhat." After all, I'd been raised to eat my feelings. I handed Hermey my empty bowl. Without missing a beat, he handed me a king cake martini.

If the Uber business crumbled, the two Christmas crusaders should really open a holiday dessert bar.

Swallowing a much-needed sip, I leaned back—mindful of the deadly decorations. "I knew Sullivan was capable of unspeakable things, but killing his own sister?"

Santa grimaced. "You sure it was him?"

"That's the problem. He and Candy were my only remaining suspects. With her out of the picture, he has to be her murderer."

"Isn't that good news? You've identified the killer. Now you just have to prove it."

"Maybe." I flashed back to Chandra rolling around in the middle of Chartres Street like a whacked out Ouija board. Of course, I didn't believe she'd channeled Dana's spirit. But her alleged message—that the motive behind Dana's murder was "so much worse" than we knew—wasn't wrong. Sullivan resurfacing qualified on that front. But now that Maybe Baby had told me he was in business with not only Candy but also another family member, I wasn't sure I had the full suspect list.

I power-ate a couple of praline snowballs from the rear console tray like they were crime-solving fuel.

One thing I was sure about—how Sullivan had gotten into my hotel room. Candy would have given him a skeleton key. That didn't bode well for the rest of my stay—or that of my family. I could move them to another hotel, but I couldn't leave.

My brother was the manager, and wedding guests were due to start arriving on Friday. Two days away.

"What I want to know is," Santa swerved around a street car, "why put Candy's body on Touchdown Jesus?"

I blinked. "Touchdown Jesus?"

"That's what the locals call the Sacred Heart statue. His arms are outstretched like he's signaling a touchdown."

Come to think of it, they were.

"Maybe the placement had more to do with the patron saint of the garden." Hermey squinted at his phone. "St. Anthony is the patron saint of animals, the elderly, expectant mothers, infertility, lost souls, the poor, sailors, the starving, travelers, and unmarried women."

The saint didn't seem relevant to the case, but Dana and Candy were definitely lost souls, and I was an unmarried woman.

Will I stay that way?

As if on cue, Dolly Parton's "Hard Candy Christmas" twanged through the speakers.

I drained my martini. "Can we skip the music?"

Hermey clicked off the stereo and poured me a refill.

Sliding lower in my seat, I caught sight of a St. Louis Cathedral snow globe on the floor and picked it up. "Right before I found Candy, I saw someone behind the cathedral. Just the hem of what looked like a nun's habit."

Hermey spun around, eyes wide. "The ghost nun!"

"I don't know." I put the snow globe on the rear console tray. "Have any of your other passengers seen a nun recently? Or Père Dagobert?"

Santa pulled up in front of Le Richelieu Hotel. "Not that I've heard."

As the car idled, pedestrians paused to stare at the vehicle.

"Well, my colleagues and I are conducting a stakeout

tonight." I sat up straighter. "If they're out there, we'll find them."

The passenger door flew open. Chandra Toccato slid in wearing head-to-toe metallic silver, which, in the context of the Christmas Car, made her look like a short, squat toy rocket.

"Ugh! Do you mind, Chandra?"

Santa raised a snowy brow. "The lady's right, ma'am. The Christmas Car is presently occupied."

"I see that, Santa," Chandra said in a frosty tone. She plunked her chain-strap Vivienne Westwood orb bag onto her lap and fixed me with a glare. "Ruth said this is how you've been getting your jollies while Bradley's in jail, but I didn't believe her."

Santa raised his red-gloved hand. "I object to that usage of 'jollies.'"

"Save it, Saint Nick," Chandra snapped. "This biscotto's about to be *married*."

Hermey wide-eyed me in shock. "You know this woman?"

"I'll say she does," Chandra huffed. "Franki and I work together."

I gasped. "Those words should *never* come out of your mouth."

Chandra's head turned so hard her solar-system earrings went out of orbit. "How many cases have we solved together now? Four, is it?"

"I solved them. And I didn't ask you to be involved."

"Hmm." She tapped a finger to her moon-pie face. "I seem to remember you paying me for my advice. And, if I'm not mistaken, Lou and I saved your life at a plantation."

Santa gave Hermey a solemn nod.

Hermey reached beneath the seat and pulled out a candy cane the size of a baguette with a paper-plate dial. "According to the Naughty Meter," he leveled a black-eyed stare at Chandra, "you're a Fudge Fabricator."

Enjoying this immensely, I sipped my martini.

"Well," Chandra pretended to examine her paddle nails, "I object to that usage of 'fudge.' And I only speak the truth."

The liquid shot from my lips. "The Naughty Meter must be on the blink. Chandra's not a Fudge Fabricator—she's a Gaslighting Grinch."

"That's not one of the presets," Hermey said, frowning.

"Put that ridiculous thing away!" Chandra shouted.

Personally, I was loving it—except that it was reminiscent of Ruth's fun meter. If I'd been wearing one, it would've been inching from Min to Med. "Listen, Chandra. I get in this car to destress. So, unless you've got something helpful to say—"

"Well, I'm stressed out too, you know," she interrupted. "Dana's spirit told us the reason for her murder was 'so much worse' than we knew, and she was spot on."

Channeled spirits were nothing if not cryptically accurate.

"And now that Candy's dead too, I could be next."

Unconvinced, I sipped my martini. "Why?"

"Because I still work at Sassy Spells, and we don't know whether Candy's sin-eating meetings with The Father were just to assuage her guilt."

"Sin-eating?" Santa glanced at me.

"An Egyptian funerary ritual. You symbolically 'eat the sins' of the deceased—basically, someone consumes bread and ale to cleanse the soul so the dead can move on to the afterlife."

"Symbolic or not," he grumbled, "I'll stick to milk and cookies, thank you."

Hermey poured himself a cocoa. "And I'll stick to peppermint bark and pretending everything's fine."

Chandra rummaged through her orb bag. "I wish Candy's spirit would get in touch with me."

"Well, I don't," I said, in case she was searching for her charm bracelet. "Maybe keep an eye on the living instead."

"Easy for you to say. You're not the one in danger."

My eyes rolled like the praline snowballs I'd inhaled.

"No need for the Naughty Meter," Hermey muttered. "She's a Nutcracker Narcissist."

Nailed it.

Chandra's tiny mouth screwed up so tight, it almost disappeared in her face. "Put a cork in it, pointy ears!"

Hermey shriveled and yanked his hat over his points.

Santa lowered his bifocals. "Ma'am, I'm going to have to ask you to exit the car."

"I'm only too happy to leave this North Pole nutmobile." She stepped out, then leaned back in for one final shot. "And FYI, Franki—if I get murdered at Sassy Spells, I'm so haunting your wedding." She slammed the door.

We all jumped.

Before any of us could react, my passenger door opened. A young man in a fedora leaned in, bracing himself on a skull-handled walking stick. "Hey, if you're getting out too, could I maybe grab this Uber?"

Santa looked over his shoulder. "Well, I don't know—"

"I know I'm supposed to use the Uber app," the guy said, removing his hat and pressing it to his chest. "But I could seriously use a break right now. I'm a ghost tour guide—Gus—and I need to destress."

Forget the dessert bar idea. Santa and Hermey just needed to advertise their special holiday kind of self-help—or elf-help, as it were. Something like, *Silent night, but screaming inside? Call the Claus-and-Elfect Counseling Car at 1-800-HO-HO-HELP.*

I scooted over, and Gus climbed in.

"Where you headed?" Santa asked.

"Anywhere. Just get me out of the Quarter."

The poor guy looked haunted—maybe an occupational hazard, maybe not. "Everything alright?"

"Yeah, but it's been... rough lately. And the cold doesn't help."

Santa shot Hermey a look.

"One Creole Milk Punch coming up," Hermey said, reaching for a cocktail shaker.

I turned to Gus. "Do you mind if I ask what you mean by 'rough?'"

"Nah, it's just..." Gus picked up the snow globe from the tray and gave it a slow shake. "This might be hard to believe given what I do for a living, but I don't actually believe in ghosts."

Hermey sniffed. "You're lucky. I do, and they scare the figgy pudding out of me."

Gus gave a dry laugh. "Well, I might be changing teams, because either I'm losing my mind, or I've seen a couple."

"A couple of ghosts?" I asked.

"Yeah. A monk and a nun."

I flinched and nearly impaled my elbow on a strand of garland studded with what looked like real holly berries—and possibly thumbtacks. "When?"

"Past few nights. Always after the bars close. The first night, the monk was singing some kind of hymn, and the nun showed up. I looked down to get my phone from my bag. When I looked up, they'd vanished."

"And the second time?" Santa asked.

"He was singing 'The Yellow Rose of Texas.'"

My stomach clenched. If I'd had any doubts that the ghost of Père Dagobert was actually Sullivan, I didn't now. He gave me yellow roses because of my Texas roots. "You know about Père Dagobert, right?"

"Oh, totally. But this guy wasn't the jolly, peace-loving friar from the stories."

Hermey handed Gus his drink. "What makes you say that?"

Gus looked out the window. "Because I saw him again last night—and he was choking the nun."

I gasped, and Hermey let out an elfin *eek*.

"They looked real. I mean flesh-and-blood real. I even shouted. He let her go, but then they both bolted behind a building."

"That's strange," I said. "You'd think she would have run *to* you—or at least *away* from him."

"I thought the same thing. So, I chased them. I just wanted to make sure he didn't hurt her again. But by the time I turned the corner, they were gone. Poof. Like ghosts."

"What time was this?" I asked.

"Three a.m., give or take."

Same time I'd seen the nun.

Gus rubbed his eyes, looking like he hadn't slept in days. "Once the shock wore off, I called the cops. No offense to anyone in the car, and especially not you, Santa, but I don't exactly buy into all this ghosts-and-magic stuff. For me, it's just a living."

I nodded. "What did the police say?"

"They listened—until I told them I was a ghost tour guide. Then they basically accused me of staging a PR stunt to drum up business."

Santa stroked his beard. "For what it's worth, I believe you."

I did too. Not because I thought Père Dagobert and the nun were ghosts, but because Maybe Baby had told me Sullivan was in business with both Candy and a so-called Mother Superior—a nun.

And if he'd been choking her, then he was either trying to silence her the same way he'd done to Dana and Candy—or she'd killed Candy, and he was dishing out his own brand of unholy justice.

14

"Does your fiancé know you're boozing it up with Santa and his elf while he's in the slammer?" Nonnone asked as I entered Le Richelieu Hotel.

This nonna was really grating on my nerves—even more so now that she sounded like Ruth. "For your information, I don't need Bradley's permission—or yours—to have a drink."

"*A* drink? Ha!" She huffed that laugh so hard, her low-hanging nose vibrated. "That's the second time I've seen you climb out of that Jingle Jalopy. What else is going on in there?"

I was tempted to say that I'd been stress-eating, but for most Italians, that was just eating. "Not that it's any of your business, but it's an Uber."

"Then why'd you have them bring you *here*? It's almost time for your fitting at Wedding Belles."

Head nonna or no, I'd had it with her meddling. "I know you think you're helping, but I've told you before—I have a wedding dress, and I'm wearing it."

A smug smirk played on her thick lips. She lifted her arms, the Souvenir della Sicilia bag swinging from her elbow, and clapped twice.

The goon nonne emerged from the hallway like a pair of hitwomen. Flattened-Nose Nonna held my wedding dress—the one Veronica and I went through holy hell to get. Salami-Fingered Nonna pushed open the door, and both of them bolted like they'd just jacked the Hope Diamond.

Veronica rushed in, eyes wide as she tracked their escape. "Franki? Was that your wedding dress?" She rushed to my side, her face alarmed. "What's going on?"

"Nonnone's staging a coup." I pointed at the head meddler, seething. "But she messed with the wrong bride."

"*Cara mia,*" Nonnone opened her arms as though she were blessing a congregation, "I don't stage coups to lose." She spun on her D&G mules and disappeared down the hallway.

"She can have this battle." My fists clenched. "But I'm winning the war. As sure as my name is Franki Amato, I'm marrying Bradley in that dress."

"Damn right you are." Veronica scowled in the direction of the hallway. "Now, how'd it go with Maybe Baby? Did you find out anything?"

I led her to the elevator. "Sullivan's running some kind of operation with two family members—a so-called 'Mother Superior' and Candy."

"*Candy?*" She covered her mouth in horror. "He killed a *family member?*"

"His half-sister." I pushed the elevator button. "But the killer could've also been this Mother Superior, whoever she is."

Veronica leaned against the wall, stunned. "We've got to find her."

"That's the problem, Veronica. Maybe Baby's grasp of the English language is shakier than Glenda in ballet flats. For all we know, she was describing a biological mother, a godmother, or just a really great mom she saw on TV."

"If there *is* a Mother Superior in New Orleans, the nonne will know her." She headed for the kitchen. "Let's go ask them."

"But…" My pitch hit peak alarm. "Marcella's in there."

Veronica turned. "So? She's connected to all the local Catholic Churches through the American Italian Cultural Center. She might even know more than the nonne."

"Exactly. We won't just get a history of every Mother Superior who was ever in New Orleans—she'll recite the complete list from the Vatican archives. By the time she's done, my entire wedding weekend will be over."

Veronica rolled her eyes and resumed walking. "She doesn't talk *that* much."

"Then I'll let you ask her," I said, following along despite grave concerns. "While she's talking your ear off, I'll get the intel from the other nonne."

"Fine."

We passed through the Terrace Lounge, and I glanced at the autographed photo of Dan Aykroyd. The *Ghostbusters* stakeout was only hours away, and I feared what we would see. Not because I was afraid of ghosts—but because I was no longer sure of *what* we'd find.

An unhinged Wesley Sullivan?

Or a murderous Mother Superior?

As we entered the kitchen, I jolted at the sight of the cannoli station, then scanned frantically for Marcella.

Thankfully, she wasn't there.

Because Mom and Nonna were sound asleep amid a mountain of pastry shells—and an empty bottle of marsala.

My mom was standing but bent over the table, using a rolling pin as a pillow. Nonna had cleared a space among the shells and fully reclined, hands folded across her chest as though she was practicing for her funeral. They were so dusted in flour and powdered sugar that even Nonna's black mourning dress had gone white. They looked like ghosts—of meddlers past.

Guilt panged my chest. My reception had reduced them to this, all for a wedding that might not happen.

But a silver lining gleamed as bright as the aluminum foil on the table—thanks to Marcella, Mom and Nonna didn't have the time or the energy to operate the Command Center they'd set up to run my wedding.

Now if I could find a way to wear out Nonnone...

I walked up behind my mother and gently shook her shoulder. "Mom?"

Her head snapped up like she'd been electrocuted. "I'm working, Marcella." She rolled the pin furiously across a recipe book. "Only twenty-five dozen to go!"

Nonna sat up mid-snore, a dish towel tied around her gray head like a bandana. "Santa Maria, take-a me to heaven! I gotta get outta this-a hell-a!"

"Relax, you two. It's me, Franki."

Nonna lay back down and resumed snoring. I wasn't sure she'd actually heard me—she had what looked like cannoli dough in her ears.

My mom's rolling sped up.

I circled around her so she could see me. Her lashes were caked with flour—and possibly ricotta. "Mom?"

"Oh, Francesca!" She pressed a palm to her chest and leaned against the table. "Thank heavens."

"Heaven?" Nonna sat up again, eyes wide with hope. "Is-a the Virgin here to bring-a me home-a?"

"No such luck, Nonna. It's just me, Franki, bringing you back to reality."

She groaned and collapsed again. "I can't-a make-a no more cannoli!"

I gasped. For a Sicilian woman, and especially a nonna, her words were nothing short of bakery blasphemy.

My mom shot me a warning look, her dark undereye circles doing most of the talking. "Marcella had better not catch you distracting us from our work."

She didn't have to tell me twice. "I'll make this quick. Do you know if any of the congregations of sisters in New Orleans still have a Mother Superior?"

"That title went out of usage long ago." My mother removed a ball of dough from a bowl. "The Ursuline nuns call their leader a 'provincial.'"

Tomato-Faced Nonna—the one whose niece didn't wear red to her wedding and ended up childless in Newark—looked up from the industrial pasta machine. "Don't forget the Sisters of the Holy Family. Their head nun is called a 'superior general.'"

I chewed a broken piece of cannolo shell. "Sounds militaristic."

"And exactly what we should call Marcella," my mother grumbled.

Tomato-Faced Nonna doused a rag with oil and shoved her arm and head deep between the steel rollers of the industrial pasta machine.

"Whoa, careful!" I stepped forward, fearing the rollers would suck her in like a lump of dough.

She pulled out and shot me a look that could curdle milk. "Are you telling me how to do my job?"

"Not at all." I held up my hands. "You're obviously an expert."

"I oughta be." She sniffed and gave the roller a final, vigorous wipe. "I've oiled my husband's cracked feet every night for forty years."

Note to self—don't eat the pasta at my reception.

"Also," she gave the machine a quasi-affectionate pat, "my nonno, Emilio, used this back in the day. Called her La Bestia."

The Beast. "The name fits."

"You're telling me. La Bestia almost killed a man—snatched his apron right into the rollers."

My stomach lurched. "And you're still using it?"

"Don't worry. My nonno told me the trick. If you can't reach the switch on the control panel, you use this." She pointed to a lever below the conveyer belt.

"A safety shutoff?"

"Uh-uh. There was no such thing as safety in the 1900s. If you push the lever forward, it sprays semolina to fix wet dough. But if you pull it back, the hopper opens and dumps the flour. Gums up the gears with grease and dough. Stops it *dead.*"

I winced at the word. "So, the emergency brake is a flour bomb?"

"A messy solution is better than no solution." She gestured for me to lean in. "Between you and me," she said in a low tone, "I'm more afraid of that Marcella than I am La Bestia. She's not right in the head, that one."

I'd had occasion—and way more than one—to witness that.

A pounding sound startled me.

Giada was at the veal scaloppini station using a meat mallet. Funeral-Faced Nonna was at the station next to her, using a razor blade to slice garlic.

Out of nowhere, I got a mental image of her husband's razor-blade toenails.

Note to self—also skip the scaloppini.

"If you'll excuse me, I need to talk to my cousin." I hurried over to Giada. "What are you doing here?" I whispered. "I thought you got fired."

"Marcella called me after Candy died," she said between thwacks. "Told me to report to work."

Of course she did. Marcella had already proven with the kitchen takeover that she knew how to capitalize on tragedy, a skill I wasn't thrilled to have associated with my wedding.

But I was less thrilled about Giada preparing food for my reception. It was hard to mess up whacking a piece of meat, but if anyone could find a way, it was my cousin.

She stopped and rubbed her bicep. "My arm is going to fall off if I don't take a break. I'll start prepping the ingredients for the lemon and caper sauce."

If my wedding happens, all my guests are going to die. "Um, maybe you should check with Marcella. She runs a tight ship—or, labor camp."

Giada's face grew dark. "I'm trying to engage with her as little as possible. I totally get why Moira couldn't work with her."

"You mean, besides the part about locking her in the janitorial closet?"

"That too." Giada went to a sink to wash her hands. "Would you mind helping me get the lemons from the walk-in?"

Might as well. Veronica was MIA, probably still listening to Marcella recount the life story of the *first* Mother Superior to arrive in New Orleans, starting with her birth. "Sure thing."

"I'll be right there."

The walk-in was by the kitchen entrance. I stepped inside, leaving the door ajar, and stared at the crates of lemons on the floor.

I thought of the lemons that had lined my windshield before Marcella had helped kidnap me for my initial bachelorette party disaster. Then the lemons in this very walk-in that Giada never ordered.

And inevitably, the lemons in the Steamboat Galliano walk-in.

Sullivan's family business... *Is he back to his old tricks?*

Dropping to my knees, I began inspecting each and every lemon for signs of tampering.

A hand clamped over my mouth, and a cloth covered my eyes.

A jolt of pure, cold terror shot through me. Whoever this was, it wasn't Giada.

Is it Sullivan?

Another jolt kicked me into gear. I began fighting. My heart pounded against my ribcage, as if it too was trying to break free.

My feet were yanked out from under me.

An accomplice. The Mother Superior?

A fresh wave of panic surged. I kicked wildly, but I couldn't connect.

And I was carried from the walk-in.

"THIS CANNOT BE STRESSED ENOUGH," I growled from a pedestal in the fitting room at Wedding Belles. "You all should be ashamed of yourselves for using my own wedding dress to kidnap me."

"Look at it this way," Nonnone said from one of two armchairs—three if you count the handbag chair for her Souvenir della Sicilia purse—"at least the cursed dress served a purpose."

The goon nonne, flanking her like Mafia muscle in mourning wear, nodded in unison.

I turned on my mother in the other chair, her clothes so white with flour and powdered sugar she blended in with the bridal gowns. "And *you*. How could you let these hooligans abduct your *own daughter*?"

Nonnone gripped her champagne glass. "Watch it with the name-calling, eh?"

The goons nodded again.

"For your information, Francesca," my mother said in a defensive drawl, "this fitting was my ticket to freedom from the kitchen. And I would give you up all over again if it got me away from Marcella."

And if it got her the champagne she was holding. "What about Nonna? You just left her there?"

"Well, I *am* the mother of the bride, aren't I?" she huffed. "And Marcella said *someone* had to stay and make the cannoli."

No surprise she'd left my elderly nonna to labor in the sweets sweatshop.

A fiftyish seamstress entered, a pincushion strapped to her wrist. She took in my plantation gown with a single glance that missed nothing and forgave less. "Well! Don't you look..."

She shoved a pin in her mouth and went to work on the hem.

Clearly, the seamstress didn't like the dress either. And how could she? The thing looked like Marie Antoinette and Scarlett O'Hara had a baby—and it had more ruffles than a drag brunch.

Thankfully, no one had suggested I wear my nonna's wedding dress. She was five-feet tall in heels and from Old-World Sicily, which meant she probably wore a flour sack. Honestly, that was starting to seem like a better option.

As was the pull-cord hoopskirt Glenda had loaned me years ago for Pirate Week—even after she'd burned the "porthole" in it with her cigarette.

Nonnone squinted. "The dress needs something."

I would've thrown up my hands in despair, but they were holding a parasol the way my mother had instructed. "You've already added a corset, hoop skirt, and six petticoats. What more could it possibly need? A steamboat?"

Her black eyes narrowed. "You should be grateful. Your mother eloped and didn't have a dress."

"Mom, you can wear this one. Because I'm not."

Her eyes sparkled—she was considering it.

My bridal consultant, Bonnie, breezed in, her slick-backed ponytail as motionless as a Botoxed forehead. "How are we doing, ladies?"

"We need a wide-brimmed hat," Nonnone announced. "Big enough to cast a shadow over that nasty nose bruise."

My mom sipped champagne. "Make it era appropriate."

"We have just the thing," the consultant said.

So did I—the blinged out bachelorette wedding veil Nadezhda had made me. I'd even carry Glenda's penis balloon over the parasol. Okay, well, maybe not.

The seamstress rose. "I've done all I can."

And with that, she left the room.

"I hate to state the obvious..." I paused to look Nonnone and my mother in the eyes, trying one last time to find an ounce of reason in either one of them. "...but I don't have time to play dress-up when I'm trying to prove Bradley's innocence."

Nonnone crossed her arms. "You need to leave the investigating to the police and focus on your wedding."

"That's just it—there won't *be* a wedding if I don't find the killer."

"Like I already told you—I've got a guy."

There was no point in protesting any longer. For Sicilian grandmothers of a certain age, the checklist for a suitable husband was short—a pulse, a confirmation name, and a willingness to eat.

And the pulse was negotiable.

Bonnie returned and lowered a massive straw hat onto my head. "This was made especially for this gown." She clasped her hands and beamed. "That completes the look."

It did—if the look was "Steel Magnolia in the middle of a long-overdue mental breakdown." The hat was as big as a satellite dish and had a wasp's nest of silk flowers, feathers, and a rogue plastic dove perched right at my forehead.

The straw hat was the last straw.

Forcing raspy breaths from my lungs, I pretended to swoon. "I can't..." I wheezed, "...breathe..."

"The corset is too tight!" My mother drained her champagne and then got up. "We have to get her out."

"Not a chance, Brenda." Nonnone leapt from her chair, surprisingly spry. "If Bridezilla goes down, she'll crush us all!"

"Get..." I gasped, staggering from the pedestal. "...scissors." Then I let myself collapse like a Southern belle with a bad case of the vapors.

My mother screamed. "She fainted!"

"Bride down in Room Five," Bonnie called into the hallway.

My mom fumbled frantically at the buttons. I didn't feel the least bit bad. She got me into this dress—she could sweat her way out of it.

"Help is on the way, Mrs. Amato," Bonnie assured.

That was my cue.

Springing to my feet, I bolted out the door and barreled down the hallway, my skirt taking out bridal consultants like bowling pins.

"Get her," Nonnone yelled, siccing the goons on me.

I skidded into the boutique, scanning for a place to hide my big plantation-gowned self. I dove into a chiffon jungle at the back, sinking behind a rack of pastel concoctions, my hoop skirt puffing out like a parachute.

My text tone sounded. Veronica.

I've been looking all over the hotel for you. The nonne said you left for a wedding dress fitting?

To which I replied, *If by "fitting" you mean being wrestled into six petticoats by a couple of nonne who could bench-press a Vespa, then yes, that's where I am.*

The dresses parted.

"Hidey-ho, Franki!" Phil Redman, the overly chipper crypt keeper from St. Cecilia Cemetery, grinned down at me.

"Hide me, Phil!"

He stepped in front of me like a gothic linebacker—wearing his signature cargo shorts even in the cold winter.

Peering between the bee tattoos on Phil's knees, I watched the rest of my bridal party squinting around the boutique.

"Where is she?" Nonnone shouted.

"If you're looking for Southern Cinderella," Phil said cheerfully, "she ran outside and flagged down a Ford F-150."

Nonnone huffed. "That's the thanks I get for trying to make her look beautiful at her wedding, Brenda?"

Beautiful? She made me look like Blanche DuBois on a bender.

My mother shook her head. "I'm sorry, Nonnone. I'm mortified."

An apt choice of words, considering I was hidden behind a merry mortician.

They exited the boutique, but I stayed low between the pastels and the sequins. I didn't trust the goon nonne.

"Thanks, Phil," I whispered. "I'm getting married soon, and my mom wants me to wear this awful dress."

"Congrats! That Bradley is one lucky rascal."

Tears stung my eyes. I couldn't get a word out of my mouth because I still wasn't sure the wedding would take place. I limited myself to a nod and emerged from the sale racks like a Southern belle swamp creature crawling out of a bedazzled lagoon.

Although I already knew what Phil was doing at Wedding Belles—shopping the sales for bodies he transported in his hearse for his Uber Undertaker side gig—I had to be polite. "What're you up to?"

"Stocking up." He patted a sequined magenta number. "Business is steady."

Because his slogan was *Uber Undertaker—When you need a body buried fast*, I had questions. But they could wait. I had murders to solve. And if I didn't, I could end up in the back of his hearse myself.

Phil flipped through the hangers. "And you? Any juicy homicide investigations?"

"You could say that. Tonight I'm doing a stakeout with some colleagues that involves ghost legends."

"A little *Ghostbusters* action, eh?"

David and The Vassals' arsenal of ecto-equipment flashed through my mind. "Actually... kind of."

Phil grinned. "Dan Aykroyd's character, Dr. Raymond Stantz, is the cat's pajamas."

Fitting, coming from a guy who had a tattoo of a cat in pajamas on one arm—to go with the bees on his knees.

"Incidentally," he pulled a red taffeta horror off the rack that was still better than the one I was wearing, "the Ghostbusters concept came from séances Aykroyd's grandfather held at the family's cottage in Canada."

The reference to Canada and the supernatural reminded me of The Father from Sassy Spells. *What was up with Canucks and ghosts?*

"What I wouldn't give to own the '59 Cadillac Miller-Meteor from the movies." Phil rubbed his hands together as if he was about to dig in to some of his infamous cemetery sausage. "I believe I've mentioned my love of her before?"

"You have," I said, hoping he'd spare me another rundown of its features.

"She's the crown jewel of cadaver transport."

No such luck.

He kissed his fingertips. "Coach-built, chrome so shiny you

could shave with it, and those iconic tailfins that just scream, 'I'm classy, *and* I collect corpses.'"

My stomach did a little flip at the "crown jewel" reference, but I managed a smile. Phil did love a good funeral wagon.

"Best part—it was a combination hearse-*ambulance*." He twisted his bushy brown beard, his blue eyes twinkling. "You know what that means."

Besides joining forces with Nadezhda for an emergency vaxing/vaccination clinic, only one thing came to mind. "You can pick up bodies from the morgue?"

"That's the dream."

"Su... sure."

"Well, I'd best pay for these and be on my way. The Big and Tall store is having a clear-the-racks sale. I do like to make the dead look dapper."

If I couldn't track down what the goon nonne had done with my wedding dress, Phil might have something I could wear to my wedding.

Then something else occurred to me. Phil worked a lot of late nights, and he knew Wesley Sullivan from a vampire case he'd helped me with. "Before you go, are you familiar with the ghost legend of Père Dagobert?"

"Sure am. I feel rather close to him in fact."

"Why's that?"

"Dagobert was a lover of food and wine, and no stranger to a tavern." He patted his belly. "I can relate."

I was glad to hear Phil occasionally ate meals that weren't made from cemetery critters. "Have you seen a guy dressed like him on any of your Uber Undertaker rides?"

He hiked up his cargo shorts. "Can't say I have. Why?"

"This is going to sound kind of out there, but... the ghost of Père Dagobert has been spotted around St. Louis Cathedral recently."

"Pish posh! Probably just some fellow in a monk costume."

"Agreed." I checked behind me to make sure no one was around. "And I have reason to believe it's former Detective Wesley Sullivan."

"The last time we spoke, you said he'd passed?"

I remembered the conversation. I'd neglected to mention the Steamboat Galliano incident. "Actually, he disappeared almost two years ago. Given the circumstances, I just assumed he'd died."

"What happened?"

"Long story short, he was running a drug ring with the mob boss Gigi Scalino, and I was investigating a homicide linked to them. One night, he tried to kill Bradley and me, and then he vanished from the deck of a steamboat."

"My word." Phil looked down and stroked his beard. "That does cast things in a new light."

"What things?"

"A couple of weeks ago, I got to the cemetery early, around four in the morning. I saw a man coming out of a mausoleum carrying a large box. Not a casket, mind you."

He would make that clarification. "And?"

"So, I shouted at him, asking who he was, but he just looked at me and walked off. And when I checked the mausoleum, nothing was amiss."

"Could you see him in the dark?"

"Oh, yeah." His eyes narrowed. "And he was a dead-ringer for Sullivan."

I stared at Phil, speechless.

What was Wesley Sullivan doing in a mausoleum?

15

———

"Thanks again for the dress, Franki." Phil shut off the hearse engine in front of the Saint Cecilia Cemetery and glanced into the back where the plantation gown lay like the dearly departed. "Some lucky soul's going to love it."

"I'm glad you can put it to good use." I meant that, too. That dress needed to be buried. My only concern was that the size might prevent a casket from closing.

"The residents will be so pleased you've come." Phil slammed the hearse door with the enthusiasm of a man about to enter a party rather than a graveyard. "They've been absolutely dying for company."

My skin started to crawl as I followed him toward the Saint Cecilia Cemetery entrance, biting back the urge to a) remind him this wasn't a social call, and b) tell him that if it were, I would've preferred to come at a time when I could mingle with the living.

Phil treated the deceased like beloved relatives who just happened to be six feet under—a trait that never ceased to be unsettling. Much like the "Rest easy in The Big Easy" sign above us, and the giant skeleton statue that sat atop a crypt, beckoning with a bony hand to passersby on Rampart Street.

He opened the heavy iron gate, and its rusted hinges screamed.

Exactly what I was doing in my head.

"Those hinges are loud enough to wake—well, you know." Phil chuckled at his own joke. "Though between you and me, some of our residents are already stirring plenty without assistance."

The last thing I needed right now. I was already being haunted by Sullivan.

Dead leaves crunched under my boots as I trailed him deeper into the cemetery, carefully watching my step. I'd learned the hard way that Saint Cecilia had a habit of revealing things better left buried. Plus, the sun was bleeding orange behind the crypts, casting long shadows that seemed to reach for my ankles.

Which didn't help.

"Since you're getting married," Phil gestured to a row of crumbling tombs, "you should consider investing in real estate at Saint Cecilia. Prime location, quiet neighbors, eternal bliss. If you'd prefer to rent, I can let you go month to month rather than committing to a long lease."

My mouth opened. As far as I was aware, a "long lease" was the only option. "That's thoughtful of you, Phil. But I'll need to run it by Bradley."

Which I had zero intention of doing.

"Of course. No hurry." He winked. "Though, you never know when opportunity might come knocking. Or when *you* might come knocking, if you catch my drift."

Leave it to Phil to casually imply my untimely demise right before a stakeout. My hand went to the small of my back where my purple Ruger sat snug in its holster. This time, I'd be ready for Sullivan.

"Ah, here we are." Phil's hands rested on his hips. "The mausoleum I saw Sullivan come out of."

The tomb loomed before us like a miniature mansion, maybe fifteen by twenty feet, complete with its own wrought-iron fence and limestone columns. It looked almost residential —if you ignored the fact that it was essentially a stone oven designed for slow-cooking the dead.

Why did I have to think that?

Phil opened the metal door and peered inside. "After you, milady."

"How chivalrous." The word slipped out before I could stop it, reminding me that this cemetery was crawling with *chevals-diable*—black "devil grasshoppers." Just what I needed when my nerves were already frayed.

Something tickled the back of my neck. My skeleton nearly launched itself from my skin as I let out a shriek that could've raised the very dead Phil was so fond of.

"Sweet Mary and Joseph!" He clutched his burly chest. "What happened?"

"Sorry." I flashed a sheepish smile. "I thought there was a bug on me."

Phil shook his head, grinning. "You nearly sent me to join the residents permanently."

It never ceased to amaze me that someone so morbid could be so merry. "Is this mausoleum usually open?"

"Never. Someone forced their way in."

Sullivan. Is he here now? Watching from the shadows, waiting for the perfect moment to strike?

A slithering sensation tickled my skin as I stepped into the sepulchral space. And the sight before me only intensified the creepy crawlies.

A life-sized angel stood sentinel in the center of the tomb, her stone eyes weeping perpetual tears of green mildew down pale marble cheeks. Her outstretched wings pointed toward rows of burial vaults—the locals called them "ovens"—that gaped like hungry mouths in the gathering darkness.

Cobwebs draped the corners of the mausoleum like tattered funeral veils. The walls, once pristine white marble, were now mottled with black mold and soot, their natural veins dark as dried blood. Cracks spider-webbed across the floor tiles, reminiscent of skeletal fingers reaching up from below.

"Perfect hiding spot for a creep like Sullivan," I muttered.

Phil stroked his beard. "And a peaceful spot for a rest."

I shivered. The air inside was bone-deep cold and damp, the kind of chill that seemed to seep up from the stone itself. My breath puffed out in ghostly clouds that made my heart race.

Although, I tried not to breathe too deeply. The mausoleum reeked of wet earth, rusted iron, and the unmistakable sweetness of decay—as if something had been decomposing in here far longer than it should have.

A scuffling sound from a back corner made me jump.

Phil's head tilted like a curious dog—that hunted critters to make deli meat. "Probably a rat. They do love to poke around the bones."

Information I would've been happy to go to my grave not knowing.

He grabbed a small flashlight from his pocket and headed toward the sound. "Let me just check on our little visitor."

The last remnants of twilight filtered through a small stained glass cross at the back of the mausoleum, casting jeweled fragments of purple and gold across the grimy floor. But as I watched, the colored light vanished—as if something large had moved in front of the window from outside.

My blood turned to ice. *Sullivan?*

No, just the sun setting.

While Phil investigated in the corner, I noticed something

odd about the shadows behind the angel's base. Moving closer, I spotted a corner of white cardboard tucked beneath the statue's draped stone robes. My heart hammering, I crouched and pulled out a plain pastry box, completely out of place in the mausoleum. The box was unmarked, but when I lifted the lid, I found a smattering of powdered sugar. Someone had been eating beignets in here. Recently.

My stomach lurched because I couldn't imagine eating among the remains of departed "residents" who couldn't.

And because I knew it had been Sullivan. I felt it in my bones. The rogue detective had been camped out in this mausoleum until sometime after Phil spotted him.

"JACKPOT!" Phil's voice boomed from the back of the tomb.

I nearly launched myself into the angel's arms, the pastry box flying from my hands and scattering powdered sugar like cremation ash.

"Seriously, Phil?" I placed my hand on my pounding heart. "We *are* in a tomb at night with a homicidal maniac lurking."

"Apologies," he called back in a cheerful tone. "But come look at this beauty! Why, this rat is as fat as a house cat—practically begging to become charcuterie!"

With shaking hands, I collected the pastry box. Phil's enthusiasm for turning grave-dwelling rodents into gourmet meats was as disturbing as the implications of the sugary evidence, and it triggered full-on panic.

The mausoleum seemed to close in on me, its stone walls pressing. I was living a Halloween-style horror show in a haunted house with no exit.

Because somewhere in the darkness, Sullivan was waiting.

And the next course on the menu?

Might be me.

~

AS I WALKED from Private Chicks to St. Louis Cathedral, I checked the gun at my back. I wasn't anywhere near ready for the stakeout, but I was rested. Since I couldn't risk staying in my hotel room, I'd crashed on an office couch and, perhaps inspired by my visit to Saint Cecilia Cemetery, slept like the dead.

A dense fog had rolled in from the Mississippi River, turning Chartres Street into a ghostly corridor. The gas lamps glowed like will o' the wisps, or "spook lights" as they were called in the South. Even for a weeknight after two a.m., it was eerie. There should have been someone out—a straggling tourist, a street musician packing up. But the fog had cleared the streets like a plague warning.

Not an ideal night to hunt a killer in the Quarter, especially when that killer was hunting me back.

Nevertheless, the fog was clearing on the case. Sullivan was running some sort of illegal business with his family at Le Richelieu Hotel, which meant it was best for him if everyone, including the New Orleans PD, believed he was dead. When he wanted to call a meeting, rather than use a traceable means like a phone or email, he disguised himself as Père Dagobert's ghost and sang hymns to summon his accomplices.

But now that Candy was dead, was the Mother Superior his only remaining partner? Or was The Father at Sassy Spells also in on the business?

Rosary-Bead Nonna's warning was at the forefront of my mind. If a regular priest and nun were bad luck for my wedding, I couldn't imagine what those two represented. *The* malocchio *and a hex rolled into one supreme curse?*

St. Louis Cathedral loomed before me, its ethereal white exterior and black Gothic spires doing nothing to calm my haunted nerves. I turned down Pirate's Alley, the same route I'd walked with Yakov. The memory of Candy strapped to the statue produced goosebumps under my clothing. My hand drifted to my gun again.

Something feels different tonight. Wrong.

Relief washed over me when I saw David and The Vassal inside the gated garden. I was glad that I wasn't tracking Sullivan alone.

Or maybe I was.

They were fully suited up in tan mechanics' jumpsuits straight out of the *Ghostbusters* movies. They'd even drawn the red "No-Ghost" logo on their sleeves. On their backs were the proton pack and ghost vac.

My sigh came out as a puff of condensation. But as long as they hadn't made a slime blower, we were good.

As I entered the wrought-iron gate, I flashed back to the beckoning skeleton statue from Saint Cecilia Cemetery. The phantom scent of musty earth and decay seemed to cling to my nostrils. I shuddered, hoping it wasn't a sign of what was to come.

"Hey, guys." I shoved my gloved hands into my coat pockets. "Looks like you're ready to hunt the ghost of a Capuchin monk —who's a very much alive guy."

"Right. But like, think about it—Sullivan's using the legend of Père Dagobert to his advantage. The real ghost energy from all the stories and sightings over the years is totally lingering around here. Our equipment will pick up on the residual ecto-plasmic signatures, and when our fake monk shows up, the readings will spike because he's disrupting the existing para-normal field."

The Vassal's head bobbed. "Exactly. It's like supernatural camouflage detection. The genuine ghost energy acts as a base-line, so when an imposter enters the area—"

"Okay, okay." I held up my hands in surrender. I already had to take on a killer. I didn't want to battle their *Ghostbusters* technobabble too.

David looked at The Vassal. "It's time to calibrate the PKE meters."

The pair turned on stud finders with telescoping radio antennas taped to the sides. Lights began blinking.

The Vassal held up his meter. "This device detects psychokinetic energy fluctuations up to 50 gigaelectron volts, and its antenna amplifies the electromagnetic resonance frequency."

"Uh-huh." I squinted at the device. "And it finds wall studs too."

"Exactly." David slid on a pair of green welding goggles with a binocular lens on one eye. "Ghosts go through walls."

In theory, they did. "What do those glasses do?"

"The Ecto-Goggles? They utilize dual-spectrum paranormal detection with enhanced thermal imaging capabilities, and the binocular lenses filter out mundane visible light to reveal the supernatural ectoplasmic aura signatures."

Tough to argue with that—because I didn't know what the hell it meant.

I looked down at a pizza box with a string attached to the lid, labeled "GHOST TRAP. BEWARE." Behind it sat a red repurposed mini-fridge with a sign that read "ECTOPLASMIC CONTAINMENT UNIT—DO NOT UNPLUG OR GHOSTS WILL ESCAPE."

I was sorely tempted to point out that they'd basically given up the ghost with the pizza box trap, but I had a pressing question. "Ghosts can read, right?"

David's gaze lowered to the box. "Uh, probably."

"Actually," The Vassal pushed up his glasses, "ghosts are curious entities, so they're drawn to devices meant to catch them."

"Uh-huh. And how does this trap work?"

"You deploy it by sliding it across the floor and use the string to reel it in."

It seemed ridiculous, but then again, I would probably fall for it, especially because the box smelled of pepperoni. "Now that you have your equipment set, let's get in place."

We took our positions inside shrubbery that lined the wrought-iron gate.

And we waited.

The fog seemed to pulsate around us, thick and alive. Every few minutes, I caught movement in my peripheral vision— shadows that shouldn't have been there, shapes that dissolved when I turned to look. My heartbeat was on high alert.

The Vassal pointed. "I see a specter!"

I glanced around. *The ghost nun?*

"No, dude." David gave a frustrated flip of his bangs. "Your glasses have fogged up again."

"Oh." He wiped his lenses on his sleeve.

We're off to a great ghostbusting start.

A drunk with a major beer belly came around the corner. He tottered along, weaved back and forth, and stopped at the pizza box. His eyes popped, and he picked it up. He glanced around furtively before resuming his tottering.

David yanked the string, but the drunk resisted, pulling it off, and went on his wobbly way.

"Well," I whisper-drawled, "at least someone's having a successful night of hunting."

David and The Vassal stayed silent.

We resumed waiting. The shadow cast by Touchdown Jesus covering the back of the cathedral cast a pall over the garden. Ten minutes passed, maybe fifteen. The fog muffled what few sounds remained in the Quarter until we seemed isolated in our own pocket of silence.

My mind drifted to Sullivan. I could almost hear him sing

Kyrie eleison through the mist. The thought made my blood run cold.

The air grew heavier. Electric.

A gust of wind blew through the alley.

The Vassal raised his PKE meter. "A significant temperature drop! Do you feel it?"

"Yeah," my voice was as dry as a West Texas summer, "it's Jack Frost."

The Vassal's slack jaw snapped shut. "You jest, but we're getting massive PKE readings—the ectoplasmic residue is off the charts!"

Also off the charts—my patience with this *Ghostbusters* nonsense. But something else was off. The air crackled with tension, charged like the moments before a storm.

The fog thickened around us, moving against the wind. And everything went silent, the kind of stillness that comes before lightning strikes. In that quiet, I could almost imagine Sullivan's voice drifting through the mist, singing to his coconspirators.

Then, coming toward us in the thick fog, I saw a shadowy figure—in a black robe.

The Mother Superior?

My hand was already on my gun when David pulled the Neutrona Wand from his proton pack, and The Vassal aimed his ghost vac.

The figure burst through the fog, arms raised like Touchdown Jesus's—except that he held a tell-tale green Hand Grenade cocktail glass in one. "WOO-HOOOOO!"

A guy in a graduation gown? In January?

He spotted us in the garden. "Today I found out I've already got enough creditsss to graduate from Tulane," he slurred. "Sssooo, I withdrew from my classses, and I'm ccccelebratin' early."

"Niiice." David nodded. "Congrats."

The Vassal smiled. "Best of luck in your career."

Through the fog, I caught the outline of a woman in a dark cloak moving toward us. My hand tensed on my gun. *The Mother Superior?*

Ruth Walker emerged in an ankle-length black cloak.

Nope. Just the Grim Reaper.

"Will you miscreants keep it down?" Ruth waved a taser at us. "While you're holding your mini cosplay convention, I'm trying to track a murderer to save my employer."

I emerged from the shrubs. "Watch where you aim that weapon, Ruth."

She turned to me, her turkey neck in knots. "I assure you, I know how to use it." Her eyes narrowed as though that were a threat rather than an actual assurance. "And if you're supposed to be Sigourney Weaver's *Ghostbusters* character, you've got the demonic possession down, but you're missing the white chiffon dress."

A huff erupted from my mouth as a cloud of mist. Next thing I knew, Phil Redman would speed up in a '59 Cadillac Miller-Meteor hearse-ambulance with an Ecto-1 license plate and chat merrily about the best bait for catching a Class-5 roaming vapor. Or maybe Chandra Toccato would pull up with her U-Haul office and offer to negotiate with the spirits rather than bust them (for a fee, of course).

This ghostbusting stakeout was a bust. Time to call it a night. I opened my mouth to tell David and The Vassal—

But I was silenced by a gunshot.

"THE SHOT CAME FROM THE LEVEE," I shouted, and I broke into a run.

As my feet pounded the pavement, I heard the group running behind me—and the clatter of *Ghostbusters* gear.

We ran down St. Peter Street, along the wrought-iron fence of Jackson Square. We got to Decatur Street, and the Christmas Car screeched to a stop, blocking our path while playing the sleigh bell recording.

"Ho ho ho!" Santa shouted. "Meeeerry Christmas!"

"It's okay," I yelled over my shoulder. "I know these guys."

"Uh," David said, "I think we all do."

"WOO-HOOOOO!" The graduate fist-pumped and leapt into the air. "Firssst I graduate, and now it's Christmasss again."

"Franki!" Santa leaned out his window. "I'm glad we found you."

"What is it? Did you see Père Dagobert?"

"Not ten minutes ago, as we were dropping off a client. He was headed toward the river."

My eyes drifted toward the water.

Hermey leaned across Santa, his black eyes earnest beneath his green elf hat. "We went up the street to the hotel to tell you, and the manager said you might be here."

I'd forgotten that I'd told Anthony about the stakeout, but I was glad I had. "We just heard a gunshot down by the water. It could be him."

Santa shut off the engine. "Let's go."

"No." My voice was tight. "You all need to clear out. It's too dangerous."

David shook his head. "We're not letting you go to the levee alone."

The Vassal puffed out his chest. "David's right."

Ruth stepped forward—instead of sprinting away. "I'm coming too." Her voice was steady, but her coat was trembling. "For Bradley."

That makes two of us, I thought without irony. "Sullivan's here for me, and I'm armed. I'll handle this."

"Bah humbug," Santa shouted in a Scrooge move. Then he climbed from the Christmas Car.

Hermey followed suit, as in the red-and-white one. "There's safety in numbers."

Even with a stadium-sized crowd around me, I wouldn't feel safe from the rogue detective. And it wasn't clear whether the safety principle applied when my "numbers" consisted of Santa, an elf, two ghostbusters, a graduate, and the Grim Reaper. I was reminded of the island of misfit toys. But in this case, I was the Pied Piper of misfit crime fighters.

We crossed Decatur to Washington Artillery Park. The levee stretched before us like a dark rampart against the fog-shrouded Mississippi. The concrete slope disappeared into shadows where the river lapped against the rocks below—a perfect place for an ambush or a body dump.

I just hoped said body wouldn't be any of us.

We passed through the park, our phone lights and flashlights cutting through the dark fog like lighthouse signals.

Rustling startled me. I raised my Ruger and jerked it left and right.

"Could you stop swinging that thing?" Ruth whisper-barked. "You're going to shoot me on accident."

"Or on purpose," I replied, tense.

She dropped back. "Nice way to speak to someone who's trying to help."

I didn't take the bait. I was too busy trying not to get caught by a predator. Plus, now that there was some distance between us, the fog seemed to swallow her voice.

If only I could replicate that effect at the office.

We arrived at the levee—the place where Père Dagobert had

once insisted on retrieving the bodies left to rot as a warning. Where the water had claimed so many souls over the centuries.

Any second, I expected Sullivan to rise from the river like a kraken, dripping with rage and a thirst for vengeance.

David's proton pack lights hit something near the water's edge—a crumpled form.

Sullivan. Still as stone in his monk's robe.

No. This is one of his tricks. A setup.

Raising my phone light as a signal for everyone to stop, I approached Sullivan with my Ruger aimed, trying desperately to steady my hand. With every step toward him, I walked deeper into his web. My heart pounded in my throat as I waited for him to spring up, to grab my ankle, and pull me underwater—to Davy Jones's locker.

As I got closer, the beam of my phone light caught a wound in his forehead. A dark pool spread beneath him in the mud.

Blood.

Wesley Sullivan was dead.

The metallic scent hit me. And instead of relief, I felt panic rise—cold and consuming like the Mississippi. With Sullivan, I knew my enemy. Now I was adrift in a sea of unknowns.

Who did this?

Are Bradley and I finally free?

Or is Sullivan's killer after us too?

"Um, I'm calling to report a murder." David's voice was calm as he spoke into his phone.

Santa swept his flashlight over Sullivan. Near his lifeless body, something glinted in the beam.

I stooped and shined my phone light on the object. Half-buried in the muddy bank was a small silver cross. The kind that might hang from a rosary.

The Mother Superior.

16

Veronica approached the Private Chicks couch with a coffee mug. "Drink this, Franki. It's a triple espresso."

From my supine position, it took all the strength I had to lift my head, let alone the cup. It was eight a.m. on Thursday, and I was running on fumes and the hazy memory of last night's power nap.

The mug read *Laissez Les Bon Temps Brew-ler*, a pun on *rouler*, but the good times weren't brewing or rolling in New Orleans.

Not when Wesley Sullivan, my prime suspect, was dead.

I knocked back the espresso like it was bathtub gin during Prohibition.

Veronica dropped onto the opposing couch. "That should perk you up."

"Let's hope." I set the mug on the coffee table between us. "Because right now, I'm just numb." I stared at the ceiling. "I've lived with his shadow hanging over me for two years. It's hard to believe he's gone."

"But he is. You saw him."

The memory of Sullivan sprawled in the mud—that dark pool of blood around his head—hit me all over again with the force of a Mississippi steamboat. "And now I'm more afraid than ever."

"Because you don't know who killed him?"

"And because whoever did must be one hell of an adversary." I tried to sit up, but gravity won. I flopped back, weak, confused, and scared—not for me, but for Bradley. Sure, he was safe from Sullivan. *But was another formidable foe still after him?*

And after me?

Veronica leaned forward. "So, what's your read on this?"

I rubbed my eyes. "I know Sullivan killed Dana, but I doubt he killed Candy. As despicable as he was, I think even he would draw the line at murdering his half-sister."

"Family business can get ugly, though."

"Which is why this Mother Superior is now my main suspect. The problem is, I've got nothing—no name, no address, not even a church—to go on."

"What about the cross you gave to the police?"

"Nothing on that, either." I shook my head. "No prints, no engraving, not even a 'Made in China' stamp."

Veronica exhaled, her gaze shifted to the floor.

Summoning my strength, I managed to prop myself up and grab my phone from the coffee table. Two missed calls from Bradley's mother. "Lillian called. I wonder if she has news?"

The door to Private Chicks slammed, rattling the opaque glass and my nerves.

The Grim Reaper—Ruth in her ankle-length black cloak— stood at the reception desk, her perpetual scowl locked and loaded on me. "She does. She canceled the rehearsal dinner tomorrow night."

The news was a punch to the gut. My wedding clock was winding down, and I was farther than ever from putting a name to the killer.

Ruth slipped from her cloak, revealing a black turtleneck

and frumpy gray wool skirt. "She asked me to pick up the flower arrangements and donate them to a children's hospital." She scoffed. "As if I have time to run her errands."

I was obviously in a bad state, because I was too tired to chastise Ruth for her lack of goodwill. I fell back on the couch. "Is this wedding going to happen?"

Ruth sniffed. "Not if you don't get off that couch and look for the killer."

As grim as The Grim Reaper was, she was right about that.

She sat next to Veronica on the couch. "I know Gigi Scalino is in prison, but he could be behind Sullivan's murder."

I'd thought the same thing.

Veronica looked from Ruth to me. "He *is* a mob boss. He could have any number of people on the outside doing his bidding."

"True," I said, "but a more likely suspect is the Mother Superior Maybe Baby mentioned."

"Who's that?" Ruth snapped.

"A family member of Sullivan's that he and Candy were running some kind of business with out of Le Richelieu Hotel. And with a nickname like 'The Mother Superior,' she could be connected to The Father at Sassy Spells."

Veronica nodded. "I'd start there, if I were you."

My phone rang.

Marcella's name was on the display. I tapped *Answer*. "Hey." My tone was somber to match the solemnity of Sullivan's murder. "I guess you've heard the news?"

"Yes, and frankly, it's left me gobsmacked. *Gobsmacked*, Franki. Like someone just told me Central Grocery stopped selling muffulettas. I mean, *what* was Bradley's mother *thinking* when she canceled that rehearsal dinner?"

It figured Marcella was only concerned with the wedding.

You'd have thought *she* was the bride. "Um, probably that her son won't be there to rehearse?"

"So? Anyone could stand in for him. It's not like walking down an aisle on your wedding day is Olympic gymnastics."

Clearly, she wasn't going to let Bradley off the hook—not even while he was behind bars. I decided to approach the cancellation from a different angle. "Yes, but his family and friends are snowed in, so I can understand why Lillian would make that decision."

"Well, it's a good thing Bradley's mother doesn't have a say in the wedding planning. It would be crazy to cancel that."

What was crazy—besides Marcella—was this conversation. "I'm glad you brought that up. I appreciate how hard you've worked on my wedding, but—"

"Stop. Right. There." Her tone was straight-up "hostage taker."

And I was the hostage. There was no telling Marcella the reception wasn't going to happen. Otherwise, I risked ending up locked in a closet like Moira—or at the bottom of the giant birthday cake like Dana Del Ray.

"Even if you don't have the wedding," she said brightly—too brightly—"you can still have a party."

"What would I be celebrating, exactly?"

"Oh," she said, as though her patience had snapped. "You want to know what you'd be celebrating, do you?" Marcella was so hot that she could've fried all three hundred cannoli shells with her breath. "Well, *Franki*, you'd be celebrating the fact that a man asked you to marry him. Because let me tell you, sister, that doesn't happen to all of us."

I wasn't sure whether it was my exhaustion or the shock, but she almost had me convinced that I needed to go through with the reception.

Then I got a hold of myself. "I'm sorry, Marcella, but no wedding, no party."

She let out a scream that could've driven the ghost of Bloody O'Reilly from Le Richelieu Hotel.

Veronica jumped, and Ruth clutched her chest.

"Give me the phone," Nonnone barked from the receiver.

"I'm not done talking, Grandma!"

A muffled scuffle followed, like Marcella was fighting off a purse snatcher.

Veronica leaned in, and Ruth cupped her ear, not wanting to miss a single blow of the Sicilian prize fight.

More scuffling ensued, and then a thud.

"Franki, it's Nonnone," the La Befana lookalike said into the receiver, breathless from combat. "You need to come to the hotel. *Pronto.*"

Before answering, I tried to process how Marcella had been overtaken by the short, octogenarian nonna. After all, she was big and strong and full of pent-up bachelorette resentment with the reflexes of a serial bouquet-catching champion. "What do I need to come there for?"

"You can't stand by and do nothing after the groom's mother canceled the rehearsal dinner. This is *war*, cara mia. I've lined up a guy for you in retaliation."

Shock ran through me, almost as extreme as when I found Sullivan's lifeless body on the levee. Nonnone was worse than Maurizio Bonsignore, *u paraninfu*, a.k.a., the Sicilian marriage broker my nonna had twice hired to find me a backup fiancé. "You can't be serious."

Veronica mouthed "What?" while Ruth squinted, trying to read my expression.

"Nonnone takes care of everything. Just ask my kids and my godchildren."

"Thanks, but no. I want my actual fiancé."

Ruth shook her head slowly, out of sync with her own turkey neck. And Veronica bit her knuckle to keep from shouting something she'd regret.

"Snap out of it, *scema*! My guy is Italian, Catholic, and he eats gluten. What more do you want? Abs?"

I was no "fool." Nonnone was nuts. "This conversation is over."

"Not until I say it is." Her voice was as sharp as a mezzaluna knife. "Think of your poor mamma and nonna, making all those cannoli."

"You're the one who wanted them, so cancel the order."

"And disappoint your guests? Madonna mia, what kind of hostess are you?"

"The kind who's hanging up now." I pressed *End* with enough force to crack the screen. Then I tossed my phone into my bag and heard a hollow thump. The pastry box from Saint Cecilia Cemetery.

Ruth clucked. "That Nonnone has some gall. But at least she's trying to solve your problem instead of wallowing on a couch."

My stare had all the warmth of a gravestone as I dumped the pastry box on the coffee table.

Her eyes narrowed. "*That's* your solution to this mess? Stress-eat pastries?"

As far as I was concerned, it was a valid strategy, but that wasn't what was happening at present. "For your information, this box belonged to Sullivan. After the shock of finding him dead on the levee, I forgot to give it to the police."

Veronica scooted forward, her eyes wide. "How do you know it was his?"

"I don't know for certain, but I found it in a mausoleum at Saint Cecilia Cemetery—that Phil Redman saw Sullivan coming out of. He was carrying a big box, probably full of whatever he was dealing."

"Drugs?" Veronica asked.

I shrugged. "Possibly. But knowing Sullivan, he could've been selling anything from stolen goods to illegal weapons."

Ruth extended her hand. "Let me see that box."

"Okay, but use a tissue, or something."

She arched a brow, and her bun seemed to tighten with indignation. "I hardly need instruction on evidence handling, thank you very much." She slid on her cat-eye readers, pulled an old-fashioned lace handkerchief from her skirt pocket, and picked up the box with theatrical precision. After checking the inside and examining the bottom, she looked at me with smug satisfaction. "It's Sullivan's, alright. And judging from the powdered sugar, he got beignets."

"How do you know?"

Ruth's mouth curved into the rare smile she reserved for exposing my incompetence. "While you were out playing *Ghostbusters* with David and The Vassal, I was conducting actual detective work. I found stacks of these same unmarked boxes in the kitchen cabinet at Le Richelieu Hotel."

Did Sullivan merely get beignets from the hotel? Or is the pastry box connected to his illicit business?

MY BOOTS POUNDED the stairs as I left the office. I needed to get to Le Richelieu Hotel and investigate those pastry boxes. They might hold the key to whatever racket Sullivan and his family of felons were running.

As I hit Decatur Street, I glanced at Sassy Spells. The Crescent City Plumbing and Palmistry van was parked out front.

Chandra was in.

Despite my brain's furious protests, my traitorous feet veered toward the door. "You've really hit rock bottom if you're going to see Chandra," I muttered. "As in, rose-quartz rock bottom."

The pastry boxes could wait. I was on a mission to ID the Mother Superior, and with any luck—make that a miracle—Chandra could help. Then again, banking on Chandra was less of a longshot and more of a shot in the dark—at the moon.

I entered Sassy Spells. The shop reeked of orange and sage, the source of which I pinpointed immediately—"Hex and The City" incense smoldering in a glittery cauldron on the empty checkout counter. No sign of The Father. Just a couple of women rifling through the spell sale rack.

I navigated the maze of shelves to the "Private Clients Only" door and knocked.

Chandra answered, her moon-pie face framed by frosted hair teased into a helmet that could survive atmospheric re-entry. Not only that. She wore a metallic silver dress stretched so tight that it looked like she was wrapped in aluminum foil, and her pointy boots would've made Hermey the envy of all elves up at the North Pole.

"What happened?" She tugged at a crescent moon earring. "Did Santa kick *you* out of his Christmas Car, too?"

"I came to talk to you about Wesley Sullivan. I assume you've heard he was murdered?"

A frustrated huff erupted from Chandra's lips, and her glare could've melted Frosty the Snowman. "I'm a medium, remember?"

This was already more awkward than I'd anticipated. There was no way I was going to admit she was psychic. Yet here I was. "I'm curious what you think."

"Ohhh." She pressed her paddle nails to her chest. "Is the great Franki Amato asking *me* for help?"

I sighed. "Don't rub it in, Chandra."

"I'm just surprised you'd consult the 'Gaslighting Grinch.'"

She was definitely rubbing it in—like salt on the Who Roast Beast. "Can I please come in? For Bradley's sake."

She stood aside. "Make it quick."

The tiny room smelled like garlic and deli meat. My stomach growled as I spotted the culprit—half a Liuzza's Frenchuletta, their muffuletta-on-French-bread masterpiece. "I'm interrupting your lunch."

"Yep. And I've gotta take Lou to the podiatrist. He's got corns and can't wear his toe shoes."

My appetite got cold feet and split. "Look," I said, sitting at the card table, "I'm sorry if I offended you with that Grinch comment."

"*If* you offended me?" She raised a plucked brow. "That pseudo Santa kicked me to the curb like yesterday's Christmas wrapping, thanks to you."

"Well, it won't happen again."

"Darn right it won't. I wouldn't step foot in that tinsel trainwreck again, even if it flew me to the moon with Frank Sinatra riding shotgun."

If Ol' Blue Eyes were alive, the only thing he'd be riding with Chandra was a restraining order.

She slurped from the straw of her Liuzza's cup while my eyes drifted back to the Frenchuletta. I couldn't remember when I'd last eaten, but the memory of that corn conversation was haunting me like the alleged ghost of Bloody O'Reilly. "Have you found out anything more about The Father?"

"No, he hasn't been around much." She inspected a paddle nail. "And when he has shown up, he hasn't done anything out of the norm."

Except for the sin-eating, the occult classes, and the relic-forging. "Then can you consult your rose quartz ball about Sullivan's killer?"

She pursed and glanced at the orb. "It's dark. I don't think it feels like talking."

Or *she* didn't feel like talking. "How about your cards?"

"Left them at home."

"Aren't they the tools of your trade?"

"I'm human, okay? We forget things."

It seemed like a psychic would sense she was forgetting something important. But I was at her mercy, so I didn't dare point that out.

Every fiber of my being rebelled against what I was about to say, but I was desperate. And we were alone, so there was no one to witness the complete meltdown of my professional dignity. "What about your charm bracelet? Can't you channel the spirits?"

"I haven't heard from Dana or Candy." She said it like they were friends who hadn't texted her back. "No word from Sullivan, either."

"Try the ball again. Remember, this is for Bradley—your relative."

Her tiny mouth twisted to the side. "Fine. I'll see what I can do."

She leaned forward, peering into the rose quartz. Unlike other mediums who put on a show, Chandra's readings were a total let down. Kind of like her, for that matter.

"See anything?" I asked, peering at the pink ball.

"Maybe."

Classic Chandra—no showmanship whatsoever. "Please keep looking. For Bradley."

"That's what I'm doing. Do you want me to strain my eyes? With Lou's foot problems, the last thing I need is an ophthalmologist visit."

"Of course not."

She huffed. "Wait. I'm getting something." Her voice pitched up. "Oh, jeez. It's not good."

I jolted forward. "What is it?"

"A powerful person." She squinted and leaned closer to the crystal ball. "Obsessed with family. And tradition. They're pulling the 'purse' strings."

"Can you see who?"

"No, just black."

The Mother Superior? "Is it a woman?"

Chandra squinted. "Maybe? But it could be a man."

"The Father? He wears black."

She sat back. "All I know is, the person's connected. Like… Mafia connected."

If Chandra was to be believed—a bigger stretch than the fabric of her metallic silver dress—then the crystal ball was pointing to Gigi Scalino, the mob boss Ruth Walker suspected. The theory was plausible since he'd once been in business with Sullivan. But with Gigi in prison, that meant the killer who'd lost the cross on the levee was one of his henchmen.

But who?

I licked my lips and realized my mouth was bone dry. "Look again and try to see whether the black you're seeing is The Father."

A sharp knock echoed from the door.

Chandra's eyes popped. "Oh, God," she whisper-shrieked. "Did I summon a spirit?"

My lips flatlined. Also classic Chandra to be shocked when she thought her psychic shenanigans might have actually worked. "Not unless they made an appointment."

Turning in my chair, I yanked the door handle.

The Father loomed in the doorway in his priestly "Mortician" garb. He stood as still as a corpse, scowling down at us both.

Then his pale eyes locked onto mine with predatory focus, making my skin crawl as though it was infested with chevals-diable.

He'd been eavesdropping on our conversation.

"MAY I HAVE A WORD?" The Father's voice was funeral-parlor quiet.

My pulse tried to make a break for it, but I forced myself to meet his stare.

Behind me, I heard the scrape of chair legs as Chandra bolted upright. "It's her you want, not me."

It figured she'd throw me under the bus. When it came to courage, Chandra made Scooby-Doo seem like a Navy SEAL.

Holding her handbag in one hand and the remaining half of her Frenchuletta in the other, she skirted the walls as though The Father had just climbed out of a coffin. Then she shot out the door faster than mourners fleeing a wake—nonne excluded, obviously. They practically tailgated the hearse.

The Father stepped into the doorway, his black-clad bulk blotting out what little light there was, and he closed the door behind him. The tiny room shrank around me, like a confessional booth with no screen—and no shot at absolution.

"I don't know who you are," he said, his Canadian accent thickening with irritation.

"Franki Amato. I'm a PI investigating a series of murders, including your former client, Candy Kelly."

"Well, ever since you first showed up in my shop, a woman has been casing the building." His pale eyes narrowed. "She even followed me to my home."

The Mother Superior. My pulse quickened. "Is she a nun?"

"You know very well who she is, so stop playing games." The pink mass between his eyebrows pulsed like an angry heartbeat.

"Honestly, I don't." I kept my voice steady despite the fact that my knees felt like overcooked linguine. "And an innocent man is facing life in prison because of a crime he didn't commit. So, if you could tell me what she looks like, it might help prove his innocence."

His laugh had all the warmth of a freezer door swinging open in a morgue. "If you keep this charade up, I'll call the police and tell them *you're* involved in my former client's murder."

I crossed my arms, hoping the gesture looked more confident than I was. "I don't believe you. If you planned to do that, you would've already done it."

Something flickered across his face—surprise, maybe, or grudging respect. "Has it occurred to you that I don't want any trouble? I merely helped a client, which is what I do for a living, and now I'm being harassed. I'd like to get on with my life and keep my business out of this case."

"What did Candy confide in you during her visits?"

He went rigid at the mention of her name. The reaction was so pronounced that I knew I'd hit a nerve—evidently, the one in the pink mass pulsating between his eyes.

"As I've said before," he ground out through clenched teeth, "we don't discuss the proclivities of our clients, particularly those who've passed."

"You've obviously been questioned by the police, so you might as well tell me what you know."

The Father leaned in, bringing that angry pink mass within inches of my face. I caught a whiff of something medicinal—antiseptic, maybe, or embalming fluid. "I assume that's thanks to you."

"Me?" I gave him my most innocent smile. "I don't even know your name. Yet."

"What I know—or don't—isn't your concern." His voice dropped an octave, gravelly and cold, like it had been dredged up from six feet under. "What *is* my concern is that black shadow you brought with you. Call her off."

The word "black" got my attention. Given his Canadian multiculturalism, I doubted he was referring to race. "So she *was* wearing a habit."

His eyes flashed with the realization that he'd revealed more than he'd intended. Without another word, he straightened and jerked the door open with enough force to rattle the frame.

The dismissal was clear, but I couldn't resist one parting shot. "For someone who doesn't want trouble, you're certainly dressed for it."

He stood silently, like a black-robed sentinel waiting for me to leave.

And I was all too happy to oblige. I hurried into the main shop, feeling his cold stare stabbing at my back like an ice pick. The customers at the spell rack had vanished, leaving only the lingering scent of the Hex and The City incense and the weight of The Father's unspoken threats.

I exited the shop into the crisp January air. The temperature had dropped significantly since I'd gone in, and storm clouds were gathering overhead like bad omens. A cold front was coming.

But the real chill came from the knowledge that the Mother Superior had me in her crosshairs. And she planned to put me on ice—permanently.

17

"Look out, baby," a local shouted, laying on his Chevy's horn like Louis Armstrong on a trumpet solo.

Startled, I leapt backwards onto the Chartres Street sidewalk as he roared past, my pulse racing like the guy's engine. *Wouldn't it be ironic if I got myself killed before the killer could do it?*

After checking both ways—twice—I crossed toward Le Richelieu Hotel and tried to focus. But my mind was on murder.

And Mafia.

Was Gigi Scalino pulling the proverbial purse strings—or was this strictly Sullivan family business?

I pushed open the hotel door as Giada stepped out of the Terrace Lounge in her chef's apron.

"Franki!" Her eyes searched my face. "Any news?"

"You don't want to know. Is Marcella out back?"

"No, she's not here. And when your mom and nonna got wind of that, they told everyone in the kitchen. The poor women were so exhausted, they all fled."

"They'll be back after some rest." After all, the nonne were to cooking what Santa's elves were to toy-making—except for

Hermey. "But it's weird Marcella would leave. She's been obsessing over my reception 24/7."

"The last time I saw her, she was frantic about misplacing a couple of things she wanted to bring for the celebration on the piazza. She probably went to see if she left them at the American Italian Cultural Center."

I almost didn't want to ask. "What... kind of things?"

"A gold sash embroidered with 'Mrs. Bradley Hartmann' in Italian flag colors. She said it would go perfectly with her Italian flag cocktail."

Not to mention the Piazza d'Italia's red-and-green lights.

"Oh, and the Bling Rings she originally bought for your bachelorette. The plastic diamond is big enough to hold a shot of liquor so you can drink it from your finger."

"What every girl dreams of," I quipped.

Giada eyed my engagement ring. "No, but a lot of girls dream of that rock Bradley gave you."

My throat tightened. I needed to steer this conversation elsewhere before the waterworks started. "Where's Anthony?"

"He drove your mom and nonna to your apartment."

Great. They'd be safe, and Napoleon would get fed, which, basically, was all he was in this relationship for. "I came to check out some pastry boxes Ruth mentioned. She said they're in the kitchen?"

"Yes, in the cabinet by the walk-in. Why?"

"Sullivan had one. I think he was using it for something shady, although his was full of powdered sugar from beignets."

"Then it wasn't from Le Richelieu. The hotel doesn't serve beignets."

Another dead end?

The main door opened.

My jaw dropped.

Then it snapped shut.

Maurizio Bonsignore, the infamous marriage broker, swept into the lobby wearing his professional ensemble—top hat, tails, and dramatic cape. He flashed long yellow teeth, smoothed his mustache with a black-gloved hand, and stretched to his full, barely-five-foot height. With a flourish of his hand, he removed his hat and bowed, revealing a triangular bald patch that mirrored his native Sicily. Rising with ceremony, he clicked the heels of his tiny loafers. "Your betrothed has arrived to save-a the wedding day!"

"Betrothed?" Giada echoed, gazing at me like she'd seen a ghost. Or a wee version of the Phantom of the Opera.

"Yeah." The word escaped as a defeated sigh. "An unfortunate incident during Veronica's wedding week in Venice. I accidentally saw him in his nightshirt."

Giada gasped. "That was *you*? I overheard your nonna at the cannoli station telling Nonnone that story. I thought she meant someone else."

"It was-a he!" Maurizio's beady eyes sparkled with predatory delight as he ogled me, mangling pronouns with his usual flair. "And he made-a me rip his-a page from my black-a book of *zitelle*."

My hands went to my hips to keep from wringing his little neck. "Only so you would stop trying to find me a backup fiancé—not because I wanted to marry you."

"Oh, this is serious." Giada plopped onto a lobby couch. "You know the custom in Sicily, Franki—you're definitely engaged."

"Maybe in the old country, but not in the U.S." I marched up to the pint-sized marriage broker and leaned down to his eye level. "I want a refund of every penny my nonna paid you."

"Carmela did not pay for this-a trip. I am-a here courtesy of-a Nonnone."

That woman meddled worse than a family member. "Fine. Then refund all the previous payments."

Maurizio's face crumpled in theatrical dismay. "It's-a not possible. My fee," he wagged one finger, "she is-a nonrefundable."

"Your fee *she is-a* refundable because you, *signore*, committed fraud. Your name may mean 'good gentleman,' but all you are is a bad con artist."

"I beg-a your pardon!" He drew himself up, cape swirling around him. "Maurizio Bonsignore, u paraninfu, is-a not a criminal."

"Then explain this—the average Sicilian bride today is between thirty-three and forty, and yet you've been charging my nonna as though I were a zitella since I was thirty. And I'm still only thirty-two!"

Sweat beaded on his forehead as his brain wheels turned, searching for a loophole. Then he looked up at me with renewed confidence. "Let's-a not quarrel, *amore mio*. The wedding is in-a two days. We have-a serious matters to discuss," his lip raised, flashing those horse teeth, "like-a your dowry."

"The only thing we're discussing is your flight back to Sicily. Today."

A car door slammed outside, interrupting us. Through the window, I saw Glenda and Nadezhda getting out of the Lucky's Liquor and Vaxing van.

Never thought I'd be relieved to see those two.

Glenda sashayed into the lobby with Nadezhda in tow, and both were in animal print. Nadezhda wore her signature snakeskin, while Glenda had opted for patches of fox fur in strategic places and stripper shoes that said "Foxy Lady" in hot pink.

"Well, well, well," my landlady drawled. "If it isn't Count von Count from *Sesame Street*. How are you doing, Maurizio?"

"*Bene*, signorina Glenda." He bowed beaming, clearly mistaking the puppet vampire reference as a reference to his nobility—which he wasn't. "But-a I live on Via Palermo."

Of course he did.

"Sorry to bust up the shindig." Glenda linked her arm through mine. "But we've got prep work to do."

"We do?" I asked.

"Yes, sugar. Your mother and Nonna sent Nadezhda and me on a top secret mission."

"Da." Nadezhda grimaced. "Mission Impossible."

My eyes narrowed. "What are you talking about?"

"Make beautiful voman."

Yet another veiled man jab. For a second, I considered confronting her about it, but that didn't seem fair since I'd been letting Maurizio call me "he" for the past five minutes.

Before I realized what was happening, Nadezhda and Glenda had flanked me like the goon nonne and rushed me into the elevator. When we got to my room, Nadezhda shoulder-checked the door like her heartthrob hockey player, Alexander Ovechkin, taking out an opponent.

Glenda grabbed the bag she and my mom had packed and began rifling through it. She pulled out the underwear and held them up. "Now why on earth do you need an adult diaper, sugar?"

"Those are my panties, thank you." I snatched them from her hand.

Nadezhda rattled off a laugh that resembled bullets from a Kalashnikov.

"Lawdy, child." Glenda shook her head. "It's a good thing your momma sent us." She opened the jar of Red Hot Body Glitter and began dabbing it on my face. "The champagne is warm, but it'll do the trick."

"What do you mean by 'trick,' exactly?" It was a fair question given that the only other thing in the bag were the chili pepper pasties.

"It's a figure of speech, Miss Franki. We've got to get you ready for the serenade."

So that's what this is about. Another freaking tradition.

"Now, put your boots on, sugar."

"Will I get two thousand dollars in seventies money?" I asked, being sarcastic. "Because that's the only thing that will make this worth it."

Glenda leaned back, her face all business. "If you put on the pasties, break a heel, and lean over the balcony, the dollars will fly, Miss Franki."

"Not even at Mardi Gras," I muttered, slipping on the boots.

Nadezhda suddenly lunged and grabbed one of my feet.

"Hey!" I tottered and fell against a wall as she wrenched off a heel. "What did—"

"Vork it, Frank." She shoved me onto the balcony. "You still owe vone tousand dollar for Rockstud Valentino."

That tightwad Communist is more obsessed with money than Marcella is with matrimony.

Keeping a death grip on my shirt hem in case Nadezhda had any more tricks up her snakeskin sleeve, I limped to the balcony railing.

Chartres Street was unusually empty.

Staring into the night, I wondered where to go next to save Bradley. I didn't have a clue where to look for the Mother Superior. And I wouldn't get a thing from Gigi Scalino if I visited him in prison.

For the first time I could remember, I truly didn't know what to do. Every lead seemed like a dead end. And this was happening during the single most important case of my life.

Tears threatened to flow like the mighty Mississippi, but the sound of footsteps distracted me. Giada and Maurizio had joined me on the balcony.

Then *he* stepped into view.

Hair coiffed. Elegant black tuxedo. Clean shaven.

Yakov.

Now that I thought about it, he was Nadezhda's friend, so he probably wasn't shaved but waxed.

He cleared his throat, puffed out his bear chest, and erupted into song—"Nessun dorma" from Puccini's *Turandot*.

Giada grabbed my forearm. "He's so talented."

I nodded, a tad emotional. Yakov's sugarplum fairy soul was really showing.

"Bah!" Maurizio flung his cape like Zorro's cranky cousin. "Who does-a this *impostore* think-a she is? Luciano Pavarotti?"

"She also loves ballet," I said, humoring his pronoun problem. "Probably dances like Mikhail Baryshnikov."

"What's-a next? She cook-a like Gordon Ramsay?"

"*Mmm*," I hedged, "more like Giada De Laurentiis. Yakov is a gentle giant."

Maurizio grimaced. "Gentle, *sì*. Genius, no. The serenata must-a be the night before the wedding, not on this-a day. It is an insult to tradition!"

Giada shrugged. "Nonnone said we had to do it tonight because Yakov has plans to wrestle tomorrow night."

Another bachelor party, apparently. I looked down. Glenda and Nadezhda had gone down to the street, and Glenda was beside Yakov doing a striptease—or maybe shedding her fur.

Too bad it wasn't Bourbon Street. She would've scored a lot of beads.

Maurizio stomped a tiny loafer. "I cannot-a stand for this-a humiliation. I will challenge this-a pretend Pavarotti to a duel."

Despite everything, I had to laugh. "Best of luck!"

Maurizio stormed from the room, cape flying behind him like that of a ticked off twelve-year-old Dracula.

Giada flashed a tired smile. "I think I'd best follow the

nonne's lead and get some rest. Is there anything I can do for you before I go?"

"No, I'm leaving too, right after Yakov wraps up his performance. I need to make sure Maurizio, the 'good gentleman,' doesn't get killed defending my—I mean, *his*—honor."

She laughed and took my hand. "You're sure there's nothing I can do?"

"I am."

We exchanged an embrace, then I followed her to the door and locked it behind her.

As I headed back to the balcony, I spotted something I hadn't noticed when Glenda and Nadezhda had rushed me into the room.

On my pillow lay a book—in the exact spot that had been stained with sambuca.

And it was no hotel Bible.

Slowly, I approached as though the book were wired to explode.

Life on the Mississippi by Mark Twain.

My stomach torpedoed.

This wasn't the work of the ghosts of Bloody O'Reilly or Ellen the Maid.

The last time I'd seen or heard of this book was on the Steamboat Galliano because it was Captain Rex Vandergrift's favorite novel.

And I knew what it meant—I was being summoned to the river by the killer.

Specifically, the levee.

THE HOTEL ELEVATOR groaned as it lowered me down to the first floor, its cables straining like my nerves. "I feel ya, pal," I muttered. "I'm not thrilled about the job I have to do right now either."

The doors opened, and I stepped into the lobby. Le Richelieu was deserted—a ghost hotel draped in shadows and silence. A clock I hadn't noticed above the reception desk ticked ominously, reminding me that I was running out of time to save my wedding. And guests would start arriving the next day.

Would I be here to greet them? Would I even be alive?

"You will," I said aloud. Determined. Or at least trying to sound that way.

My hand reached for the door handle, but then I let my arm fall to my side. Before I faced off with the Mother Superior at the levee, I wanted to know what she, Sullivan, and Candy had been doing in the hotel.

The answer had to be here.

Starting with those pastry boxes.

I pivoted and entered the Terrace Lounge. The giant birthday cake that had held Dana Del Ray's lifeless body was still in the corner, a macabre reminder of her murder.

Exiting quickly, I walked past the pool. The chlorine burned my nostrils as I made my way to the kitchen.

And I went in.

The huge room was pitch black—the darkness so complete it was like stepping into a void. I felt around until I found the light switch.

The kitchen lit up. Without the nonne bustling around, filling the space with their chatter and the aroma of garlic and herbs, it seemed far less inviting. Cold. Clinical.

And the industrial pasta machine didn't help the atmosphere. La Bestia was a fitting name, because it overtook the far end of the room like a mechanical monster—with a digestive system that included teeth.

I went to the pantry-style cabinet beside the walk-in, my boot heels echoing on the tile. As Ruth had said, the pastry boxes matched the one Sullivan had at Saint Cecilia Cemetery —plain, unmarked.

But what was the powdered sugar for if not beignets?

I scanned the room, my gaze sweeping over stainless steel surfaces that gleamed under the harsh lights. Someone had dropped a notebook on the floor near the cannoli station.

Probably recipes. I stooped and flipped through the pages, expecting to find measurements for ricotta, marsala, and pistachios. But the pages read like a mob accountant's fever dream.

50 CANNOLI = 45k

   25 cannoli = 25k

   100 cannoli = 90k

MY STOMACH DROPPED FASTER than the hotel elevator. "What the hell is in those cannoli? *Gold?*"

The notebook fell from my hand to the counter with a thwack.

The gold bar-shaped drugs in the lemons on the Steamboat Galliano.

Sullivan had never stopped dealing. After laying low, he'd roped in his relatives to help him run the business. *And what better front for drugs than Italian pastries made by Sicilian nonne?*

My cousin Giada had been right. The powdered sugar in the pastry box wasn't from beignets. It was from cannoli—that had packets of drugs in the filling.

I paced the length of La Bestia, my thoughts turning like the rollers in the machine. The lemons on my windshield, in the Le

Richelieu walk-in—Sullivan had been taunting me for outing his and Gigi Scalino's smuggling operation, subtly letting me know he was back at it.

The levee was the last thing on my mind now. This was bigger.

I yanked open the walk-in door. Kneeling on the cold floor, I examined the lemons for the veal scaloppini, one by one. All intact. I rose and scanned the shelves. Other than the fruit, the main items in the walk-in were veal, cheese, and eggs. "If there were drugs in here, Candy or Sullivan must've cleared them out."

Then it hit me like a rolling pin.

Dana.

Follow the dollars.

She'd been distributing drugs for Sullivan during her private gigs. She wasn't just a dancer—she was a dealer.

Hands shaking, I fumbled for my phone and dialed Bruno Messina.

"Franki, baby," he answered on the first ring. "I thought you'd never call!"

That made two of us. "Bruno, I need to ask you something vitally important."

"The answer is *yes*, doll! I'm free tonight."

My eyes rolled like cannoli shells. "This isn't about a date. I need to know whether Dana Del Ray offered to sell you drugs."

Silence ensued.

"Is this some kind of setup?" His voice had lost its flirtatious edge, replaced by something more guarded.

"No, Bruno. I'm trying to solve Dana's murder, remember?" I gripped the phone tighter, my knuckles white. "Now will you please answer the question?"

"She offered me some coke. But I'm not into that stuff."

Because if his mamma, Santina, caught wind of it, he'd be sleeping with the garbage bags. "Did she say who she worked for?"

"Not by name. She just said, 'The Godmother.'"

The phone almost slipped from my palm. Maybe Baby had confused "mother superior" with "godmother."

The killer wasn't a nun. She was a laywoman.

Who sold cocaine in cannoli.

My knees buckled, and I grabbed onto the counter for balance.

The handbags. The Santa Sicily bag full of cannoli. The Souvenir della Sicilia bag with the cannolo keychain. And Chandra—she'd said a powerful person was pulling the "purse" strings.

Nonnone.

The big boss nonna who'd been seemingly obsessing about my wedding was a freaking drug kingpin.

And who wore fine jewelry from Dolce & Gabbana's rosary-inspired line. The silver cross next to Sullivan's body was hers.

"Yo, Franki!" Bruno's voice seemed to come from far away. "You still there?"

"Gotta run." I hung up, shoved the notebook into my bag, and turned to go. Not to the levee, but the police station. With the logbook, I could take down Nonnone and save Bradley in time for—

A shadow fell across the doorway.

Nonnone entered in her signature black Dolce & Gabbana—a black top and floor-length skirt with a scarf around her neck. On her shoulder was a canvas bucket bag featuring the phrase "Il bel paese L'Italia" and a couple dancing the tarantella.

How fitting that she'd chosen a bag depicting a dance, because we're about to tango.

Her eyes were locked on the logbook in my hands. "You found my notebook."

"I did. And your drug ring, *Godmother*."

She reached into her bag. But what she pulled out wasn't a cannolo.

It was a gun.

18

———

Two zip ties flew at me like strands of al dente fettuccine.

"Drop the notebook," Nonnone barked. "And bind your feet with those ties. Tight."

That was abrupt. "We're not going to talk about this?"

"We've talked enough." She waved the gun with practiced ease. "Now do as you're told, *signorina*."

The "signorina" was akin to a slap since it indicated my single status. But the gun left no room for a fight. I let the notebook fall to the floor. Then I bent, slowly, my fingers trembling as I wound one of the ties around my ankles. I had to buy time.

"Don't try anything smart. You already screwed me when you didn't show at the levee last night. I had it all planned—you and Wesley, nice and neat. A murder-suicide."

I shuddered. Nonnone, not Sullivan, had been the one to put the Mark Twain book in my hotel room, unaware that I'd planned a stakeout and had no intention of staying in Le Richelieu after the stain-on-the-pillow incident.

"Well?" She stared at me. "Don't you have anything to say for yourself?"

My head cocked. "You... can't expect me to apologize for not showing up."

"Yes, I can! Do you have the faintest clue how hard I worked to plan that? I had to watch three episodes of *Dateline* to get the angles right."

Somehow, I struggled to feel sorry for her. "Why *did* you kill Sullivan, though? I thought you were family—or his godmother."

Her laugh was as bitter as rancid garlic. "Are you kidding? The guy was *Irish*, for crying out loud!"

An equal-opportunity godmother Nonnone was not. It was a good thing Giada's friend, Moira, hadn't heard her. On second thought, I wished she had. Moira would've taken out the big nonna with her bare Irish hands.

"Tighten that tie," she barked. "Now!"

I did as I was told and rose.

Nonnone's lips curled with contempt. "None of this would've happened if it weren't for your brother."

"Anthony?" My voice cracked. "What does he—"

"When he got the manager job, we had to shut down our entire operation." Her eyes flashed with anger. "Wesley's half-sister, Candy, came up with a plan to scare him away with ghost stories."

"The haunted hotel rumors," I whispered. Bloody O'Reilly and the ever-terrifying maid, Ellen.

"So we could resume business as usual. But then Anthony went and invited your fiancé to have his bachelor party in the Terrace Lounge."

The pieces clicked together with sickening clarity. "Wesley wanted revenge."

"For what happened on the Steamboat Galliano." Nonnone's smile was stiletto sharp. "He couldn't resist the temptation."

My teeth clenched. "By killing Dana Del Ray."

"Exactly. And Anthony made it easy by hiring your cousin, Giada. She posted her daily menu on her fancy food blog, and Candy told Wesley."

Then he had Candy tell Giada that Dana had to eat a meal before she got in the cake.

Nonnone placed her bag on the cannoli station. "That fool thought it was hilarious to frame Bradley."

"You told him not to." It wasn't a question.

"Of course I did. But we had to do something about Dana anyway." She shrugged. "She wanted out of the private party business."

My stomach lurched. "So you killed her."

"She threatened to expose us if she didn't get money to fund her krewe. What choice did we have?"

I could think of many. "So, Sullivan stole the cyanide from the Pharmacy Museum."

She shook her head. "Too risky for him to be seen in public, what with the New Orleans PD looking for him. No, he had Candy steal it, and she paid some woman to say she saw Bradley do it."

That explained why the woman didn't know the ghostly pharmacist who worked at the museum—and why she'd asked my name. She wanted to make sure she misidentified Bradley to the right person.

"But Candy was weak. She felt guilty about Dana's death because they used to be roommates. That's when she ran to that fake priest at the witch shop."

Chandra—she'd told Marcella and Nonnone about Candy's visit to Sassy Spells when she ran Ruth by the hotel on their way to The Big Teasy.

Nonnone hmphed. "And for a sin-eating ceremony, of all things. That's against the Catholic Church."

"So is murder."

"*Silenzio!*" Her expression was homicidal. She waved the gun at the remaining zip tie I was holding. "Put that around your left wrist, then both hands behind your back."

As I obliged, she stepped behind me, her breath warm on my neck. She yanked the plastic tight enough to cut off circulation.

And I thought about the flash of black fabric I'd seen disappearing around a building behind the St. Louis Cathedral. It wasn't the habit of a mother superior and certainly not a ghost nun. It was Nonnone's Dolce & Gabbana.

She walked around to face me.

And I stared her down. "You killed Candy for talking to The Father, and Sullivan turned on you, trying to kill you in retaliation. That's why you're wearing that scarf—to hide the bruises from when he choked you."

She raised her chin. "I've never been so disrespected in my life. I told Gigi that Wesley had to be eliminated."

The "Gigi" echoed in my head like an explosion. "You work for Gigi Scalino, the mob boss?"

"*Work* for him?" She let out a harsh laugh. "I'm the brains of this operation. Haven't you noticed a pattern here?" She shrugged her shoulders. "Men ain't too bright, Francesca. You're a PI—look at the evidence. Bradley's in jail, Wesley's dead, and Gigi's rotting in prison. I was Gigi's *comare*, but then he went and got caught—by *you*, no less."

My stomach twisted. I'd put her lover behind bars. Not a good look.

Nonnone took a step toward me. "I've been to hell and back because of you." She adjusted her grip on the gun. "I lost my house and my car when Gigi couldn't pay the mortgage. I shuffled back and forth between my kids' houses until I ended up with one of my godchildren, whose golden retriever chewed my twelve-thousand-dollar Sicilian *carretto* bag."

Something told me the D&G purse was the thing she was most angry with me about, and not Gigi being in prison.

"Do you know how long it takes to get a luxury bag repaired? The line is longer than confession at Easter!"

Suspicion confirmed.

Her eyes hardened. "But I got to thinking... Gigi being side-lined was no reason to shut down a profitable business. So, I got in touch with Wesley, and since Candy was working here, we decided it was the ideal front."

"To sell drugs."

She flinched. "How else was I gonna keep myself in Dolce & Gabbana?"

I'd heard of women maxing out their credit cards for couture, but she'd taken it to a whole new level—like, "The Devil Wears Prada and Packs Heat" level. Except that this devil wore Dolce & Gabbana.

Nonnone squinted at me. "I have a question for you."

"Fire away—uh, *metaphorically*, that is."

"Did you learn nothing from the nonne at St. Mary's Church?"

Evidently, she'd heard about my Big Fat Sicilian Wedding Superstition Sermon. "What do you mean?"

"You threw away your life to save Bradley's! Why? One man's the same as the next, Francesca. You marry one, have your family, then—if you're lucky—you have your fun on the side. Otherwise, you live to regret it."

Nonnone was a female chauvinist pig. Granted, I *would* regret being in Funeral-Faced Nonna's razor-blade-toenail-and-nose-hair-clipping predicament. But I wasn't going to admit that now. "The only thing I regret is not realizing that your spiel about the three hundred cannoli being a celebration for a fruitful new life was complete BS."

"It wasn't." She sneered. "They're a celebration of *my* new life, not *yours*. As soon as I've taken care of you, I'm starting over somewhere with palm trees." She gestured toward La Bestia with the gun. "Get on the conveyor belt."

My blood turned to ice water. The industrial pasta machine loomed at the far end of the kitchen—fifteen feet of gleaming steel and grinding gears that had once pumped out ten thousand pounds of pasta a day. Its conveyor belt could carry lumps the size of a casket, and its rollers could crush a casket too. "La Bestia?"

"Sure. This has to look like an accident." The corners of her mouth tilted down in mock sadness. "Poor Franki must've slipped and fell into the pasta machine." She patted La Bestia's side almost affectionately. "The same one that almost killed a man back in the day when his apron got caught in the rollers. Only this time, you won't be able to save yourself."

"The remnants of these zip ties will prove my death was no accident."

"Doubtful." Her smile was as cold as January wind off Lake Pontchartrain. "They'll be pulverized along with everything else."

Desperate, I had to stall. "Tell me—did you invite your drug clients to my wedding to pick up cannoli? Is that why you were so adamant I have a reception without a groom?"

"Smart girl." She moved toward the cannoli station and grabbed a handful of powdered sugar from a bowl. "Too bad you're not smart enough to mind your own business."

Before I could react, she flung the powdered sugar in my face.

The world went white. Sugar coated my eyes, my nostrils, my throat—I gasped and choked, tasting sweetness mixed with panic. Blinded, I stumbled backward, my bound hands useless behind me.

La Bestia's motor roared to life.

"Help!" I screamed, hoping someone—anyone—was in the hotel. But my voice echoed in the kitchen. I blinked frantically, trying to clear the sugar from my eyes. Through the white haze, I made out Nonnone's dark shape moving with the patience of a hunter who knew her prey couldn't escape.

My hip cracked against a prep table edge, sending pans crashing to the concrete floor like cymbals.

Seizing the moment, I hopped toward where I thought the exit should be, ankles screaming against the zip ties. But the kitchen had become a maze of shadows and gleaming steel. My shoulder slammed into the walk-in door as I stumbled past it. If I could just reach the kitchen exit, make it to the lobby—

The gun barrel cracked against my skull with a sickening thud. White-hot pain exploded through my head, and my knees buckled.

The last thing I saw before darkness claimed me was the cannolo keychain swinging from her handbag—the key to the entire case.

Then I knew nothing at all.

MY HEAD THROBBED with the kind of jackhammer rhythm usually reserved for the day after Mardi Gras. A wave of nausea washed over me, and the air tasted thick, dusty, and vaguely of yeast. I cracked an eye open, then another, and the world swam into a blurry, terrifying focus.

I was lying on my back, staring at the rust-stained tin ceiling of the old macaroni factory. The low, mechanical rumble of La Bestia's motor vibrated through me.

Nonnone had somehow hoisted me onto the conveyor belt— and tied me down. My feet would enter the rollers first, promising a slower, more agonizing death. The thought was scarier than the scarifier at the old Pharmacy Museum.

She hadn't told Marcella to resurrect the old machine to make food for my reception. She wanted it to make macaroni out of me.

Oh, God. Am I really going to die by pasta machine? The food that had literally fed me all my life? The irony was devastating.

But my mom and nonna would be proud.

Nonnone's long, witch nose appeared in my line of vision, which was more jarring than La Bestia's movement, and I noticed a significant detail—her Dolce & Gabbana necklace was lined with small silver crosses, and one was missing.

She hadn't realized that she'd left a cross at the crime scene.

Would the police ever connect it to her?

"You're awake. *Bene.* I prefer my victims conscious for the dinner theater." She flashed an amused smile.

"Nonnone," I rasped, my throat feeling like sandpaper. "You don't want to do this."

"I do." She belly-laughed, the tip of her nose bouncing with each guffaw. "Too bad you'll never get to say that at the altar."

That reminder stung, and tears pricked my eyes. But I would sooner be flattened into a giant lasagna noodle and cut into strands of spaghetti than cry in front of her. "You won't get away with this."

"A classic line, cara. But woefully incorrect."

"Is it? You left a clue next to Sullivan's body, and I gave it to the police."

"You're lying." She hiked her handbag higher on her shoulder. Then her eyes narrowed. "What was it?"

Not wanting her to get rid of her incriminating necklace, I had to lie. "Strands of hair."

"I don't believe you. They wouldn't have found my hair in all that mud."

"Believe what you want."

"Even if it *is* true, it won't matter. In a few hours, I'll be on a plane with a new identity. By the time they find what's left of you, I'll be sipping sambuca in a country with no extradition treaty."

Panic, cold and sharp, jabbed at my ribs. At the same time, I was incensed at her flip reference to the liquor she and Sullivan had used to kill Dana. I wriggled my wrists, trying to loosen the ties, but I was trussed up like a holiday turkey, seconds away from becoming the main ingredient in Nonnone's parting dish.

She gave me a mock salute. "*Addio*, Francesca. I'd say it was a pleasure, but let's be real—it wasn't."

"Agreed."

With a dramatic flourish, she pressed a switch.

Nothing happened.

She pressed it again, harder this time.

Still nothing. The conveyor belt remained motionless.

"What the—" Nonnone muttered, jabbing and pulling various switches on the control panel. "Move it, you piece of junk!"

I watched her growing frustration with a mixture of terror and vindictive satisfaction. Even La Bestia wasn't cooperating with her murder plans.

She turned to me with exasperation. "Do you know how to work this thing?"

"Seriously?" My head shot up. "You want me to help you kill me?"

"Fine. Be difficult." She bent over the control panel, squinting at the faded labels. "I'll do it myself."

After another minute of angrily pushing and pulling switches, the conveyor belt lurched to life and began inching me toward the first set of steel rollers. And from my vantage point, they looked like they could flatten a semi-truck into a pizza crust.

God, this is so Lucy and Ethel at the candy factory. But I'm not laughing!

Nonnone laughed, as if reading my mind. "I'd stay, but I don't want blood and guts all over my nice outfit."

She turned and went to the exit. Then she switched off the light, leaving me to my fate.

The door shut behind her, plunging the kitchen into a dark gloom.

"Okay, Franki. Think." I yanked at the zip ties, my nails scraping uselessly against the tough plastic.

The rollers were now ten feet from the mouth of the beast, turning slowly but with such force that their power radiated through the air.

The rhythmic, grinding squeak... groan... squeak... groan of the massive steel cylinders filled the factory. The moment anything—hair, clothing, skin—got caught in that gap, the machine would take over with an irresistible pull, like being caught in the gears of a clock the size of a car. The sheer, immense force they radiated was a physical presence, promising a swift and very flat end.

Nine feet.

Frantic, I thought of the Rescue Remedy drops that Pharmacist Francine had sold me—not that they would help, even if I could access them.

"Where is Marcella? Or Anthony? I'll even take Maurizio Bonsignore!" Without one of them—or anyone—I probably wouldn't survive to get married. I twisted my wrists harder. "Why hasn't at least one nonna come back to cook? Their work in the kitchen is never done!"

Then it hit me. It was Thursday afternoon. All the nonne were at the cunzata del letto—rigging my bed.

Eight feet.

"Damn traditions! I will never, *ever* observe one for the rest of my life." Which, given my current location, was going to last about another minute.

Overcome, I glanced at the ceiling and thought of the St. Mary's Church mural of the Virgin Mary ascending to heaven. *Is that what's going to happen to me in mere seconds?*

My mind raced, scrambling for an out. What I needed was a miracle from said virgin. I mean, how many times had I recited the "Hail Mary"? Ten thousand, give or take a few thou? So, where the hell was she when I needed her?

Seven feet.

Then, through the fog of my concussion, a memory surfaced. The words of Tomato-Faced Nonna, oiling La Bestia—and her husband's cracked feet. *"A messy solution is better than no solution!"*

The release lever!

Turning my head, I tried to see down the side of the machine. But I couldn't. I gave a series of hard jerks against the straps and managed to look down.

There it was. The greasy, old-fashioned lever, underneath the conveyor belt at the first set of rollers.

My only shot at survival.

Six feet.

The space between those heavy steel rollers was set for an enormous lump of dough—bigger than me. The machine would apply hundreds, maybe thousands of pounds of force, concentrated into that narrow line where the two rollers met.

Contorting my body, I bent my knees and tried to roll onto my side, despite the straps Nonnone had used to tie me to the conveyer belt. It was hard, but I managed. I had to reach that lever.

Five feet.

The air grew warmer, humming with the power of the

machine. I could see the whole room, the potential path to safety. But I was on a one-way trip to being flattened. Then shredded.

I straightened my legs, my bound feet reaching, straining, for the lever. Tomato-Faced Nonna had said to pull it back. And from where I was laying, that meant I needed to push it forward. And not just push—I had to shove the lever all the way forward. "Hard to do without hands!"

Four feet.

The vibrations rattled my teeth.

I can't die now. I didn't put on the clean underwear my mom packed for me. Plus, I'm wearing Red Hot Body Glitter.

And I'm still a zitella!

"Wait. I'm not a zitella. I never was!" The rage began to build, not at Nonnone but at my mom and nonna. "I'm going to *live* to get married."

Three feet.

The point of no return was approaching—once my feet entered that gap, the machine's grip would be absolute.

Time to channel Saint George slaying the dragon. Or, in this case, Saint Glenda—in the form of her Grit Getter Kit—slaying La Bestia. "I don't have champagne, but I've got the glitter and the boots."

My boots!

The heels were high and just might reach the lever.

But my ankles were bound too.

Two feet.

There wasn't time to try to slip one of my feet from the boot, so I aimed my legs just off the side of the conveyor belt.

With a surge of adrenaline, I kicked out and missed the lever. Then I remembered—Nadezhda had broken off my heel for the serenata!

One foot.

With bent knees, I angled my body further to the right and put every ounce of my fear and fury into one last, convulsive kick with my left heel.

The lever was stiff—it probably hadn't been used since the Roosevelt administration. Teddy, not Franklin.

But with a groan of protesting metal, the lever gave way.

The effect was instantaneous. And biblical. The hatch flew open, and a volcano of fine semolina flour erupted into the air.

WHOOMPH!

A massive, choking white cloud engulfed the machine, the kitchen, and me. I coughed, my lungs burning, and the flour turned to paste in my mouth—a glue that threatened to choke me.

The giant plume hit the gears and rollers with the force of a dry-chemical fire extinguisher. The machine groaned. The gears ground against the powdery onslaught. The once-steady hum sputtered.

And just as Tomato-Faced Nonna predicted, the belt, now coated in a thick layer of white powder, lost all traction. It slid, went slack, and with a final, pathetic squeal, the entire machine shuddered to a halt.

The sudden silence was deafening.

I lay in the white-out, a human cannolo, my heart hammering against my ribs. The flour had gotten between the zip ties and my skin, and I'd broken into a sweat from the adrenaline and exertion. The combination of fine powder and moisture created a slippery paste around my wrists. I twisted against the slick mixture, feeling the plastic give a little. I pulled again, harder, gritting my teeth as the edges cut into my skin.

With a final, raw-knuckled wrench, the tie on my wrists snapped.

I sat up, tearing at the binding on my ankles. It came free

more easily. I scrambled off the machine, and my boots slipped on the now perilously slick floor.

And I broke the left heel.

It was like chapter thirteen of Glenda's memoirs, except that I was in a race to catch a killer, not strip to make two grand—in seventies money.

My bag was on the ground by the walk-in. I rummaged through the contents, shocked to find my phone still inside. Apparently, Nonnone had been convinced I wouldn't make it.

At one point, I had been too.

My hands shook so badly it took me three tries to unlock my phone. But the phone wouldn't turn on. "A dead battery? Really?"

I would have to call the police from inside Le Richelieu.

Moving as fast as my wobbly legs and broken heels would take me, I entered the lobby and stopped.

Thumping came from the door behind the reception desk. Rhythmic. Desperate.

The key hung on the doorframe, but I stood immobile.

Nonnone?

No, impossible. She was on her way to the airport.

Another of her victims?

Entirely possible.

Chewing my lower lip, I grabbed the key and inserted it into the lock. Then, wielding a stapler like a club, I threw open the door.

Three sets of eyes stared back at me from the dark closet.

"Oh, geez!" I leapt backwards. But as my eyes adjusted, faces came into view.

Then I saw the gags.

And the zip ties.

"Marcella?" I stumbled forward. "Anthony? Wait. *Maurizio?*"

The D&G-loving boss nonna had overcome us all.

Dropping the stapler, I went to work removing the gag from Marcella's mouth—the gold Mrs. Bradley Hartmann sash.

She took a deep, oxygen-starved breath, her smoky-eyeshadowed eyes bright with what looked like sheer terror. "Franki," she wheezed. "For the love of all that's holy—so, *Italy*—please tell me I didn't miss my wedding reception!"

19

"Wait up, sis!" Anthony shouted, running from the hotel and trailing me, Marcella, and Maurizio. "Don't leave me heuh alone!"

Tires shrieked through the evening air.

A '59 Cadillac Meteor-Miller hearse-ambulance screeched to a stop in front of us, chrome tailfins gleaming like freshly polished devil horns.

Phil popped out onto the street, eyes shining brighter than the grill. "This is a chance encounter! I was on my way to Private Chicks to show you my new ride." He gestured to the car with both hands like a game show host. "Either I manifested her, or the Saint Cecilia residents gave me a belated Christmas gift."

Speaking of the holiday, I would've preferred Santa and his seventies sleigh, but this wasn't the time to be picky about paranormal-themed transportation. "Phil, the killer's at the airport. Can you take us?"

"Pile in!" He patted the hood with pride. "This beauty holds multiple bodies."

Marcella parted her hair curtain and peered out with one

smudged smoky eye. "And if anyone gets hurt or killed, we're already in the right vehicle."

Not what I wanted to hear.

Maurizio opened the passenger door. "A woman must have-a the chaperone."

"In the 1800s, Maurizio." I turned to my brother. "Anthony, you stay at the hotel."

He went as white as cannoli filling. "With these ghosts? Hell no, I'm going in the *Ghostbusters* car."

It was nothing short of a miracle that Candy's plan to scare him off hadn't worked. "You have to. You're the manager, and some of my guests will be checking in."

Marcella tapped his chest. "And this wedding is happening!"

Technically my line—but she'd delivered it like a prize-fighter defending her title, so I let her have it.

Anthony wiped sweat off his brow, even though the temperature was barely above freezing. "Fine, but I'm staying outside."

And he would. All night long.

Still coated in flour, I threw open the Ecto-1's front passenger door and climbed in beside Phil, probably looking like a ghost.

Maurizio stomped a tiny loafer outside my window. "You sit-a with this man? This is an affront-a to my honor."

My skull hit the vintage pleather headrest.

Marcella smoky-eyed him. "Why is it an affront to *you*?"

"We are betrothed." He got in the backseat. "She saw my nightshirt in-a Sicily."

She huffed and slid in next to him. "Honestly, Franki." She slammed the car door. "How many men are you trying to take off the market? We're going to need a spreadsheet to keep track of them all."

What we needed was a padded cell.

Phil hit the gas, and the car lurched forward. "You've notified the police?"

"Yes, but I need to call Veronica. Can I use your phone?"

Marcella handed me hers. "I've already dialed her number."

"Thanks." I put the receiver to my ear. The call went to voice-mail, so I called the office.

"Private Chicks, Incorporated," The Vassal answered.

"Vassal, is Veronica there?"

"No, she's at the police station. Bradley's attorney managed to get a flight from Boston."

Music to my ears. "This is vital. I need you to call Veronica until she answers. Tell her Nonnone is the killer, and I'm on my way to the airport to stop her from skipping town."

"Oh, my," he exclaimed. "Shall David and I bring the ghost-busting equipment?"

My head lowered. The kid was so smart, and yet so clueless. "This isn't a haunting, Vassal. It's a homicide."

"Ow," he shouted. "Those chains hurt!"

Muffled sounds of a struggle followed.

I blinked. "What's going on?"

The sounds continued. I worried the goon nonne had invaded the office and restrained him, and possibly David. "Are you in danger? Who's there?"

"Me," Ruth growled into the receiver.

The Grim Reaper. The chains were no doubt from her cat-eye glasses.

"Now I know why you've been MIA at work today. I heard from your cousin you've already rounded up a Sicilian fiancé."

Forget the headrest. I hit my forehead on the dashboard.

"Where are you now?" Ruth snarled. "Catching a flight to Palermo?"

That's it, I thought. Nonnone lied about going to a country with no extradition treaty. She's going to flee to Sicily.

"Answer me, missy!"

"No, but the killer probably is." I hung up, handed Marcella her phone, and glared at everyone in the Ecto-1. "None of you say another word until we get to the airport. Otherwise, our next stop after Louis Armstrong International will be the hospital or the morgue."

For the next fifteen minutes, the '59 hearse-ambulance was as silent as a tomb, except for the roar of the engine.

As Phil pulled into the airport, I put a hand on his arm. "She's fleeing the country, so drop us at Concourse A."

Marcella leaned forward between the seats. "Too bad she's not at Concourse B. They've got an Angelo Brocato's."

I turned and cleared my throat.

She eased back and glanced at Maurizio. "A legendary New Orleans Sicilian bakery and gelateria," she whispered. "Gelato, cookies, and cannoli."

"*Santa ricotta!*" Maurizio threw up his gloved hands. "Don't-a mention the cannoli no more."

For once, I agreed with my faux fiancé.

"That-a Dolce and Gabbana *diavolessa* lock-ed me in-a the closet because I want-a to duel that-a Siberian soprano."

Which, of course, would've involved the cops—something Nonnone couldn't risk until I was dead, and she was halfway to freedom.

"But don't-a worry, *cara mia*. I will-a defend your honor."

"You do, and you'll be back in that closet."

Marcella leaned into Maurizio, glowering. "And I'll put you there."

"If you don't believe her," I said, "talk to my cousin's friend, Moira Mulligan."

He shrank into the door panel, holding his top hat like a shield.

Phil pulled up to the airport entrance. "I'll park this baby and meet you inside."

We piled out of Ecto-1 and ran for the doors.

Maurizio bowed with a flourish of his cape and let Marcella go before him.

She gasped and fluttered her eyelashes. "How classy is that, Franki?"

Needless to say, I didn't answer. The electric door opened, and I was hit by the smell of burnt coffee, stale pretzels, and the jarring sight of the green "plane de lis" logo, a plane merged with a fleur-de-lis that made absolutely no sense.

The airport was chaotic. Departure announcements echoed through the concourse, luggage wheels rumbled on the tile, and somewhere a toddler was having an epic meltdown.

As I scanned the check-in area, I spotted something that made my stomach drop.

Ruth and Chandra.

Chandra's eyes met mine, and she screwed up her mouth. She marched toward me in a white, lunar-themed motorcycle ensemble that made her look like a moonstruck storm trooper —or a Stay Puft Marshmallow Woman.

I didn't see a helmet, but she didn't need one with her head of hair. "How did you beat us here?"

"We took Lou's motor toilet." She glared at Maurizio. "I was at Private Chicks when you called. Ruth summoned me on account of your second fiancé here."

Marcella turned to the mini marriage broker. "It's a motorized toilet her husband made for the Krewe of Commodus Mardi Gras parade last year."

Maurizio removed his top hat and fanned his face, which was the colors of the flames Lou had painted on the toilet. "The hearse-ambulance seems-a like a good choice now."

"Listen, all of you. Nonnone is armed and dangerous. You all need to leave the airport and let me handle her."

"Nothing doing, two-timer," Ruth growled. "I'm making sure the granny gangster goes to the hoosegow."

"What Ruth said," Chandra boomed, her Boston accent blasting through the airport. "I'm Bradley's blood relative, and *I* ID'd the killer."

"Too bad you didn't ID her to me, because she tried to kill me with the industrial pasta machine."

She put a hand on her plump hip. "That's your fault. You were there when I saw her in my rose quartz crystal ball."

"Chandra," I got down in her face, "the only thing you saw was black."

"Yeah. Nonnone in black fabric."

If I had one regret about marrying Bradley, it was that I'd have to deal with the mad medium for the rest of my life. "Welp, since you ID'd her, let's get to finding her. She's probably bound for Palermo."

Ruth slipped on her readers. "We can't get to the gates without boarding passes."

Valid point. I chewed my cheek trying to come up with a strategy to get us through security.

Then the answer presented itself.

David and The Vassal had entered the airport—with their ghostbusting gear. The Vassal's vintage canister vacuum gleamed with Christmas lights, while David's military-surplus frame buzzed with its attached PC tower covered in glow sticks. Both contraptions were beeping, whirring, and generally creating the kind of spectacle that made TSA agents break out in a cold sweat.

"Oh, God," I muttered. "They're going to get arrested."

Ruth put her hands on her hips. "They're doing it to create a diversion to help Bradley."

"All the same, I can't let this happen." I took off at a sprint.

But TSA had already surrounded them.

"Sir," a harried agent waved her hands at David's proton pack, "you cannot bring these... devices... through security."

"You don't understand." The Vassal adjusted his glasses as his PKE meter beeped. "We're detecting massive psychokinetic energy readings throughout this terminal. There's definitely supernatural activity here."

A second agent approached David's apparatus with the wariness of someone approaching a bomb. "What exactly is this?"

"Proton pack." David assumed a grave expression. "For subduing hostile spirits."

The Christmas lights on The Vassal's vacuum flashed. "The readings are off the charts!" He pointed the handheld PKE meter around. "There's definitely a Class 5 full-roaming vapor in the vicinity!"

More security agents converged on the scene.

"Couple o' crazies," a sixtyish man exclaimed to his female companion. "They're gonna shut down the whole airport."

Every TSA agent within a fifty-foot radius clustered around the ghostbusting equipment, trying to determine if it was dangerous, decorative, or just plain deranged.

And we slipped through the checkpoint.

"Please don't touch the containment unit," The Vassal shouted. "You could release every spirit we've captured since Tuesday!"

We broke into a run through the terminal. I was in the lead, despite having no heels on my shoes, followed by Marcella, and Ruth in her Keds. Chandra was in the rear, bogged down by her motorcycle boots and helmet hair.

Maurizio's little loafers slipped on the slick tile, and his tiny legs worked furiously but couldn't keep up. "Wait-a for me! These-a shoes, they are not-a made for the running!"

"Forgive me, Maurizio," Marcella yelled over her shoulder. "But I've got to save my wedding reception!"

I dropped back and shot her a wry look. *She* was the bridezilla, not me. And she wasn't even a bride.

"Do we know the gate?" Ruth shouted.

"No," I gasped, out of breath. "We have to... check... them all."

Midway through the run, Chandra dropped off.

Then Ruth.

Marcella and I kept going, breathing hard. We scanned passengers at three different gates with no luck.

And then I spotted Nonnone at the gate for Newark—where Tomato-Faced Nonna's niece, Rosa, lived childless.

She sat near the door to board in a blonde wig that was anything but inconspicuous on an eighty-plus-year old woman, and it wasn't only the color. The cut was spiky like the one on Bruno at the strip club. To further disguise herself, she'd ditched her Dolce & Gabbana. As it turns out, the heat-packing devil *did* wear Prada.

She rose and came to meet us, her hand in her black tote. "Try to stop me," she said in a low tone, "and I'll shoot you both."

My mom rushed up with a rolling pin, followed by my nonna, who was wielding her handbag medieval-mace style.

Fear rose to my chest. "You two shouldn't be here. I can take care of myself."

Nonna's eyes blazed with fury. "We're not-a here for you, Franki."

"She's right, dear." My mom's face hardened, and she raised the rolling pin like a battle axe. "We're going to take out Nonnone for forcing us to make three hundred cannoli!"

"Try it, Brenda," Nonnone said through clenched teeth, "and you and your-mother-in-law will have more holes than Swiss cheese."

"*Swiss* cheese?" Marcella cried, her face registering shock and horror. "You should've said Provolone!" She lunged at Nonnone's legs.

Apparently, the boss nonna hadn't learned that Marcella only spoke in Italian food.

Nonnone stumbled, and the tote dropped to the ground, revealing the pistol in her hand. "Freeze!"

Marcella went rigid on her stomach, eyes wide.

"She's got a gun," a female passenger shouted.

Travelers shrieked and dove behind chairs, luggage flying everywhere.

A horn blared.

And I spun.

Chandra was commandeering a terminal shuttle with Ruth and Phil as passengers.

"Stay back!" Nonnone waved the weapon, her wig askew. "All of you!"

Extending my arms, I held back my mom and nonna to stop them from making a fatal move. "Put the gun down, Nonnone."

Her eyes narrowed. "I'm boarding that plane." She backed toward the boarding door, keeping the gun trained on us. "None of you are going to stop me."

"No, but the airport just did," Phil called out from behind us —still cheerful, despite the firearm. "All flights are grounded."

Nonnone's head whipped toward the service desk.

"I am-a arrived, *amore mio!*" Maurizio came sliding across the polished airport floor in his tiny loafers, finally catching up. His arms windmilled as he tried to stop. But he crashed into Nonnone's legs like a bowling ball hitting pins. They both went down in a tangle of limbs.

As I tried to spot the weapon, my mother pushed me aside and jumped in. She ripped the blonde wig from Nonnone's head and did her signature move—a vicious hair pull.

Chandra and Ruth joined the fray.

"For the cannoli," my nonna shouted. Then she flung herself on the pile as though it were a coffin.

The gun skittered across the floor.

And I scooped it up. "Got the weapon!"

Everyone scrambled to their feet—except Marcella and Nonnone.

Marcella went into wrestling mode, pinning the boss nonna in a move that Yakov would've admired, using her knees to immobilize the elderly woman's shoulders.

I aimed the gun between Nonnone's eyes. "Looks like your only destination is to Orleans Parish Prison—with Gigi Scalino."

THE CLOCK READ ten thirty a.m.—twelve hours since I'd arrived at Central Lockup, and I was pretty sure I was serving a sentence of my own.

Marcella had left to prep the American Italian Cultural Center for the reception, and Maurizio had gone with her, refusing to stay and see my "first-a fiancé." But I was wedged between Ruth and Chandra like a shrimp in a po-boy.

Even worse, Ruth kept nodding off on my shoulder, snoring straight into my ear canal. Every time I shoved her upright, her head flopped right back like a possessed bobblehead.

Chandra, meanwhile, had turned her hair into a personal pillow and was sleeping silently, which would've been peaceful—if not for the Category 5 hurricane raging on my other side.

"Yoohoo, Miss Franki." Glenda waved as she strutted up the hall in her Strip Search outfit—just in case. Per usual, Nadezhda was in tow. "Any news?"

"Not yet."

"Well, shoot." Glenda stomped a stripper shoe.

I hoped she wouldn't set off her police sirens again, because they would set me off. My nerves were in knots, and my stomach was no better. I was seriously concerned that Bradley wasn't going to be released.

"Don't you worry, sugar. Miss Ronnie's gonna get your fine fiancé out of jail in time for that wedding tomorrow. She'll have Maybe Baby, David, and The Vassal there too."

"I just wish it wasn't taking so long."

Glenda smoothed a lock of hair from my forehead, and if it hadn't been for the handcuffs holding up her loincloth, I'd have sworn she looked almost maternal.

The door buzzed open, and I shot to my feet.

Maybe Baby emerged in a pink vinyl blazer and miniskirt, a red rhinestone bra, and red Moschino inflatable wedge heels. The look was pure Barbie-meets-bounce-house, totally appropriate for her party supplies business.

"I'm glad you're out." My eyes darted to the door. "Did Bradley get released too?"

She looked on either side of her. "I don't think so. I don't see him."

That was kind of my point, but I didn't point that out.

Glenda planted her hands on her handcuffs and jutted out a hip. "How does it feel to be free, Miss Maybe?"

"Good, but that Detective DiMaio's a real piece of work. After locking me up for almost a week, he offered me a job."

Nadezhda perked up at the mention of earning money. "Doing vhat?"

"Police dispatcher."

Not an ideal fit given her communication style, but if Maybe Baby was any indication of the New Orleans PD's hiring practices, it explained why so many locals complained that they were unreliable.

Maybe Baby snorted and hiked up her bra. "I told them I don't have time to be sewing patches because I've got my party supplies business to run."

Glenda blinked blue metallic lashes. "What patches, Miss Maybe?"

"You know, on their uniforms. They probably get coffee stains on them, so they need new patches put on." She adjusted her blazer and tried to look professional, which was difficult in a garment that squeaked. "But I'm designing a new product—inflatable wedding altars."

It reminded me of Bruno's pitch for a wedding chapel to Lucky's Liquor and Vaxing. "Nadezhda, meet Maybe Baby. With your brains and her... well... *your* brains, the two of you will make a killing together."

The door buzzed open, and I jumped.

David emerged followed by The Vassal.

Although I'd hoped for Bradley, I was relieved to see them in their tan Ghostbusters jumpsuits rather than Central Lockup's orange ones. And I was even more relieved that their equipment hadn't made it out with them. "What's the verdict, guys?"

David flipped his bangs. "Innocent, thanks to Veronica."

The Vassal gave a solemn nod. "She convinced the DA that a canister vacuum covered in Christmas lights doesn't meet the legal definition of an improvised explosive device."

David cocked a brow. "And she argued that hunting ghosts doesn't constitute impersonating federal agents."

I exhaled. "So, you were looking at domestic terrorism, disturbing the peace, and impersonating ghostbusters?"

The Vassal pushed up his glasses. "And reckless endangerment of travelers, but Veronica said our 'scientific demonstration' fell under free speech."

I managed a weak smile. "Remind me to triple her retainer. But seriously, thank you both for what you did at the airport. Nonnone would've escaped if it hadn't been for your performance."

The Vassal's brow wrinkled. "Performance?"

I rubbed my temples. "What about Bradley?"

"We didn't see him, but we did see Nonnone. Detective DiMaio had her in handcuffs."

"And orange." David grinned. "No handbag."

Despite my stress, I cracked a smile. The cannoli kingpin killer was finally getting her just desserts.

The door buzzed open, and I bolted to it.

Veronica came out, her face grim.

She didn't even have to say it, but of course, I intended to make her. "Please tell me they're letting him out."

"I just talked to his attorney. The DA's office won't release him—not yet."

Her words were a punch to the gut. "What do you mean *not yet*? Wesley Sullivan killed Dana, and he's *dead*. The case is closed!"

"Not officially." She grimaced. "They think Bradley might've been in on it. That he helped cover it up. The cyanide was in *his* coat, Franki."

"Sullivan planted it. Bradley didn't even know Dana Del Ray."

"We know that, but they don't. And with no living suspect to question, the DA's playing it safe. Unless the judge decides to push it through—or someone can produce hard evidence—they won't reconsider until Monday."

Monday. *After* the wedding. I dropped back into the chair. "So, he's going to miss the wedding."

"Sugar," Glenda dropped into a stripper squat to look into my eyes—and given the loincloth, I wished she hadn't, "can you think of anything you might've missed?"

"Da," Nadezhda urged. "Tink, Frank."

I glared at her and then buried my face in my hands, trying not to cry. I'd done everything I could to save Bradley and our wedding. And it hadn't been enough. And all because of Sullivan and that girl...

My head shot up. "The woman with the pink-blonde lob at the Pharmacy Museum! Candy paid her to lie about Bradley stealing the cyanide."

Veronica gasped. "Let's go find her!"

"Where?" I raised my palms. "She walked into the museum, got behind the old pharmacy counter, and pretended to work there." I stood and paced the hallway. "I should've known something was up because instead of a lab coat, she was wearing a tight yellow sweater with orange-and-pink striped sleeves."

"Hey..." Maybe Baby pushed blonde locks from her eyes. "A woman in my cell has that same sweater. What a consistence!"

More proof—along with the patch discussion—that she wasn't cut out for the police dispatch job. "Did you talk to her?"

"Sure. She got busted for trying to sell drugs." Maybe tapped her lip. "The weird thing is, she stole them from an old museum."

Veronica and I embraced.

And Glenda set off her police sirens.

Nonna grasped my arms to steady me. "*Calmati, Franki.*"

"Your nonna's right, dear." My mother gave me a pointed look. "You've got to calm down. We'll figure this out."

Of course, she said that while pacing the lobby of Le Richelieu Hotel and wringing her hands.

The St. Louis Cathedral bells began to toll.

We all went still.

And I mentally ran down the list of warnings from my Big Fat Sicilian Wedding Superstition Sermon. *Are tolling bells a bad omen?* One never knew with Italian traditions, especially since a bird pooing on a bride was considered good luck.

My dad walked up, adjusting his tie. "What's the matter?" he asked in his nervous stomach voice. "Did somebody die?"

"Madonna mia!" Nonna made the scongiuri gesture.

"Joe!" My mother put her hands on her hips. "This is no time to joke."

"Who's joking? People have been dropping dead lately. Isn't that why Bradley went to jail?"

"Sonny," Nonna patted my dad, "now that-a he has been-a freed, let's-a not bring-a that up anymore, *eh*?"

"Okay. Then what's the tragedy?"

My mother threw up her hands, not staying calm at all once again. "The limo has been in an accident, Joe. They can't send a car to drive Franki and Bradley home from the reception."

"Is that all?" He smiled at me. "We can drive you, honey."

"Uhhh, like Mom said," I hurried to intervene, "we'll figure this out. Later tonight."

Not to sound spoiled, but the thought of my parents driving Bradley and me home in the Ford Taurus wasn't how I envisioned starting off my marriage. My nonna would for sure sit in the back seat between us. And the mere thought of the conversation was cringeworthy. Also, I could guaran-freaking-tee that they'd sit in my driveway and watch Bradley carry me over the threshold before leaving.

A shudder racked my body.

My brother entered the lobby, looking surprisingly civilized in his black suit. "Yo, Sis. You got something on your forehead."

Looking *civilized but not* acting *it.*

My hand moved towards my face—but my mother blocked it in mid-air. "Don't touch, Francesca! Not after what we paid that makeup artist."

My mother measured everything in terms of money.

"Fine. I'll just look at it." I headed for a mirror.

My nonna practically threw her body in my path, stopping me mid-step. "*Ma sei impazzita?*"

"Why would you ask if I'm crazy?" I huffed. "I just want to look at my makeup."

"*La sposa può guardarsi allo specchio soltanto togliendo una scarpa, un orecchino e un guanto,*" Nonna singsonged.

My mother shrugged. "It's the tradition, dear."

Even though I'd sworn off traditions while being carried to the mouth of La Bestia, I decided to follow the wedding-day ones, just in case. I'd already been through the wringer—and almost a pasta cutter. I couldn't risk any other calamity, particularly on my big day.

"Okay," I said with a sigh. Maintaining traditions was hard work, and this one was especially onerous. I removed one satin slipper, one pearl earring, and one silk glove before looking in the mirror.

And I got a shock.

The nose bruise my mother had caused was gone, thanks to a visit to the Voodoo You-th Spa, but somehow, despite a hot bath and the pro makeup job, I still had some Red Hot Body Glitter near my hairline. I started to wipe it off, but I stopped myself. Glenda and her Glitter Grit Getter kit had helped me save Bradley from a life in prison, so it seemed fitting to wear a little to our wedding.

Plus, a bit of sparkle was in order.

I stepped back and did a final check. Fortunately, the goon nonne had returned my wedding dress in one piece. The design was inspired by Grace Kelly's iconic dress—something I'd be sure to keep from Marcella, given Grace's Irish heritage—and it took my breath away every time I looked at it.

"Oh, Francesca." My mother pressed her hands to her cheeks. "You're stunning in that dress. The style really complements your figure, and it's the perfect shade of white."

Too bad it was only going to be white at the church. As soon as I stepped into the red-and-green lights of the Piazza d'Italia at the American Italian Cultural Center, the dress would look like the Italian flag for the rest of the night.

Anthony gestured to the door. "Time to go, Sis. And might I say, you're lookin' like a million bucks."

I grinned and gave him a hug.

Veronica squealed from among the throng of my relatives.

"Did Anthony say it's time?" She emerged from between two of my dad's cousins in a burnt orange matron-of-honor dress, a nod to the University of Texas, where we met. "We've got to get you to that altar, girl. Let me get your gown."

She picked up the hem of my dress, and following the Old-World Sicilian tradition, I led my wedding party from the hotel —sans the requisite torches, despite my nonna's protests.

"Shake your money-maker, Miss Franki!" Glenda yelled from a group that had been waiting out front.

We'd made an agreement that she would be fully covered for the church, and she'd stuck to the deal—in her own way. She wore a sheer catsuit adorned with strategically placed crystal snowflakes. And stripper shoes that read "Snow" and "Ho," respectively.

As I waited for my army of relatives to file out of the hotel, I scanned the other guests. Of course, Nadezhda was with Glenda in maroon satin snakeskin that matched her hair spikes to perfection. Also among the guests—Maybe Baby, Carnie Vaul, Ladonna Cucuzza, Shona Helper, Wendell Baptiste and the members of his band, The Tremé Tribe. Oh, and my mother's best friend, Rosalie Artusi.

When everyone had gathered behind me, I turned to take a look. A hundred people, mostly family, had come to see me get married. And these were just our *close* relatives, according to my nonna.

No wonder I didn't remember I had a cousin Giada.

Anthony opened the parasol my mother had bought and held it above my head. Thankfully, the plantation wedding gown that went with it was dead and buried—literally, according to an update from Phil. But I'd agreed to the parasol, because that was a common bridal tradition in New Orleans.

Wendell made eye contact with me and winked. Then the band broke into "When the Saints Go Marching In."

My cue to walk.

Flanked by my father and none other than Maurizio Bonsignore, a concession I'd made to my now ex-second fiancé when I'd broken our engagement, I began the block-long walk down Chartres Street to St. Mary's Church.

"Franki," Nonna shouted, "eyes-a to the ground-a."

Right. I absolutely did not want to see a priest, nun, or black cat.

Tourists and locals stopped to watch our Sicilian-style second line, cheering me on and taking pictures.

A group of frat boys raised their Hand Grenades. "Bride! Bride! Bride!"

Strands of Mardi Gras beads dropped from a balcony.

"*Bonne chance, chère,*" a woman shouted.

A young man stepped into the street. "Marry me, beautiful!"

Maurizio came to a halt and stood as erect as a soldier—a toy version. "Sir, I challenge-a you to a duel!"

"Maurizio," I stopped short, causing my entire entourage, starting with Veronica, to domino. "That's not your responsibility anymore, remember?"

He removed his top hat and bowed. "Of-a course, signorina. Please accept-a my sincere apologies." Then he turned to the young man. "Sir, I retract-a the challenge."

"Party on," the guy replied.

The walk resumed.

A tour guide with a group of cruise ship passengers pointed excitedly. "And here we have an authentic French Quarter wedding procession, folks. How fitting that our Carnival Cruise passengers get to witness a real carnival parade in the Carnival City!"

"It's-a not a carnival," Nonna shouted. "It's-a my grand-a-daughter's Sicilian wedding!"

Honestly, it *was* kind of a carnival. And by the time my krewe got to the reception in Piazza d'Italia, we would be able to rival any New Orleans Mardi Gras.

We arrived at the entrance to St. Mary's Church, and the butterflies in my stomach might as well have been badgers.

My father opened the heavy wooden door.

Following the warning of Rosary-Bead Nonna, I entered the old church with my right foot—even though she never said what would happen if I didn't. But after hearing about Funeral-Faced Nonna's "obstacles," I would've been insane to chance it.

The contrast struck me immediately. I'd gone from being surrounded by cheering tourists, brass band music, and the chaos of a hundred relatives, to hushed whispers, soft organ music, and the reverent quiet of sacred space. I breathed in the calm and the scent of incense and old wood. This was the start of a new chapter, a new beginning.

With the love of my life.

A dizzy spell made me swoon.

My mother's face grew concerned. "Are you alright, Francesca? The doctor did say you have a mild concussion from that blow to the head."

"It's not that, Mom. It's just nerves."

My nonna approached. "It's-a time to rip-a the veil for good-a luck."

"Nonna, I'd like to keep it intact." But then I remembered La Bestia. "Actually, you'd better rip it. Tear the hell out of that thing."

She ripped the veil and then pulled a piece of metal from her handbag. "Now, put-a this-a iron in your bodice to ward off-a the bad luck."

Iron? On my chest? What would those Italians think of next?

Mom handed me a handkerchief. "Here's your something red for love and fertility. You don't want to end up childless in Newark like poor Rosa."

"Where am I supposed to put this?"

"In your bodice with the iron, dear."

"Mom, I'm going to look like I have a third boob."

"Francesca! You're in a church, for God's sake!"

Rich, coming from a woman who'd just blasphemed in said church. But I kept my mouth shut and shoved the stuff into my dress.

Then, I peered into the Church. My ushers, David and The Vassal, stood near the doors in their tan Ghostbusters jumpsuits. After their selfless sacrifice at the airport, I asked them to wear the outfits. After all, they were kind of like military uniforms, and this *was* New Orleans.

I also looked at all the guests on Bradley's side, so happy they'd been able to make it after the blizzard. I was especially grateful to see his mother, Lillian, and grandmother, Cordelia, seated in front.

Next, I looked at Bradley, and my heart skipped a couple of beats. He was absolutely dashing in his black suit. Tears welled at the thought of all we'd been through to get to this day, but I willed them away. None of that mattered now.

Because Bradley was about to keep his promise to see me at the altar.

"Francesca," my mom tapped me on the shoulder. "We're about to start."

"Hang on, Mom." I had a few more people to mentally acknowledge.

First, I looked at the statues of St. Lucy and St. Gabriel, both of whom had played an indirect part in my journey to the altar.

Last but not least, I stared at the mural of the Virgin Mary ascending to heaven and winked. She might've helped me get off that awful conveyor belt.

"You ready, honey?" My dad's voice cracked.

Even though my father was ecstatic for me, I knew it was

hard for him to give his only daughter away. I nodded, kissed him on the cheek, and wiped tears from my eyes. *Stop crying, Franki,* I thought. *Don't ruin your makeup.*

Think Glenda grit.

And her strategically placed snowflakes.

But the tears continued to flow.

Then a thought hit me that stopped the tears and made me smile from ear to ear. *Dear God, I'm finally free, FREE, of Mom and Nonna's meddling!*

"Anthony," my Mom whispered, "go tell the organist we're ready to begin."

"On it, Ma." He left.

My mom and nonna lined up at the door to wait for David and The Vassal to escort them to their seats.

My dad and I stood behind them, arm in arm.

Nonna elbowed my mother. "We did it-a, Brenda. Franki's-a getting married."

"We *did*, Carmela." My mom's voice came out a squeal. "Thank God for the St. Joseph's Day lemon tradition."

"Sì! And-a only sixty-eight-a more days until-a the next-a one." She leaned in. "You know what-a that means-a!"

The door opened, and David extended his arm for my nonna.

But I pulled away from my dad and grabbed the old woman, holding her back. My eyes narrowed to slits as thin as a communion wafer. "Nonna," I said in a low, throaty growl, "why are you counting down to St. Joseph's Day?"

"Francesca," my mother admonished, "let go of your nonna! The wedding is about to begin!"

"Not until you two tell me what's going on."

Nonna shot a worried glance at my mother, who shook her head hard—and fast.

"Talk," I ordered, "or I don't walk."

My mother broke into a sweat. "Fine. The steal a lemon tradition works two ways. It can help you get engaged—and also get you pregnant."

Nonna raised a finger. "You don't-a want to be childless in-a Newark like-a poor Rosa!"

The room tilted. "The meddling isn't over," I whispered. "It's never going to end."

"Franki!" Nonna called.

"Francesca?" my mother shrilled.

But I didn't answer. I was too busy watching lemons circling my head.

"Damnit, Brenda," my father shouted. "Why the hell did you have to bring that lemon stuff up now?"

"Why do you always blame *me*, Joe?" she yelled. "Your mother started it!"

Plump, round, yellow lemons, all in a ring...

Nonna stomped a foot. "I did-a not-a start it!"

No, not *yellow* lemons...

Pitch black.

"MRS. HARTMANN," Bradley slid his arms around my waist and pulled me close, "your carriage awaits."

Please, God, I thought, *don't let my dad be outside the Piazza d'Italia in the Ford Taurus. Or Phil Redman in his Uber Undertaker hearse-ambulance.*

Bradley lowered his head and kissed me passionately. My knees wobbled—not from the mild concussion, but from the kiss.

Okay, *mostly* from the kiss.

"Franki!" Marcella shrieked.

I jolted from my husband's arms.

"*Grazie a Dio* I caught you in time. You almost forgot the extra Nutella for your bomboniere and this!" Marcella held up the gold, Italian-flag-themed *Mrs. Bradley Hartmann* sash.

While I was glad to have the twenty-five leftover jars of Nutella, I was sad to see that sash. I'd stashed it under a table, hoping she wouldn't remember it. "Whew! Lucky you found that." I took the bag of Nutella and the sash and pointed to my head. "Must be the mild concussion."

Her smoky-eyeshadowed eyes locked onto my lace sleeve, and her brow rose. "Is that dress like the one—"

"Sophia Loren wore to marry Cary Grant in *Houseboat*?" I gushed. "Yes!"

"Ohhh..." She smiled and nodded. "Now I see it. For a minute I thought it was inspired by Grace Kelly." She stuck out her tongue and rolled her eyes like she'd lost it. "You'd think *I* have the concussion."

Moira, who stood behind her, raised the Irish flag cocktail she'd made to spite Marcella. She knew the actress—and princess—who'd inspired the dress.

Bradley leaned in. "Excuse me, babe. I need to say goodbye to my mother."

"Take your time, Mr. Hartmann."

Maurizio Bonsignore strode up in his tiny loafers. His top hat was smashed, and his neck was slanted to the left, thanks to an amused head pat he'd received from Yakov after challenging him to a duel.

Marcella looked down at him. "You were so valiant to challenge that big Russian beast for calling me 'mortadella' instead of 'Marcella.'"

"It was-a my duty, signorina. He compared you to cold-a cuts-a."

"He didn't do it on purpose," I said for at least the tenth time. "His English is limited."

"That does-a not make it-a better." He put a gloved hand on his throat. "Because my neck, he still have-a the crick from that pat."

"Let me help you with that." Marcella gripped his shoulders and began to massage.

He jerked from her grasp, gave a mighty flip of his cape, and clicked his heels. "Signorina, you have touch-ed my naked skin-a. In-a Sicily, we are now betrothed."

"*Betrothed*? ME?" Marcella looked at the night sky. "Thank you, Virgin Mary!" Then she swooned.

Onto me.

"Help me," I wheezed, trying my hardest to prop her up. She was big enough to crush both me and the mini marriage broker. "And bring water!"

Ruth ran up in her Keds and threw a glass of water in her face—and mine.

"I meant water to *drink*, Ruth."

"She's unconscious. How could she drink?"

Ruth was playing innocent, but we both knew she'd doused me on purpose. "Just help me get her to a chair."

We seated Marcella next to the accordion player—because the music was so grating that it could rouse the residents of the Saint Cecilia Cemetery—and I patted her cheeks.

Ruth slid on her readers. "What'd you do to her, Franki?"

"Nothing!" I patted Marcella's cheek a little too hard. "She's happy because Maurizio proposed."

Ruth sniffed. "First you collect fiancés like baseball cards, now you're pawning them off on other people."

"Ruth, I didn't intentionally collect fiancés. All of this happened because of a silly Sicilian tradition."

Maurizio stepped forward. "Sì, she saw me in-a my nightshirt."

"Stay out of this, Maurizio." I gave Marcella a slap. Then I turned back to Ruth. "I love Bradley, and he loves me. And now that we're married, you're just going to have to accept that."

Her mouth drew up, and her turkey neck followed. "Well, you managed not to get him arrested or murdered today, so that's a start."

For Ruth, that was progress. I patted Marcella's cheek.

Finally, her eyelids fluttered open.

Maurizio flashed his Osmond teeth and dropped on one knee, producing one of the comically large Bling Ring shot glasses Marcella had bought.

"A proposal?" Her eyes rolled back, and she fainted again. Then her head popped up. "Yes! I'll marry you!" And she was out once more.

Giada hurried over. "Is she alright?"

"She's just overexcited." I gestured to the piazza. "She finally got her dream American-Italian wedding reception, and just now she got a husband."

Giada blinked. "I'm sorry. What?"

I waved off the question. "Don't try to make sense of it. You can't."

"If you say so." She bit her lip. "Listen, I didn't want to say anything before the wedding, and I definitely don't want my family to hear this." She paused and looked from side to side.

And I did too. True to their word, the Montalbano side of her family had worn mourning clothes to my wedding to protest her divorce. "What is it? Does it have something to do with Wolf?"

"Indirectly. Moira and I are leaving for Italy in a few days. We've both been offered jobs with a luxury food tour company."

That godawful soup sauce leapt to mind. "You're...*cooking*?"

"No, I'm going to be a tour guide. You know, take clients to fabulous restaurants and various sites. They said I could hire my own assistant, and since Moira needs a job, she's coming too."

"That's amazing, Giada. I'm so happy for you both. Bradley

and I will take one of your tours." And we would eventually, now that I knew she wasn't cooking.

"I'd better run. So much to do. But congrats, cuz." She hugged me. "I knew this wedding would happen."

She left, and I glanced around for Bradley.

"Miss Franki!" Glenda sashayed toward me in her reception attire—a Versace-inspired number consisting of four gold Medusa heads and a set of gold lamé wings that had turned the Piazza d'Italia into a red-and-green Studio 54 every time she moved.

The two goon nonne, who'd forced her from her sheer snowflake catsuit into a somber navy sack dress for my wedding service, emerged from the crowd, latched onto either side of her, and pulled her towards the ladies' room.

"Help, sugar! These large Lilliputians are gonna strip me bare again—like Sunny backstage."

I gaped all over again. It still shocked me that Glenda had an issue with nudity. I started after her, but Bruno blocked my path.

His hands were in his pockets, but his chest hair was on full display. The champagne on his breath was evident as he came way too close. "You know, I always figured we'd hook up."

"I never thought that. Not even once."

"It's not too late to change your mind."

"Um, it is?" I tapped my ring finger, which now had an added gold band.

A gleam I didn't like entered his eyes, and he leaned in. "Now that you're married, you're finally unattainable. That's hot." He leered. "Whadya say we skip this joint, and head to Lake Charles."

The obvious choice would've been Las Vegas, but Bruno didn't have the logic skill. "Or," I said brightly, "I could knee you where it counts in front of all of my guests and let you explain what happened to Bradley." I gestured to Yakov. "And to my big Russian wrestler friend."

The gleam left his eyes, and he leaned back. Then, he casually sauntered to the exit—and broke into a run.

Bradley approached and extended his arm. "I hope you let your would-be third fiancé down easy just now."

"Not so much."

Chandra strolled over in a blue sequined dress with her usual moons and stars, and her husband, Lou, was in tow behind. He was walking stiffly, probably because of his corns combined with the unfamiliar loafers. This was the first time I'd seen him in anything but toe shoes, and I considered it an unintended wedding present.

Chandra shot me a self-important smile. "Lou and I wanted to welcome you to the family, Franki."

"Yes, welcome," Lou said, ever a man of few words.

"Thank you both," I managed, biting my tongue. Chandra had only recently learned she might be related to Bradley. But if she made a habit of this kind of talk, I was going to trace the family tree to prove her wrong.

She ran a hand over her helmet hair. "I was just talking to Cordelia about how we're possibly related, and she invited us to the family compound in Nantucket for the Fourth of July."

Chandra at family gatherings? I staggered back, unable to fathom a future of charm-bracelet channeling at family functions.

Bradley slid his arm around my waist to steady me. "It's too early for us to decide, Chandra. If you'll excuse us, Franki and I need to get going."

But I had regained my composure. "One thing you should know, Chandra. The family summer home is old, and they have a ghost maid and a butler."

"Dear, Gawd!" She staggered back, and I was pretty sure her

supernatural Crescent deodorant from Sea Witch Botanicals abandoned ship in that moment. "S- s-spirit servants?"

Satisfied that Chandra would now turn down any Hartmann-family invitation, I let Bradley lead me from the piazza. But I stole one last glimpse of all the people who'd come to celebrate with us. I hated for the reception to end, but on the other hand, we had an early flight to Rome.

And I was anxious to start our honeymoon.

Not only that, so far no one from my family had carried out the tradition of kidnapping me and making Bradley rescue me by solving riddles. And frankly, I wanted to keep it that way. I'd already been kidnapped enough for one week.

We exited into the street, and I gasped.

My carriage could not have been more perfect.

The Christmas Car—with cans strung on the back and a sign that read, "Just married."

Santa opened the car door with a jolly wink.

Hermey stood beside him like an elf sommelier, holding two champagne flutes with candy cane stir sticks.

"Franki, wait!" Veronica ran up and threw her arms around me. "I know I've said it a hundred times already, but I'm so happy for you."

"Thanks, bestie." I squeezed her tight, and the iron in my bodice pressed into my breast bone. "If it hadn't been for you offering me a job, I never would have met Bradley."

She wiped away tears. "You two would've found each other somehow. It was destiny. Now, get out of here before someone ropes you into another tradition!"

Awesome point. I hugged her again—despite the alleged good-luck iron—and shed a few tears myself.

Several members of my wedding party began pelting me with wheat, an ancient Sicilian tradition that was basically a grain fertility grenade.

"Friendly reminder," I shielded my face, "that tradition only happens when the bride leaves the church."

Nonna hit me with a handful. "We do it again-a, for good-a measure."

"We want a baby, dear," my mother shouted, tossing wheat at my stomach.

"Mamma mia," I muttered. I was right about the meddling. It was never going to stop. I could really use one of Marcella's Jell-O IV shots about now, but champagne would have to do. I took a flute from Hermey, drained it, then took Bradley's.

As I climbed into the car, my mother was so overcome that she burst into "O Holy Night."

21

"Tell me, Mrs. Hartmann," Bradley pulled me closer to him in the backseat of the Christmas Car and kissed the top of my head, "what was your favorite part of the night—besides marrying me, of course?"

I nuzzled into his side, grateful Hermey had put up a partition to give us privacy. "Someone's awfully sure of himself."

"Well, you almost missed out. Technically, Marcella shouted 'I do' a split second before you answered the priest."

And my mother had almost taken her out with a hymnal, but I didn't want to relive that event. "I'm not worried about Marcella. She's marrying Maurizio."

Bradley's head jerked back, narrowly missing a boiling bubble light. "The marriage broker?"

I nodded.

"How's that going to work? I mean, he's what? Four feet? And she's at least—"

I put my finger to his lips. "Don't ruin our wedding night, Bradley."

He let out a laugh. "That reminds me, did you see Yakov dancing with Ruth when we left?"

"Yes, but he was just grateful she found his ballet slipper pendant at the hotel."

Bradley cocked his head. "I think it was more than that. He was holding her—"

My finger flew back to his lips. "Again, don't ruin our wedding night."

"Yeah, you're right." He reached for a Schnapps bottle from the mini bar. "I'll wash that thought away with a shot of peppermint."

As he poured himself a drink, I opened the bedazzled green "I Love Italians and Cash" bag Marcella had given me for the cash wedding gifts. My eyes widened as I did a quick count of the bills. "Oh my God."

"What is it?"

"There's two thousand dollars in seventies money in this bag."

"O-kayyy... And in today's money?"

"Ten grand."

"Whoa." He let out a low whistle. "Our guests didn't mess around."

The Christmas Car slowed, and I peered through an opening in the fake-snow-covered window. We were on my street, by the creepy cemetery—and a bush moved.

"Everything okay, babe?"

"Yeah, I just..." I rubbed the knot on my head. "...thought I saw something in the cemetery. Probably a cat."

"That reminds me, on my way to the church today, I saw a Subaru with a priest, a nun, and a black cat in the backseat."

The car lurched as Santa pulled into the driveway, but not as hard as I had when Bradley dropped that Sicilian superstition trifecta bomb.

I'd said I wasn't going to observe any traditions after today, but the sighting was so shocking that it rattled my resolve. The sparkle of a turnip-shaped ornament covered in glitter caught my eye. And I stiffened—with Glenda grit.

There was no way I was going to live the rest of my life haunted by tradition. I flat refused. And besides, why worry about what was to come when I had Red Hot Body Glitter, twenty-five jars of Nutella, and ghostbusting coworkers? Not to mention two thousand dollars in seventies money and chapter thirteen of Glenda's memoirs.

"Hey, you two lovebirds." Santa knocked on the partition. "You're ho-ho-home!"

Bradley held up a hand. "Stay where you are, Mrs. Hartmann. I'll get your door."

As he walked around to my side of the car, I gave Santa and Hermey some large bills from my wedding stash.

Hermey's black eyes remained typically wide.

But Santa's eyes popped. "Ho-ho-holy smokes!"

"Thank you both, truly." I grabbed my bag of leftover Nutella. "I'll be in touch."

Bradley opened my door and helped me from the car.

As the Pontiac Catalina drove away, the recording of sleigh bells played. "Ho ho ho!" Santa cried. "Meeerrry Matrimony!"

"Not exactly a sleigh," Bradley said, "but close." He took the bag from my hands, and we walked up the driveway. "I fully intend to observe the tradition of carrying my bride across the threshold."

After everything I'd been through with traditions, this was one I could get behind. "I'd like that."

Bradley pushed open the door, and Napoleon shot out—not to see me, but to escape Bradley's wheaten Cairn terrier, Trixie.

"Napoleon!" I called, but Bradley had already swept me off my feet.

As he carried me through the doorway, I looked over my

shoulder. I couldn't shake the feeling my parents and nonna were watching—maybe from the cemetery.

Bradley set me down in the hallway and paused to give me a long, sweet kiss that made my knees wobble all over again.

When he released me, Trixie leapt at his feet, wagging her tail and possibly batting her eyelashes. He knelt to scratch her head, and she licked his face. As he rose, Trixie flashed her teeth at me, then snapped at Napoleon—all in stealthy silence so Bradley would remain oblivious to the canine cold war.

"Would you lock the door, babe?" I asked. If my family was outside, I wanted to make sure my mom didn't barge in and break into another round of "O Holy Night."

Bradley locked the door and switched off the porch light. "Do you think the dogs will be alright with Glenda while we're in Italy?"

Glenda wasn't the problem. "Napoleon loves her. She feeds him food from Thibodeaux's."

Trixie gave a low growl, and Napoleon darted into the bedroom. A bell rang, and he yelped.

Bradley looked at me. "What was that bell?"

The cunzata del letto!

"A dog toy," I fibbed. It was awfully early in the marriage to be lying to my husband, but I needed to get a look at what was in that bed before he did. Otherwise, he was likely to have the marriage annulled.

"Um, if you'll excuse me for a moment, I'm going to slip into something more comfortable."

He flashed a dazzling smile. "You're excused, Mrs. Hartmann."

I attempted a sultry look and slipped into the bedroom. The mattress was as lumpy as my bodice after I'd stuffed it with the iron and red handkerchief. I dropped to my knees and peered under the bed.

Napoleon stared back at me—lodged between a bell and a cheese grater.

"Nonna," I groaned.

"Uh, Franki?"

Bradley's voice startled me, and I bumped my injured head on the bedframe. Then I pulled myself from under the mattress. "Yes, babe?"

"Trixie just brought this into the living room." He held up one of Glenda's acsexories. "And what's going on with the bed?"

I stood, as he pulled a jar from beneath the covers. "Red Hot Body Glitter?"

My face was probably the color of the glitter. "It's a Sicilian wedding tradition."

His brow shot up. "Edible body glitter?"

"No, stuffing the bed with all kinds of things. Apparently, Glenda helped my mom and nonna." I pulled back the bedspread with dread.

Lemons, at least twenty of them, scattered across the sheet like landmines—instead of the coins, booze, and chocolate I'd been promised.

Bradley ran a hand through his hair. "I thought you were done with those after I proposed."

"Me too." I sank onto the side of the mattress. "But apparently, Sicilian women also steal lemons to help them get pregnant."

He sat beside me and slid an arm around my waist. "Since you brought it up, I'd love to have a little Franki. Or two."

I placed my palm on his cheek. "I don't think we'll need a lemon to land a little Hartmann. But if we do, I will happily raid every St. Joseph's Day altar from New Orleans to New York to have a family with you."

A knock sounded at the front door.

The dogs barked, and Bradley rose from the bed. "It's after midnight. Who would be here at this hour?"

"Francesca," my mother shrilled, her voice drilling through the door. "Your nonna and I brought the leftover cannoli. It's for you, dear, not Bradley."

"It's-a bad for his weak-a digestion," Nonna yelled.

The room began to spin.

"Franki, eat-a the cannoli for break-a-fast. It bring-a the good-a luck."

"And possibly a baby!" my mother hummed.

Still in my wedding gown, I grabbed my hobo bag from the nightstand. Then I climbed among the citrus fruit, lay on my back, and pulled the bedspread over my head.

"I'll just go get those cannoli," Bradley said.

Meanwhile under the covers, I pulled the Rescue Remedy from my bag and drank more than the two recommended drops.

Love, lemons, and lunatics, I thought, summarizing my happily ever after in the dark. *What could possibly go wrong?*

SURPRISE PREORDER!

Welp… remember that surprise job offer Giada and Moira got before Franki's wedding? Turns out it was more than just a plot twist—it's the start of a *whole new series*!

The Pasta & Piazza Mysteries are coming—and you'll want a first-class seat on these Italian food tours. Giada and Moira are leading luxe foodie adventures across Italy, where the cuisine is divine… and the crimes? Deadly.

Preorder their first mystery today!

CAPRI, CANNOLI, AND CONSPIRACY
(Pasta and Piazza Mysteries, Book 1)

A luxury food tour in Capri? Yes. A corpse in the Blue Grotto? Not on the itinerary.

When a cannoli-loving boat captain turns up dead during her first group trip, travel guide Giada Adair's dreamy new career takes a deadly detour. One minute she's sampling lemon linguine and soaking up the sun, the next she's dodging questions from Carabinieri, a cannoli king, and a tourist group full of amateur sleuths. Between a siren-obsessed professor, shady fishermen, and a secret society that reenacts ancient island rituals, Giada's got more suspects than flavors of gelato. With help from her street-smart assistant and a distractingly handsome inspector, she'll have to navigate myths, murder, and mascarpone—before someone decides she's next on the menu.

BOOK BACKSTORY

Thank you so much for reading *Sambuca Scarlet*! Can you believe Franki is finally married? I cannot! I mean, it only took 10 books, six short stories, and a novella to get that girl to the altar. It was hard work, so I definitely sympathize with her mom and nonna. :D

As always, I like to point out some of the things that inspired the story. First, Le Richelieu Hotel and its ghosts are all real—if you believe in spirits, that is. I'm not sure where I stand on that, but I can tell you a spooky story. Even though I was never a huge fan of the *Ghostbusters* movies, I just *had* to include a ghostbuster subplot in this book for some reason. And when I paid a recent visit to Le Richelieu Hotel for book research, I was shocked to see an autographed picture of Dan Aykroyd hanging in the tiny Terrace Lounge.

Fun fact: Dan Aykroyd dreamed up *Ghostbusters* thanks to Abbott and Costello movies—and a grandfather who held séances in their Canadian cottage. Only in Canada!

The history in *Sambuca Scarlet* is true, as well. Père Dagobert de Longuory, General Bloody O'Reilly, and the poor souls who lost their lives in the Creole Revolt were all real individuals. Their stories live on in the various haunted tours around New Orleans.

Incidentally, the blood stain on the pillow in Franki's room was inspired by a TripAdvisor review. According to a man who stayed at Le Richelieu Hotel, he woke up to find blood on his pillow—that wasn't from him.

Finally—and this is my favorite New Orleans history discovery —the Sicilian macaroni factories and spaghetti houses were actually the reason that pasta went mainstream in the United States. I know that I, for one, owe the memory of those men and women my deepest respect. Pasta is my favorite food—after cake, of course.

Now, I've been asked whether Sambuca Scarlet is the end of the Franki Amato Mysteries. It's not. Franki will return, but first she's got to go on her honeymoon and settle into married life. I've put the poor girl through a lot these past twelve or so years, so she deserves a rest and some peace and quiet that she won't get, thanks to her mom and nonna—and now her cousin, Giada. She's going to need Franki's help from time to time in her new Italian venture. *Mamma mia!*

Stay tuned!
   Traci

COCKTAIL

ITALIAN FLAG COCKTAIL

This is Marcella's version, so drink at your own risk! The original uses grenadine for the red section of the flag, and not sambuca. Also, if you want to make it an Irish flag cocktail, do what Moira did and swap the sambuca with arancello for an orange layer.

Ingredients
    ⅓ oz Red Sambuca (bottom layer - red)
    ⅓ oz White Chocolate Liqueur (middle layer - white)
    ⅓ oz Green Crème de Menthe (top layer - green)

Pour the red Sambuca into a shot glass first. Then, using the back of a bar spoon, slowly layer the white chocolate liqueur over the Sambuca. Again using the back of a spoon, carefully layer the green crème de menthe on top.

Layering Tip: Pour each layer very slowly over the back of the spoon to prevent mixing. The different densities of the liqueurs will help them stay separated, creating the red, white, and green stripes of the Italian flag.

Cent'anni! (Although I doubt you'll live "one hundred years," as the toast states, if you drink this version of the recipe!)

PRIMO (MAIN COURSE)

SPAGHETTI ALLA SAMBUCA

I couldn't resist including this recipe, even after what it did to poor Dana Del Ray. Of course, that was the fault of the potassium cyanide, which is definitely not included in this recipe! Interesting note about this dish—it's considered Italian American and not authentically Italian, which means Marcella freaking loves it!

Ingredients
    1 lb spaghetti
    ½ cup olive oil
    1 tbsp chopped garlic
    1 tbsp chopped shallot
    1 lb large shrimp, peeled and deveined
    1/4 cup Sambuca liqueur (but not the red!)
    ½ cup dry white wine
    ½ cup chopped tomatoes
    1 tbsp chopped fresh tarragon

½ cup unsalted butter, cut into pieces
Salt and black pepper to taste

Bring a large pot of salted water to a boil and cook the spaghetti according to package directions.

While the pasta cooks, heat the olive oil in a large sauté pan over medium heat. Add the garlic, shallots, and shrimp, and sauté for 1–2 minutes until fragrant.

Add the white wine and Sambuca to the pan. Stand back and carefully ignite the sauce with a long match to flambé. Wait for the flame to die out.

Stir in the chopped tomatoes, tarragon, salt, and pepper. Continue to cook for 2 minutes.

Remove the pan from the heat and add the butter, stirring until the sauce is slightly thickened.

Drain the cooked spaghetti and toss it with the sauce in the pan until everything is well coated.

Serve immediately, and garnish with fresh parsley if desired.

Important note on flambéing: Igniting the Sambuca is for both flavor and dramatic presentation. Giada didn't flambé hers in the book—but the recipe ended up killing Dana, anyway. But, as you know now that you've read the book, that wasn't Giada's doing.

If you decide to flambé this dish, please proceed with caution. Work in a ventilated area, away from flammable objects. And definitely make sure to turn off your exhaust fan to prevent flames from being drawn upward. Also, use a long match or a grill lighter, and keep your face and body away from the pan when lighting the alcohol.

Mangia!

ALSO BY TRACI ANDRIGHETTI

FRANKI AMATO MYSTERIES

Books
Limoncello Yellow
Prosecco Pink
Amaretto Amber
Campari Crimson
Galliano Gold
Marsala Maroon
Valpolicella Violet
Tuaca Tan
Nocino Noir
Braulio Brown (a Thanksgiving novella)
Sambuca Scarlet

Box Sets
Franki Amato Mysteries Box Set (Books 1–3)
Franki Amato Mysteries Box Set (Books 4–6)
The Franki Amato Mysteries Big Box Set (Books 1–7)

Short Stories
Franki Amato Mini Mysteries
(short mysteries free to newsletter subscribers only)

PASTA AND PIAZZA MYSTERIES

Capri, Cannoli, and Conspiracy (preorder now!)
Rome, Ravioli, and Revenge (forthcoming)

DANGER COVE HAIR SALON MYSTERIES

Books
Deadly Dye and a Soy Chai
A Poison Manicure and Peach Liqueur
Killer Eyeshadow and a Cold Espresso

Franki Amato also investigates with the sleuths of Leslie Langtry, Arlene McFarlane, and Diana Orgain in the

KILLER FOURSOME MYSTERIES

Books
4 Sleuths & A Bachelorette
4 Sleuths & A Burlesque Dancer
4 Sleuths & A Barnstormer

ABOUT THE AUTHOR

Traci Andrighetti is the *USA Today* bestselling author of four humorous and murderously fun mystery series: the Franki Amato Mysteries, the Pasta and Piazza Mysteries, and the Danger Cove Hair Salon Mysteries. She's also a co-author of the Killer Foursome Mysteries.

Before plotting murders in Italy and New Orleans, Traci was an award-winning literary translator and a Lecturer of Italian at the University of Texas at Austin, where she earned a PhD in Applied Linguistics. But then she got wise and ditched academia for a life of crime—writing, that is.

Want in on her latest capers? Visit www.traciandrighetti.com.

www.ingramcontent.com/pod-product-compliance
Lightning Source LLC
Chambersburg PA
CBHW071211210726
48293CB00002B/381